A Palace of Smoke & Mirrors

The Gift War: Book Two

Loren Little

LOREN LITTLE BOOKS

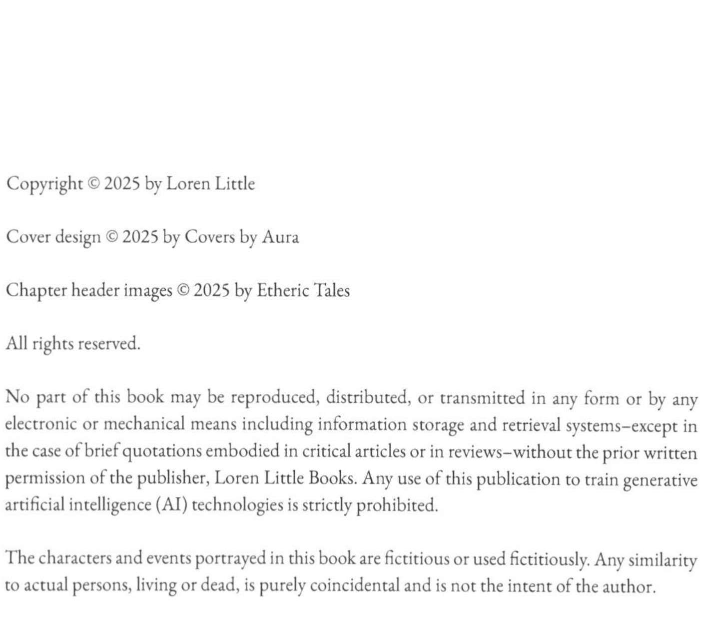

First edition 2025.

A PALACE OF SMOKE & MIRRORS

Contents

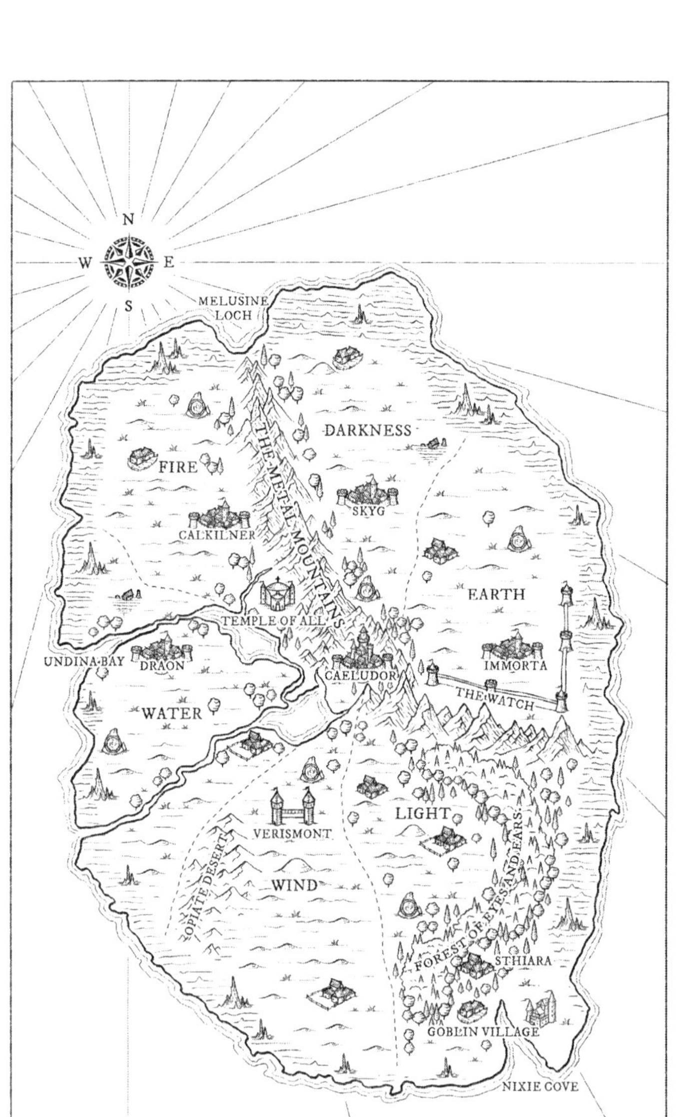
N
W
E
S
MELUSINE LOCH
DARKNESS
FIRE
THE METAL MOUNTAINS
SKYG
CALKILNER
EARTH
TEMPLE OF ALL
UNDINA BAY
DRAON
CAELUDOR
IMMORTA
THE WATCH
WATER
LIGHT
VERISMONT
OPIATE DESERT
WIND
FOREST OF EYES AND EARS
STHIARA
GOBLIN VILLAGE
NIXIE COVE

Author's Note

Dear Reader,

This is the second book in a dark romantasy series called *The Gift War*. The first book, *A House of Cloaks & Daggers*, must be read first or else we are all going to be disastrously confused. That said, this book remains a sound choice of gift for a friend or a partner—and if your grandchildren have already started the series and they are grown up, then I think we'll be safe with your selection this year.

The mature and explicit content in this series intensifies with an updated list of content at www.lorenlittle.com/themes for this book. Please note *The Gift War* is dark in both tone and theme. Reader discretion is always advised.

I must inform you that I am still an Australian writing in AU/UK dialect with no signs of stopping. I greatly appreciate your grace and patience with me—even more so for not reporting ill-presumed spelling errors on Amazon. For my much beloved international readers, your pronunciation of certain letters and words remains superior to ours, and I will continue to defend your honour in these matters.

Thank you for picking up this book from the depths of my anxious, battle-scarred heart. The world of publishing is a business and being an author is my career, but this book was a labour of love. And it was all for you. You are truly the reason I can tell my stories, and I am grateful for you every single day.

Please accept my apologies in advance. Eventually, it's going to be okay. All my love,

Loren x

P.S: I forgot to provide my long-suffering editor with a copy of the updated glossary, but it is in the back of this book for you. I also heard that you wanted bonus scenes from an alternate point of view, so there's one or two of those in here too. *Don't skip to the end for them now.* If you do that, I'll know. It's so much better for you to read them at the end of this book for maximum emotional damage, so please, let's be reasonable. When you're done with it, come and find me! We can hyperventilate and sob together.

Playlist

LISTENING TIP: For maximum emotional damage, I highly recommend listening to **Distraction by Sleep Token** at the end of this book even if you don't normally listen to music as part of your reading.

Winner — *Conan Gray*
The Love You Want — *Sleep Token*
Is It Really You? — *Sleep Token*
Just Pretend — *Bad Omens*
God Complex — *VIOLENT VIRA*
Mary On A Cross — *Ghost*
Dark Signs — *Sleep Token*
Silver Spoon — *Erin LeCount*
Lead Me On — *FLETCHER*
Castles Crumbling (feat. Hayley Williams) (Taylor's Version) (From The Vault) — *Taylor Swift, Hayley Williams*
Distraction — *Sleep Token*

Lonely is the Muse — *Halsey*
Who Knew - Edit — *P!nk*
F**kin' Perfect — *P!nk*
CONCRETE JUNGLE — *Bad Omens*
Sorry — *Halsey*
Lead Me To Water — *Alec Benjamin*
"Slut!" (Taylor's Version) (From The Vault) — *Taylor Swift*
Missing Limbs — *Sleep Token*
Creatures in Heaven — *Glass Animals*
Feel Me Now — *If Not For Me*
Middle of the Night — *Amy Shark*
The Hills X Creepin X the Color Violet — *LonelyEve*
Take Me Back To Eden — *Sleep Token*
everything in my mind — *Nevertel*
You And I – Stripped — *PVRIS*
The Arsonist — *Alec Benjamin*
Eyelids — *PVRIS*
Wonderful Nothing — *Glass Animals*
Crush — *FLETCHER*
Oil & Water — *PVRIS*
Roses — *Awaken I Am*
Hangfire — *Wind Walkers*
Masterpiece — *Motionless In White*
If I Killed Someone For You — *Alec Benjamin*
Rain — *Sleep Token*
you're like — *Jamie Fine*
this is me trying — *Taylor Swift*
Marble Arch — *Erin LeCount*
If Our Love Is Wrong — *Callum Scott*
Fall For Me — *Sleep Token*
A Tear In Space (Airlock) — *Glass Animals*
traitor — *Olivia Rodrigo*
(Bonus Scene)
Gethsemane — *Sleep Token*
Infinite Baths — *Sleep Token*

For Adeline.

"I give myself very good advice, but I very seldom follow it."
— Alice in Wonderland (1865)

One

An Eleven-Year-Old Girl

Blood stained the white fabric between my fingers.

I scrubbed and scrubbed at it with a bar of soap, rinsing and repeating, but the marks wouldn't fade. The water ran red first, and then pink, and still the bloodstains on the sheet remained.

Fingers numb and bones aching from the icy water, I dropped the linen with a flat, wet slap. Let it gather at the bottom of the sink, suffocating the drain as I pushed myself up on the tips of my toes and stretched over the steel basin to turn off the faucet.

It shrieked, metal against metal, and I sighed to break the heavy silence that followed. The dead quiet of the house weighed on me like a ball and chain around my ankles, like my bones had been replaced by iron bars. The leaden weight inside me was the only thing keeping me tethered to the earth, the pressure on my lungs the only thing preventing me from screaming until flesh shredded and bone shattered.

His flesh.

His bones.

I found him in the kitchen.

Standing beside the stove with a beer in hand, staring at the array of empty bottles littered across our small wooden table. Glaring at the brand-new highchair next to it, a pattern of blue bears and silver balloons on its padded seat and an unnaturally, immaculately clean feeding tray attached. He didn't look up at me as I approached, though I trudged into the room with my invisible ball and chain in tow, dragging my heels along the floor.

"We need new sheets," I said. My voice was sweet, youthful, and monotone—like a flatline on the hospital monitors in the throat of an eleven-year-old girl.

A grunt was the only response offered to me by the hollow-eyed man near the stove.

Then he took a swig of beer.

The ugly smell stuffed itself up my nose like mouldy fruit left in the fridge for too long.

"We need new sheets," I repeated.

Bloodshot eyes slid to mine. "I heard you."

"You haven't moved."

His eyebrows slowly crumpled into a frown. "You want me to go right now?" he asked, pointing towards the door with the neck of his beer bottle.

"There are no fresh sheets," I stated. *Careful. I have to be so careful.* "She's going to need them changed again by morning."

"It's late. Put some in the dryer."

A rush of cold seized my chest, but I put a hand on the back of the nearest chair to steady myself. Calmly—like I wasn't repeating myself all over again—I told him, "They're stained."

He made a dismissive gesture at the ceiling and began to stride for the doorway. "At least they'll be dry," he muttered. "I'm going to crash on the couch."

Something alive and tangible inside of my chest lunged for him with razor-sharp teeth and talon-like claws—but instead of sinking into its prey, the hateful beast stumbled headfirst into my heart with a ferocious, painful *thump*.

"No."

He paused in the doorway. "What?"

"*No*," I said again with emphasis. My chest rumbled faintly as if the beast was feeling its way around the obstacle of my blood organ, still determinedly set in its pursuit.

There was no way I would replace her bedding with bloodstained sheets. Again. She deserved clean, untainted linen, even if it didn't stay that way for long. She was in there sobbing and bleeding and in unimaginable pain. She was hurt in ways that could never be healed, losing parts of herself that could never be replaced because of him—

Because of *him*.

"You don't want to push me tonight, Auralie," he warned in a voice laced with violence and suffering and the only promises he ever kept.

The dark things hiding beneath that voice were my constant companions, so my knees did not buckle beneath the weight of his threat. Instinct cautioned me against it, but I opened my mouth once more inside of an unpleasant smile.

"Three days," I observed quietly. "Is that a new record for you?"

He turned slowly. His eyes were foggy, glazed by the liquor, and he strained to pull his focus onto me. "What?"

"It's been three days since you last threatened me," I clarified, my cheeks swelling with a vitriolic grin. "If you don't count when I was a baby—which I don't, because I can't remember any of it—or the months you spend on the run, I'm sure this is some kind of record."

The air between us trembled and pulled taut.

He clenched his fists, eyeballs swimming in his head, and spent a moment searching for something...

Alas, all he could come up with was more anger and irritation. Shoulders twitching, he shook the beer bottle in his hand and screwed his nose up at me.

"Shut up," he spat, droplets of saliva spraying from his mouth.

Silently, I lifted my middle finger in the air between us.

The atmosphere cracked.

"Shut up!" he roared again. The bottle went flying and exploded against the wall behind me in a spray of beer and glass that tickled the back of my neck. "Shut up! Shut the *fuck* up!"

The words assaulted me like a punch in the nose, but I latched on to the abuse like a starving beast and greedily devoured the ugly expression on his face. My own heated to near the point of delirium as blood flooded to my cheeks and filled my head—a warmth, a sensation I hadn't felt in weeks.

Something. *I'm feeling something—*

"Hit me!" I screamed back at him. My voice box felt like it had caught on fire, positively quivering in the wake of the falsetto, but it was too late for me to stop. "Go ahead and *do* it!" I shrieked. "Just get it over with! Because if I have to spend *one more moment* in this house, I am going to fucking *kill* you, you asshole!"

He took a thunderous step towards me. "Aura—"

I didn't wait for him to finish. I couldn't take it any longer. I could not be in that house with him, sleeping with one eye open every night, chewing nervous holes through my blankets every time I heard a creak from one of the floorboards down the hall. I couldn't do it. I *wouldn't*.

Heaving an enormous breath that stretched my lungs to bursting point, I released the most blood-curdling scream I could muster and closed my eyelids against the darkness that splintered across the room in flashes of nightmares and artificial lights. There was the sound of my terror and loathing as I spent every last scrap of my voice at once in that single scream, followed by a symphony of what sounded like bullets raining down on me—and then there was nothing.

Complete and utter silence.

Part of me prayed that someone had heard me and intervened, but I couldn't sense the presence of anyone else in the room. It was only me and the monsters...

Or perhaps it was only monsters.

Before I opened my eyes, I tried to gather enough saliva to force down my swollen throat, but my vocal cords were paralysed and my stomach was in knots. I felt the chilling heat of my scream settling in my chest, curled up between my collarbones like a dragon. When I tried to take a breath of air in through my nose, I was hit with the stench of exposed flesh and burning wood. I doubled over and nearly choked as a mouthful of my own blood came hurtling out at an alarming speed, and my eyelids were ripped back on instinct.

All the lights were out.

The whole room would have been in complete darkness had there not been some kind of fire glowing in the cabinet underneath the kitchen sink and a second blaze sparking against the doorframe behind my father's body.

Limply, he lay on the linoleum with his arms and legs spread out, bent in unshapely forms. Everything around him was in jagged pieces—cutlery, crockery, wooden furniture, and chunks of plaster. I was seeing all of it in black and white. Even the dark blood pooling beneath his head, which was turned away from mine.

My stomach churned around a knot of unease once more, and I dropped to my knees as I retched and spat another mouthful of metallic-tasting fluid onto the ground. Seconds later, my head followed and turned the whole world off with a skull-splitting slam.

I slept for a long time.

I almost thought I'd never wake up.

I almost hoped I wouldn't.

When the white-haired woman appeared in the doorway, I must have been dreaming.

And when I did eventually wake up, it was daylight, and the world was colourful again. I was in my bedroom, tucked under the covers. The fires were all out. The light globes were working. The parts of our kitchen that had appeared to be shattered and broken were whole. My mother had fresh, clean sheets.

And my father was gone.

Two

Little Beast

Something brushed against my upper lip, tickling my nose. I shrugged it off because I was trying to get the sleep I so desperately needed. The world was finally dark again, and I was so, *so* tired—

Sniff.

There it was again. Scrunching my nose up, I turned my head away, making sure to keep my eyes tightly closed against any rebellious flares of light because I—

Sniff.

It came back with a vengeance, with the persistence only a sentient being could demonstrate.

Alright, I thought. *That's it.*

My head thrashed from side to side as I tried to rouse myself from the depths of my dream-snared reprieve. Heavy as iron balls, my eyelids felt tender and swollen when I attempted to pry them open using sheer will alone. With my arms feeling like jelly, I couldn't seem to call upon my own hands for help.

Loud roaring echoed in my ears like cars speeding down a newly paved highway, irritating me further. *I have to find the window and close it so I can get some rest.*

A bright particle of light sliced through my vision as my lids slowly pulled apart. It *hurt*. My eyes watered, lashes fluttering with the intensity of broken butterfly wings while I fought to unravel the circling lines of shooting stars. With some difficulty, I managed to force my sight to wade through the blurry whirlpool of shapes and emerge on the other side of the obnoxious luminescence beyond them.

A white thing with feathered edges bleeding into the murky background swiped across my vision, making my nose tingle, and I shouted at it even though I knew it was likely some sort of insect and would not care to hear my protests. I bent my neck from left to right, rubbing the far corners of my eyes against my shoulders, and searched for my sense of balance.

When I found it, I shouted again—an incoherent gurgle of annoyance at discovering my new surroundings. I was sitting in a carriage, slumped against the wall, and the roaring in my ears was the sound of the wind and earth falling away through an open window as we travelled over the countryside at an alarming speed. A red velvet curtain was pulled halfway across it, guiding a beam of light with firm, rigid boundaries to pour into the space in front of me and land...

...all over Wren.

No. I frowned. That wasn't right. Not Wren anymore. Lucais. *The High King of fucking Faerie and my ill-fated fucking mate.*

It had only been days since I learned that the High King of Faerie, my fated mate by order of the Oracle, was not the man I had been introduced to when I first arrived at the House. Instead, it was his arrogant best friend, who had brought me there under false pretences, lied through his teeth to me for months, and forced everyone else to go along with his harebrained schemes.

And why? Because he was an asshole, inextricably linked to me by forces beyond even his own control, and yet he was repulsed by me in every possible way. I was only a *half*-faerie. I was more human—in all of the worst ways—than I was anything else, with little to no control over the complicated powers making a hollow inside my soul, and he wanted to make me suffer for it.

Fortunately, I felt the same way about him and all of *his* flaws.

He grinned at me, and I groaned. I couldn't remember the last thing that had happened, but his expression was evidence enough that it had all gone terribly wrong. I was about to pose the question when I spied what he was holding in one of his large, long-fingered hands.

"Where did you get a feather?" I mumbled accusingly. My words were slow and my voice was thick with the exhaustion of someone roused prematurely from their sleep.

In a flash of white and gold, Lucais flicked the feather out of the open carriage window. His eyes never left mine, and his smile only faltered for a singular moment, which was surely deliberate and done to add melodramatic effect.

He blinked at me innocently. "What feather?"

Throwing my head back into the wall, I closed my eyes and let out a soft whimper, silently begging the High Mother for it to be another one of my nightmares from the human world. If my memory hadn't been triggered by the resurgence during my first night in Faerie, I wouldn't be able to recall a single thing about those awful dreams, and I found myself wishing for that again. Like I could wake up and forget it all.

I was groggy and nauseous, and the thought of wading through Lucais's defences churned the acidic contents of my stomach. With effort, I opened my eyes, and I swore filthily under my breath when I didn't wake up quite literally anywhere else in the world.

"Good morning to you, too, little beast," crooned the real, blond-haired and golden-eyed, aggravating and cocky, High King of Faerie and Bane of My Existence, Lucais Starfire. His voice was smooth as velvet and sweet as honey. I wanted to take a vegetable peeler to his throat so it could never send warm shivers down my spine again.

I scowled at him, feeling a knot forming somewhere deep inside my heart, tightening around a vital artery. "Little beast?" I repeated with distaste. "Since when is *that* my pet name?"

Lucais's smile only grew wider, but his eyes darkened until the gold blended into amber. It carried a serious, silent threat. "Since the last time I quite affectionately referred to you as *bookworm*, you stole the light from my sky and tried to bolt," he told me. His tone was pleasant and conversational, but his eyes were smouldering. I suddenly felt hot and uncomfortable—almost ashamed. "So, no. From now on, you shall be referred to as what you truly are. A *little beast*."

I forced myself to hold his stare as I crinkled my nose. "I don't like it," I said.

"Demon?" he offered, arching one golden eyebrow on his beautiful and hateful face.

"No."

He leaned forward, bracing his elbows on his knees, and flashed his sharp teeth at me. "*Wretch*," he continued, pursing his lips around the word. A mischievous light danced in Lucais's eyes, his brows flicking up towards his ruffled hairline.

I scoffed. "*No.*"

The High King did not miss a beat. "Monster."

My pupils flared. "No!"

He rolled his eyes, feigning exasperation—I was certain that he had an entire thesaurus of derogatory names to call me, and he quite enjoyed reciting them—and sat back in his seat with a dull thump. "Villain?"

"Ugh—" I broke off, distracted. I'd moved to smack the palm of my hand against my forehead, and that was when I realised I was in chains.

High Mother help him in a minute or two.

He had put me in chains. *Again.*

But this time, they were not tethered to him. A set of thick, convict-style iron manacles encircled my wrists, fixed to chains that were bolted into the floor on either side of my feet. Anxiety curdled in my stomach. I straightened up, looked down at my confines, and pulled against them instinctively.

Nothing happened.

Blood flooded my cheeks until my face felt swollen.

I knew nothing would happen, but the panic overtook every other sense and logical thought in my mind. With a racing heart, I waited for the cool iron to warm and scorch my skin, but—

"It was a necessary precaution," Lucais began quietly. His voice was an echo down a very long, dark tunnel. "After the stunt you pulled in the Court of Light, and in front of Enyd's Court, no less—"

"It doesn't hurt," I cut in, looking up at him with fear bleeding from my eyes. *Why doesn't it hurt?* I scanned the cuffs around my wrists, on the brink of hysteria, and shot a panicked glance at the High King when I found nothing. "The iron doesn't hurt me."

Lucais gave me a bewildered look. "You think I'm trying to punish you? To...*torture* you?"

Confounded, all I could do was shake my head. "No, I-I don't know. It doesn't matter." I heaved an enormous, shaky sigh. "Shouldn't the iron *hurt* me?" I yanked, grinding my teeth together until my jaw ached, and pulled against the chains so hard that the cuffs scraped the first layer off my skin. Another wave of tears pricked at my eyes. *Please, please, please.* "I have magic," I hissed at the floor, at the chains, at the iron. At the cold and empty universe. "There was magic."

The High King's expression had softened by the time my eyes found their way back to his face. He opened his mouth, then sighed, and said, "Little beast, you're a human. There is already iron in your *blood*."

Abandoning my endeavours with the chains, I blinked away my tears. They rolled down my cheeks like fat, useless drops of acid. The iron didn't need to tell me what I already knew; the magic stalking me through Faerie had ghosted me as soon as I gave in to it—which was what I'd been afraid of the whole *fucking* time—and to wish for any further, physical proof was borderline masochistic. The truth was staring me in the face, cold as death and firm as *iron*.

My powers had disappeared again, exactly as they had done in the human world when I'd needed them most at the hopeless age of eleven. They stalked me, haunted me, tempted me, and then bailed.

Fuck them. I turned my attention back to Lucais, focussing on his words instead, searching for a loophole.

"Being part-faerie, you have less than there is in a full-blooded human woman, but trace amounts nonetheless," he concluded.

My eyebrows drew together, and I cocked my head to the side. "Are you saying I have low iron?"

Lucais's upper lip curled. "I'm not a doctor."

"You're not a lot of things, you know." I contained a laugh because none of it was actually funny, and he was looking at me the way he did when he wanted me to feel stupid. "Besides, I already know I have low iron," I complained.

I'd been diagnosed anaemic as a child, and neither the supplements nor the injections worked because my iron and transferrin saturation levels never went back into the normal ranges. The doctors gave me doses high enough to counteract my vegetarian diet, but beyond that theory, they couldn't figure it out. In hindsight, though, it made sense.

A blood test couldn't have determined that my mother cheated on her husband with my flaky faerie father many years after a brutal war permanently separated faeriekind from human beings. Ergo, at the point of conception, my body was damned to become a battleground for magic and iron as the consequences of other people's actions played out inside my genetic code.

I sighed. Very briefly, I entertained the thought that I'd like to meet another half-faerie and ask them if they ever suffered the same problems. But that was too distracting, so I packed it away for later.

"I don't understand why iron can hurt you and not me when both of us are supposed to have access to magic," I went on, my voice adopting a calmer edge than a few moments prior. "Aren't faeries supposed to be allergic? How do you suppose I've ever had magic at all if the repellent *lives* inside of my body?"

That would explain a lot, actually.

Lifting a shoulder nonchalantly, he replied, "Well, at the moment, you *don't* have any magic. It's dormant. I'm working on a theory that you might react to contact with iron when it's active if your body treats it as a foreign substance externally, but I don't think you'll allow me to test it out on you because it's going to fucking hurt." Lucais's eyes flared as if to emphasise his point. "Besides, it doesn't really explain what I tasted in your blood." His throat worked, and his tongue darted out to swipe across his upper lip as if he were recalling the experience fondly.

I grimaced. My blood had cured him of locust poisoning, yet the experience had been anything but nice for me. All of two seconds after finding out he'd betrayed my trust in the most absurd and damning of ways, I was being asked to save Lucais's life. And I did save him. Because I wanted to yell at him, and because—

No. Any other reason would be insane. I just wanted him to be conscious when I yelled at him, obviously.

After a moment, the High King huffed and said, "Honestly, the very existence of half-faeries is a mystery to begin with, and it's one I haven't had the inclination to study until"—he looked me up and down—"recently." Frowning, he turned his gaze towards the carriage window. "We'll find the answer eventually."

Inhaling deeply through my nose, I curled my hands into fists around the iron chainlinks. "How do you know I don't have any magic right now?" *Have you suppressed it? Can I steal it back?*

Lucais jerked with the motion of a short, sharp laugh. "What's the last thing you remember?"

Studying the dark wood stain behind the High King's blond head, I tried to recall what had happened after I unleashed my magic.

It had been relentless, a whispering presence following me throughout the House, playing me for a fool again for old time's sake. While the High King and his Hand were away, gallivanting across Faerie doing only the Oracle knew what, I had occupied myself in the House by reading, futilely searching for a dungeon to satisfy my in-built, inherited system of denial, and slowly reacquainting myself with magic during my final days there.

At first, I didn't have a choice. I tried to ignore it while it pushed and pushed and *pushed*. But after the day in the field with the caenim and Wren—no, with *Lucais*, who I had believed to be named Wren at the time—the closed door of my mind cracked open, and I lost an inch or two of the leash I had tightly wound around temptation.

Then another inch.

And another.

I let it go until the voice of mystical misguidance was wrapped around my body like an invisible constrictor python, squeezing the resistance out of my bones like the breath from my lungs. The only reason I had even considered using it to flee was because he had told me in the armoury that I could learn how to create a shield for myself and other people. Something that could go undetected but protect my little sister from harm.

For Brynn? For the sake of something—and *someone*—good? I'd agreed to do it. I'd agreed to try.

Apparently, I hadn't tried hard enough.

All I wanted was to replicate the flood of darkness I had unleashed in the bathroom the day Delia's beautiful white hair had turned black—preferably without the non-consensual hair dye—to create a distraction long enough for me to escape unnoticed.

The darkness was there, waiting, asking to be let out, but I had overshot my own abilities because I'd never physically rehearsed the action of evanescing. My deep, immobilising fear of flying prevented me from being able to bring myself to try it out in advance; however, because I'd read about it in the House's library, I thought I knew enough to put it into practice when the time came. I figured I wouldn't jump out of a plane wearing a parachute for fun, but if the plane was on fire and I knew the logistics of how to operate the parachute, then that entire scenario would be a completely different story.

Unfortunately, instead of ending up in the Forest of Eyes and Ears, where I would have been safe and hidden, I ended up in the back of the High King's carriage in chains, where I was flustered and mortified.

"You locked me up," I accused instead, lifting my wrists for emphasis.

The High King's eyes rolled back in his head. "Do you remember when I mentioned the exceedingly real risk of you imploding and taking out Sthiara in the process? Well, I don't know what you were trying to do back there unless you were trying to murder me, but you completely short-circuited. You used too much power too fast and burned yourself out. I thought *you* died. Wren was—" He stopped abruptly, a war of frustration and guilt using his facial features as their battleground.

Wren.

My heart thumped in my chest like a blow to the head, pain shattering across my body in waves of betrayal and regret. I felt my pulse picking up a new, unhinged rhythm and would have bet that the High King was listening to it as he watched my cheeks flushing pink with guarded, slightly narrowed eyes flaring sparks of gold and amber.

"I put the cuffs on you to protect you," he confessed after a moment, changing the subject with as much ease as opening a door with rusted hinges. "And to protect my realm. I warned you that what you were doing toed the line of dangerous territory, but you didn't listen to me." He ran a hand over his mouth, dragging his fingernails across the glittering stubble. "Nobody has ever stolen the light from my Court before, Aura. Nobody has ever dared to try, and they've certainly never done it by *accident* simply because they were pissed at me."

I blew out a harsh breath of air. "I suppose we're on the way for you to hang me for treason, then?"

It was an attempt at dark humour to lighten the mood, but I realised too late that I'd committed more than one conceivable crime against the High King of Faerie—and it was not stealing light from his sky for a mere moment in time that hung tension so thick it threatened to strangle me in the air between us. I had fallen in love with his best friend, and we'd done unspeakable things with each other under his roof and on his furniture.

Although Lucais detested the fact that he was destined to bond with a half-breed mortal who needed to be saved from flesh-eating monsters every other week, and he didn't really want me to do those things with him instead, it had to feel like he was being wronged. Lucais had to be at least a tiny bit pissed off himself.

Even if it was *at* himself.

"No, little beast," he said at last, resignation colouring his eyes a solid, stunning gold. "I won't let them put a noose around that pretty little neck." Lucais gazed out of the window as if he could see our destination, though he was facing the way we'd come, and his voice dropped in pitch and volume. "I won't tell anyone if you don't."

I nodded slowly because I knew he wasn't talking about the stolen light. "Them?" I repeated, so quietly I almost thought he wouldn't hear me. My voice cracked as I tried to amplify the whisper with my next words. "You mean the people in Caeludor? That's where we're going?"

Why would they put a noose around my neck?

He nodded, his expression tight. "I know you had other plans, and I would be thrilled to hear all about them, but we need to get ahead of the rumours after what the Court of Wind witnessed at the House. News of the caenim attack will spread to the city, and there will be chaos if I'm not around to calm their fears."

"You can't order Enyd to keep her mouth shut?"

He regarded me like I had suddenly grown a tail. "It's not Enyd who will send word."

The urge to roll my eyes at him was intense, but I managed to keep it at bay. *I have got to be civil if I want to get out of these chains.* "You can't silence her soldiers?"

Lucais was already shaking his head at me. "Do I look like the High Mother to you?"

Fuck civility then.

I ignored him. "Can you let me out of these chains?"

He ran his tongue along his bottom lip as he considered. "I *can*."

Glowering at his obviously misleading truth, I remembered all the times he had manipulated our language to lead me astray while keeping within the bounds of his inability to outright lie. It made my blood boil. I had enough to worry about and work through in my head without having to wade through the unlimited variations of phrasing the High Fae took advantage of whenever they spoke. Something as simple as *"You can call me Wren"* had almost ruined the both of us completely.

He acknowledged my irritation with a raised brow and went on to ask, "How likely is it that you'll attack me if I do?"

Chewing on the inside of my cheek, I shrugged. "Like you said, I have no magic."

"It is actually your fists I'm afraid of."

"I would nev—"

"You've done it before," he interrupted, giving me a pointed look.

And though I loathed to admit it, Lucais was right—I had slapped him across the face in Dante's Bookstore.

"That was before I knew who you were," I argued miserably.

Lucais chuckled. The sound was dark, low, and sensual. I tried to shake it off, but it gripped onto my hips like a pair of hands and sent a bolt of something entirely unwanted between my legs.

"Does it really make a difference who I am?" he purred.

Defeated, I shook my head and let my shoulders slump forward.

It wasn't worth the effort it would take for me to lie to the King of Deceit himself.

"The cuffs remain until I am certain that you won't run for your life once I let you loose," he declared, like I truly was a beast he was rehabilitating before releasing back into the wild. "You don't see it like this now, Auralie, but we're lucky that all you did back there was black out. If you disappeared, you'd find that there are worse things than scorned High Kings in Faerie, and you'd be tripling the reward for your own neck." He shook his head. "I don't want to be your enemy. It makes no difference if you like me or even if you trust me, but if you could just try to refrain from betraying me again—at *least* until you stop being such a liability—then we'll be fine."

I snorted. *Hypocrite.*

Lucais's eyes flashed as if he'd heard the private thought, but he said nothing. He simply ran a hand through his hair and readjusted his position, resting his elbow on the windowsill and propping his chin on his fist. The High King was so handsome; he would make a stunning portrait posing like that, and I hated it. I absolutely hated it.

Until you stop being such a liability.

He was too beautiful to be so cruel.

Bored with our conversation and wilfully ignorant of my charged gaze, Lucais occupied himself by watching the scenery flash past us outside, and I decided to do the same—

Except I couldn't. Because I was chained in place.

I don't want to be your enemy. Lucais couldn't lie to me outright, but he could trick me into believing things that were not true. Crucial things—like his identity and the Oracle only knew what else.

So what is it now? He doesn't want to be my enemy, but he will be? He already is? He wants to be friends even less? Oh, it's giving me a headache.

The urge to rub my temples to ease the pressure building inside my skull was intense, and the fact that I was restrained from doing so made me want to cry. But I didn't. I would not play those games with him, not when the odds were stacked against me so high that I was destined to lose count every time I tried to calculate the distance I needed to cover in order to get ahead.

Glaring at Lucais's side profile, I vowed to never allow myself to be made into such a fool by a faerie again. A fool who was tempted by fate only to find out it was a lie. That everything was a lie.

No.

He could never win at the mindfuckery. I'd do anything. I'd refuse to play—or I'd cheat.

I settled back against my seat and closed my eyes. *You don't have to be my enemy, but I want nothing more than to be yours.*

I knew he could hear me that time.

Three

You Can't Pick a Fight with Irons and Expect to Win

Somewhere between one place and the next, I lost my battle with the carriage and succumbed to the rocky movements and whooshing white noise conspiring to lull me to sleep. When the carriage came to an abrupt halt, it yanked me back to alertness. I fell forward, only managing to catch myself a second before I landed face-first in the High King's lap.

He was wide awake, lounging in his seat with his legs uncouthly spread apart, one hand resting atop his knee and the other raised in the air as if he wasn't quite sure what else he was supposed to do with it. For a split second of pure and unfiltered insanity, I imagined that he was going to place his palm against the back of my head, fist his hand in my hair until it almost hurt, undo the buckle of his belt with his other hand, and guide my face the rest of the way down to where he wanted my mouth.

Then I shoved that absolutely obscene train of thought *out* of my head and right back into the asylum from which it had obviously escaped unbidden. Halting my descent into madness, I glanced up at him from beneath my lashes and glowered at the hideously charming smirk creeping across his full mouth.

Ew. He's having the same thoughts. Ew, ew—

Using the tension of the cuffs and chains, I pulled myself upright and pushed my spine against the carriage seat until I felt the wood digging into me through the cushion.

"Not right now, but thank you for the offer," the blond fiend began, visibly fighting for his composure despite the even tone of his lovely voice. "I'm afraid we've come too close to civilisation, which wouldn't ordinarily be an issue for me, except that I *am* the High King and someone is about to open"—he paused, casting an expectant look out of the carriage window right before the door swung open and blinding light flared into the space between us like a prison spotlight—"that door."

I was preparing to pull an immature face at him when I noticed who that someone was.

Wren.

My heart punched my chest like it was trying to make a hole there so it could see him, too. Something became lodged in my throat—something that couldn't be swallowed or spoken—so I just stared at him with round eyes as he turned to face me. The exchange felt like it had to be happening in slow motion because an eternity spanned between us in mere milliseconds. A vision of warmth and heat bursting against the sun-brightened background, his broad figure took up almost the entire carriage doorframe and cast an overly large shadow across the floor. He was all dark eyes, dark skin, and dark curls...

And a dark look that unravelled across his face as his gaze snagged on the handcuffs chaining me in place. Without sparing a single moment for logical thought, Wren reached for me. His eyes were widening with horror, and his hands were fast.

Too fast.

I couldn't move out of the way in time.

The dark-haired faerie grasped my wrists, locking his fingers around the iron cuffs in an automatic attempt to pull them apart and release me. But the iron scalded him, smoke and sparks flying, and a violent hiss marked the sound of the manacles devouring his skin.

He yelled—loudly and with vulgarity—and jumped backwards, shaking the hand that had copped the brunt of the damage. Pulling the chains taut, I hid my hands behind my back so he couldn't make a second attempt. Judging by the feral look on his gorgeous face, I was certain he would try.

Wren's stare sliced into me, deep chestnut eyes narrowing into slits when he marked the deliberate removal of my hands from his reach, and so he turned to Lucais instead.

"Are you out of your fucking mind?" he demanded. "*Let her go.*"

Lucais was gaping at him with obvious disgust. "Me? Has a Bogeyman possessed you, Wren? You can't pick a fight with irons and expect to win. I've never seen anyone do something so foolish..."

The High King continued his tirade of ridicule, but it all simply faded from my mind. Everything from the moment that he uttered the name *Wren*.

It was the first time I'd truly heard him use it since the day we met when he had tricked me into believing it was *his* name.

But it wasn't.

He was Lucais Starfire, the High King of Faerie, and hearing him address the real Wren directly for the first time broke the spell of lingering confusion I'd been caught under since the truth was revealed.

I stared at him like I was seeing him for the very first time. His tousled blond hair, the sharply carved jawline and high cheekbones, his thick golden eyebrows so often elevated with distaste for me, and those eyes filled with starlight, sunlight, and the burning heat at the core of the earth. The man from my dreams—both nightmares and daytime fantasies—with broad shoulders, strong legs, and tattooed arms corded with muscle. His glistening crystal earring, the twin necklace to my own with the shared insignia of our homes peeking out from his loose white shirt, the defined column of his throat, and his full mouth of baby pink lips and teeth as sharp as the words he so often spoke.

"Lucais," I murmured absently.

He broke off mid-sentence, elongated and delicately pointed ears pricking further, and turned his face to me, head tilting ever so slightly to one side. Golden eyes smouldering, he doused me with an expression of incredulity, and his tongue came out to wet his lips just as I thought they were beginning to curve upwards into some semblance of an affectionate smile. They didn't, though.

He gazed back at me for what felt like thousands of years, and then clicked his tongue and returned to his one-sided conversation with a clearly agitated Wren. I was too bewitched by my revelation and too embarrassed to peer up at Wren and discover if he looked as hurt as the palpable tension between us immediately felt. It was the first time I had ever properly acknowledged one of them by their true names. Both out loud and in my own head. And I had picked the High King—without even thinking about it, without even meaning to choose him.

"Auralie is *fine*," the High King stressed to his friend.

Are they still friends?

I hadn't even asked.

Did I ruin that, too?

"She is ready to punch me in the throat and make a run for it at the earliest opportunity, though," he added, lowering his voice into a harsh, sardonic whisper and cupping a hand over his mouth and nose to conceal it from me. "I think she's bored of me."

Wren wore a furious expression when I at last looked back at him. "Are you fine?" he bit out.

Fine? Such an interesting question, especially coming from you. I felt my lower lip begin to wobble, so I snagged it between my teeth with a sharp intake of breath. *Exhale.*

Fixing him with a hard look, I asked, "After what you did to me?"

Wren's beautiful face fell. His anger dissipated, replaced by a profound look of remorse. The pull I felt towards him strained, like the iron chains the High King had used to secure me to his carriage were wrapped around the feelings his best friend and I had for each other instead of my wrists.

Even if I wanted to, I couldn't go to him. I *refused.* He was not the man I had thought he was. Wren was dangerous because he could seriously hurt me. He *had* seriously hurt me.

Hadn't he?

Lucais was Lucais, and I'd found a way to reconcile myself to that because he was the same no matter what name I called him. When he was pretending to be Wren, he had tried to drug me in Dante's Bookstore with silver powder. And when he was leaning into his true name of Lucais, he had tried to wake me by sticking a feather up my nose. Even when he was pretending *not* to be the High King, he still acted like one...

Oh, the irony.

The day I teased him for thinking of himself as a Prince in Brynn's dreams must be the funniest day of his stupid, immortal life.

His name never changed him, not even a little bit, and I didn't like him any differently between one name or the other.

But the real Wren? I had absolutely no idea who he was. I did not know who the man standing in front of me with a broken heart and burned hands was when he wasn't pretending to be somebody else—and doing a damn good job of it, too.

I really liked him when we were roleplaying soulmates, but he was doing it without my informed consent and lying to me through his perfect teeth.

Was it all a lie, though?

"I will be fine," I conceded, turning my head away from him. My eyes burned with the threat of hot tears. Some strange part of me was flailing as if caught on something underwater, blowing ferocious air bubbles to the surface with a message that popped before it reached my ears. Shuddering, I tried to shake it off. I shot the High King an impatient look, and his eyes grew large with theatrical indignation. "Are we far from these gates?"

Blinking slowly, he shook his head. "About a twenty-minute walk."

"We're walking?" I frowned. I couldn't see out of the carriage door, and the window on the other side was covered by thick velvet curtains. *Is there another town like Sthiara out there?*

"No," Lucais replied. "I'm not, but you are." He gestured between his right-hand man and me with a long finger. "The palace is protected by wards that are so strong even I can't evanesce through them unless I am alone. Everyone comes and goes on foot. And for this trip, at least, I need to travel to the palace gates by myself."

I was about to ask why, but he waved a hand—

And pushed me outside.

It had to have been the force of his magic because Lucais never physically touched me, and yet the chains tethering my handcuffs to the floor were released, and an invisible wind picked me up and carried me out through the door. It dropped me rather unceremoniously onto the ground. Instinctively, I went to throw out my arms to steady myself, but the chains on my handcuffs had been linked together, and the action set me completely off-balance.

Wren's strong arms caught me before I fell flat on my face on the gravel road. He supported me as I found my feet, and by the time I was able to look up again, the High King had slammed the door shut, and the carriage was being pulled away by a team of six black and white unicorns with an alarming number of spiky horns.

Jackass.

The sound of a horse's snort came from behind me, and I glanced over my shoulder to find Elera standing in the middle of the dirt road, ogling me. Her large, dark eyes were wise but regarded me with an element of caution. I nodded to her in greeting, and she hesitated a moment before bowing her head to me—lower than a simple hello would warrant—until the tips of her three curved horns brushed against the ground. Elera didn't spare a glance in Wren's direction when she lifted her head and broke into a gallop after the High King's carriage.

I turned back to him. "Why is he going alo—*what are you doing?*"

Wren's shirt was already over his head by the time I finished changing the question, and then I'd completely forgotten what I'd originally been intending to ask.

While he politely ignored me, I stood there and eyed him in wonderment.

How did he fool me into thinking he was someone that he was not?

He was the man from my dreams—or at least he would have been if my night terrors weren't actually about Lucais Starfire. The prisoner in the dungeon of my mind was the High King of Faerie, who had glamoured his tattoos to hide them from me and pretended to be someone else when we had met, but I'd seen Wren in the dark. *Hadn't I?*

They'd tricked me, and I was no longer sure about anything.

I stared at the man I had thought I was trying to save every night—the man I thought I was going to love. Exuding heat, his scent was that of a roaring fire in the dead of winter. His skin was a rich, sepia brown and soaked up the sunlight until it practically shimmered with golden light and warmth; and he was tall, broad-shouldered, muscular—

And impossibly strong.

The chain linking my handcuffs broke apart with an aggravated shriek as Wren freed me, using his shirt to protect himself. Carefully, he broke the cuffs apart using only his fingers wedged into the space between my wrists and the irons. When they split into pieces, Wren tossed them into the gully and took my hands in his, dutifully inspecting my wrists and forearms for damage. He was the embodiment of warmth in both his looks and his personality, and that made it so much easier to believe he was—that he could have been—the High King under the rule of the Court of Light.

And he didn't have a choice. And I loved him—

"You're fine," Wren surmised, reluctantly releasing my hands. I took them back into my own custody and rubbed my wrists, feeling strangely light and hollow without the cruel pieces of jewellery gifted to me by my mate. "Physically, at least."

"And you're shirtless," I commented, mostly as an excuse to let my eyes wander down his chest.

I navigated his breastbone, like a valley between his pectorals, over the peaks of his dark brown nipples, and then through a maze of his abdominal muscles, which shuddered beneath my gaze as though my eyes were a physical touch. I stopped myself before I went any lower, before I remembered—

"I can't stand it," he said quietly. "The sight of you in chains is blasphemous. The way he treats you—"

I put my hand up between us, though I didn't really understand why. "Stop," I pleaded. My chest felt tight, my heart fracturing a little under the pressure of the enormous breath I pulled into my lungs. "You played along with his games, and whether you were a willing participant or not is beside the point. You treated me every bit as badly as he did. Worse, even." *Because it fucking hurt more from you.*

Wren sighed and bent his head towards me, dark curls falling across his eyes. "Don't misunderstand me when I say this because I am sorry for hurting you and I wish it had been different, but I did not take anything from you that you were not willing to give me, and your feelings for me developed of their own accord. Believe me when I say *that* if you believe anything at all. You don't love me because of the Oracle, Aura. You love me *in spite* of it."

"I don't have feelings for you," I snapped. I felt the tang of warm metal grace my tongue and swallowed it down. "I don't love you at all."

"Liar," he accused.

"Manipulator," I spat, but the voices in my head agreed with him. I sent a mental blade after their throats.

Brown eyes boring into mine, his mouth curved into the faintest smirk, and when I sucked my lower lip between my teeth, his gaze dropped, tracking the movement. I stepped back because something brutally honest and gasping for air told me that I didn't stand a chance if he tried to kiss me.

Wren sighed. "I need to give you more time, I know." He gazed down the road to where the carriage had disappeared over the hill. "The city is beyond the crest. The reason he has to go alone is because we haven't permanently resided here for quite some time. Every pair of eyes within sight or sprinting distance of the royal carriage will be scrutinising it today."

I rolled my eyes. *If Lucais disdains me so much that he can't stand the idea of being seen with me in public, why can't he bear to let me travel freely through his realm?*

Probably for some highly suspicious and nefarious reason. As if lying about his identity could ever be the worst of his secrets.

"Aura?" Wren waved a hand in front of my face. "Are you hatching a plan to flee? If so, you won't need to fight me off because I'll let you go. I'll go *with* you—anywhere you want, any time you like."

Shaking my head, I glanced back at him and smiled ruefully. "No, I've had a change of heart. I'd really like to see what and who the High King is so desperate to hide me from, actually. He wanted to smuggle me into Caeludor like some sort of contraband, so let's go." I tucked my necklace beneath my shirt and smoothed it down, brushing a hand over the scar on my forearm left by the original manacle from our trip through the Forest. "Take me into the City of Light."

As promised, Wren acquiesced without argument and offered me a respectful nod of his head. We were almost at the top of the hill when a thought occurred to me.

"He called you Wrenlock in the House when he was poisoned, but when he gave me your name in place of his own, it was Wren. Which do you prefer?"

"Wrenlock," he answered immediately. "He gave me Wren as a nickname when we were kids to poke fun at me for my affinity with birds, and he continues to use it to this day because he knows it annoys the hell out of me."

Nodding to myself, I swirled my tongue around behind my teeth. *Figures.* I pursed my lips and tried his real name out. "Wrenlock."

It was the first truth that intruded upon me as we stepped up to the top of the hill and found an enormously wide and deep valley carved into the ground below our feet.

Wren, one way or another, is dead.

It is only Wrenlock and Lucais now.

And I had a sinking feeling that Wren had taken his bookworm out with him in a murder-suicide that could never be corroborated in the papers by the only true witness—an enchanted House.

Four

Pretty Little Neck

Caeludor was not the city I had imagined.

In fact, I hardly considered it much of a city at all. It was more like a wasteland. Lucais had spoken of the Ruins to me when we first travelled through the Court of Light and encountered the Banshee on the road. He'd said it was a vacant and discarded place to which they had been exiled—and if I didn't know any better, I would think that I was descending upon it with Wrenlock.

The mist was incredibly disconcerting because it obscured most of the infrastructure from my view. Fog as thick as rain clouds and dark as a lightning storm had settled over the city like a heavy blanket, barely allowing the tallest buildings the space to breathe. I could discern the shadowed outline of certain architecture with telltale features in their designs, such as the buildings lined up on winding streets with chimneys ascending from slanted rooftops or the symbolic spires floating over larger buildings. Even some half-dead trees were visible, anchored in the mist like macabre beacons. Overall, though, visibility was severely restricted, and it was much darker and colder than I'd have ever thought possible during the rule of a High King from the Court of *Light*.

Caeludor, I had learned through my studies in the House's library when I was alone, was a neutral part of Faerie. The *only* neutral part. There was a permanent ceasefire in place that even the Gift War had not violated. It was home to the High King or High Queen of the time and their inner circle, as well as faeries from any other Court who wished to make the city their home.

Predictably, it was protected and fuelled by the magic of its High King or High Queen, and as a result, the colloquial name changed to match the primary element of Faerie's ruler in different reigns. It was the City of Light while Lucais Starfire was High King, but had Enyd become the High Queen, it would have been called the City of Wind. Because of that, the city's bones and soil thrived on every kind of magic. One might have even found Witches living in Caeludor, according to some of the books I'd read. I'd never seen any pictures of it, but if it was truly the same city I was venturing into, I could understand why there were no visual depictions.

There would simply be no point in painting it when the canvas would have to remain so incredibly bleak. The artist may as well spill milk onto a blank page and call it a day.

Built in a valley, Caeludor emerged from the ground like a felled beast between the tall peaks of four mountains. At my back, the hillside was a walk through a field of daisies on a warm, sunny day compared to the three striking monsters in front of us that curled around the north, south, and east of the city like a scaled serpent. I was certain they were the Metal Mountains because they looked to be made from the blades of fallen swords and had a sinister, mystifying hue.

Steel glinting in the surviving light from the persistent skies above, the peaks were jagged and appeared fragile at their highest points. It was as though their astounding height was artificial, and the structures were in as much disrepair as the city beneath them.

"Why do they look like that?" I asked my sullen companion, who was a quiet and constant warmth at my side despite his lack of a shirt.

Wrenlock had discarded it on the ground near the handcuffs, and when I peered down at them to discern why, I realised the iron had found a way to burn through the fabric to get to his skin when he had freed me. At the sight of his shirt, riddled with scorch marks and holes, the newly formed ice around my heart began to crack again. I was fearful that a chunk of it might be due to fall off soon if I wasn't careful.

Is it really that bad? Isn't he hurt, too?

"The Metal Mountains?" he asked, confirming my suspicions. "They're covered in the swords of fallen soldiers from the Gift War." He squinted as he peered up at them, the ghost of long-buried sadness catching in his eyes before he blinked. "After it ended, there was so much weaponry left discarded across the realm that we didn't know what to do with it. Especially since there were so many families who never knew for certain when or where their loved ones had died. We couldn't identify and return all of the lost possessions, but we couldn't destroy them all, either. Lucais decided to drop the swords on top of the mountain ranges around Caeludor as a tribute...and a reminder of the price we paid."

A shudder buried itself at the base of my spine and began to snake its way up to the nape of my neck while he spoke. The landscape surrounding Caeludor had such a gruesome history—it was no wonder the city looked like a graveyard with its tombstone buildings and corpse-like flora crawling up out of the mist.

"And the fog?" I enquired, as we made it to the base of the slope, and a few figures became partially discernible on the road up ahead. They moved about like wraiths beneath dark waters. "Is this another one of those faerie-ruler-mood-swings?"

Wrenlock regarded me doubtfully, as if he was trying to recall when we'd had that conversation. He wasn't the one who had told me, though. It was Fake Wren—the wolf in sheep's clothing, draped in romantic faelight beside the bookcase in my bedroom at the House. The High King of Faerie, undercover. *The jerk.*

"No," Wrenlock replied at last. Raising his brows, he stretched a hand back to rub his shoulder thoughtfully.

I faltered a step. His arm was smooth, the skin entirely unblemished. My stomach twisted, a pit of ravenous vipers curling against the sides, striking me with truths. For so long, I had been looking at Wren and imagining him with the tattoos from my dreams hidden beneath the long sleeves he always wore. But he'd never had any tattoos at all. He wasn't the man from my dreams—except he *was*.

"This is essentially the perpetual state of the weather here now—most days, at least. I can't even tell you why, but I *can* tell you that it wasn't always like this. In its glory days, Caeludor was a powerhouse of magic, infinite in its beauty. Underneath all this," he continued, waving a hand at the fog as if he could wish it away, "I'm sure it still is."

I wonder if I'll get the chance to see it—

Mid-thought, I stopped myself, because that was not helpful. *Who cares about the city and what it looks like underneath the eerie fog?*

I could not afford to get caught up in thoughts like that. Caeludor's cryptic horror and ambiguity were merely another set of lines on a very long list for me to scratch off, and the paper was about to be scrunched up and discarded. I didn't even care to figure out the nightmares I'd had about Lucais anymore. The thought of *trying* sent a wave of heavy exhaustion straight to the marrow of my bones, and my head positively swam with it in all of the worst ways.

Truthfully, the High King had made his bed. If someone abducted and tortured him in a dungeon, he probably did something to deserve it.

I'd believe it. A jury wouldn't be hard to convince, either. And even if he *didn't* deserve it...

Why should I care?

He lied to me. He lied to *me*, of all people. He knew that I was supposed to be his fated mate, and yet he palmed me off to his traitorous best friend—or former best friend, I still hadn't figured that out yet, and it was another line I didn't care to waste my limited energy reserves on crossing out—and then he had the nerve to get mad at me about it. Like it was *my* fault, like I'd done something wrong.

And his best friend. *Wrenlock.* Something incredibly annoying and sticky was telling me not to hold him so personally responsible for the actions he took during an elaborate hoax that his High King had concocted and forced his hand in, but that seemed to go against all of my better instincts. I just couldn't *shake* it...

But I couldn't trust him, either.

Or Morgoya. Or anyone I'd met in Faerie at all.

They wanted me to find my biological father—yet *another* man I couldn't care less about.

My list of deplorable men was getting longer every single day, and it was truly beginning to concern me. Nonetheless, why should I have cared about a man who had a one-night stand with a married woman, knocked her up with his half-breed offspring, and then abandoned them both? Why would I want to find him only for another controlling man to try to lay his claim on me?

No, thank you.

Not even with a thank you. Just no and fuck off.

Even the Court of Darkness, too.

Blythe? I didn't know her.

What do I owe her? What do I owe any *of them?*

Nothing.

I was sick and tired of Faerie, and all of its lies and deceit. Sick to the point of violence. I wanted my magic back—even though *it* was a snivelling little traitor, too—and I wanted to go to the Forest of Eyes and Ears. I could trust the Forest in a way I could never trust any living person—*or* their horses *or* their Houses, for that matter. The Forest would protect me while I practised some of the more basic magic tricks, and once I'd mastered a shield for myself and Brynn, I would go home.

Even if I couldn't build a shield in the end, at least I'd go home knowing I tried.

Fuck Wrenlock. Fuck Lucais. Fuck Caeludor.

The Malum? Over it.

Court of Darkness? Not interested.

The Oracle? Unsubscribed, bitch.

"Aura." Wrenlock's deep, rumbling voice cut through my consciousness, and I shook my head as I resurfaced in the present moment, blinking rapidly to realign myself with my surroundings.

We'd stopped in the middle of the road, which had transitioned from dirt and sand into cobblestone, and some of the mist had cleared enough that I could begin to make out the colour in the windows of nearby stores and houses bleeding through the gloom.

"You went off somewhere in your head again," Wrenlock remarked. "Are you okay?"

I pressed my fingertips into my eyes and rubbed them, trying to wake up properly. *Why do I feel like I keep falling asleep? Probably the aftereffects of burning myself out with power, I suppose.* "I'm fine," I answered tersely.

He didn't look convinced, but we continued to walk.

Barely a few steps further into the outskirts of the city, I noticed someone staring at me—a girl who looked about my age with fire truck red hair that made her stand out against all the grey. She was carrying a wooden bucket down the road in the direction Wrenlock and I had come. Pausing, she hiked the bucket up on one hip and cocked her head to the side as her eyes sought out mine. As soon as I glanced over, she gave me a small wave with the hand she'd freed—a wave with a delicate flare of pure flame.

Fire magic.

My eyes nearly bugged out of my head at the sight of someone holding fire burning in their bare palm. It was beautiful and terrifying, and it made something awaken deep in my stomach, twisting up into my chest. I gave her a small albeit awkward wave back, and her brows drew together as she watched like she'd been expecting something else and I had disappointed her.

Quickly, my eyes darted away, and the only fire I experienced again was of the flames licking at my cheeks as we moved into clearer sections of the city.

I am still a human in Faerie.

I'd do well to remember it.

Caeludor was not like Sthiara in its streets. Where Sthiara had been quaint and reminiscent of the Victorian era in Belgrave, Caeludor was something out of a gothic nightmare in the Middle Ages. The buildings were multi-dimensional, leaving cavernous spaces between their high ceilings and long walls, and the structures were taller than they needed to be. Everything was elaborately decorated with spires, overlaid tracery, and carvings of cauldrons, broomsticks, and unicorns. It was also largely bland and greyscale, whereas Sthiara had been bursting with colour. I could easily tell that not only the fog was to blame.

Somehow, though, the resident faeries were more diverse. A few of them even presented as human in their appearance—but, if I looked closely enough, I could spy an identifying trait such as a tail or a third eye. None of them looked remotely interested in us as we walked through their streets, even though Wrenlock was the only person partially undressed, and I didn't have the pointed ears that were so commonplace.

For a moment, I felt like Livia waking up on solid land for the very first time. Then, another thought struck me, and my heart sank.

"Have you put a glamour on me?" I asked, turning to Wrenlock with tears already welling in my eyes. They didn't fall, but I still wanted to slap them away.

Why does my heart feel like it's breaking all over again at the thought?

To my relief, he looked genuinely horrified. "No," he promised. "No, Aura, I would never do that to you."

Another crack speared through the ice. "Then why isn't anyone looking at us? I'm human, and you're...half naked."

Wrenlock smiled at me warmly. "I'll show you, if you like." He held his hand out with his large, smooth palm turned up towards the sky. "Do you trust me?"

"No," I countered honestly.

"What I meant was..." He sighed. "Do you trust me enough to evanesce a few hundred metres further into the city with me?"

"Oh." I chewed on my lower lip as I considered. *It might be good practice for my ultimate escape.* "I suppose so."

Taking his hand, I felt a jolt of electricity and familiarity strike me at the touch. It was not unlike the moment we had experienced in Lucais's bedroom in the House—back when the High King was still pretending to be Wren—where some twisted and confused part of me had recognised him as my soulmate.

Although, as he squeezed my hand and I stepped into his embrace, I began to wonder if that recognition had stemmed from something else. *Is it possible that I—*

My scream caught in my throat as Wrenlock's power sucked us into a vortex and we vanished in a fit of wind, swept up from the quiet street like runaway ribbons. With my stomach flipping and twisting angrily, we landed inside a mini tornado down an alley off the side of a bustling street. Dampness hung in the air, hand-in-hand with an icy chill.

Teetering to the side, my hand found purchase on the grooves in a wall covered with slimy moss to hold myself up. Feeling violently unwell, I wondered if there was another way to travel using magic that I could learn to master instead.

This particular mode of transport will simply not do.

When I reassembled my wits about me again, Wrenlock put a finger to his lips and beckoned me to follow him to the opening end of the alley. He crouched down behind a stack of crates filled with vegetables waiting to be brought through the back door of a nearby establishment—perhaps a restaurant or a bar, if the animated echo of voices spilling out into the street every time a door swung open was anything to go by. I was surprised to see how many of the supplies looked like normal, human-grown food items.

Judging by the crowds of people walking or flying up and down the street, we were much further uptown than I'd expected.

Giant frogs, the size of small dogs, hopped up and down along the side of the road. Cats lazed on top of the slanting rooftops, tails flicking over the edges of the guttering, taunting the frogs who were jumping up to try to snatch them with the end of the long, red tongues catapulting out of their mouths. Children—faelings, they were called—were racing each other through the street. I'd never seen a faerie child before, and it was like being punched in the gut.

Brynn.

But with wings.

Tiny little wings like those of a dragonfly were attached to the shoulder blades of the faelings. They were translucent, patterned only by the barely noticeable, wafer-thin bones that stretched up and down each wing, reinforcing their delicate structure as they beat with all the force of a lady beetle and the stubbornness of a human toddler. For all of their efforts, the faelings barely made it a footstep or two into the air each time.

They were chasing orbs of light, balls of fire, droplets of water, and little hurricanes of wind up and down the street, playing with them as if they were snowballs. Older faeries were watching, talking, and waving—

Waving with the elements.

My brows drew together as I studied the way those people were greeting each other. Every wave of a hand displayed a very small, harmless show of the faerie's power. But my train of thought was brought to a grinding halt by a sudden, intrusive silence.

All at once, everyone and everything *stopped*.

Wrenlock nudged his head towards the road, and it clicked that he had brought us up ahead of the High King's carriage. The clip-clop of the six sets of heavy unicorn hooves on the cobblestone was unmistakable.

Some people vanished. They simply evanesced from the street—there one moment, gone the next. Many took faelings or large frogs with them, while others hurried to usher the young off the road, either hiding them behind their legs or shoving them behind doors. The faeries with wings took off into the sky or settled to the ground and folded their wings behind their backs in a motion that seemed very redolent of a human putting their hands in front of their face as a mark of self-defence.

Somewhere, a window slammed shut, and the sound of a set of curtains being drawn followed it, the sharp scrape of the metal eyelets against the rod distinctive and ominous.

And then there was Lucais's carriage.

I couldn't see him inside it, and I wasn't sure if anyone else could, but there was no mystery shrouding its ownership or doubt surrounding its occupancy. His presence was as powerful and naturalistic as a change in the weather outside or a drop in the temperature in a room.

The six black and white unicorns pulling the carriage were frightening in a spine-tingling way when I observed them up so close. Their dark grey horns looked like a mess of tangled vines, like thorny brambles growing atop their heads. Truly, I couldn't tell where one horn began and another finished. They were much larger than Elera—if that was even possible. They looked proud, strong, and absolutely menacing.

The carriage itself appeared to be carved out of a giant shell. White and gold shimmered like that of a pearl, a faint sheen of luminescence falling over it in a blanket of light—a striking contrast to the darkness pouring out from the inside.

Lucais wasn't using his magic at all. Didn't even seem to be in touch with it.

Normally, he was light magic on legs. His hair, his eyes, and his skin unfailingly glowed with some semblance of light. Even under a grey sky, even on a foggy street...but the inside of the carriage was pitch-black. No light lined the tiny gaps in the curtains. Nothing glowed or even glimmered from within.

I almost started to convince myself it was empty and my sixth sense was actually the result of deeply-rooted paranoia until I saw it—a single, mildly flaring golden eye. Just one, peering out through a slit in the curtains. I couldn't tell if he was staring at me or not, but I felt the urge to hide overcome me like a handkerchief dosed with chloroform.

Wrenlock took my hand and pulled me closer to his side, and for some reason, I let him.

The High King must have seen us because he turned his head, and I heard a few stifled gasps from across the road as onlooking faeries spied the single gold eye glaring out at them.

When the carriage moved on and Elera disappeared with it, the clip-clopping of hooves fading from earshot, Wrenlock and I stood up and tried to brush the dampness from our knees.

"Why?" was all I could ask him. I knew to be specific, but I couldn't bring myself to do it.

"I told you," he began slowly, refusing to meet my questioning gaze. "We haven't been back here for a while."

A bitter rush of anger shot up my throat. "Define *a while* as it pertains to my question of why these faeries are acting so strangely around him," I demanded. Evidently, we still were not past the language and lying barriers, and I had no choice but to be exceedingly careful about my phrasing.

Lucais was from the Court of Light, and they were acting as though he'd just risen up from the shadows of the netherworld—or whatever their equivalent was that did not involve Merfolk. *Is their equivalent the Court of Darkness? No...*

"I can't," he repeated, vigorously wiping at the fabric on his knees. With a shaky sigh, he straightened, brow furrowing. "Honestly, Aura, I cannot remember the last time he was here because he does not tell me everything. Case in point—the fact that he was going to deceive you about his true identity and force me to do the same. I received no warning about that. My best guess is that it would be at least fifty years since Lucais has held court with the public in Caeludor—maybe even a hundred—but if you discover that I am wrong, please do not accuse me of misleading you on purpose."

"A *hundred* years?" I pressed my tongue against the roof of my mouth to counteract the sensation of my jaw hitting the ground.

He cleared his throat, shrugging. "Time passes differently in Faerie than it does in the human world. And we've had some issues, you know."

"Oh, I *know*." My eyes flashed when they locked with his, and I thought I saw him flinch. "But a whole century? That doesn't make any sense."

"It does when you factor in all the things he's done," Wrenlock retorted. His voice was tight, a muscle in his jaw flickering.

"Like what?" I scoffed before I could really consider what it would look like. Three hundred years in power—or more, potentially—was a great deal of time to accomplish or ruin a great many things. "Freeing the slaves?"

A beat of hesitation. It was a telltale sign that I was knocking on a door that did not wish to be opened. Morgoya had explained it to me once—that when the High Fae told the truth, they tended to tell the whole truth and nothing but the truth. And they *loathed* it.

Wrenlock scraped the toe of his boot across the stonework. "Among other things."

Ugh. I rolled my eyes. No more secrets, we had agreed.

Liar, liar, liar.

It wasn't really worth me fighting with him over it, but part of me was incensed. When Lucais had said the House was the High King's safe house, I'd assumed he meant from the Malum, yet Wrenlock made it seem like Lucais was hiding from his own people—like he had good reason to do that. *Why would a High King need to use a safe house to escape the fear and censorious looks from his own subjects?*

Then it occurred to me. Everything he'd said and done indicated he felt a lot of frustration and shame over me, which felt like a good reason to keep me concealed. Perhaps he *was* hiding me from them for my own protection, after all.

I won't let them put a noose around that pretty little neck, he'd said.

But why would they want to put a noose around my neck, Lucais?

I tried to reach him down the bond using the strange and unreliable mental telepathy we had been experimenting with both willingly and unwillingly since the day we met, but there was no answer. Realistically, I was probably too far away from him to even *feel* the bond properly, and I still wasn't really sure what the feeling represented.

Annoyance? Yes.

Irritation? In spades.

A connection I can't shake off? That, too.

The bond I felt with Wrenlock was vaguely similar and yet even stronger, though try as I might, I couldn't make sense of it. Nevertheless, I was glad that nobody looked at me, the human mate of the High King of Faerie, and the shirtless man walking down the street beside me. Morgoya's words echoed in my head once more—*they have a lot of questions we don't know how to answer yet*—because I actually understood what she meant. For all intents and purposes, the goddamn High King and his inner circle had dragged me into their twisted political disaster and made me an accomplice to their crimes.

Discreetly following the path of the royal carriage, Wrenlock and I navigated our way through streets that became clearer the further into the city we walked. The fog remained above us, hovering like an ever-present ceiling until, at last, I spied the gates ahead—but I had to strain my eyes to locate any sight of the palace beyond them. For some reason, the fog fell in much heavier clouds behind the boundary of the half-open, heavy metal gates, though the street we were striding through was almost as clear as a normal day.

I refused to take my eyes off the space before me where Lucais's palace surely belonged—refused to even blink—and eventually, I spied a few walls and turrets peeking through the mist as it shifted and swirled. We stepped through the gates, the sentries recognising Wrenlock with a brief nod, and together, we entered the High King of Faerie's palace.

At least, what was left of it.

Five

The Locust and the Love Declaration

Maybe I'd imagined it.

Stranger things had definitely happened in Faerie before. *Many* stranger things. It was actually far more likely that I was hallucinating the ruination of Lucais Starfire's palace than it was that the High King of Faerie's home had been allowed to fall to pieces and not a single creature had done *anything* about it whatsoever.

Wrenlock and I followed the cobblestone road across a bridge that was barely wide enough for a single carriage to cross with any degree of comfort. Squinting over the low-set stone parapet to see what was hiding below, I discovered a river of mist snaking beneath the bridge, completely obscuring my vision of the ground.

The fog condensed, an immaterial fabric tightening its hold as it wrapped itself around us like hessian bags falling over the heads of prisoners before the guillotine. It was something akin to a sentient being guarding the palace, almost like a dragon or three-headed beast in a fairytale, prowling around the perimeter. It felt poised to swallow any potential threats into its opaque mists, sentencing them to an eternity of wandering lost through an endless and inescapable fog.

The idea made a grim sense of claustrophobia gather in my chest, squeezing my heart.

Breathing deeply in spite of the damp chill clawing at my lungs, I searched for a physical anchor for my eyes to settle on to help me hold the panic at bay. I could hardly make out the shape of a building ahead of us, let alone see where the bridge ended or if anything was coming our way. I did, however, spy the far side of the palace's exterior as I cast my eyes around. For a brief moment, the mist thinned, and I saw the crumbling stone again. It was like a sandcastle that had weathered the touch of too many waves, falling into collapse in jagged fragments and dust.

I tried to catch another glimpse so I could make a more thorough assessment of the damage, but the fog didn't shift again, and soon enough, we had reached ascending steps. With my hand tightly secured in Wrenlock's gentle grasp, I navigated them unsteadily. A new pair of sentries—dressed in the white and gold uniform I had seen before but coated in a sheen of gloom that had not been present at the House—opened the tall, arched doors for us like they were weightless.

Stepping inside the palace felt as though we were escaping a rainstorm. Relief seized my shoulders and forcibly released the tension I was carrying in them until I could feel my chest deflating like a balloon.

The comfort brought to me by four walls—wherein my sight was restored, and the bitter chill in the air was trumped by some type of presumably magical heating element—was so strong that I sighed blissfully and slumped against the nearest one. My head lolled back, gaze drifting up towards the high ceiling. I studied its intricately painted surface until a familiar heat grazed my throat, bringing my eyes back to the man standing a few feet away from me.

Wrenlock watched me, a hot flare of desire evident in his dark eyes, twinkling like the flame of a lighter being held beside a candle wick. He was a wild element, burning up all of the oxygen in the room in his timeless pursuit of me. I was motionless as I stood there, a rope covered in wax, unable to react but wanting more than anything for him to set fire to me so I could burn with him.

He didn't move to close the distance between us, but I remembered when he had—when he'd pressed me up against the wall in the House's hallway right before we evanesced through it, desperate to find somewhere safe to land in each other as we tumbled onto the bed.

In my peripheral, a figure appeared in one of the nearby doorways and strode over to meet him. Silently, they handed something over, and he accepted it without breaking eye contact with me for even a second.

The faerie disappeared.

After holding onto me with his eyes a moment longer, Wrenlock's gaze fell, causing heat to bloom beneath the places it landed on my body. He tore his eyes away from my flesh like it was something sticky and then slipped the item—a black tunic—over his head with ease, leaving me gasping for breath, my chest heaving as I stumbled forward, glaring down at the stone floor so he wouldn't have access to the regret watering my eyes like dead flowers.

It's too late. He hurt *you,* I reminded myself.

He didn't mean to, a wicked and intrusive voice whispered in reply.

Irritated, I shoved the voices into a cage in the back of my mind and slammed iron doors shut, locking them twice. I steeled myself, pushing my shoulders back, and stormed past Wrenlock without another look as I headed towards the staircase.

One fated mate who had the power to keep his promises, but never did simply to spite me. And one *whatever he was* who would do anything I wanted if I asked nicely enough, but didn't have the power to see it through.

The High Mother and the Oracle must be clinking their teacups together and laughing at me.

I walked beneath an enormous chandelier, stumbling a step as I craned my neck to look up at the lights. The heavy black frame must have existed for decorative purposes since there were no candles to illuminate the room; instead, Lucais's orbs of faelight bobbed up and down in place of the flames, a mix of whites, yellows, and oranges.

It occurred to me as I redirected my line of sight and focussed on taking the thin, gold carpeted steps two at a time that the palace did not belong to Lucais—it belonged to whoever the High King or High Queen was at any given point in time, and must therefore have many different features leftover from many different rulers. I'd not seen a chandelier like that at the House, so it was likely a relic left behind by the Court of Fire. Absentmindedly, I wondered who it was and how long it had been since they lived there. A few hundred years, at least, based on what Lucais, Wrenlock, and Morgoya had told me about the Gift War.

Do all the Courts leave something behind? Would the Court of Darkness, too?

For a building so old, the High King of Faerie's palace was certainly not in a dire state of disrepair inside, which cemented my belief that I'd imagined the crumbling exterior. If the foundations of the building were truly so weak, I would surely have found partially collapsed walls and ceilings clouded with stone raindrops waiting to fall upon me within.

On the contrary, the palace looked to be in relatively good condition for its age; its firm stone floors and walls had minimal cracks and chips, chandeliers were polished to the point of sparkling in the dark, glass casings around the empty lanterns had been wiped so clear they were almost invisible, and clean tapestries and stainless rugs of gold or white adorned the halls.

At the top of the large, cascading staircase were carvings of dancing pixies and land-dragons—known as dinosaurs in the human world—high on the walls and low between the posts on the stone balustrades.

I paused, assessing their depictions as I contemplated my next move. The heat brushing my back told me that Wrenlock was following but quietly keeping his distance. Somewhat regretfully, however, he was not the man I needed to see. The jury was still out on whether he was the man I *wanted* to see—or if I even wanted to see either of them at all.

Walking on, I moved deeper into the palace. The orbs of faelight did not respond to my presence the way the ones at the House did, and longing stabbed my gut. I had raged against the magical presence of the House during my stay there, but it had been so nice to not feel alone. The palace felt empty and cold, lacklustre for all enchanted purposes.

A few twists and turns later, though, I found one similarity—cabinets of magical relics and historical tokens.

Like a museum, the hallway displayed paintings and ornate mirrors along the walls between finely woven tapestries preserving memories from otherwise forgotten ages. Custom spaces had been carved into the grey stone to fit treasures like delicate oil lamps, wooden carvings of mythical creatures, gold vases, twinkling crystal lamps, and glass figurines of creatures from the water.

It looked to be priceless, like something Lucais would be placed in charge of as High King, rather than something he would have brought with him from his own personal collection.

Perfect. It was exactly what I needed.

On cue, like we had rehearsed it for an audience of one, I felt him appear behind me. Then I heard him take a single step, weighed heavy with hesitation.

"How was your walk?" the High King of Faerie asked, and the sound was a velvet caress against the inner chambers of my soul.

"It was fine, Your Majesty," I answered in a lilting voice.

Slowly, I pivoted and met his curious gaze. Lucais wore the same clothes—a loose white shirt with string instead of buttons, left to hang open at the collar, with his sleeves rolled up to his elbows to display the tattoos he'd only recently revealed to me, and fitted black pants. He didn't carry his weapons belt. In the faelight, his crystal earrings and the Court of Light insignia hanging around his neck sparkled, and his golden eyes mirrored the shine as they narrowed on me with suspicion so strong it could have given me a strip search.

I watched him fold his arms over his broad chest as he leaned against the wall, and my roguish heart fluttered idiotically.

"Call me Lucais, please," he purred, and then he cocked his head to the side. "Or baby." His full mouth pursed as he regarded me thoughtfully. "No, wait"—he held up a finger between us, his eyes dancing—"how do you feel about *schnookums*?"

Smiling at him with all of the false pretence I could muster, I reached for the closest item—a glass carving of a unicorn, slender with a long mane and a single, straight horn. Gingerly, I picked it up and sidestepped off the gold-tasselled hall runner so I was standing on the granite-hard stonework.

And then I dropped it.

The unicorn smashed into a thousand pieces of glass, like hail on the ground.

Lucais lifted a brow. "I'll think of something else, then."

"So thoughtful of you," I murmured absently, stepping around the mess I'd made. "Tell me why you don't want the people of Caeludor to see me."

"I never said that."

My cheeks filled with air before the breath escaped through my lips in a whoosh. I stopped in front of a small mirror, edged with an elaborate design of frosted-glass flowers, hanging in the centre of the wall. When I reached for it, I caught a flash of movement in my peripheral vision and glanced back to see that Wrenlock had stepped forward as if to intervene. Lucais held his hand out, halting him.

"Now, now, Wrenlock." Lucais's golden eyes were piercing as they locked with mine. "If my future High Queen feels the need to dispose of items in this palace that are not to her personal taste, I will caution any man against trying to interrupt her creative process."

My stomach flipped—and then dove behind my rib cage when I tried to kill the feeling with my mental tenacity. *I have to do this.*

Not only was he still playing with me, but he was the greatest half-liar and total brute in all of Faerie. If he wouldn't answer a question plainly and of his own free will, there had to be something that would force his hand or trip his feet. It was simply a matter of finding it, and then figuring out not only what he was hiding from me, but *from what* he was hiding *me*.

Taking a deep breath, I held the mirror in one hand as I traced the other across my reflection. Aside from the darkening circles beneath my eyes—which had not been so purple since I'd been plagued with relentless nightmares—I did not look any different.

My cheekbones had hollowed out somewhat, but my hair was still the colour of paprika and had barely grown in length, a waterfall of bloody curls spilling over my shoulders. My freckles were soft and splattered over my nose and cheeks, and my eyes were as blue as the day I was born.

Worse than any symptoms of sleep deprivation or malnourishment, though, was the rounded curve on both of my plain old human ears.

No. Magic. *No.* Power.

I had nothing but the desire to set fire to things because I was fucking pissed.

"This is nice," I remarked, glancing up at my intended soulmate. "Is it expensive?"

He rubbed the stubble on his chin with one hand, his expression unreadable. "Yes."

"Hmm." Nodding agreeably, I peered at myself again. The birthmark painted onto my skin through one eyebrow matched the colour of my lips, which were dry. I wet them with my tongue before I threw the mirror onto the ground with all of my might, where the flowers imploded and my reflection cracked. As I sighed sharply, my chest seared with heat and trembled with galloping beats. "Shame."

Wasting no time, I snatched a crystal lamp and sent it flying into the glass door of the display cabinet behind me. The sound of glass shattering was so loud it almost caused me to wince, so I filled the corridor with the sound of damaged and broken things to help me acclimate.

As the volume increased with echoes of damage, the palace atmosphere began to match the way my world sounded inside my own head. Flinging open the doors on the next cabinet, I reached in and gathered items between my wrist and elbow without even checking to see what they were. Using my forearm, I swiped them off the shelves. *Bang. Crash. Clink.* I tipped vases from their resting places on the walls, yanked tapestries from their hooks until they tore, and flicked glass figurines onto the stonework. *Bang. Crash. Clink.*

Lucais didn't speak, didn't try to stop me. He was waiting me out—testing me to see if I'd cave first.

So, I gritted my teeth and kept going.

Pausing in front of a suit of armour halfway down the hall, I tilted my head to the side, and a heavy silence fell upon me as I examined it, quieting the other voices in my head. I pushed the whole suit of armour over because I had to keep up the commotion, keep mimicking the sound in my mind. If nothing else, at least it was cathartic.

The suit shattered another cabinet on its way down, sending broken pieces of glass and ceramic spilling across the floor like a flood of treasure out of a pirate's chest.

"You do realise that you are destroying your own alimony?"

I faked a laugh to cover the sound of my relief that the High King was still standing there, at least interested in what I was doing, if not perturbed. "Aren't you listening?" I hissed. "I don't *want* it."

"Fine." His tone was clipped.

Good.

Reaching out blindly, I seized something else from the wall and sent it careening against another cabinet. *Bang. Crash. Clink. Bang. Crash. Clink—*

"I swear to the High Mother," Lucais grumbled at last, and I whirled, glaring at him to disguise my investment in what he had to say. All I needed was one truth—a single, solitary, straightforward answer. But his eyebrows shot skyward, and he flung out a hand towards me, looking pointedly down at the suit of armour. "You're as destructive as a pet wolf and about as friendly as one, too."

My eyes rolled back into my head. "Wrong answer," I seethed.

"Is there a *right* answer?" he shot back, flinging both of his arms out to the sides with a desperate, pleading look in his golden eyes.

I shook my head in disappointment, bending to pick up the sword from the fallen suit of armour. To my surprise, both Lucais and Wrenlock flinched, the latter ducking behind a painting I hadn't fully knocked off the wall while the former took cover behind a nearby cabinet. The glass had made an ocean all over the floor, but the gold frame was still intact.

My brows pushed together. *Is the sword magical?* It looked like any boring old sword, but maybe I wouldn't know the difference. My gaze bounced between the two men, irritated, as my chest rose and crashed back down with heavy breaths. "What are you hiding from?"

"You, in a minute, by the looks of things," Lucais retorted, his tone bordering on the edge of hysteria as he peered at me between the shattered shelves. "Will you put that thing down?"

It took everything in me to stop my mouth from falling agape. Recovering quickly, I shot back, "Will you tell me the truth?"

"I *have*—"

"No!" I screamed, rage taking the reins.

Fuck, this is worse than the silent treatment I used to get as a child!

A frustrated scream built between my collarbones, and I slashed the sword wildly above my head. It cut through a tapestry hanging on the wall like a stick of butter, and the weight of it swinging through the air nearly sent me toppling over and falling into a pool of glass on the ground.

I grunted quietly and sought my balance with a deep breath. "You have *not.* You lied to me, Lucais, and you *just*"—bracing myself with my feet shoulder-width apart, I raised the sword high above my head with two hands on the hilt—"*keep*"—glass rained down on me as it collided with an empty lantern, which blew apart against the sword's razor-sharp edge—"*doing it!*"

As I brought the weapon down, aiming for the dramatic finish of the blade striking the floor with a clang, I misjudged the grip required for its weight distribution. The sword slipped from my hands. It flew through the air, turning hilt over end straight down the hallway until it landed—

Oh, no.

Embedded in the chest of a very unfortunately placed man.

He was a pale, maroon-skinned faerie I'd never seen before who had turned the corner and come to a sudden stop in the middle of the hallway. I didn't know what race of faerie had three eyes, but he had a third one in the middle of his forehead above an expertly sculpted nose, and they all turned glassy at the same time. Collapsing, he landed flat on his back, the suit of armour's sword standing straight up in the air.

My stomach dropped, the impact of its fall sending bile shooting upwards, where it burned a hole in my chest. Everything felt like a live wire, tingling with unhinged electricity. My hands went to my mouth to stifle a scream that never came.

Fuck, fuck, fuck.

I had about a millisecond to regain control of my expression before Lucais and Wrenlock, who had turned their heads to track the course of the sword, looked back at me.

Focus, focus, focus.

Clamping my tongue between my back teeth so hard I tasted a metallic tang, I regained ownership of my expression and forced it into a mask carved from stone. Emotion slipped away like a balloon in the breeze, replaced by a masquerade I hadn't practised since I was eleven years old.

Lucais turned to me first—eyes wide, cheeks flushed, mouth slightly agape. I was at a standstill, snared on indecision between the urge to run and hide behind his arms or run and hide behind the suit of armour. His gaze bounced off the ceiling before he pinned me to the spot with a smouldering copper stare and sighed brusquely.

"The *staff* aren't part of your *alimony*, bookworm," he said through his teeth with a head shake. He pinched the bridge of his nose. "Spectres defend me, I'll be Marked for this. Clean that up before anyone sees," he ordered Wrenlock, who pulled a face at him behind his back. "Apparently, the future High Queen and I have a considerable amount of work to do on our communication skills before we're fit to be seen in public—let alone the privacy of what is *supposed* to be our own home."

Hopelessly, I gaped at the sword protruding from the body and found myself barely able to comprehend a single word the High King had said. Wrenlock didn't look at me again; he simply turned and walked in the opposite direction, although I noticed that his silhouette did an excellent job of blocking my view. I wasn't sure if it was intentional, but I imagined so.

Lucais roughly pushed a hand through his hair, gesturing to the doorway at the far end of the corridor. His blond locks were mussed, sticking up in places like he'd just risen from a fitful night of sleep. "After you, bookworm."

I was on fire. My veins were burning with a sensation of soul-deep horror, but I had to force it down. I could not let it rise to the surface where it would very likely consume me.

Oh my god. I'd killed an innocent faerie. *Murderer. I killed a faerie. Brynn would be mortified...*

No. *It was a* faerie, *for fuck's sake.*

Faeries are cruel and vicious by nature, right?

Besides, I had done much worse things in my short life already than *accidentally* skewering a faerie on a sword that part of me had thought was a prop when I first picked it up.

I swallowed a painful lump and waited until I felt its leaden weight hit my stomach before I started walking in the direction Lucais was pointing. Surprise slackened my mouth when I realised that I was capable of walking at all.

"I don't think I like *bookworm* anymore," I managed to say, as our steps drove the shrapnel of my explosion deeper into the fibres of the pretty hall runner.

Each movement echoed with a crack over shards of glass, grinding them into the bottoms of our shoes. It reminded me of the day that Lucais—masquerading as Wren at the time—had been poisoned by a locust. The way the glass had felt slicing into the soles of my bare feet as I hauled his half-conscious body back to my room only minutes before he told me he loved me and insulted me in the same breath.

I'm so in love with you, it's made me sick.

"Fine by me," he replied curtly. "You really are a nasty little beast."

A sigh expanded in my chest and rushed out through my nose.

The day with the locust and the love declaration was well and truly behind us indeed.

Six

Dungeon

Waiting for the High King's fury to surface was like waiting for the walls to start talking back.

Aside from the short outburst immediately preceding the manslaughter—or rather, the faerieslaughter, I supposed—Lucais didn't seem to be upset with me.

As we walked in a bland silence, I began to wonder if maybe he disliked that particular employee and I'd done him a favour. Then I wondered if I'd committed a crime that perhaps *would* result in a noose being placed around my neck, effectively bringing his prophecy to life if I wasn't more careful. *He may be the High King, but is he powerful enough to prevent a witch hunt—or was it a human hunt?—led by an angry mob if he's been hiding from his own people in the remote, heavily protected House for a century or so?*

That train of thought delivered me right back to the station of the original problem, which was the fact that he was a dirty rotten liar, and I was sick of it.

"Are you mad at me?" I asked him plainly. *Would you still love me if I were a worm? Would you still love me if I butchered your butler?* But he hadn't loved me in the first place—not really, not in a way that was safe for me to accept—so, instead of that, I added, "About the staff member back there."

Lucais eyed me sideways, continuing to take long strides down the hall. "No," he said, tone clipped. "I am not mad at you about the staff member back there."

I grimaced because for some reason that made me feel even worse. "Shouldn't you be?"

Stopping in his tracks, he whirled on me with a huff, eyes blazing like a summer sun. "I should be a lot of fucking things since I met you," Lucais snapped. He began listing them off on his fingers. "A neurosurgeon, a coroner, a cauldron-worshipping death-wielder—which would come in handy right about now, ironically—a water faerie, a doctor..." He scowled down at his hand, which had run out of fingers to lift, and then raised his head to narrow his gaze on me like a laser beam from a sniper as he took a step forward. "Have I *missed* anything?"

I shook my head. "I...I don't know."

"Right," the High King barked, and in the same breath, he exhaled a humourless laugh. "Of course you don't. *I'm* the one keeping all the tabs. I'm your fucking executive assistant now, too." He swiped the back of his hand through the air between us, causing a burst of cold to rush over me. "Do you realise that you've hardly left me a *moment* to be the High King since you quite literally crashed into me like some sort of faulty vehicle or wayward bird?"

Heat clouded my head, curling like smoke in my nostrils. Lucais could be right about many things, but he didn't have to be so *rude*.

"Like it makes a difference!" I shouted, throwing up my hands. The way my voice echoed against the walls bolstered my confidence. "When you've been hiding out in a safe house from your *own people* for a century, I can't imagine you'd have many *better* things to do!"

Lucais's eyes flashed. He leaned towards me, raising a hand between us with his pointer finger extended, and opened his mouth to speak—but then he shut it, eyes crinkling at the corners, and pressed his lips together in a tight line. Stepping back, he very forcefully pointed towards the end of the hallway and the door to which we had been en route. My lashes touched my eyebrows as I glared up at him. Lucais held my stare for long moments with the same rigid control he used to keep his arm and pointer finger firmly in place. He took deep, measured breaths that filled his chest and stirred the curls of my hair as each exhale swept over me with the scent of ink, musk, and the heat of a midday sun.

Oh, fine. I see how it is.

I couldn't be sure which one of us relaxed first, but that was all it took. Somewhere between the two of us, a singular muscle twitched, giving in, and then the tension of our stand-off collapsed into the space between us like a fallen house of playing cards.

"The High King of *Liars*," I muttered, sullenly folding my arms over my chest as I began to walk again.

"The High Queen of *Beasts*," he returned, pinching me on one of those arms.

I ignored the sting of his cruelly playful touch. Ignored the way it *lingered* far longer than it should have.

As our silence bloomed once more, so did my discomfort. The palace expanded, the ceilings getting further away and the windows rising higher up the walls with the growing distance we put between ourselves and the scene of the crime. Every corridor we turned down was empty, as though I'd killed the only staff member in the whole palace.

I killed him. I killed someone.

"Where are you taking me?" I questioned, breaking the quiet spell of guilt as Lucais walked with purposeful strides.

"To the dungeon," he replied stoically.

I skidded to an abrupt halt in front of a closed wooden door, the colour draining from my face.

Lucais tossed a smirk at me over his shoulder. "Not to throw you in there, you insufferable woman," he promised, completely misunderstanding the source of my panic.

Even if he did try to lock me up in a dungeon, I would simply scream until he got so sick of hearing my voice that he let me out again. Or, in the worst-case scenario, I was fairly confident that Wrenlock would come to my rescue.

No, it's not me that I'm worried about.

It was the image of *Lucais* in the dungeon that crossed my mind, sending a storm of sickness to the pit of my stomach, wreaking havoc against all of my internal organs like a battered ship fighting to stay afloat against the wrath of the water gods. The sound of his voice when he screamed—which had happened in the months that he was bruised by iron weapons and drowned in buckets of icy water—indicated that an insurmountable amount of pain had been inflicted upon potentially the most powerful man in the world.

I hadn't had a nightmare about it since my first night in Faerie. I'd actually started to convince myself it was merely a conjuring of my imagination and had nothing at all to do with the suspiciously timed Oracle's prophecy, the disappearance of the Court of Darkness from a Map I was yet to see for myself, and general tomfoolery of faeries and their war-central politics. *But if it was—*

"Tell me what that look on your face is for," Lucais said, the demand long and drawn out with languid trepidation.

I could have sworn I detected a whisper of concern for someone other than himself in his voice, but it was surely a symptom of post-murder trauma on my part.

"It's nothing," I muttered, dropping my gaze to the floor.

Even if I wanted to tell him—and I *didn't*—I couldn't.

I'd never been able to talk to anyone about my dreams because something beyond my control always stopped me. I'd experienced it often enough at the House to realise what it was—a big step from my tormented winter nights alone in my room—and I could recognise it as magic. I'd felt it myself in the House and even tasted it inside Wrenlock's mouth. Some kind of magic had been threaded into my dreams, and while my presence in Faerie had lifted the spell far enough for me to remember what they were about again, I didn't think I could say it out loud. My tongue tingled with the threat of going numb even when I did nothing more than consider it.

"Little beast," Lucais purred, stepping towards me with a note of warning in his voice. He donned the skin of a predator effortlessly, his eyes taking on a feline glow. "If we are to be honest with each other, you need to realise there's some work to be done there on your end of our bargain."

I rolled my eyes. "You are *such* a hypocrite."

He scoffed. "Hardly. As a matter of fact, I think what I'm about to show you will go a long way in my favour where you're concerned."

"Oh, like you care what I think."

The plain wooden door clicked open as Lucais placed one palm flat against it, the other hand patting the space on his chest above his heart. His eyes captured mine, sparkling like stolen gold.

"You wound me," he lamented.

"I wish," I mumbled in reply.

Climbing down the stairs with my hands firmly pressed against my sides, we cleared a few flights before we arrived at another door. A chill crept along my arms, the tiny pinpricks like those of a rat skittering up to find a perch on my shoulder. The second door was bound by iron, and when Lucais extended an arm towards it, I couldn't reign in my reaction in time. I couldn't even control it. I grabbed his wrist with an unyielding grip, pulling his hard, heavily muscled forearm against my chest.

His brow furrowed as he cast me a downwards look, head tilted to the side. Without trying to recover his arm, he turned his body and used his free shoulder to push the door open, keeping between the reach of the iron reinforcements.

The air rushed out of my lungs all at once when it swung open and, using the arm I was still fiercely holding onto, Lucais pulled me through the doorway. I let go of him, and he placed his hand on the small of my back, the puzzled look remaining fixed in place until he closed the door, and his face was consumed by the immediate onslaught of shadows.

The dungeon was cold and pitch-black.

For a moment, all of my anger and apathy left me for dead. I was paralysed by fear for the man at my side as liquid dread rose up my throat.

This is it. The moment my most wicked dreams come true, born of selfishness and greed. I couldn't let him go, and now I'll pay the price.

My dreams had been warning me about it for months before my twenty-first birthday—before I met the High King and stepped through the gateway into Faerie. It was the vision the Oracle had chosen to show me in the human world, a prophecy from fate, and I had allowed it to be decreed because I willingly watched it happening to him. How shamefully I had *longed* for it every night.

Strength abandoned me, and I leaned into Lucais's side, though I didn't know what use it would be. I couldn't save him. I hadn't figured out who was hurting him—although the Malum were the most obvious guess—or how they'd managed to entrap him. I didn't know why I was there with him in the first place, aside from the instantaneous and glaring idea that he'd brought me down to the dungeon to show me something and they'd ambushed him—

Light.

A flare of light split the room into a million pieces as an orb appeared at our side, dozens more following it, and Lucais moved with the speed of an apex predator, pinning me to the closest wall. I gasped. The damp stone was bitterly cold as it seeped through my clothes in search of skin.

"Little beast." Lucais's mouth was at my ear, his breath warm and sweet as it caressed my face, the scent of him intoxicating. Tingles shot down the side of my neck, straight to my nipples, and then lower, causing a heated tension to wake up and stretch in my belly. "You're starting to make me nervous."

I gulped. "You should be," I whispered thickly.

And for the very first time, I actually wished I could tell him.

Nose skating along my cheekbone, his lashes tickled the bridge of my nose, and his mouth was dangerously close to mine when he murmured, "*Why?*"

Because—

Something clutched my throat, cutting off the oxygen.

I haven't even opened my mouth yet.

Fear nipped at my fingers and toes. At that moment, I realised I was going to die trying to tell him the truth. I was going to die because there was an ancient and powerful magic willing to kill me to prevent the words from leaving my lips, and I suddenly could not *stand* the fact that he didn't know what would happen to him down there.

Death was the better option.

God, I wished things were different. But Lucais needed to know, and I needed to be the one to tell him. I had been scared and silenced for far too long, and I wasn't about to keep doing it.

My head bobbed, my throat working as I tried to force a breath of air inside my body, to swallow, to do *anything—*

Alarm flashed in my eyes, and Lucais's head reared back, an incensed type of confusion marring his features.

"Auralie." He scanned my face, catching the tension in my throat, the terror in my eyes. "*Auralie.*" His voice was strained, tighter than normal. "What is it?" he asked, palm slapping against the stonework beside my head. His eyes were frantic as they assessed me from head to toe. "*Where* is it?"

My hand searched for his, snatching it and placing it flat against my rib cage, directly beneath my breasts, where my lungs had been disabled. I couldn't move them—couldn't even *feel* them. His forehead creased, mouth twisting as he made the connection, and then he moved his hand to my throat while I choked on magic. He felt the muscles contracting, felt the absence of air, and put his hand over my mouth.

Oh, like that's helpful—

Wedging his thumb and forefinger between my lips, he pried my mouth open, but even then, the air would not come in.

"You really can't breathe," he exclaimed, and my annoyance was dulled by my current predicament. "Fuck. How—"

Thank the High Mother, Lucais figured out that the question he was about to ask was an insensitive waste of my very limited time because he didn't complete it. As his voice broke off, the edges of my vision went black and blurry, and the orbs of light he had summoned into the dingy little room with us began to look more like stars. He grabbed both of my hands in one of his, pinning them to the wall above my head and ignoring the withering look I tried to give him.

Then he took a deep breath, and his lips crashed against mine, searing with heat and bursting with oxygen.

Lucais's mouth sent an entire lungful of air into my body, breaching the boundary line sewn between my lips by the magical entity working to subdue me forever.

My chest was heaving as I breathed him in hungrily, the feeling of his mouth on mine like breaking through the surface of a murderous ocean, and every time I gulped down one breath of fresh air, I found myself clawing at him for more so I could keep my head above the water.

Dazed, I thought I might have bitten him in my desperation—but he tasted like honey, not blood. I angled my head to allow his mouth to cover more of mine, to facilitate deeper access, begging him for *more, more, more*.

He gave it to me, his hand forming a tight manacle around my wrists as he took my breath as his own and replaced it with everything I'd ever been missing. At last, my violent gasps softened into something less destructive and more desirable, and it was then that his tongue flicked out to taste me.

The movement was quick—so quick I wondered if he'd even meant to do it at all, but then he groaned and pushed his body onto me, crushing me against the wall, his chest flush against mine, his hips digging into me. His hand fell from its place around my wrists and moved to cradle my face as his tongue pushed inside my mouth, the other hand gripping my side with enough force to bruise in the exact shape and design of his fingerprints as I met each stroke of his tongue with one of my own.

The sound of my panting morphed into a moan as a feeling of desire swelled in my chest and reached for him. I was begging him. My *body* was begging him, desperate to make up for a thousand years of lost memories, like nothing he gave me would ever be enough to cover the eternity for which we were destined. Lucais responded as if he knew that and would never stop trying.

My whole body was alert and alive, my heart pounding wildly in my chest. My lungs felt so full of oxygen that I might never need to break my mouth away from Lucais's again.

As my hands fell from the wall, any resolve to steer clear of him crumbling away like that sandcastle underneath waves of perseverance, I tangled my fingers in his hair, whimpering with ecstasy as his teeth nipped my lower lip. His hair was as soft as silk. My fingertips felt like they were being coated in pure, molten gold as they combed through the messy strands, pressing into his scalp like they'd find somewhere permanent to land. I gripped a handful and tugged gently and—

You better fucking stop that.

His voice was in my mind. And his tone... He wasn't annoyed that I had pulled on his hair. He was *turned on*.

I writhed against him, a small groan escaping from my throat that Lucais swallowed into his own, and he slowed the kiss, pulling my tongue into his mouth and sucking. He explored me so deeply that the back of my head scraped against the wall, the stonework grinding into my hair and scalp with the intensity of his touch. Then he moved, the hand digging into my hip relaxing so he could wrap his arm around my waist, pulling me flush against him. I felt his erection pressing into me, thick and hard and pulsating above the place in my body where it belonged.

My chest heaved, but as my tongue tangled with his and I explored the edge of his top teeth, a thought occurred to me. A very dangerous yet necessary idea.

I have to show you something.

I waited to see if it had worked, if he could hear me through the bond the same way I'd heard him. He nipped at my mouth and nodded his head, still half lost in the kiss. As he licked over the spot his teeth had caught, I wrapped my arms around the back of his neck so tightly it would have been a stranglehold on anyone else.

And then I showed him.

While I did, Lucais kissed me, indulgently turning his head from one side to the other to ensure he was taking advantage of every possible angle into my mouth. His movements were slow and gentle, the pleasure inflicted upon me by his tongue, teeth, and lips both unrelenting and maddening.

Even as I showed him memories of the nightmares in which he was tortured, he sent pulses of ecstasy and heat rippling through me, his mouth never leaving mine.

The dungeon. A cold, damp floor. Thinning bed of straw in the corner, an overturned bucket plated with iron at its side, and a threadbare blanket crumpled on the ground. Your shoulders trembling beneath the grip of two dark figures. I can't make them out. I don't know who they are. I'm trying...

Lucais's hand slid down from my lower back, cupping my ass and squeezing. He hitched one of my legs around his waist, securing my body against his, and smoothed his hand beneath my thigh, leaving a trail of warmth behind.

Your tattoos. They shove your head into a bucket. Repeatedly. Hold you there. I see the mist from their breath clouding above your head. It's so cold and damp. Your body falls still. Limp. They pull you out, your head lolls to the side, and they drop you on the stonework. The sound is gutting. I can't move. I can't reach you. I never reach you.

Lucais's tongue swiped my lower lip as he murmured, "*More.*"

And I knew that, while the evidence of his enjoyment was still straining against his pants and wedged up against my body, he was not talking about the kiss.

The sharp scrape of an iron bar being dragged across the ground. The hollow ring echoes. It hurts my ears. You're coming around again. They move so fast the bar whips through the air like a whistle, cracking like thunder as it makes contact with your—ugh! I don't know what. Okay? I always close my eyes here. I don't want to look. You're covered in burn marks and bruises. There's blood all over your body, the ground. It's been going on like this for months. Lucais—

"Hmm." He hummed into my mouth, tugging at my upper lip with his teeth, and I sensed that he was about to pull away.

My fingers tightened in his hair and yanked his mouth back to mine. Our profiles fit like pieces of a jigsaw puzzle. We stood with our foreheads pressed together, panting into each other's mouths.

Lucais, they're going to kill you.

His voice entered my mind again, the sound a sensual caress without a hint of distress. *No, little beast, they're not. But you might if you don't let go of me.*

Like a rubber band snapping, my arms fell away from him, and the High King stumbled backwards until he hit the opposite wall with a sudden thud. It knocked the breath out of him in a ragged sigh. His lips were swollen, glistening with my kisses, and there was a wild look in his eyes as he stared at me, chest heaving.

I touched the place he'd bitten me with the tip of my tongue, tasting the tang of my own blood mixed with the honey-sweet remnants of his mouth, and then I tried to speak to him in my mind again.

I'm sorry.

With a sharp exhale of breath, he rested the back of his head against the wall and responded out loud. "For what?"

"For all of that."

He laughed—softly, weakly, but it was real. "Little beast, don't worry. That is not the kind of torture I am destined to suffer through at your hands. You don't need to apologise for it."

I gawked at him. "I would have tried to tell you sooner, but..."

"I'm glad you told me now," he said, his tone full of composure and reassurance. It made me question his sanity. "I was growing concerned for you."

Had he not seen what I'd seen?

Maybe I'd convinced myself it was Wrenlock back in the House because he was a nicer option than my snarky blond escort, but the visions were as clear as day in the dungeon. Lucais was being tortured in my mind, and I'd just given him a front-row seat.

"You were?" I arched an eyebrow because I was growing concerned for *him*.

Lucais's shoulders moved with a sigh, and he slipped his hands into his pockets. "Aura," he began with a stern look, "I've wanted to know about your nightmares since the very first time I learned you'd been having them."

I blinked at him in a stupor. That was...*months* ago. My mother had spilled the beans in front of him in our kitchen, after he saved her life during the caenim attack and sat upon our antique washing machine like it was a throne, talking about how the High King of Faerie was the most handsome and clever person we'd ever met—

Oh, isn't hindsight a bitch?

I chewed on my lower lip. "Why didn't you ever ask?"

The High King blew out a long breath, filling the chasm of space between us with the echoes of magic and a place to call home. My stomach clenched with desire at the sight of him relaxed against the wall, his clothes and hair dishevelled by my hands, his mouth swollen and plump with the effects of what it had done with mine.

I felt a tug, like he was trying to call it back on his end, and so I slapped the feeling away.

Disowned it.

"I wanted you to come to me with them when you were ready," he confessed, glancing up at me through long lashes. "You made it quite clear that they were private, and you wanted me to have nothing to do with them in the first place. But I figured out that, at the very least, they involved me somehow."

I frowned, and the corners of his mouth twitched.

"You woke up screaming my name in that cottage like you were dying," he explained, and I remembered how he had come rushing in to comfort me when I woke up in a confused, petrified sweat, only to drop me onto the hard floor when I'd ordered him away. "Based on that alone, I imagined that what you were dreaming about was pretty gruesome because that's certainly not the way you scream my name when I make you come."

I pulled a face. "You haven't—we haven't had sex—"

"Yet," he interrupted, inclining his head suggestively. "I was referring to when we do it in my head."

My heart thudded, but I rolled my eyes. "That will absolutely never happen," I vowed, trying to make my expression resemble a deeply rooted sense of disgust. "You'd die trying."

The colour in his eyes flickered with heat. "I do love to prove you wrong, don't I?"

"You'll be waiting a while. A *long* while."

"Will I?" he challenged. "Because you were halfway there with only my mouth on yours. Imagine what I could do when I put it elsewhere."

I scoffed, but I felt my saliva thickening in my throat. "You've been misinformed."

"You should close your legs then because that's where my informant lives." He paused, surveying me with a feline gaze. "Unless the scent of your arousal is lying to me, and you're thinking about someone else when I'm kissing you."

My thighs squeezed together as blood flooded to my cheeks, igniting them with a toxic concoction of shame and desire. I hadn't been thinking of anyone else, but there was some merit to the argument that perhaps I should have been.

"I really thought you didn't care about the dreams," I admitted, offering up a different truth for the sake of changing the subject.

Lucais hesitated as if he didn't want to speak the next thought that came into his mind. "Why didn't you try to tell anyone else?" he wondered. "Like...Wrenlock?"

Is that jealousy in his eyes?

"It won't let me," I confided. "What happened then... It happens every time, and I didn't trust any of you. I still don't trust you now, but when I first arrived here, I didn't know who anyone was or what they wanted. Thanks to *you*." I glared at him, and he held his hands up, palms facing me in mock surrender. "None of you were worth it. Not even..." I trailed off, unwilling to say the High Lady's name.

He rolled his eyes, half-shrugging as he pushed away from the wall. "Fair call. Stupid, but fair."

A sense of fury reared its head in my chest again, taking the place of the heat from his touch. "Don't call me stupid!"

The High King gave me a scornful look. "Don't act like it then."

"Oh," I groaned. "I *hate* you."

"Mmm." He stepped over to me, and I bristled as he brushed his thumb across my lip, wiping the last and final traces of his kiss away. Then he rubbed it off on the hem of his shirt like he couldn't stand to have any remnants of me left on his skin. "I hate you, too, little beast," Lucais murmured. "In fact, I think we should start *hating* on each other more often, don't you?" He cracked his neck. "Ease some of that tension..." Arching a brow suggestively, his eyes roamed down my body. "I'd certainly like to ease mine into you."

My eyes widened when I caught his meaning, thinking back to the way his stone-hard cock had throbbed against my belly and imagining how he'd feel if he was permitted to work all of that pent-up frustration out on me and inside of me—and I shoved him backwards. "No."

His laughter was the most beautiful sound in the world, echoing through the chamber of his ultimate demise as he turned and led me further into it like a fate-stricken lamb to the slaughter.

Seven

The Mercy of a Taxpayer's Money

My body was a traitorous vessel, its nerves singing from the lingering traces of the true High King of Faerie's touch, but my mind—which, for arguably the first time in my adult life, had all of its wits fully intact without being chemically rebalanced by prescription medications—was spinning, falling, reeling.

Lucais had watched me smash priceless heirlooms into smithereens, and he didn't try to stop me. He had witnessed my faerieslaughter of a member of his staff, but he didn't reprimand me. He had kissed me, and then he wiped it off. He had watched his own body being brutally tortured inside of my mind, but then he propositioned me for sex.

Infuriating High Fae, High King bastard!

I was so enraged that I thought steam would start blowing out of my ears. As it was, however, only my breath clouded in front of me as Lucais opened the second door of the dank chamber and brought me into the real dungeon. The room rapidly dropped to subzero temperatures, causing me to lose all sensation in my fingertips, and the moisture-laden air made every breath feel small and heavy in my lungs.

An inane sense of fear invaded my nervous system, and I searched for Lucais's hand at his side.

For a split second once our knuckles touched, I was convinced he was going to pull away, but Lucais flexed his fingers around my hand before he threaded them through mine. Warmth engulfed me from the inside out—a sensation he was providing using his magic to combat the bitter chill chipping away at my bones. I hadn't realised that my teeth were chattering until they abruptly ceased under the command of his power, and then I squeezed his hand back.

Our footsteps were stiff but heavy against the damp, uneven cobblestone ground. The echoes were sharp, serenaded by an occasional *plop* of water dripping from the iron bars of the empty cells on either side of us. There would have been no illumination if not for the orbs of Lucais's faelight spinning around us as we moved because the cells had no windows. If not for that little detail, the dungeon would be identical to the one from my nightmares.

My neck twitched against the temptation of a shudder, and Lucais glanced down at me. His eyes were a startling contrast against the gloom and darkness—vivid gold, deep enough for me to climb into and hide from the monsters who lurked within the memories of the room.

We walked by rows upon rows of small, tight cages protected by thick, wrought-iron bars. All of them were empty, haunted, foreboding.

At the end of the path, the space opened up.

A long, worn bench sat in the middle of the floor beneath a wall with hooks and large nails hammered into a wooden beam at crooked angles. Weapons hung from them, though the shadows were especially dark and made them harder to discern, and Lucais's faelight orbs remained obediently tethered to our sides.

Bravely, I took a step out into the open space and let his hand drop from my grasp. A single orb of faelight accompanied me, alongside the warm relief of his magic stretching out to soothe the distance. My gaze was trained on some kind of blade hanging from the rack. I thought it might be familiar, though I couldn't be sure. One more step, and—

Clang.

My head whipped in the direction of the sound, its shallow echo sending a bolt of anxiety rolling down my sternum. The orb of faelight by my side hesitated, then eventually followed my line of sight. Its weak, yellow-tinged glow illuminated the corner of the dungeon in a watery light, and my gasp of shock became lodged in my throat like a stone.

Hands flying to brace themselves against my stomach and chest, I banished all the air from my lungs by trying to scream. For all of my efforts, the noise I made amounted to nothing more than a strangled cry, muffled by the inability of my own lips to fully come apart.

The mangled figure of a man, strung up by his hands in iron cuffs chained to the ceiling, barely flinched beneath the sudden onset of faelight. His skin was coated in dried blood, his wrists so raw the bone was exposed where the iron had burned his skin and flesh down to the remnants of a few loose flaps of ligaments and muscle. The chains clanked together as he attempted to lift his head, bloodshot eyes spearing straight into mine.

My stomach gurgled with gall and spiralled downwards. I recognised him as the sentry from the clearing in the Court of Light who had struck me. Face pale and drawn, his matted hair was plastered to a forehead smeared with blood and dirt. His eyes barely held the strength of a single blink before his head snapped forward with enough force to sprain the tendons in his neck.

"Hanson," I whispered.

Lucais's shoes scuffed against the ground as he came up beside me. I felt the warmth of his palm hovering within an inch of my lower back.

"What the fuck have you done?" I breathed, shaking my head as Hanson's body finished swaying. My words were wisps of grey mist in the shadows between us.

The High King let out an agitated breath, mingling with mine. "This is not what I wanted to show you," he muttered.

"Why did you do this?" I demanded softly, emphasising each word.

He shrugged in my peripheral vision. "He hit you."

A tense, lengthy pause strained between us while I waited for him to elaborate. He stared at me like he was trying to figure out what more there was to say.

"You're my mate," he said at last, "and the High Queen of Faerie—or you will be, one day—and that means I could have someone executed for looking at you the wrong way if the mood struck. But, if you recall, you were not enthused by my suggestion of his execution, so"—he made a wide, reverent gesture towards the sentry with both hands—"I put him here. *Alive.*" A heartbeat later, suddenly his voice was light and the words were coming out fast. "I cut out his tongue for the way he spoke to you, but he *is* alive. Can we move on now?"

My eyes were as round as a full moon and equally tormented as I steered my gaze back to the High King's former sentry. I knew it was stupid and, quite frankly, *infuriating* for me to feel badly about a man who had put his hands on me with harmful intent, but old habits were hard to break. I felt something pulling at a loose thread of my heart as I scanned Hanson's condition one last time.

The former member of the Guard had aged considerably since the last time I saw him, as if the magic preserving his immortal features had been drained from his very blood. He suddenly looked like a great-grandfather, almost blurring the lines of mortality; a relic of humanity with wrinkles and skin sagging beneath his eyes and chin.

Lucais had rendered him helpless. Stripped him bare. Robbed him of his strength and the power he possessed—derived from the position he had held in the High King's Guard and for the simple fact that he was a man. He came armed with the implied maturity and intelligence of all the years and all the weapons forged for him by his predecessors. He had expected the world to honour it. And then Lucais took that, too.

I had to admit that part of me was thoroughly disgusted by the sight. Part of me was flattered, though. Even pleased.

A man had hit me, and Lucais had strung him up in the dungeon like a butcher's kill of the day. He had not even given him the privilege of sitting down in his own cell, never mind the notion of a fair trial or the bail granted to reoffend at the mercy of a taxpayer's money. He had done that. For me.

When I realised how deeply concerning it was for me to be romanticising the actions of a psychopath, my forehead creased. My therapist would have been mortified—but my therapist had tried to keep me out of Faerie with pills, so I decided that I couldn't really be bothered about her opinion anymore.

Lucais put both hands on my shoulders, his fingers reaching so far down that the tips softly curled underneath my collarbone. He gently spun me around, bending his head to speak into my ear. "Don't try to scream this time," the High King whispered.

And then my eyes met the serpentine gaze of my father through a set of iron bars.

The scream coiled beneath my rib cage, ready to spring loose at the flip of a switch. It was tight, electrified, and raw. Lucais's hands held it at bay, the soothing tendrils of his power coaxing a sense of calm and strength throughout my trembling body as pure, instinctive fear gripped my heart and nearly ripped it right out of my chest.

My father. In Faerie.

Lucais wrapped an arm around my waist, a life ring in rough seas. *You're safe. I'm here.*

He was right.

I wasn't alone. And when I wasn't alone, I was always strong. I always had been, and I always would be, whether we were facing each other down in the human realm or in the land of the faeries.

Loosening my grip on the High King's arm with my next steadying breath, I noticed that my nails had been digging crescent moons deeply into his flesh and felt a flood of regret colouring my face.

The ice-cold, emotionless eyes in the cell pierced me like the point of a fencing sword. They were the eyes I had once believed to be the mirrors of my own, as blue as a lagoon to reflect the seas in mine. After all, they were the only feature we shared. The long lashes, the clear colour.

But my mother had blue eyes, too, and my father wasn't related to me at all. I was the unlucky product of a faerie fling—the result of my mother's infidelity within the first year of her marriage to the blue-eyed man presently behind bars. The faerie father was nameless to me, and I had no desire to learn of his identity, but that did not change the truth.

The man in the prison cell was not my father.

But he *was* the man who had haunted me throughout my childhood and into my adult life.

He was the man who used his voice to silence the rest of our household. The man who used his fists when that didn't work. He was the man who wore a bad mood like a cloak he never took off that dragged along the floor, leaving a trail of sadness and discomfort in its wake. He was the man who tread heavy footsteps down the hall, whose weight caused the floorboards outside my bedroom to creak as he approached in the middle of the night. He was the man who never stepped across the threshold, but sometimes paused to reconsider his decision to leave me alone after he'd already turned and started to walk away.

In truth, I didn't know what he would have done if he hadn't left. But I would try to stay awake for as long as I could afterwards, and then I'd fall asleep picturing his hand around my throat as he squeezed the last of the air from my body because that's what I thought I heard him thinking about.

He wasn't capable of doing that any longer.

My father figure was alive. The mortal louse had been preserved. Although, he didn't look like he was really aware of my presence or capable of coherent speech as he stared directly through the iron bars between us. I moved, tilting my head from one side to the other, and watched him, waiting for a reaction.

None came.

He was breathing, but not responsive.

The terror invoked by his face subsided as quickly as it had risen. I covered my mouth with my hand and waited for the indignation to take its place. I waited for some kind of anger to boil to the surface, for fury at Lucais for what he had done to come and slap me back to my senses.

It didn't. I suddenly realised I would be waiting forever because it never would.

Lucais Starfire had done the one thing I'd dreamed about doing for longer than anything else. The desire was my earliest memory, my first big dream. Lucais had exacted the vengeance that all of my previous boyfriends had sworn to do in defence of my honour. He succeeded in the task that most of my father's friends had set out to accomplish, and he did it without making a mess. He did it without seeking glory for besting the monster. Lucais had no trophy scars. No war stories. No expectations of me. He simply had the man incapacitated in his dungeon, and the safety of his mate and her family secured.

I blinked up at him in a stupor and cleared my throat before I tested out my shaky voice. "You have had my father here this whole time?"

The High King nodded, staring intently at his prisoner through the bars. "Yes."

I'd killed a man earlier in the day in a fit of rage. I'd fought back a self-righteous smile at the sight of the sentry who had hit me strung up like prey. And now I was about to *thank* the person responsible for both of those atrocities—the High King who had tortured his own man, kidnapped my father, and then discarded them both in a dungeon without so much as an acknowledgement in the newspapers.

It was the end of the road for me. I could never go back—and I didn't even want to because the truth of the matter was that the situation I was in with Lucais was where I had been trying to go my whole life. Ever since I was a child, as deranged as I knew it may very well be.

I swallowed the emotional lump in my throat, trying to calm my racing heart and reel in my ecstatic, livewire nerves.

"Please let him go," I said quietly, doing my best to mimic a businesslike and professional tone. I swallowed, and the sound was audible. "Before I actually fall in love with you."

A heart beat twice in separate chests.

"Ew," Lucais scoffed, scrunching his nose as he gave me a sideways glance. His eyes slid back to my father with the ease of an oil slick, but I thought I spied the corner of his mouth twitching. He flattened it immediately and adjusted his shirt. "Control yourself, woman."

A gurgle of laughter rose up my throat and burst out of my mouth, the sound of a dam overflowing after many years of heavy rainfall under immoveable clouds and poor maintenance of the overall structure.

I laughed until I couldn't breathe, until my sides cramped, and I almost fell over. I laughed until Lucais picked me up and carried me out of the dungeon, his faithful orbs of faelight trailing us for the whole journey to a bedroom somewhere high up in the palace. I laughed until tears streamed freely down my cheeks, into my ears, over my throat, and between my breasts. I laughed until my jaw hurt and my throat was raw, until I forgot why I had ever begun, and until I fell asleep.

Eight

Wrenlock Elumos

My laughter eventually died inside dreams of the dead faerie. His three eyes haunted me that night. I watched the light leaving them like fireworks all through the dark, flickering on and off as though I were bewitched by a looping reel that could not be paused or closed. Unable to fall into a deep sleep and unable to wake up enough to dispel the images, I succumbed to a form of sleep paralysis that I truly thought I'd left behind in the human world.

At the very least, I was convinced I'd left it in the cottage on the road into the Court of Light. It made sense, since that was the last location in which I'd experienced a nightmare, unless—

Had the House... No, it couldn't have. But what if it did?

An enchantment such as the one on the House might have held the power to ease the burdens locked inside someone's mind. To take the edge off the guilt and self-loathing. In the Forest of Eyes and Ears—brought to life with a similar spell—I had felt a sense of peace unlike any other. Maybe the House had attempted to provide me with something akin to that by scaring off my nightmares and quelling my daytime fears. After all, I really hadn't grieved for the loss of Jonah's life in the bookstore. Not like I grieved for the maroon-skinned faerie with three eyes, whose name I didn't even know.

When I woke up, thoughts of Jonah, the House, and its attempts to soothe me in the forefront of my conscious mind, I felt wetness stuck to my lashes and cheeks. Tears had started to flow once more, escaping from the corners of my eyes before they had even opened to the melancholy morning. My heart hung heavy in my chest, a low-lying anchor in the sky of my regrets.

Guilt closed an iron fist around my soul and shook me senseless when I stumbled out of bed, a sudden cramping sensation roiling through my stomach. It was like someone was scraping out my insides with an apple corer.

Arm across my mouth, I rushed into the bathroom and dry heaved over the sink. There was nothing in my stomach for my emotions to forcibly eject, so the action only served to create a burn down the back of my throat from the acidity of my saliva.

After rinsing my mouth out, I slipped into the shower and tried to wash off the sadness that drenched me when I realised I had to do those tasks all by myself again. It wasn't because I had any type of aversion to the act of turning on taps and fetching my own towels; it was the loneliness that the previous night had drilled into my bones, leaving me hollow and wanting for companionship. For *friendship*.

The House never spoke to me, so it had never had the chance to lie to me, but in place of words of affirmation, it communicated with acts of service—a constant and unfailing false sense of security that I would have to learn to live without again. Even when it was shunning me, or it had mysteriously gone quiet, the House had given me Delia in its place to make sure I always had someone to take care of me if I needed it.

And I shouldn't have been so sad about leaving. I knew that.

But I hadn't realised until it was too late that the House had shown me what most of my friends had grown up with when I was in school. What I had tried so hard to be for Brynn.

It had taken care of me. It ran my baths, it brought me fresh and clean linen, it cooked all of my meals, and it chased away my fears in the dark. Yes, I had fought with it—in the only way one could fight with something like an enchanted House—and I cursed at it when it didn't do what I wanted. However, I started to figure out that was all because it cared. And I didn't say thank you.

I hadn't even said goodbye.

Wrapped in a towel, I walked into the middle of the bedroom, traipsing water all over the scuffed wooden floorboards as I surveyed my new surroundings. The room was nice if Halloween was the occupant's favourite holiday.

Smaller than my room at the House, most of the space lay between the floor and the high coffered ceiling, which loomed above me like a dome. There was a huge, unused candelabra pendant welded from obsidian fixed in the centre, dusted with cobwebs. Fixtures of a similar design were fitted to the walls, furnished with candles that appeared to have had their wicks pulled out. Two steep, arched windows made from stained glass were featured against the far wall. They provided a restricted view over the palace's primeval buttressing and tinged the dismal, fog-weakened light with colour as it slanted into the room between window panes.

An oversized bed sat against a blank wall, adorned with elaborate carvings on its ebony bedhead, the spires of which almost touched the ceiling. I could tell that the blankets were dyed in deep golds and strong whites, but beneath the stained glass they appeared cerulean and turquoise. They were ruffled, an unchecked ocean ready to swallow me whole. I had no clue what the time was, but there was no way I would willingly place my body back at the mercy of that mattress.

There was a large, antique wooden trunk at the foot of the bed. I ransacked it for a change of clothes and found that not only did the enchanted Houses fail to offer underwear, but the creepy palaces in Faerie did, too. To my surprise, however, I found some normal clothes—normal by faerie standards, at least.

Once I was dried, I dressed in a pair of plain, well-fitting black slacks and a long-sleeved shirt with buttons and a neatly pressed collar. The fabric was cool against my skin, so I put a long coat over the top and pulled on a pair of pile-lined boots. If it was not safe for me to wear dresses in the House, it was certainly not safe in a city where I could not see past the end of my arm if I stepped outside into the fog.

Hunger had started to stab me below my ribs, clenching and unclenching my sides. The nausea still gurgled, emotions warring with basic need. I took a deep breath and blew it out in a huff of air that clouded in front of my face. As much as I didn't want to stay in the bedroom, I didn't want to leave it, either. That would mean facing up to the things that hunted me across time and portals, leering at me when they thought I wasn't looking.

But I was on my own again.

The palace was not the House.

There was no magic there. No enchantment. Its cruel hardwood and vicious stonework did not care about me. Still, I decided to give it a chance. If my magic was lost, maybe it had taken my ability to properly sense other kinds of magic along with it.

I sucked in a breath through my teeth, the sound too sharp and loud in my own ears. My eyes wandered over the palace's interior, looking for a friendly surface and finding none.

"Hello?" I asked into the quiet vacancy. "Are you here?"

"Hello," a smooth voice replied.

Whirling at the unfamiliar sound, I stumbled and nearly fell over from the shock of finding Wrenlock standing in my open doorway. I had not heard his footsteps or the door opening. He was a vision of shadows in the low lighting; black clothing, messy dark hair, unblemished skin cooled by the melancholy lighting.

"Was that you?" I asked, cocking my head to the side.

"Was what me?" he returned, pushing off the doorframe and striding towards me.

"I said something, and you..."

Wrenlock raised an eyebrow. "You did?" He stopped in front of me, taking in my outfit, and then reached up to tuck my hair behind my ears. I eyed the skin on the palms of his hands, noting the burn marks had been healed. "Are you talking to yourself, babe?"

If looks could set people on fire, he would be ash.

"*No.*" I shrugged his hand off from where it had come to rest on my shoulder and folded my arms over my chest. "Forget it."

He sighed deeply. "I'm sorry, I shouldn't have teased you. I just came to see if you were hungry because you don't know your way around this place yet." As if it heard him, my stomach let out a feral growl, which caused one side of his mouth to quirk to the side. "I see," he stated, and then he offered me his arm. "Look, Aura, I'll take you to breakfast. No strings attached. In fact, when you stab your fork into your food, you can pretend that it's my heart."

Groaning, I hooked my elbow around his arm and told myself it was because I was weak with hunger pains. Though relief chilled the fire in my veins slightly as we exited the macabre bedroom and stepped onto a thin navy-and-gold rug in the hall, it was momentary.

We were on a level of the palace that was basically an entire wing of bedrooms. There were closed doors separated by colourful portraits within copper frames placed in a square formation around an open, gaping drop leading down to the lower levels, walled by a solid ebony railing of modest height in the middle of the floor. High windows ushered in murky, silvery daylight that beamed down in a tight formation and exposed clouds of dust leisurely floating across the space.

The urge to throw myself over the bannister came and went in the blink of an eye.

"I do not want to stab you," I snapped, glancing up at Wrenlock. Everything felt so hot and cold around him, and all of it was out of my control. "You broke my heart. You broke my *trust*. You were the nice one who took me under your wing—and then took advantage of me. I don't want to stab you, Wrenlock. I want to look at you without hurting."

"Hmm." He placed his free hand over my forearm and squeezed it gently as we moved through the shadows. "But you want to stab Lucais?"

My upper lip curled. "Is that some perverted standard of affection with you people?" I demanded. "You don't care that the sight of your face physically *hurts* me, but you care about how violent and aggressive I'd like to be towards your High King because you think that's some type of fucked up foreplay for us?"

"Aura—"

"No!" I shouted.

Shoving his arm away, I stepped backwards and felt the eyes of the portrait paintings along the walls dart towards me, intrigued. I glared back at one set of painted black eyes for a moment before shuddering and returning my attention to the man in front of me.

"No. You know what? *Fuck* you and *fuck* your *fucked up* standards of love! Because the truth is that I would *rather* have Lucais fat-shame me to his unicorn and slut-shame me in these halls, every day for the rest of my life because the Oracle disappointed him with me, than have to remember what it felt like to have a complete *stranger* put his fingers inside me, his tongue in my mouth, and make me believe it was *fate*."

Wrenlock dragged a hand over his anguished face.

Guilt roared deep in my belly, devouring the scene with wicked delight. It was a greedy, starving beast I had been feeding all my life. My chest heaved with breaths I scarcely managed to pull up from the catacombs of my lungs as we stared at each other across the hallway. Wrenlock's eyes were glinting in the reflection of light from somewhere, the chestnut dark as oblivion. For the very first time, I could feel the vexation radiating from him.

"Go off, Aura," he hissed, the precision of his gaze cutting into me. "Please, keep going. Get this *out* of your system because you are not doing us any favours by playing the victim." He took a step forward, and I stepped back, even though the distance between us suddenly felt like a void between worlds. "I *know* that what I did was wrong. I *know* I hurt you. If I could have done anything about it, I would have. Don't trust me, fine. But trust *that*."

I took another step backwards until I could feel the ridge of the carpet edge beneath my foot. He remained in place.

"I am *bound* to him by a magic stronger than anything else in the world," he went on, raising an apprehensive hand in the space between us. "The same magic that hides this realm from yours. The magic that ended a war so intense it created human beings. The magic that *almost* managed to reverse the curse of the Malum." Wrenlock's eyes shone with silver again, and I realised it wasn't light.

Those are tears.

"He came so close, Aura." Wrenlock's voice cracked, the sound of something precious breaking. "He acts like the Court Jester, but you have *no* idea how powerful he is. You have no idea how many enemies he has because of that power, because they crave what he is capable of doing—the things he is capable of creating and destroying and commanding—and what you saw in my behaviour is just a *drop* in the ocean of that." He paused, angling his head to one side. "Did you know the High King before him was only in power for a single year before he was ousted by Lucais?"

I swallowed hard and shook my head.

"Never has a ruler in our history had such a short reign," Wrenlock told me, shaking his head as if he could hardly fathom it himself. "Lucais came into his power as a mere faeling. The youngest of the High Fae to possess enough power to challenge the High King. The crown sought him out decades before it was expected to do so, and he only grew stronger once it did." He sighed roughly. "I would tear down mountains and burn bridges for you with my bare hands, Aura, but consider me fairly. *That* is what I was up against."

I opened my mouth to reply, but no words came out.

Wrenlock seized the opportunity and stalked towards me until I was pinned against the wall. His hands flattened against it, one each above my head and my shoulder, and he leaned down until he was close enough that I could see the flecks of amber in his irises.

My breath caught in my throat.

"The day you arrived from the human world, I came upstairs," he murmured, his voice gentle and warm. "You were in the middle of a conversation. I corrected him on his misbegotten recollections of the Gift War, fully intending to follow that by introducing myself to you as Wrenlock Elumos. I thought you knew he was the High King. I thought you knew he was your mate. Why else would he have brought you back? Why else would you have *come back* with him? It was too late for me to do or say anything by the time I realised I was wrong. I tried to talk him out of it, Aura. Believe me, I *tried*. I begged Morgoya for help, went to Batre when she tried to refuse, and fought against my feelings for you until they consumed me.

"It was never my plan to fall in love with you, but I did it anyway," he swore, so close to whispering. "I fell in love with the *fire* in your soul. You love books. I never read, but suddenly, I want to spend my days inside a library. You want to tempt fate by stumbling around the boundary lines of the wards, and I can't think of any better way to spend my time than to stand around and watch you. You are angry and defiant, and sometimes you jump to miscalculated conclusions, but you're clever and kind when you want to be, and what we did to you was not your fault. It is not a reflection of your intelligence but a sign of the times in Faerie. I *physically* could not tell you my name until *he* had told you *his*."

A single, stray tear slipped down my cheek.

"But I need you to hear it now." He inhaled deeply. Released it as a controlled breath. "I am Wrenlock Elumos. I was born to Hairem and Maylace, and I have three sisters. When I was a kid, I had a pet crow; the other kids used to tease me because they said the crow was my familiar, and only Witches have familiars, but I loved that bird. We went everywhere together because I didn't have any friends. My father often worked away, and my sisters never wanted to leave our front porch with their dolls in case the wheels of their little prams got too muddy because we lived on a farm. I enjoy music and dancing, but I'll sit and read a book with you until we fall asleep any day of the week. I met the High King when I was only a boy myself. When he asked me to come to Caeludor as the Hand, it was the greatest honour of my life. Until I met *you*. And I swear, I had no intention of falling for the fated soulmate of my best friend, whether he's an idiot who doesn't deserve her or not."

The confession hung in the air around us like the perfume of a spell wafting from a bubbling cauldron. The truth about Lucais, about his power—and Wrenlock's helplessness, the magnitude of his struggles while we were living in the House. It was too much. All of the revelations were too strong.

I couldn't think of anything to say other than to remark on the thread of solidarity that rolled out between us. Normally, I didn't find common ground with other people, so it felt precious to me.

"I didn't have friends for a long time, either. I wasn't allowed to have people come to the house because of my father, and it sort of...scared everyone else off."

Wrenlock's mouth pulled up in a sad, understanding smile. He leaned back from the wall and extended his hand to me. "If you don't want me to touch you, I won't. I can't lie outright to you. You know that. When I told you to slap me if my hands go anywhere you don't want them to be, I meant it."

I laid my palm against his. His eyes lightened back to chestnut brown as his fingers closed around mine. We walked, hand in hand, down the winding staircase to the lower levels of the palace. My stomach growled ravenously right up until the moment we passed the corridor of magical relics and heirlooms. The stain of the maroon-skinned faerie's blood was still on the rug—or maybe it wasn't.

Wrenlock pulled me from the doorway, and I blinked so quickly I couldn't be quite sure what I had seen. I questioned him about it, though—asked him who the three-eyed faerie was, his name, his family, if there was anything that could be done to fix it—but he told me it had all been taken care of, and it was better if I didn't know the details. Wrenlock also told me it wasn't the first violent death to occur in the palace, whether by accident or intent, but that tidbit didn't provide me with the solace he thought it would.

By the time we made it to the dining hall, I felt nauseous again. And when I stumbled into the room, one hand gripping my stomach, I fell to my knees beside the nearest pot plant and vomited all of my stomach's acid into it.

Nine

Low Blood Sugar

"Oh, High Mother." Morgoya's lilting voice carried across the room. "Wrenlock," she chastised. "Tell me she is *not* with faeling."

The sound of a glass shattering pierced my ears, and I managed to lift my head high enough out of the pot plant to find that Lucais was sitting at the head of the breakfast table with a pile of broken glass at his feet. He had one hand in a fist before him, his wet skin and shirt sleeve stained pink with the contents of his former glass mug, and the other pinching the bridge of his nose. The High King's eyes were tightly closed.

Are you okay?

His voice in my mind was composed, but I felt the thunderous echoes restrained by sheer willpower behind it. It was obvious to me that a mental conversation was all he had the capacity to hold at that moment in time. I, on the other hand, did not have the strength to even reply in my mind. Another empty wave of nausea rose up, pausing at the halfway mark behind my sternum and wreaking havoc on my ability to breathe properly, and I ducked my head back into the pot plant. My mouth watered as my stomach heaved, and my throat tightened rhythmically.

If I can just force it out for good, I'll be fine—

"No," Wrenlock replied, speaking through his teeth. "She killed someone yesterday."

"Oh," Morgoya quipped. "Well, that's alright, then."

"Though," Wrenlock pushed on, "I am glad to see where your priorities lie, Your Majesty."

I groaned into the bottom of the pot at the inference, and the sound echoed around the gap between the decorative ceramic and the plastic container housing the actual roots. The suggestion that Lucais was more annoyed with the idea of Wrenlock and me creating a life together than he was at the fact that I had *taken* a life the previous day was preposterous but probably very accurate. Even so, both things were equally horrifying in my personal opinion—especially considering that Wrenlock and I were not mates.

The laws of soulmates and procreation in Faerie were very ambiguous. I had been informed that conception between a pair of non-soulmate High Fae was believed to be strictly impossible, but that left me with a plethora of questions about how a human woman could carry a half-faerie child without conforming to the soulmate rituals of the High Fae. I knew my mother certainly hadn't accepted a bond with my biological father because he had *left* her.

Perhaps they didn't know. Or perhaps I was wrong, and they weren't really soulmates. In any case, it certainly wasn't common enough to have been studied properly yet—if it actually ever happened at all.

But that was the least of our worries because, fated mate tropes aside, there was also the whole *practical* side of things.

"I am not pregnant," I mumbled, bracing my hands on the ceramic rim to push myself back onto my feet. "It is not possible." I straightened and paused, my eyes darting around the room, feverish and unseeing as I wondered at the most absurd possibilities. "Unless...faeries don't..."

Wrenlock raised an eyebrow at me when my gaze crash-landed on his face. He understood where my train of thought was headed. "No, Aura. It's not possible." His eyes flicked to the High King. "Unless—"

"Oh, by the Elements, will you listen to yourselves?" someone said. I jerked, tracking the sound of the voice to Batre's face, and was genuinely pleased to see her sitting at the table beside the High Lady of the Court of Light. "This is—"

Morgoya's emerald-green eyes widened as she lowered a teacup from her mouth, and she elbowed her girlfriend in the ribs. "Stop it, this is delicious," she demanded under her breath, nodding her head towards us with a meaningful look.

Batre rolled her eyes but said no more.

"No," I answered Wrenlock, as I walked over to the rectangular table in search of water or tea to wash down the acrid taste in my mouth. He had essentially confirmed that faeries conceived the same way humans did, so I was confident. And *relieved*. "It is not possible."

The High King kept his head in his hand, thumb and forefinger on either side of his nose, pinching the space between his eyebrows. He relaxed his other fist and reached for the dainty glass teapot in front of him. Without a word or an upwards glance, he poured a steaming cup of purple tea into a porcelain cup printed with dandelions and sunbeams, stirred in two cubes of sugar, finished it with a splash of milk from a pitcher labelled with painted almonds, and lifted it by the saucer.

It took me a moment longer than it should have to realise Lucais was offering it to me. As I reached for it, he moved his head almost imperceptibly and looked up at me from beneath furrowed brows.

The sight of his face from that angle—from *any* angle, honestly—made my heart flutter and stomach flip. Meeting his golden gaze left me with a nonsensical feeling of accomplishment, like earning his attention was worthy of a prize. It was such a foolish schoolgirl feeling, but it made me giddy nonetheless.

"Thank you," I murmured, sinking into the chair beside him. A muscle in my core flexed and tightened at the proximity, at the ease of taking up space next to him. The conflict of my emotions provided precious little assistance to settle the nervous ache in my belly.

The High King had an empty seat on his other side, straight across from me. Morgoya and Batre took up the two seats down from it, clearly wanting to sit beside each other and anticipating that Wrenlock and I would be joining Lucais on the left and right.

Though it was steaming, I took a sip of tea straightaway. It was sweet and woodsy, the taste like nothing I'd ever experienced.

"The sugar was a lucky guess," I commented, noting that he had made it to my exact tastes, but he had never seen me make a cup of tea before in his entire life.

"No, it wasn't," Lucais replied, lifting his head entirely from his hand at last. He looked exhausted. "You need all the sweet things you can get."

And there it is. The reverse compliment. The pointy ends of his teeth showing through a smile.

Spine straightening, my free hand curled into a fist, though I didn't have the energy to bang it on the table or shake it at him. "For once in your life, can you not be so unpleasant and cruel to me?" I whinged. "Just for the first hour of the morning, please. Two hours on the days when I am unwell."

He screwed his beautiful face up at me. "What are you talking about, you deranged creature? You have low blood sugar. I tasted it last night—"

Morgoya spat her mouthful of tea all over Wrenlock, who had made a poor choice in taking the seat next to me—directly across from her—instead of the spot they had purposefully left for him on the High King's other side. Batre shouted in alarm, though it sounded as if it might have begun as a laugh, and I closed my eyes, covering my face with a hand as I sank down further in my seat. I wished the floor would open up and swallow me whole.

Do they have sinkholes in Faerie?

I made a mental note to look into it.

The High King tossed a cloth napkin at his indeterminate friend. Wrenlock accepted it with a nod of acknowledgement and began to wipe the tea from his face with a stoic expression, his eyes trained on the High Lady, who sat in front of him with a slim-fingered, perfectly manicured hand splayed across her open mouth. His dark, tea-dampened curls stuck to his forehead, and his brow creased as he glowered up at the strands and tried to push them back into place with the napkin.

"I am so sorry," Morgoya apologised. She immediately switched her attention back to Lucais. "What did you say about last night?"

The High King let out a long-suffering sigh. "Nothing."

"He bit me," I interjected, because something had to be said about it since the mention had already been made. *I think I actually bit him, too, but that's not important.* "There was an accident with one of the staff here. I had a—"

"A tantrum," Lucais muttered at the same time as Wrenlock offered, "A crisis of mental health?"

"More like a breakdown," I amended, side-eyeing them one after the other, "mentally speaking, and—"

"Glad your illness has come with a newfound sense of self-awareness," the High King said under his breath.

"—I accidentally lost control of a sword," I continued, completely ignoring his jibe. "One of the staff caught it." I paused, gnawing on my lip, then added, "In his chest." The unease in my stomach rose again, but I managed to hold it down. "Lucais and I had some things to work out afterwards."

Morgoya's eyes flickered back and forth between us, a thin eyebrow reaching for her dark hairline. "But you haven't—"

"No," Lucais repeated firmly, for what was starting to feel like the hundredth time that very morning.

I ground my back teeth together.

For High Mother's sake. Nobody is having sex.

I wanted to ask why it even mattered, although I technically wasn't speaking to her. We weren't actively avoiding each other; I simply hadn't seen her since the House, and I didn't know what to say. I wasn't ready, so I fixed my gaze on Batre instead and smiled.

"I'm glad to see you again," I told her honestly, marking the hurt that flashed across her girlfriend's face in my peripheral vision. My stomach twisted, but I didn't know what to do with the feeling. I had no room for it.

"You too, Aura," Batre replied. Her gaze darted to the side, aware of Morgoya's reaction.

It may not have been the nicest thing for me to do—especially if it would pit the two lovers against one another—but I genuinely liked Batre. She was the only person who hadn't lied or kept any secrets from me while I was living in the House. In fact, she very nearly gave it away, played a significant part in making me realise the truth, and had actually been the one to confirm it in the end.

Morgoya, on the other hand, had been a much closer friend to me—and she had lied through her teeth, covering for Lucais and stringing me along in silly little games designed to drive the real High King mad while I fell deeper into my involvement with the fake High King, Wrenlock.

Batre, to my knowledge, had played no such games with me.

"What a reunion," I whispered, training my eyes on my plate as Wrenlock began to pile it high with different faerie foods. I spied the paperdove eggs, berries, pancakes, thick slices of toast he generously buttered before placing down, and strips of colourful melon.

"Eat," he urged, gently nudging my arm with his elbow.

Yes, Auralie, eat. Lucais's mental voice was in my head, and I detected the mocking edge to his tone. *Try using a dining table for its intended purpose this time, and do let me know what you think of the experience.*

My back stiffened, and then I emphatically ignored him.

But I did eat. Because I was starving—and because I was surrounded by people who didn't seem to care that I'd killed a man beneath their very roof, most likely because they were faeries who did worse things themselves before getting out of bed in the morning. And whether it was right or wrong, that fact eased some of my guilt considerably.

"Who says I don't care?" the dark, hollow voice from my bedroom hummed in my ear.

I jumped in my seat, my knees hitting the bottom of the table, causing the cutlery and glasses to clatter. The force made a pitcher of milk tip over and spill all over the table cloth.

Shit—

Batre was quick to act, mopping it up with a napkin and preventing the liquid from running off the sides and into Morgoya's lap, but my heart still raced like a wild horse, and blood flooded to my cheeks as if it could defend me.

I waited for someone to yell or swear, and I found it hard to swallow my uncertainty when nobody did. It was an accident, and accidents always attracted the worst attention—like broken dishes over spilled milk from a man who walked past holes in the walls every day without blinking. My muscles were impossibly tense, every joint in my body locked into place, anticipating the imminent way in which I was about to be shattered. I blinked, then looked at the expression on the closest face. Wrenlock was at my side, his mouth full of pancakes as he stared at me with a wide, probing gaze.

"I'm sorry," I whispered, the two simple words sounding broken and battered as they exited my mouth.

Hey.

Before I could move or speak again, the dull thump of something else falling over grabbed my attention, and I turned to see that Lucais was casually flicking cups and saucers over with his forefinger. His lips were tilted up in a warm, devious smirk as coloured liquids rushed out across the tablecloth like oil spills over an ocean. He clumsily knocked over a bowl of grapes that began to roll towards me, picked up a breakfast scroll with icing and cinnamon, tossed it up into the air above the table—

And then, with a musical laugh and a snap of his fingers, the table was set back to rights as if none of it had ever even happened.

Breathe, bookworm. Easy fix.

Batre snorted, and Morgoya picked up a green grape from the bowl that had reappeared properly centred and filled in the middle of the table. With questionable aim, she threw it at the High King, who leaned back on his chair legs with expert balance and caught it in his mouth. That earned a chuckle from Wrenlock, too.

A nervous relief itched the corners of my mouth, but I was still holding onto my breath until I felt Lucais's boot nudge mine underneath the table. He winked at me when I glanced towards him, laughing around a mouthful of grapes. The air tumbled out of me in the rhythm of amusement, though it was quiet and partnered with a shameful sting as my nervous system rebooted.

The sound of jokes being made and giggles ensuing joined in with the breakfast dishes and cutlery clanging—and the occasional slurp when Batre took a long sip of tea—to break up the tension in my shoulders as I dined with the group.

Every time they revealed a new fact about themselves to me, the concrete in my veins softened a little more.

I learned that Wrenlock had once proposed marriage to a streetlamp on the way home from a bar crawl in Caeludor's lower town, and that Lucais had been banned from a tavern in the Court of Light because the owner had been hexed with short-term memory loss by a Witch, so he didn't realise that he was the High King.

Instead of letting him forget about it and resuming his normal patronage, Lucais started a tradition where the group paid a visit to the tavern and he did the exact same thing that got him banned in the first place—which was to ask the enchanted lute in the corner to play the tune of the song the owner's ex-girlfriend wrote about him post-breakup, and bespell all of the objects in the tavern to dance while Lucais stood on top of a table in the middle of the room and serenaded the owner.

Batre thought it was a little redundant, but everyone else thought it was hilarious. They did it once a year on the same day of the original incident.

Things took a slightly darker turn when Morgoya and Wrenlock compared how many battles they'd won during the Gift War only for Morgoya's count to score higher. And Batre revealed that she'd accidentally turned her first girlfriend into a pot plant during an argument—before losing track of her after someone put her out in the garden when it rained—but even that revelation didn't frighten me like the spilled milk.

I'd asked them where Delia was because I hadn't seen her. I hoped that she might have been able to join us, but I was informed that she'd returned to her own home. Apparently, she only lived in the House when it was occupied, and never travelled into the city. I tried to bury my feelings about that.

The dining room was small and cosy compared to the rest of the palace, and the High Fae were warm and open.

Walled with bookcases, the room had a low ceiling, and empty space was filled by large stone pots housing exotic plants with deep green leaves. Together, we sat at a modest table neatly garnished with antiques between a plain glass casement window and a blazing hearth. Laughter rebounded off the walls as they told me their stories, encasing me until I had no choice but to join in and laugh until water leaked from my eyes, which made Morgoya laugh even harder.

Eventually, when it seemed that everyone had finished eating and Batre had the hiccups from giggling so hard on a full stomach, Lucais pushed his plate away and drummed his fingers on the white tablecloth.

"On that note," he began, flicking his golden gaze towards mine. My eyes shuttered, bracing myself for his next words as the collective mood stalled and then began a slow, inevitable downwards spiral. "I have to address the Court this afternoon, which gives me only a few hours to visit the Map. I'll need a statement printed for distribution in the lower town," he advised Wrenlock, before shifting his gaze to the High Lady. "And I'll need you to make arrangements for the carousal tomorrow."

Both his High Lady and his Hand nodded in complicity.

I flicked an eyebrow up and asked, "What about me?"

"You were so curious about the Map when I first mentioned it," Lucais replied smoothly, brushing a crumb of biscuit from the tablecloth before smiling up at me with his lethal brand of innocence. "I thought you might like to see it."

"So I'll go with you?" I tripped over my own voice, clearing my throat. "Alone?"

The High King of Faerie swept his smouldering gaze around the room before turning it back onto me like the barrel of a gun. "Is that a problem, little beast?"

I was already shaking my head in response to everyone's eyes falling on me. *Play it cool.* "No. Why should that be a problem?"

Brushing a hand through the air between us in what I hoped was a nonchalant gesture, I rose from the table with very little grace right as the blond fiend began to send images into my mind of our kiss the night before from his point of view.

They assaulted me like repeated flashes of lightning striking my cerebral cortex. My temperature spiked, heat pouring out beneath my skin, dripping down my middle and pooling between my legs. I tripped on my chair leg, and Wrenlock's arms came out to steady me, wrapping around my waist with a fluidity honed by practice.

The images abruptly ceased.

"We'll reconvene at the assembly," Lucais announced, standing so quickly his chair nearly toppled over behind him. He straightened the lapels of his long coat—black velvet with elaborate stitching in golden thread—and glided across the room with the grace of a bird soaring through the air.

When his hand came out to rest on my lower back—a gesture no doubt intended to guide me out of the dining room with the faintest semblance of ease—he wiped the invisible traces of Wrenlock's touch from my clothing first. And I felt four pairs of eyes burning into our backs as we left the room without another word or backwards glance.

Ten

How Do You Turn You Off?

The Map of Faerie was kept in the very heart of Caeludor.

That was all Lucais would divulge as he escorted me down the hallowed halls of his palace to the same foyer I'd walked through the previous day. Above us, the obsidian chandelier hung from the ceiling like a guillotine over my *pretty little neck*. My throat tightened in response, and I didn't take a breath until we had crossed from one side of the room to the other.

The High King and I had not seen another soul. I couldn't decide if they were hiding from us, glamoured, or simply non-existent. We must have travelled through at least four empty floors by the time we made it back to the entrance, but the only signs of life were stationed outside the palace doors. Lucais waved a hand in a very forceful and elaborate motion as he strode towards them without missing a beat, and they swung open to reveal the same pair of sentries from the day before. I stared back at them quizzically as I descended the steps, holding hands with the High King for balance, but they gave none of his secrets away in their eyes.

Repressing a sigh, I glanced away.

For a High King of a land as vast and encompassing as Faerie, I thought, *his circle is small, and he doesn't seem to have a very robust staff. And for a palace so hollow and spacious, there doesn't seem to be enough bodies in the entire damn world willing to fill it.*

It was perplexing.

Lucais's frightful carriage was waiting for us within the stony gloom in front of the palace. It was clouded in wisps of fog, six almighty unicorns snorting and scuffing their hooves against the cobblestone impatiently.

With a great deal of alarm, I recognised there was no driver. The carriage door simply *opened* for us as we approached as if at the behest of a phantom footman. I glanced at my companion for a blink of reassurance or a word of explanation, but the High King merely bowed his head to me and pointed to the interior with one long, demanding finger. Regarding him with suspicion, I did as he bid me to—after a fleeting look inside to assess the risk of being chained and cuffed to my seat again.

There were no chains, no handcuffs. The floor was smooth and polished, bearing no evidence of the bolts that had been secured to the wood only a day earlier.

Claiming the same seat, I crossed my arms over my chest, firmly tucking my hands away behind my elbows. Lucais did the same, reclining back at his leisure, his legs spread widely apart in the most crude fashion. He hung his head, eyes heavy and half-lidded, the gold smouldering in the dim lighting so fiercely the placement of his gaze could have burned a hole straight through my head. I felt the touch of an invisible hand trickle down my throat like spilled blood, and with a rush of deep-seated panic, I remembered the body of the faerie I'd—

"We have time now." His voice was a seductive purr, his downcast glance an illicit suggestion laced with temptation. Lucais sent me an image in my mind from his perspective the day before—the back of my head, my face hovering in perfect position between his legs—and even as my traitorous mouth watered, I thought my eyes were about to pop out of my skull.

Blushing furiously, all I could think to shoot back at him in reply was, "How do you turn you off?"

My regret for my choice of words was dealt swiftly and justly.

"I don't know," Lucais crooned, a brazen smirk playing on his full mouth. "You really only seem capable of turning me *on*."

I tried so hard not to look, but his words were like a tangible force tugging my gaze down, and the subject matter was beyond *evident*. Memories of the way his erection had felt pressing into me the previous night and the hot flare of basic, instinctual need that had been lit inside of me as a result started to creep into my mind. Hastily, I shut them down, shoved them away, and locked them back up.

As soon as I regained one measly ounce of self-control, I ripped my eyes away. If the carriage had not been in motion, I would have leapt out of it. Even though we were already on the bridge, and the thick fog floated like impenetrable clouds outside of a plane's window forty thousand feet in the air, I still considered throwing myself out. Impaling myself upon a sharp, jutting rock down the side of a ravine was surely better than impaling myself upon...*that*.

Reverting my focus to the mysterious, low-lying clouds, I risked straining my eyes as I sought another glimpse of the crumbling exterior of the palace, but it was impossible. Adamant. *Deliberate.* To my displeasure, Lucais's gaze was on me like a hawk, and I had an inkling that he was the reason the mist had suddenly become fixed in place like a quantifiable substance. We were taking one step forward and two steps back, and it seemed like we were due for another blind retreat.

"What is it with all the fog?" I asked, pouting at him.

His simpering expression remained, but he shifted just a *smidge* in his seat. "Privacy?"

"Can you be serious for a moment?"

"I can."

"*Will* you?"

"One day."

"Oh, spare me." I groaned, eyes circling the interior of the carriage as I demanded, "How far away are we from this Map?"

The carriage bounced as the High King puckered his lips and lowered his gaze, feigning bashfulness as he gestured towards his lap with his eyes. "I did already indicate that to you."

Steadying myself with hands splayed to the sides, I gave him my best deadpan look and retorted, "Close then, are we? A few minutes away? Yeah, that's not even surprising."

"Feisty little thing." Lucais clicked his tongue and pointed to the floor between his legs, one hand placed with his palm flat against the ceiling to help him remain seated as the carriage jostled us around. "Would you like to get on your knees for me and find out for certain?"

Another bump in the road sent me bouncing on my seat with a small yelp. I clenched my thighs together in an attempt to block out the rocky vibrations of the carriage beneath me. Lucais was certainly doing it on purpose, but he was nowhere near as funny as he thought he was. *What petty sort of person abuses their powers like this to manipulate a carriage ride? And what's he going to do if I actually—*

"Bookworm?"

"If I do," I managed to say around a heated knot of nerves and desire, "how will I know when to stop? Do I just count to thirty, or will you let me know?"

He scoffed and averted his eyes. "*Beastly* woman."

"Arrogant *prick*."

The High King's perfect face grated on my last nerve. I couldn't stand it any longer; I shuffled as far away from him as I could get on my seat, pressing myself up against the carriage wall, and glowered out the window as the fog lifted and the unicorn fleet pulled us deeper into the city of Caeludor. He was trying to take me apart like some kind of wind-up toy, and I'd be damned if I let him succeed.

Our ride remained bumpy. I had every muscle known to humankind tensed and ready to stop me from jolting forwards and landing back in his lap should we hit a particularly rocky piece of road again. The tension in my abdominal muscles was dangerous but necessary.

Lucais, on the other hand, was like a lazy house cat perched precariously on top of a washing machine, watching me with a glint of satisfaction shining in his eyes.

I wondered what went on inside his head. Under the circumstances, the only conclusion I could draw was ugly—that he was a sadist, toying with me because he liked me best when I was upset, and part of me contemplated the idea that I might actually be the masochist he'd been searching for his whole life.

The thought struck a chord, so I buried it—like throwing a blanket over a bell to muffle the sound.

Caeludor, at least, was neutral.

The city was waking up for the day as we travelled through it, like a yawning dragon blanketed by smoke. The gloom never entirely dissipated, but the upper town was distinctly clearer than the lower, most likely due to the sloping angle of the city's overall design and the fog's inexplicable pull towards the palace itself. It was as if Lucais's home was a magnet.

There was no logical, scientific explanation. The fog was magical by nature, possibly sentient, and seemed to prefer to rest in higher places like the palace spires. It coiled around the building like a serpent rising from the ground to the sky. I just couldn't work out *why*.

Out my window, there were faeries flitting from one place to the next, completely oblivious to our presence as we trotted through the streets. Their lack of attention was an immediate red flag. Even if the occupants of the carriage held no interest for the townsfolk, there was no chance that not a single one of them would experience the reflex reaction of looking up to search for the cause of the resounding thunder the unicorn hooves created when two dozen of them hit the cobblestones in unison.

I felt the sting in my chest as part of the ice around my heart reformed.

Lucais saw me righting myself in my seat, heard me suck in a sharp breath, and arched a brow.

"You've put a glamour on me again," I stated quietly.

The game was over, and we'd both lost.

I fell back from the window abruptly as my cheeks flared with an uncontrollable, searing shame. Disappointment sank to the pit of my stomach and rolled around there—a marble at the bottom of a bowl, weighed down like a sword thrown into a lake and buried to the hilt upon its bed. It hurt so much, and I couldn't explain why. I only knew that it felt worse than what Wrenlock had done to me.

It felt worse than anything.

"You keep putting glamours over me," I whispered, blinking dubiously at his boots. He didn't want me to be spotted—he was making sure there were no witnesses. "So why wouldn't you just let me leave when I tried? You know I would have laid low. Why pick me up and chain me to yourself again?"

A sharp intake of breath, and then the High King said, "You really want them to see you, little beast?"

I shook my head. "It doesn't matter what I want."

But I *did*. I wanted them to see me, and I wanted them to see what he was doing to me. The hot and cold torture, the trickery and deceit, the spells that cloaked me in their streets while I grappled with the fate he'd sealed for them during a war before I was even born. I wanted them to know me so they might understand why I didn't want to be their High Queen and live out the remainder of my sentence of eternal servitude at his side. I wanted them to see so that, one day, they might forgive me.

Lucais's voice cut into my thoughts like a steak knife into a fillet. "I want what is best for the people of this realm," he told me plainly. "I hope that, as their intended High Queen, you would want the same."

"And I am not what is best for them," I mused. *On that, the High King and I might agree.* "So your solution is to stow me away inside of your spells like some kind of fucking mistress."

Lucais's head swung from side to side. "Nope. Try again, you maniacal woman. That is not what I said."

"Okay." I sat forward, feeling a pleasant shift in the atmosphere between us as the carriage moved smoothly around a bend. "Then what's the problem? Why the glamour, Lucais? It can't be the Malum or the caenim. You said the city was secure—"

"It *is* secure."

"Is it Blythe and the Court of Darkness? Do you think I am indispensable in your quest to find her and figure out what went wrong, and you don't want anyone to know you've brought in reinforcements?"

"I don't care about finding her."

"Then *what* is it?" I threw my hands up, and they landed with a slap on my thighs as I leaned back again. "Is there something about me you find so utterly atrocious you cannot bear to reveal it to your people?"

He blinked at me. The High King just stared at me, blinking like an idiot for long minutes.

"Nothing," he answered at last. "In fact, if you're so ready for them to meet you, let's get it over and done with. I am not here to stand in your way, Your Future Highness."

"I don't understand—"

With a wave of his hand, Lucais cut me off, and the top of the carriage opened up like a sunroof. He was on his feet in seconds, his arms reaching for me and hauling me to mine. Eagerly, I scrambled to find footing to hoist myself up high enough to see below the tree line. Lucais scooped me up with one arm around my waist, the other laid flat upon the carriage rooftop, and held me with my back flush against his chest and his chin resting against my ear.

The city was absolutely *beautiful* and filled with—

That's a lot of people.

Everyone crowding together on the street stopped, turned, and looked at us. Every. Single. Person. There were so many faeries out in the gloomy light of day, meandering about their mornings, and I drew in a sharp gasp of air as they simultaneously stopped what they were doing and every last one of them bowed.

They *bowed*.

Faeries dropped to their knees or hung their heads low in a startling display of deference. As far as my mortal eyes could see, there were faeries offering respect to us in a way they had not even attempted to replicate when it had been Lucais in the carriage alone. I wanted to turn to the High King and ask him why it was happening, but I was acutely aware that they were listening. I knew they could hear us since the glamour had been lifted for possibly the last time, and they would be curious.

I spoke to him in my mind instead. *What is this for?*

His answer was simple. Fast. *For you.*

The idea was absurd, but my eyes were not playing tricks on me. The pathway through Caeludor became marked by faeries of different races, colours, shapes, and sizes, all bowing their heads or entire bodies. Lucais did not elaborate on his thought, but he remained a steady presence holding me upright as the carriage continued its journey to the city's heart.

They had seen the Oracle's prediction. They recognised me—or at least remembered enough about me to make the connection. Lucais said the Oracle didn't show faces, but he caught a glimpse of flame-red hair in the vision.

My curls were freed by the wind, the strands pulled loose and teased in the air as the carriage picked up speed down a long, straight stretch of road. The High King's heart beat into my chest in an unsteady rhythm, his lungs expanding with even breaths, caressing me with each inhale. I felt like I was on a float in a parade, but there was no music, and nobody was making eye contact with anyone else. They were simply watching, processing, and...

Wiping away tears?

Finally, Lucais loosened his grip.

I practically collapsed back into my seat, breathless and exhilarated.

"Happy now?" he demanded, sounding anything but overjoyed himself. "You wanted them to see you and know that you're here, and now everyone who's ever set foot in this place before in their whole immortal life will get the message—including the Malum, probably. But what the hell, right?"

"Don't be so dramatic," I sniped. The experience was strange and thrilling at the same time, but I had low hopes where he was concerned because the High King had a track record of ruining everything for me. "That display was all you. I only wanted you to stop *hiding* me."

"Really?" he sneered. "Who's hiding who again?"

I scrunched up my nose, shaking my head. "If you're talking about *Wrenlock* and the bond—"

The High King cut me off with a lethal look as the carriage lurched to a halt. "We're here."

"Lucais—"

He held up a hand. "Enough, Auralie. There are people out there watching us. For once, I am going to need you to fucking behave yourself, or I'll not only glamour you again, but I'll see you back in those chains on both your hands and your feet, and I'll let the whole of fucking Faerie see it too."

I recoiled from him like he was a venomous snake. Lucais didn't react or give me time to think; he simply straightened his clothes as the door opened by itself, and then deftly stepped down from the carriage, avoiding my eyes when he held his hand out to help me down after him.

The people in the vicinity pretended not to stop what they were doing to watch, but everything moved in slow motion. The way that hands swung, feet stepped, heads turned, and mouths opened for words... All of it was delayed as they kept one eye trained on us. I didn't feel any malice or distrust, even though I was sure I'd seen some of them crying. The air was charged with raw inquisitiveness and a tinge of shocked relief.

Lucais snatched my hand and pulled me into a small, unmarked building. It was different from most of the grotesque structures in the city; a tiny, textured flat with a white picket fence and flower garden wedged between two towering multi-storey buildings on a street lined with weeping willows and crawling wisteria vines. A black signpost shaped like a wilting rose stood out the front with a wooden sign, but the paint had been sanded away.

The bell above the door jangled on entry, and I had a momentary flashback to Dante's Bookstore. Homesickness grabbed for me with hands of desperation as the smell of mothballs and fresh ink rushed to greet my nose.

A rainbow of spines lined the walls from the ceiling to the floor on shelves of golden timber and long-stemmed plants with drooping leaves were suspended in midair above our heads, some tethered from macrame hangers on ceiling hooks and others seemingly bespelled to levitate. Obsidian jars housed long quills, glittering like a starry night, and a large, gliding wooden library ladder was in the corner of the room beside a stack of half-opened book cartons.

We had entered a faerie bookstore.

Something in my chest pulled, and my lungs constricted, remembering the last time we had been inside an establishment like it.

I'm sorry, lassie, but ye must go.

A short, portly man with a large, crooked snout and two elongated ears like those belonging to a horse stood behind the counter. His head was mostly bald save for some tufts of white hair at the top, and his skin was a speckled tangerine. Huge round eyes, rimmed with tight creases, were raised to welcome us, and he smiled with a wide mouthful of slightly discoloured teeth. After disappearing beneath the countertop for a moment, he rounded the corner half his height, walking with a slight limp that had him leaning heavily on a gnarled tree branch serving as a cane.

"Your Majesty," he greeted Lucais pleasantly. The small man's voice was a smooth rasp, and I buried my unreasonable shock at hearing an unfamiliar person referring to the arrogant bastard at my side as royalty. His dark, eager eyes moved to my face, and he licked his plump lips. "This is she?"

Lucais both looked and sounded less than impressed when he glanced down at me and confirmed it flatly. "This is she."

"And so she is found." The short man reached for my hand, nodding his head enthusiastically. Not knowing what else to do, I gave it to him, and he held it snugly in his thick-fingered grasp, bending his head with reverence. "It's an honour to finally meet you, milady," he said, his voice filled with conviction. "A real honour."

My face paled. *Milady?* "Than—"

Lucais clamped a hand over my mouth. "Uh-uh. Zip it, you. Never give thanks to a malevolent faerie or they will take it as a debt owed."

I licked his palm to get rid of his hand, and his eyes flared before he pulled it back. "Malevolent faeries?" I repeated. *Are they not all a little bit malevolent?*

"Eyes on the prize, bookworm. This is Eldrick," Lucais said by way of introduction. He suddenly sounded bored. "He's the only Hobgoblin in town I trust with my precious artefacts—" The High King broke off with a small choking noise, noticing that Eldrick had taken advantage of our distraction and started to lick my hand with small strokes of his purple, catlike tongue.

The Hobgoblin's eyes were closed, and he moaned softly as if he were licking chocolate from my fingers. I tried to conceal the cringe, but I was exceedingly glad his eyes were closed because I could not keep the expression from flitting across my face. The rest of my body was tense, frozen in place by the stupefaction and unfamiliarity of local customs. My track record with the Goblin race was indigent at best, and I still had the taste of Lucais's skin on my own tongue.

With a quiet groan, Lucais tugged me firmly against his side and reached across me like he was brushing away a cobweb, effectively snatching my hand back from the storekeeper. "*You* are obviously not included in that," he muttered, eyes darting to mine. He sighed wearily. "Eldrick, please. We're here to see the Map."

"My deepest apologies," the Hobgoblin said, bowing repeatedly as he backed away. He gave me one last, longing look as his tongue swiped over his mouth again. "It has been *so* long since we have had a High Queen, and such a treasure is she."

Lucais had the nerve to roll his eyes. "Indeed."

"A Hobgoblin?" I hissed at him when Eldrick shuffled back behind the counter and started opening and slamming drawers with a ferocity that put John Dante to shame. I wiped his saliva off on my clothing as discreetly as I could manage. "I thought you said they hate to be observed. Didn't one of them try to attack us on the road into Sthiara?"

Lucais gave me a scornful look. "Not *us*," he replied. "*You*. Besides, that was a *Goblin*. They're quite different." He paused, thoughtful. "Do you learn anything when you read, or do you just like to look at all the pretty words? All those books you ransacked in the House's library—and for what?" he muttered.

I shook my head, too dazed to bite back, and watched as Eldrick returned carrying a large key on a periwinkle ribbon. Lucais followed him as he hobbled into the back room, dragging me along behind him, and looked on as Eldrick carefully placed the key on the floor.

Using his free hand, the High King clicked his fingers, and blinding light exploded from within the key in a circle, opening a portal out of thin air in front of us. Before my mouth could finish falling open, the High King stepped through it, his figure becoming veiled by a thick coat of magic—almost like a sheer blanket woven with luminescent golden threads—and then he used the hand still wrapped around mine to yank me inside too.

Eleven

What Shadows?

I attempted a scream, but the High King twisted our arms and covered my mouth with his free hand again.

Stunned, my chest heaved as I registered the shape of his body pressed against mine from my shoulders down to my knees. His arms were around me, one across my chest and one looped over my waist. The heat from his skin was a searing touch, the vile thing between his legs growing thicker and harder with every passing second pressed into my lower back, gently pulsing with need.

His full, insistent proximity stirred a flurry of butterflies between my legs—tingles that travelled up and down my spine like unwanted passengers on a broken elevator with one blissful, inevitable fate. My head lolled back against his shoulder, and Lucais's breath was a honey-sweet pant in my ear, the sound of a sinful promise that might condemn me simply for listening.

To break the spell—and I *really* had to break the spell—I surveyed our new surroundings.

The portal had transported us into a small room. A cottage kitchen with herbs and spices lined up on the windowsill, pots and pans hanging from the ceiling, and a round table carved from heavy wood sat in the middle of the space. Through the lace curtains, I glimpsed the paradisiacal expanse of an open forest bursting with coloured flowers, filled to the brim with particles of light and accompanied by a rushing crystalline stream.

"What is this place?" I whispered.

Lucais let me go, and the removal of his arms from my body felt like he had stripped me bare of my clothing and the first layer of my skin. "The Map."

Shivering, I gritted my teeth and scowled. The Map was quite obviously sitting in the centre of the table, but that's not what I had asked him. The place we were in was not the Map; it was the part of the world in which Lucais had chosen to store the Map, and I wanted to know why.

"It belonged to my family," he explained curtly. "They lived here during the Gift War. We're not..." He sighed and waved a hand around the room. "We're not actually *here*. This is all decoration to colour the rip between worlds so it tricks our minds into remaining calm while we're in a state of existing and not existing between everywhere and nowhere. The real cottage burned to cinders and ash during the Gift War."

Flames licking the walls, thirst of fire so greedy and gluttonous. Screaming, voices boiling in a cauldron of death and destruction. The chokehold of smoke and ash. Falling, falling. One by one, the walls come tumbling down. Heat rolling, crashing in waves. A spray of ashes and sparks crackling in the air of destiny's undoing. Empty spaces, clean slates, cleansed by the fires burning, burning. Too late. Darkness, for now and ete rnity—

A cupboard door banged, violently wresting me from the scene playing out in my head like a waking nightmare in broad daylight. Lucais was oblivious, rummaging through the kitchen cupboards and drawers by the window across the room.

I shuddered to dispel the illusion and faced the Map head-on instead. "So this is it?"

"Yes," the High King replied absently, crouching down to reach one of the lower shelves.

The Map of Faerie was an old drawing on discoloured parchment paper, dotted with lines and embellished with swirls. Its edges were curled in, smooth but not straight. Approaching it, I examined the depiction of Faerie.

My eyes narrowed. Vaguely resembling the outline of a live human heart in its shape, the land was cut halfway down the middle by a grim depiction of the Metal Mountains—portrayed like stitches woven through flesh on the page. Six sections were carved out to represent each Court, with a seventh expanse of land left undefined around the border. It rolled in like a dark sea, covered with shadows and sparse outcroppings of dead flora—the Ruins.

The six Faerie Courts were stacked unevenly, sliced into two rows of three. To the east, from north to south, there was the Court of Darkness, the Court of Earth, and the Court of Light. To the west, from north to south, there was the Court of Fire, the Court of Water, and the Court of Wind.

The Metal Mountains were sharp, jagged peaks that ran from the northernmost point between the Court of Fire and the Court of Darkness directly down to Caeludor—which sat roughly in the middle of the map, a tiny borderline triangular shape with its flattest base facing west—cutting a line of separation on the east, between the citadel and the Court of Earth.

The jagged outline continued down the page on an angle, further serving to divide the Court of Earth from the Court of Light.

In Lucais's Court, I saw the scribbling whorls depicting the Forest of Eyes and Ears stretching from the far outer corner through the centre of the land. Bordering but not quite touching the Metal Mountains and the Ruins, it bloomed in a long, twisty line down the perimeter. I spotted the Goblin Village and Sthiara leading the way up the coastline to the House, sitting against the little inlet protected from the Underworld by heavy iron nets.

Enyd's Court of Wind was home to the Opiate Desert, which spanned across the north-western corner against the Court of Water and her slice of the Ruins. Similar townships and villages were marked, as was her portal into the human world, but none of it looked familiar to me. No corner of her land touched the coastline directly; all possibilities were consumed by the Ruins.

Other landmarks were considerably harder to discern, portrayed by smudges and circles with swirling underlines or small, partially incomplete shapes and dotted lines. I could almost make out something in the far north above the City of Light that could have resembled the Temple of All because it was shaped like a religious cross, but it might have simply been an outcropping of trees near the Metal Mountains.

The Court of Water had the only other open inlet allowing faeries to access the beaches along the coastline. Bodies of water took up much of the space, annexing a large portion of the land and flowing back into the ocean. It was the only Court in all of Faerie with direct access to Caeludor, unrestricted by the brutal mountain range encasing the city on all other sides, but the pathway must have relied on bridges due to the amount of water gathered around the border. It made me wonder if we'd travelled through Enyd's Court from Sthiara in order to get into the city by carriage—or if we had taken tunnels beneath the Mountains, the way that Morgoya and Wrenlock had suggested was being done by the caenim with help from the High Lord of the Court of Earth.

I didn't ask because it seemed far too dangerous a choice for Lucais to use tunnels that were being exploited by his arch nemesis and their sick, vicious little pets. That meant I must have slept through my time in the only other two Faerie Courts I had technically visited.

As I studied the Map a little closer, I found that each Court had some kind of magical illusion placed upon it.

Beneath the surface of the Court of Fire, there was a crackle of sparks and flare of heat rising from the paper without leaving a single burn mark, though the increased temperature created refractions in the air above it.

The Court of Water rippled as if there was a pool of water beneath the page, but while the area felt cool when my fingers hovered above it, the paper remained dry and flat on the surface.

Wind whipped between the edges of Enyd's Court, blowing the lines of ink and depictions of towns or landmarks like trees bowing in the breeze. I could see it coasting across the page like the exhale of breath.

Lucais's Court glowed with an unparalleled luminescence, appearing on the Map as if someone had been digging into Faerie and struck gold on the way down.

The Court of Earth rose up from the page as if piled high with dirt and rock, though the paper remained smooth and unblemished.

And, as Lucais had once told me—back when he still had me believing that he was Wren—the Court of Darkness was completely swamped by shadows. All the other Courts had different smudges of ink and drawings on them, and there were clear blotches of darkness moving about within the Ruins like living tumbleweeds of wickedness and spite, but pure shadow and oblivion swallowed up Blythe's Court.

Consuming it.

A bitter, callous chill traced the outline of my spine. There was an unscented reek of nothingness wafting from the northeastern corner of Faerie, as if the shadows over the Court of Darkness were eating it alive.

No—more like feasting on its corpse.

Unthinking, I reached out to touch the Map. The urge was instant and indescribable. I had to see if any of it was real—the Elements, each using the Map like a playground to demonstrate the powers that made their home in each respective Court—and the pads of my fingers grazed the old parchment paper before I could stop them. My hand went nowhere near the northeast, but the shadows ran for their lives and simply vanished along the edge of the paper like I was a drop of oil in inky water.

I hummed, tilting my head to one side. "Lucais," I called softly, keeping my eyes on the page. Beneath the shadows, the Court of Darkness looked like all the others, albeit murkier and with more of those evil tumbleweeds rolling about. "How long does it take the shadows to come back? And what do you think it means?"

"What's that, my love?" he murmured vaguely. His voice was muffled, his nose buried in a book on the other side of the room.

"I *said...*" I swallowed the ball of nerves threatening to affect my voice and turned to look at him. "When do the shadows come back?"

"What shadows?" he questioned, slowly dragging his gaze up from the pages. He lowered the book from his face like it was a pair of reading glasses and he was deep in a completely different train of thought.

"The ones covering the Court of Darkness."

"No," he remarked, already turning back to his book. "They've been there for years and never move. They won't budge."

"Well," I huffed, shrugging one shoulder that felt like it had spiders crawling all over it. I glanced back down at the Map to double-check I wasn't just seeing things. My mouth twisted, and I clicked my tongue before telling him, "They literally just did."

He slouched against the counter, slapped the book against his thigh, and rubbed his temple with his free hand. "Come again?"

I gave him a beseeching look. "They're *gone*. The shadows over Blythe's Court have exited stage left, evacuated the building. They're on vacation, gone fishing—"

Faster than lightning, the High King leapt to his feet. A light bulb moment must have exploded on top of his head at last. His book was discarded, thrown over his shoulder with such force that it crashed against a shelf and sent preserving jars clattering into the sink below. One jar landed on the bench, the high pitch of heavy glass rolling across the marble countertop all I could hear for the longest moment in history as Lucais dove across the room like I'd tossed a grenade into the sink.

His eyeballs scraped the Map, registered the absence of the shadows, and grew to twice their normal size. And then his arms were around me, yanking me back from the table while his hands pinched my arms in a death grip. Frantic, he searched me from head-to-toe as if checking for the entry and exit wounds of a gun that hadn't been fired outside his own mind.

When he found nothing except the quizzical look on my face, he returned to the Map, tugging me with him. The colour drained from his skin until there was nothing but a deathly pale hue where the golden glow of pure light belonged.

His fingers were still burrowing into my flesh.

"Lucais," I said, loudly. "What is it?"

He met my gaze again, his face stricken, and we stared into each other's eyes, swapping anxious dread with brutal understanding. We stood as still as statues for devastatingly prolonged moments.

I clocked weakness in him for the very first time.

Finally. *Finally.*

The High King's golden eyes had dimmed to a barely-there yellow—it was the colour of the final straw, the one that would snap and break the faerie's back if I so much as breathed upon it. His face hovered in front of mine; close enough to kiss, close enough to blow out the candle burning in his eyes if I wasn't careful.

But I could not hold my breath for long.

After all, much like the High King himself, I was not a water faerie.

"What the fuck have you done?" I hissed.

One step forward. Come on.

His eyes shut as my words hit him, and his grip on my arms slackened. When he spoke, his voice was hollow. An echo. "I was wrong."

He was wrong?

I frowned. "What does that mean?"

"It means I was wrong, Aura. That's what it fucking means." His long fingers flexed around my arms, and something inside his throat tensed and bobbed like he was trying to choke it back up. "The Court of Darkness never disappeared at all. It's there, and they're in there. Alive. They're still alive," he whispered. "And they have been all this time. For sev—for seven years."

My heart was thumping against my chest painfully, coated with the dread oozing from him like blood from an open wound. Still, I had to ask. "Is it not a good thing that they're alive?"

"*In exile.*"

Then, he let me go.

He was sinking.

I could not think of moving my arms fast enough to catch him, and suddenly, it was too late.

The High King of Faerie was on his knees before me.

Twelve

The Lapsus

How many fractions of a broken kingdom make a High King? *One High King. One thousand pieces of him scattered through time and space. Light. Darkness. Water. Fire. Earth. Wind.*

Ruins. Caeludor. Fog. House. Palace.

Humans. Soulmate. Land-dragons. Slaves. Gift War. Secret-Keepers. Prophecy. Forest of Eyes and Ears. Portals. Keys.

Mind. Body. Soul.

Kingdom. Crown.

Caenim. Curses. Mother. Father. Friend. Witches. Banshees.

Malum.

Me.

The most powerful man in all of Faerie was crumpled up at my feet like an unwanted love letter.

Time stood still while I teetered on the brink of something finite, my mind reeling as it played flashbacks of the day in the field outside of Sthiara when the caenim snapped and drooled all over the beautiful blond man I had believed to be named Wren. I had made a split-second decision not to save him back in that moment because I had been absolutely convinced he was working against the High King of Faerie.

Aura, my love.

Will you please pick up the dagger at your feet and kill *it?*

I'm so in love with you, it's made me sick.

But he *was* the High King of Faerie.

And I didn't want to make that mistake again—even if he insisted upon repeating his own blunders.

"Lucais," I murmured, delicately lowering myself to the ground in front of him. I sat on my knees, one hand in a fist, touching my knuckles to the cool floor for balance.

The High King was coiled up, his head hung low between his legs, his hands knotted in his thick, golden locks. I laced the fingers of my free hand with his, softly untangling each thread like I was handling sunbeams in physical form, and slipped my hand beneath his chin to coax his head up until I found his eyes.

They were haunted, bled of their colour and power. The one thousand pieces of a High King were sharp and jagged, slicing into Lucais as they orbited his mind, trying to return home to complete the picture in a frame that something had shattered once upon a very different time.

The light in the room began to dim ever so slightly. I didn't risk tearing my eyes from him to check if the sun was setting outside in the make-believe sky. Even if it was, there was nothing I could do to save it.

"Your truth is safe with me," I whispered. It was my final effort—the only idea left in my arsenal. All I could do was hope that he would believe me.

He has no reason not to.

One step forward.

The High King shook his head, nuzzling his cheek into my palm, a solid and harmless warmth. "Aura..."

I waited, watching him expectantly. Lucais's hand came up to grip my wrist, holding it firmly as he dragged it down until my palm was sitting directly over his heart.

Thunk-thunk-thunk-thunk-thunk.

Faerie hearts beat in threes, I'd learned in the House's library, but I counted five echoes inside of the High King's hollow chest. Over and over again, his heart slammed into my palm with five consecutive beats. I didn't question him about it in the moment, choosing instead to hold space for him in my quiet.

At last, he spoke.

"There was something trying to get into the Court of Darkness," the High King of Faerie revealed in a low voice. His eyes were closed, his face tilted up towards the ceiling. "Or maybe it was trying to get out. It created such an intense, chaotic pressure in there that I couldn't actually be sure which way it was headed when I picked up on it."

"In where?" I enquired softly, my hand still resting atop his rebelliously fluttering chest.

"In the *lapsus*," he replied. "It's what we call the place between one location and the next. When we travelled through the gateway between your hometown of Belgrave and my empty field"—he slyly opened one eye to gauge my reaction, and then closed it when I poked my tongue out at him rudely—"we had a singular moment in time where we were in the lapsus. Here, there, everywhere, and nowhere. That blink-of-an-eye moment."

I pursed my lips, observing the homely cottage interior around us. *A place between one place and the next.* "Like this?" I asked. "The cottage is a lapsus?"

He shook his head, ruffling his blond locks. "Not quite. You can't stay long enough in a lapsus to build anything like this," he explained. It was funny to watch him talk with his eyes closed. I found myself smiling at his eyelids. "This is a permanent establishment, built onto an outer corner of tangible existence with a doorway spelled into a key, and it *requires* a lapsus in order to reach it just like anywhere else you can't get to through a physical door."

"Okay," I said gently. None of what he was saying made any sense to me whatsoever, but he was so pretty when he was being polite. I didn't want to risk deterring him from doing it again.

"When we use a gateway in or out of Faerie, or we open a portal from one place to the next, or even when we evanesce, we encounter a lapsus," he informed me, seeming to sense my confusion. "But there is also one within the wards—which is how people are able to get through them—and there are wards up between every single Faerie Court. There have been ever since the Gift War, but they don't extend to the tunnels beneath them. If someone wants to get into the Court through the tunnels instead, they have to be let in by someone on the other side of an iron door." Lucais lowered his head back down and opened his eyes, staring at the fingers I still had splayed over his heart.

I quickly withdrew my touch.

Lucais grabbed my hand and made a prisoner of it in the cage of his long fingers. And I let him.

"The wards serve to function as protection more so than they do in the capacity of teleportation. We never needed them for travel before the Gift War, and I control them all now, which means that I can see who is entering and escaping from each Court," he admitted. "I don't use them to track the comings and goings of regular faeries—or even the interesting ones, really—but if creatures like caenim or Banshees try to gain entrance into one of the six Courts, I can very quickly and easily reinforce that ward's protections and shut them out. Or, as it so happened with Blythe's Court, I can trap them inside of the lapsus, too."

"How so?" My brow creased. "If you can't stay long enough to build anything..."

"The passage of time in the lapsus is not continuous," he replied. "At best, it's singular, and at worst, it's repetitive. They are not stacking moments in time on top of one another like building blocks to move forward like we do. The lapsus is climbing and falling all over the same, single block." He sighed deeply. "I imagine... I don't think it would be pleasant if there is anything sentient trapped inside of it. It would be like reliving the same, single split second of time again and again. The lapsus is filled with electricity. Whatever is living inside of it now must be feeling like it's being electrocuted continuously—zapped back in time by a split second every single time it tries to move forward."

The hairs on my arms raised, even beneath the warmth from the long sleeves of my shirt and coat.

"It all started years ago," Lucais went on softly. "Blythe hadn't shown up to any of our normal events for a while, and she hadn't been spotted outside of her own land, which was also a little bit darker and quieter, according to reports from neighbouring towns. To be fair, though, this wasn't totally out of character for her or anyone who lives in the Court of Darkness. That's why we didn't think anything of it—which means that nobody knows exactly when she first went missing or when the shadows overtook her place on the Map." He shook his head, staring past me at the wall.

"I last saw her seven years ago across the room at a party, so my guess is that things went awry shortly after that. But I didn't start investigating what happened until the first human body showed up beside the gateway in the Court of Light two years later—when I realised Blythe might actually be missing, and her Court was vanishing, too."

"You said it was a Malum infestation," I reminded him. He'd started to explain it to me on our first day at the House, but he hadn't been forthcoming with information, and we'd gotten off track about the Gift War and my family history. Then Lucais—Fake Lucais—had walked up the stairs, and the lies swept all of us away.

The Real Lucais nodded, meeting my gaze with hooded eyes. "I thought it was at the time." Worrying his lower lip, he bent his head to the side, cracking his neck. "Because the Court of Darkness is shadowed by default, I had to guess. I couldn't actually see any of those insidious little balls of angry black ink that represent the different hordes of Malum on the Map. They weren't out in the Ruins like they always are, so I assumed they had infiltrated the Court of Darkness. I thought maybe there were just so many of them that it created an entire wave of shadow that spread over her land, but I was wrong. I think I was very wrong. I realise now that they were probably hidden inside the tunnels, and Gregor was already helping them."

Glancing down at our hands, I rubbed the pad of my thumb over one of his knuckles. Even for hands so slender, one of his could still completely engulf both of mine. "So the northeast corner of the Map went dark, the Malum vanished inside of the underground tunnels..." I clicked my tongue. "I am not understanding how the Court of Darkness was sent into exile."

Lucais's throat bobbed. "I think they were cornered by something in there, and it took me far too long to realise. Seven years ago, around the time I last saw Blythe, I caught something in the lapsus of the Court of Darkness's wards. I felt it—the immediate, undeniable sense of *wrongness* within it—but it disappeared. When it returned two years later, I acted before it could move one way or the other, lest it escape from my reach again." He pinched the bridge of his nose with his free hand, squeezing his eyes shut.

"I didn't realise I had shut down the entire function of the wards around Blythe's Court, effectively locking everyone in and everyone else out, until it was too late. I'd never had to do something like that before. We were busy trying to work out where the fuck Blythe had gone, why the shadows were playing up on the Map and obscuring her Court—not to mention figuring out why all of those human women were showing up murdered inside the gateways. Then...something *moved*. It was like a monstrous snake beneath the water, dangerous and stealthy, and it swam right into my net."

Cringing at the analogy, I pulled my hand back from his grasp and wrapped both of my arms tightly around myself. Lucais looked down at his hand like I'd cut off part of his finger in the process.

"I tried to find a way around it," he carried on after a moment, "but the *thing* was using the ward's connection to me as some kind of conduit. It started feeding on my power, draining me of a microscopic drop of my energy each day. The more attention I paid to it, the more it took. I have reserves of power in spades, so I was able to ignore it for a while, but the problem was finding a solution for everyone else. The few soldiers I sent into Blythe's Court never returned, and the risks quickly outweighed the potential benefits, given that there are numerous other threats worthy of my attention." The veins in his neck pulsed, his throat tightening. "The Malum, for one. The numerous faeries living in my city who would like to see me either ruling differently or decorating their table as an exquisitely handsome blond centrepiece, for another."

I gave him a dubious look. "How do you know the thing in the lapsus *isn't* Malum?"

"I don't." Lucais dragged one hand through his hair, leaning back on his other. The hem of his shirt rode up, and I avoided peeking at the slip of skin it revealed. I deliberately didn't notice the curve of his hip, the line of taut muscle, the deep grooves and outline of something that travelled lower and longer.

"The Malum have a distinct presence on the Map. Have done ever since they came into existence," he reminded me, oblivious to my straying interest. "They're back to skirting the edges of Faerie within the Ruins again, and I can't spot any inside of Blythe's Court now that you've scared all of her shadows away. Besides, the Malum should not contain anywhere near the amount of power or skill I can feel inside of the lapsus." He smacked his hand on his thigh. "Until the human killings began, the Malum had lived—well, not peacefully, but they weren't violent, either." The High King shrugged.

I cocked an eyebrow at him, but he wasn't looking at me. He was staring off through the window.

Not violent? I thought. *Pfft. They were violent before they became Malum. They planned to rape the Witches.*

"To be honest, I had a very strong suspicion that Blythe was the *thing* in the lapsus," he confessed, sounding as though he was still partially convinced of it. "Would've sucked to be her in that case. If it was, though, then it wasn't really *her* anymore. Blythe may be a raging bitch, but she's not vicious—and whatever is in the lapsus *is*. I could feel it attacking me, each strike like a snake biting me repeatedly and injecting a speck of weakness into my powers every single time. With each blow, it took something from me and used it to strengthen itself." Lucais stared at the wall in serious contemplation of his next words.

"Blythe is a bad decision maker, a sore loser, and she has one of the most unhinged belief systems I've ever had the displeasure of arguing about, but she's not a thief. She wouldn't try to steal someone else's power. Wouldn't know what to do with it if she did, honestly. She's a purist."

I choked down an unexpectedly sour taste in my mouth. "You know her that well?"

He frowned quizzically and turned to me. "I know everyone that well, little beast. It's my *job*."

"Pity for everyone, then," I muttered, rolling my eyes skyward.

"In the end," he continued, speaking those three words through his teeth, "I had to make a decision. I had more pressing matters to attend to, which required most of my power to be conserved and not *tainted* by whatever was in there. So, instead of holding the wards closed on both sides, keeping the *thing* away from whatever might be left in the Court of Darkness and the rest of Faerie at the same time..." He took a deep breath. "I dropped the inner ward. I used a fraction of that power to further reinforce the outer ward, ensuring that it couldn't be broken through and endanger the rest of Faerie..."

A tense, lengthy pause.

"And effectively trapping that *thing* inside of the Court of Darkness, along with any of Blythe's surviving faeries and any Malum who had actually infiltrated their Court." The atmosphere grew dark and heavy. His voice became a rasp. "They were alive, Aura. The whole time... I'd ignored them for two years. Protected them in exile for five. And then, one day, I just stopped..."

His irises were sparking like fireflies trapped in a dark jar.

"I didn't let the monster out. *I sealed it in with them*."

No. My mind was an echo chamber of desolation and disbelief.

Lucais heard it. His own reply was grim. *Yes.*

Burying my face in my hands, I took a deep breath and spoke directly into my palms, cupped over my mouth to muffle the sound. "How long ago did you drop the inner ward?"

One. Two. Three seconds. Four.

"Lucais." I parted my fingers so I could glare at him. He was already shaking his head at me softly, eyes crinkling, lower lip caught between his teeth. "How. Long. Ago."

The High King exhaled in a long, melodramatic sigh. "When. I. Met. *You.*"

Oh, High Mother.

Hands falling from my face like boulders from a volcanic mountainside, I leaned back as far as I could go without tipping over and made an incoherent shouting noise at the roof. A thick, hot lump of saliva caught in my throat and burned when I clarified, "*Because* of me?"

Lucais wore an expression of great offence on his face, though I was beginning to memorise the cracks in his mask. "I could not concentrate when I was with you, thank you very much," he snapped, sitting upright with his elbows braced on his knees. He stared me down, the steady smoulder returning to his eyes. "I was too distracted. And you can wipe that look *off* your face, you blasphemous vixen, because I told you to go away, but you simply had to come back, didn't you?" He waggled his finger at me angrily.

I rolled my eyes, biting the inside of my cheek to hide an incredibly inappropriate smile triggered by the memory of that day.

He had been so obnoxiously confident—and unsavoury—as he waited for gratitude that would never come after he'd torn apart my bookstore while saving my life.

"Well, thanks to you," he pressed on, swapping his eyes on my face for the kitchen window again, "the *thing* in the lapsus caught onto the fact that I was preoccupied—saving the life of the fucking bane of my existence—and doubled its efforts." Lucais scoffed. "You probably made it jealous. It was like it could sense you through my thoughts, like my power reacted to you and gave everything away. So *fine.*" He whipped his head back to look at me, his golden eyes searing with determination and desire.

Innately, I wanted to shy away from the conviction in his gaze, but there was a part of me emerging from the shadows around my heart that wanted to lean forward to greet it.

"You can win this one, Auralie. Maybe I wasn't *desperate* to reclaim the extra power I was using to hold the *thing* in the lapsus at bay. Maybe I didn't *need* to forsake the hope for all of those faeries," he said, his voice rising in volume. "Maybe I *shouldn't* have condemned Blythe and her Court simply for being the *nuisances* that were taking my attention away from *you*."

Me. My heart balked.

Lucais paused to drag a ragged breath into his lungs, eyes flaring wildly as they drilled into mine. His voice was scathing in the most romantic way when he spoke again, the tension in his shoulders buckling and collapsing. "But I couldn't take any chances with you, now, could I?" he said. "Not with you. Never with you. You just had to be the one thing I can never risk, and you had to fall straight into my lap, glaring up at me with those perfect blue eyes like I was the one who put you there."

I was falling, spiralling, sinking.

I'm so in love with you, it's made me sick.

Aura, my love.

Will you please pick up the dagger at your feet and kill *it?*

You're going to be the death of me, bookworm.

I wish it was different, bookworm. I really do.

I have a mate.

He's a very lucky man.

Bookworm.

"Lucais."

"Auralie."

My heart, a thunderous stampede of wild horses trapped within the flesh cage of my chest, was on the verge of stopping. If not for the fact that it simply could not keep up with the heart of a man who beat five times for every pump instead of two, then for the fact that it looked like he wanted to kiss me until he could learn to tolerate it well enough to do it as part of his morning routine every day for the rest of an exceptionally long life. And I *couldn't.*

I felt the pull of his mouth like a hand cupped around the back of my head. I could feel the mating bond stretched across my body, intertwining with every cell and flowing through my veins. The answer was right there within my reach. *Yes, yes, yes.*

But I couldn't take it. I knew I couldn't take it—at the very least, not until he gave me answers.

All my other concerns and grievances aside, I knew that kissing him again would wipe my memories.

If I allowed myself to fall, I'd fall so hard I'd give myself a concussion. I'd stop caring about anything else but him—the beautiful blond man with eyes like the molten core of decaying stars and hands that could shelter my entire heart in a house of skin and bone. I would get tunnel vision through a secret pathway that led straight from my heart into his, following a string that fate had woven between his rib cage and knotted inside of mine.

I couldn't let that happen.

I couldn't see that tie made, that bond formed, that fate signed and sealed away like the faeries in the Court of Darkness.

Because what had he done to me? What had he done to his own people? Everything he revealed to me was recent, but he locked himself away inside of the House long before then. *Why?*

All I'd wanted when I trashed the palace was for him to tell me the truth, but he would rather watch me destroy priceless heirlooms than open up to me. If enough pressure was applied in the right way, he might be inclined to respond with honesty. But if I was his mate, his intended High Queen, I deserved to know things for no other reason than *that.* I should not be held solely responsible for seeking out answers using faerie-friendly phrasing.

Not with him—not with anyone, but *never* with him.

It was like asking me to move across the world for him and then leaving me alone to speak in broken French to strangers.

Lucais had riddles of his own to solve, and I suspected that he planned to play me in his games like a pawn while keeping me in the dark so I didn't give his position away.

Finding my father in the Court of Darkness? Is that idea even real, or another ruse? What else is he planning that is so important he has to chain me to his carriage to ensure his schemes are protected?

He would never tell me.

I wasn't *worth it* to him.

This is futile.

"Are they still alive?" I broke the silence with a metaphorical dagger jammed straight into the heart of the conversation and waited for the blood to leak out around us. When nothing happened, I probed. "Can you tell by looking at the Map?"

Lucais's gaze had settled comfortably on my face. "I am unsure."

My eyes flickered between the High King and the table. "Why...is...that?"

"Because presently," he began concisely, his voice a velvet-smooth purr, "I am too busy looking at you."

Oh, the insufferable fool.

Inhaling a deep breath through my nose, I climbed to my feet and walked over to the other side of the table, leaning over the Map to examine the Court of Darkness in greater detail. The shadows had returned, misting over the space allocated to Blythe's land without imposing upon the other Courts. An enigma, a great temptation. With considerable strength, I resolved not to touch it again.

Why did my hand scare them away?

"If there are faeries still alive in there," I mused, as Lucais adjusted his position on the floor so he could see me, "does that mean the *thing* isn't as malevolent as we assumed?"

I heard the surprise in his voice when he repeated, "We?"

"You." I blushed at my faux pas and hoped he couldn't see the tinge to my cheeks. "It's *your* fault. I don't know why I said *we*."

"And you say you don't want to be High Queen," Lucais muttered. Begrudgingly, he climbed to his feet. "You terrify me, little beast. I cannot turn my back on you within striking distance lest you try to behead me for my crown."

"You're not wearing a crown—" I broke off as I glanced up at him. My eyes narrowed. "In fact, I've *never* seen you wear a crown. Why is that? Is your head too large?"

Lucais gave me a withering look and came to stand opposite me against the table. "I'm saving it for a special occasion, whereupon I shall wear my crown and absolutely nothing else."

"Am I in this daytime fantasy of yours?" I questioned with a long-suffering sigh.

"Indeed, you are."

"Well." I slapped my palms on the wood and beamed up at him. The sting was worth it for the dramatic effect. "At least if you're wearing a crown, I'll have *something* to hold my interest."

"Vicious wretch," he grumbled, bracing his hands on the table as he hovered over the Map and stared daggers down at it. The humour in his expression quickly faded. "If the Court of Darkness truly survived the absence of their High Lady and the presence of this blight in her place, they may very well try to kill me for what I did to them."

I felt as if he might have been saying that more to himself than to me, but I responded nonetheless. "You don't know that anything bad actually happened to them, though, right?"

"No, I don't. It's still in there, angrily prodding me, zapping flickers of magic. Maybe it left them alone, or maybe they're all dead." He turned on his heels, pushing away from the table with a little too much force. "But I have to find out."

"How do we do that?"

Cocking his head to the side, Lucais threw an amused glance at me over his shoulder.

"How do *you* do that, I mean?" I cleared my throat with some degree of discomfort. "Because, like I said, this is completely and utterly your own fault."

"*I* will have to let the ward down again, but on the outside this time." He strode to the kitchen window and began collecting books and pages that had been thrown into disarray upon our arrival. "There is no one-way travel through these wards. That kind of magic has been outlawed since the Gift War. So, if something can enter, then something can escape at the same time. Which means—"

"Wait," I interrupted, circling the table. "Why is it outlawed?"

Lucais stopped what he was doing but didn't face me. "It's a safeguard." His voice took on a dark edge. "The wards were made in a time of warfare you could not imagine, a little beast though you might be. Faeries used to lure humans—their own kin, who had only just been rendered powerless—into portals to entrap them. And then they sent through hideous creatures to torment them to death. They'd place bets on how long the human would last before they screamed, bled, begged for their mother, or died."

Something in my stomach flipped over, cold and slimy. I covered my grimace with one hand as I stepped up to his side. "That's horrible."

"I'm sorry." Lucais glanced down at me with a wry smile, not looking like he'd ever been sorry for anything before in his life. "I thought you expected that sort of thing from us."

"From you, maybe."

He pulled a face at the window. The sun was, in fact, setting in that imaginary world between places. I watched it paint his features in beautiful colours and brutal shadows as our reflections stood together in the glass.

"I've never done something like that," he stated. "If I wanted to kill a human, I'd do it myself with my bare hands. I'm not *lazy*."

"How reassuring." The space between my shoulder blades tingled as I tried and failed to stop myself from imagining him doing a lot of other things with his bare hands. "How exactly do you plan to protect the rest of Faerie when you let down the ward?"

"Two ways," he replied matter-of-factly. "I'll create another lapsus outside of the border. Balancing them up against each other like that is precarious, though, so if that fails to contain it, the *thing* will probably take the opportunity to escape into Faerie rather than hide in the Court of Darkness any longer. Which means...we need to shrink Faerie."

"*Shrink* Faerie?" I repeated, disbelief widening my eyes. "How do you intend to do *that*?"

"Not by scale," Lucais clarified, turning to me at last. He folded his arms across his chest and looked down his nose at me with a mixture of apprehension and remorse warring on his features. "I'll have to reduce the size of the ward around the outskirts of the six Courts—the one that stands guard between us and the Ruins. That will allow me to approach the Court of Darkness from the far northeast, hopefully luring that *thing* to the outskirts."

"What about outlying towns? Are there none?"

"They'll need to evacuate."

I frowned. "So you're going to tell them—"

"No," he interjected, finality resounding in the air between us. I was suddenly struck with a feeling of impending doom. "They're going to decide to move further in towards Caeludor by themselves."

I groaned. My suspicions that he was not headed somewhere I'd like were correct. I could already taste the ire budding on the tip of my tongue. "And you're going to orchestrate that by...?"

Lucais grinned handsomely. "Well, bookworm. We need to find some more of those pesky caenim."

Thirteen

Inter-Realm Travel

Lucais's power scared me, but the idea that it could be challenged terrified me even more.

That was why I asked him to stop the carriage and throw a glamour back over us before we reached the palace gates on our return from the faerie bookstore and the secret portal to the Map.

"Are you quite well?" he demanded, one eyebrow arching sharp as a right angle as he regarded me in the low lighting of the carriage's interior. "Have we not already had this fight? And did you not already *win* it?"

Taking a breath of air in through my nose, I let my eyes fall closed for a moment while I unjumbled my response. For once, I could admit that the High King's reaction was compatible with the situation, but I still needed to make my request of him. And I had to do it in a way he would not find insulting.

The sudden dip in my confidence wasn't personal, and the timing of the favour I required was merely strategic. It had been lingering in the back of my mind beneath a pile of other matters, and the visit to the Map had illuminated the urgency. I simply needed to convince Lucais to do it before he was no longer *capable* of doing it—before his attention was dragged away to fight with the lapsus or squash an uprising or make a determination on the fate of the Malum once and for all.

Lucais had disappeared for weeks at a time when we were at the House, so there was no telling how long he'd stick around the palace. The idea that he was required to expend so much of his magic on fighting invisible adversaries made me extremely nervous.

Truth be told, the faerie bookstore had also made me dizzy and disconsolate with homesickness. Perhaps I hadn't felt it before, or I suppressed it, but the ache to be amongst familiar surroundings and see that leaving was the best decision for everyone involved hit me like a kick to the stomach.

Even though I wasn't in love with Faerie, I didn't think I wanted to go home for good, either. The Forest was out of the question according to the High King of Exceedingly Questionable Morals, and neither of us had the energy to spare on bickering about it. A visit to the human world wasn't entirely selfish, despite the fact that my heart was being pulled between two places, a phantom pain needling me between my breasts.

"I'd like to take a trip back to Belgrave."

The High King's expression was as baffled as I'd expected it would be. "Auralie," he chastised. "I hardly think now is the right time to go on vacation."

"It's not a vacation," I argued, fisting the cuffs of my coat to reinforce the calmness I promised myself I'd display. "I left in a rush that night to escape the caenim, thinking my family would forget me, but you gave me a loophole for a reason. You spelled it so I could lead the caenim away from my home, but return if I desired it in the future, didn't you?" Inhaling deeply, I stared into his eyes with conviction, travelling so far into their colour I could have fallen through a portal into a new world. "I need to go home, Lucais, and I need you to come with me."

He stared back, resolve wavering like a white flag in the wind. "Why?"

"Because I imagine that you're about to get very busy, and I want to ask a favour before we get to the point where it's asking too much from you."

The look he gave me suggested that we might already be at that point, but he cast his gaze to the slit between velvet curtains and nonchalantly waved a hand in the air. We came to a sudden stop, and for once, I could almost *feel* the glamour falling over us. It was like a sense of inexplicable déjà vu.

"What is it?" he demanded softly. I felt his refusal to look directly in my eyes like a hand reaching for me through the darkness.

My mind flashed back to the afternoon I'd spent with Morgoya on one of the only beaches in all of Faerie that were safe for the High Fae to visit. She'd told me about the Gift War and remarked on the history of land-dragons and sky-dragons, overwhelming me with good intentions and an intricate history of things that crashed together to create the world in which we lived. One of the comments she'd made had circled around the ability of magic to serve its wielder as required—even to the extent of altering their physical forms. The idea might have sounded superficial to some, but I had immediately thought of my sister, Brynn, and her best friend.

"Brynn has a friend." I swallowed the ball of concrete in my throat and straightened my spine so I didn't feel so much like I was begging him for help. "Morgoya told me about the High Fae's ability to change anything about themselves to suit their needs. Brynn's friend was born into the wrong body, and she would..." The words were tangled together on the tip of my tongue. "I don't fully understand half of what you can do," I confessed, "but I thought that you might be able to help her feel safer and more comfortable to be who she is, given your power."

Lucais turned his eyes on me with the scrutiny of a hawk. "We cannot alter other people," he told me, his tone a little gentler than it had been a moment ago. "It can be done with dark magic and sacrifice, but it's not something I'm prepared to dabble in, and I don't think you'd want me to do that because the consequences are often quite ghastly."

I clenched my teeth together, breathing in deeply and evenly. "No, I just wondered if you could give something back to counteract the consequences of humans losing their magic. Like maybe a protection spell. Morgoya said..." I trailed off with a sigh, realising I was asking him for the impossible. If he could have given the humans their magic back, I'd have bet he would have done so by the end of the war. "Never mind."

"Bookworm..." Lucais leaned forward, elbows braced on his knees, and ran both hands through his hair while hanging his head. "If we go back to the human world, there's a good chance the Malum will follow us. There are probably still caenim sniffing around the borders, though they've at least stopped murdering your lookalikes. I don't know how long we'll be able to stay before it becomes too dangerous."

"I don't need long," I whispered, hope sparking in my chest. Tears of conflict welled in my eyes despite my best efforts to hold them at bay. "We can be there and back in an instant."

He rolled his golden eyes at me. "Obviously."

There was no time for me to question Lucais's reply because the instant I touched the hand he extended towards me, I was swept up in a gust of air warm as a summer breeze, and his arms were around me like my favourite blanket.

My stomach rose and fell with a sensation of being pulled against gravity by forces outside of the bounds of nature. I buried my face in Lucais's chest as the carriage fell away from us and we evanesced across Faerie. Caeludor became a distant feeling, the cool air and biting fog dispelled like smoke in the breeze, and the soft tinkling of windchimes grew louder and louder as we approached the Court of Light.

Surrounded by an empty field, I landed with the High King of Faerie on solid ground only a few heartbeats later. Swapping all of the fog-drenched, miserly sky in the city for the magnificent kaleidoscope of light once more warmed something deep in my bones, though I tried to conceal it.

The gateway rose up in front of us like a wall of glass, and Lucais's hands gently and meticulously brushed the hair back from my face when I turned towards him, a memory of my nightmares coasting over the forefront of my mind. The depth of his eyes distracted me beneath the light of his homeland, scintillating sunsets chasing sunrises around the midnight of his pupils, and I lost my train of thought.

"We cannot stay long," he informed me sternly. "I wish I could give you more time, but it's not only for us. The longer we stay outside of Caeludor's wards, the more attention we'll draw from the Malum if they're monitoring inter-realm travel, and the greater the risk to the people who live in Belgrave." Lucais's fingertips scraped against my scalp with a gentle pressure as he threaded his hands through my hair again. "I put a pliant shield up around the town when we left the first time, but there are limitations to it, and you need to understand that I don't care what happens or what you say to me while we're there."

I was tempted to make a snide remark about how Belgrave wasn't the only place in the world where my opinions and demands meant very little to him, but since he was doing me a favour, I refrained.

"Are we clear, Aura? You're my one and only priority."

A concoction of pleasure and dread mixed with his words in my mind, and I could only nod with vague enthusiasm because it felt like a deal-breaker for him if I tried to argue the point. "I know. It's okay."

"Alright." The High King of Faerie gripped my hand, his touch like a safety net beneath my skin as I stepped through the gateway, but—

I was wrong. It wasn't okay at all because when Lucais and I stepped through the wall of glass, the world we walked into was not the same one I had left behind.

Fourteen

A Couple of Months Ago

It's not your fault. It's not your fault. It's not your fault.

The words circled my mind like vultures as I drifted through Belgrave as a ghost. Whether they were a positive affirmation or the binding command inside a spell made no difference to me. The minute I stepped through the gateway, I knew something was very wrong.

The empty field that existed miles out of the small township of Belgrave was a vast expanse of undisturbed land and long, golden grasses when I'd followed the High King into Faerie, so the industrial estate that existed there as we stepped back through the glass-like wall was new to me. Behind us, the soft symphony of wind chimes coming from the lilac wheat stalks with azure-tipped spikes was quickly replaced by loud, obnoxious beeps, truck reverse alarms, and rumbling engines. Voices took the form of shouts in the distance as men in hard hats and fluorescent vests clamoured around in different lots, waving their soot-smeared forearms above their heads or driving forklifts back and forth in private concrete yards encircled by chain-link fences.

Lucais saw the sharp rise of fear and dread in my demeanour—or perhaps he felt it stabbing him through the bond—and grabbed my hand to pull me across the obscene display of modern industrialisation and development. I watched as brand-new warehouses, truck and car yards, mazes of side roads—some of which were still being laid down and marked—and parallel parking spots whooshed past us in a smooth gust of golden-tinged wind.

We arrived beside the river in the heart of town, and I dropped his hand again. Everything was wrong.

It's not your fault. It's not your fault—

The docks had been redeveloped to make room for a restaurant. It extended over the water on a collection of white-painted wooden stilts, with fairy lights decorating the alfresco dining area behind a set of clear plastic curtains that could be rolled up or down, depending on the weather. There was a large, peeling sign like a billboard, advertising boat rides for tourists over to the next town along the water. Squinting at it, I read the words, though none of it made any sense to me whatsoever.

My stomach flipped with foreign uncertainty because the next town had barely hit a population of three digits when I'd left Belgrave a couple of months ago—*a couple of months ago!*—and yet it had suddenly become an attraction for tourists to go and see the site where a bushranger's remains had been discovered during a level-crossing project—

"Lucais," I said, my voice wobbling. *It's not your fault. It's not your fault. It's not your fault.* I sucked in a harsh breath that burned my lungs, and my voice rose with panic. "Lucais!"

"Aura," he answered. His tone mirrored my confusion while he reached for me, and I whirled, snatching his hand like I knew what to do with it as I registered the utter disbelief etched across his face.

He never finished the sentence he was forming. The touch of our hands sent a spark of amber light shooting into the atmosphere like a firecracker on somebody's birthday, and then we were spinning through the air until we were halfway up the main road that cut through town.

I wasn't sure which one of us was in control of the direction we moved when we evanesced in each other's arms—or if either of us could honestly say that we were.

While the High King didn't seem to share my terror at our findings in the human world, he did seem to share my horror at the way things had changed since we were last there.

To make matters worse, the first building my eyes fell upon in the main street was my favourite.

And, to my utter dismay, Dante's Bookstore was closed.

The windows were boarded up, the sign on the door advising that the shop had permanently shut its doors and would not be reopening, and the insignia on the rosewood had been scratched off. Whether intentionally or not, I couldn't be sure.

A sob of disbelief and raw sadness ripped free from where it had tethered itself at the bottom of my throat, and I would have fallen to my knees if Lucais's arms hadn't been wrapped tightly around my waist, fixed under my arms. He stood behind me and cast his eyes around the crowded street that was filled with traffic lights and crosswalk signs, despite the fact that almost half of the shopfronts looked like Dante's Bookstore. It had been turned into a one-way street to accommodate some of the more insufferable rear-to-curb parking spaces, and I—

"Watch out!"

A cyclist tore down the street, almost plowing straight into us as we stood on the curb, and threw a middle finger up above his shoulder as he sped away after having almost knocked us into the pathway of an oncoming tram. Bleary-eyed, I blinked at the slow-moving monolith of public transport that pulled up to a signpost beside us as a robotic female voice filtered out through a set of speakers I couldn't quite trace, alerting its passengers to the name of the stop.

"Please alight for Main Street, *visitors to the city's* Tourist Centre, *the* Docks, *and section* Twelve *of the* Heritage Society Tour.*"*

I hadn't even noticed the tracks they'd laid down in amongst the cobblestone or the new power lines criss-crossing through the sky. Lucais tensed as a large group of people poured out of the tram and spread out around us like a nest of ants, dissipating into the existing crowd within moments.

"Please stand clear. Doors closing."

The tram began to crawl along the tracks again with a faint metallic buzz. It stuck out to me like a sore thumb in an alien world, full of sensory overwhelm as the sounds of nonsensical human chatter, the perfume of beautified chemicals and car exhaust fumes, and the scratch of polyester shoulders brushed up against us.

A tram—in Belgrave! They're fucking joking—

"We have to get to the townhouse," I said, my voice thick with the tears that were flowing freely down my red-hot cheeks. I felt feverish, burning up, even though it was very clearly winter again in the human world and the wind was bitterly cold.

There was no guarantee that my mother and sister would still live in the same townhouse, given that the rest of the world seemed to have changed in unimaginable ways during my absence. But with my father out of the picture, I had a feeling that my mother wouldn't have found a good enough reason to change anything about their living situation. After all, the only times she had moved us in the past were because of him. They were separating and he wanted to sell the house, or he'd punched too many holes in the walls for the real estate not to notice, or she couldn't afford to absorb the rent increase once he'd left.

So I wasn't surprised to find that my mother's car was sitting in the same government housing driveway as if I'd only been gone a few days—not the way that I was surprised to see the little black hatchback parked beside it.

"No," I whispered, racing towards the front door. Another shot of déjà vu attacked my nervous system as I fumbled with the door handle, banging my other fist into the wood. My head was swimming with emotion as I grappled for the off switch in the new reality playing out before my tearful eyes. *If I can only wrench this fucking door open and step back into the hallway, it's fine. It'll be fine.* "No, no, no, no, no, no—"

"Aura." Lucais's voice was tight, even as he reached around me and knocked on the door like a perfectly normal person would do under perfectly normal circumstances. Neither of which were applicable to us. "Aura, I didn't—"

The front door swung open, cutting his voice off like a guillotine, and revealed a teenage girl.

Dressed in a white crop top and baggy grey sweatpants, she had shoulder-length, pale blonde hair with hot pink dye on the ends. She was very pretty with her blue eyes, light splattering of freckles across her nose and cheekbones, and the glimmering sheen of makeup dusted across the high points of her face. I could tell she had her eyebrows professionally threaded, and possibly her lashes done, too.

A part of me was assaulted by an unexpected twinge of jealousy as I recalled all of the normal things I'd missed since I left—like hair salons and makeup, and wearing dresses without fear of getting caught on brambles whilst running for my life.

The girl looked between my face and the face of the High King as if we were trying to sell her something or ask if she had the time to talk about our Lord and Saviour Jesus Christ, and my shoulders began to relax. For a moment, I almost believed we were at the wrong house, and I'd misremembered the number plate on my mother's old car. Or maybe she'd sold it to pay rent.

But it was only for a moment.

Only until the girl rolled her eyes at us and turned her head to call out over her shoulder for someone in the house.

"Mama, Aura's home!" Brynn shouted.

And then she turned and walked away from me, leaving the door between us wide open—and sealed permanently shut.

Fifteen

A Handmade Crown

The years of practice I'd had of trying to conceal my pain and tears from my mother to prevent worsening the condition of her own state of mind should have served me well when she appeared in the doorway. But they did not.

The sight of my mother with more grey in her hair than strawberry blonde, wrinkles and sunspots decorating her complexion, and the loss of so many missing years in her light blue eyes cracked something permanently in my soul. The High King must have felt it coming on. Before the scream left my dampened lips, the whole world came to a grinding halt.

Everything around us froze. The roaring sound of traffic on busy nearby roads, the hum of tourists talking and laughing down at the docks, and the ticking of the grandfather clock in the hallway behind my mother that hadn't been there during any of the years I'd spent living with her. The chirping of birds in overhanging tree branches, and the barking of the neighbour's dog behind the gate next door. The blinking of my mother's eyes. The way her mouth had automatically begun to curve up into a grin, and the way her hands had already started to reach out to pull me into a hug.

All of it stopped, paralysed in time and space.

Paused so that nobody except for the High King himself could witness me breaking into pieces.

In the very back of my mind, I felt stupid. The shame burned like a branding. As if I'd been tricked again—as if I'd *let* myself get tricked again. But there were layers of other emotion piled thickly on top of that feeling—all-consuming films of rage, betrayal, desolation—and I couldn't wade through it to find my own foolishness, cradling that feeling of naivety so the edges didn't turn sharp and begin to slice me into ribbons from the inside out.

Buckling under the pain, I folded myself in half, clutching my stomach as my head grew heavy and hot with fast-rising congestion.

"Take me back," I wailed, slamming my fist into the brick wall beside me. Pain shot through my knuckles, radiating across my wrist and up through my elbow to my shoulder. My skin scraped against the rough surface, but it only made me smash my hand harder against it as I hiccuped sobs and wild, animalistic sounds of sorrow and desperation. "Take me back! Take me back! *Take me back—*"

"Aura, I'm sorry." Lucais's presence was a distant warmth, a sun orbiting the void. I felt the sincerity in his apology and found the sensation strange. "I'm sorry. I'm so sorry, but I can't. I'm not a—"

Time traveller.

Through the bond, I completed the sentence. The ache in my wrist became so profound that I had to stop hitting the wall, so I turned, barely managing to locate his face through the blur of tears in my eyes as a violent sob wracked my shoulders, and slid to the ground. When the fibres of my coat caught and pulled against the rough surface of the bricks, making an unbearable scraping sound on my way down, I shrugged out of the sleeves. I didn't care that it was freezing cold outside. I curled up, crestfallen, on the concrete slab that made up the front porch of my family's home.

My chest was on fire. Pain so intense it felt like a heart attack coursed through me, rolling out across my body in flares of sadness and regret from where my heart was splintering into a million different pieces. I didn't need him to say it out loud. Lucais was many things, and he lay claim to many different powers, but we'd walked into the one thing he couldn't do. The one gift he couldn't give me. It was the limitation of a man who could do anything—

Anything but give the Malum their High Fae powers back. *Anything* but give the humans their connection to the High Mother back. *Anything* but give his soulmate the years she'd missed from her little sister's childhood back.

"I thought you knew," he said into the eerie quiet of the new world, sounding shell-shocked himself.

Shaking my head, I replied with a croaky, "No." My throat felt swollen and raw from the hysterics, and there was a pounding bass drum in my head.

"A part of me suspected it was why you asked me to make them forget you," he went on. "When you agreed to come with me without hesitation, I assumed you didn't exactly plan on returning."

"No," I said again, my voice flat, dead. I glanced up at my mother's body standing like a wax figure in the doorway—a person I knew well, yet at the same time the face of someone I'd never met. "I didn't know what I was doing," I admitted, so low he wouldn't have heard if my confession wasn't literally the only sound left in the entire world. "I still don't. But I've seen this on television." I choked down another miserable sob that was nearly a laugh and lifted my head back to rest against the brick wall. "I take it that I'm not going to crumble into dust now or something?"

Lucais was already shaking his head. "You're part-faerie," he reminded me gently. "But if you were completely human, it would depend on how much time had elapsed. Time operates differently in Faerie than it does in the human world because the lack of magic here means that what could be days for us ends up being months for them. Their lives can end in the blink of an eye—and so can their childhoods, their youths, their years." He tipped his head towards my mother, his brow furrowing. "They know it too. Talk about it endlessly. Magic sustains the High Fae through the ages, and appeals to the humans who find out about the real world and travel into it to live with us. With the limitations removed, we can theoretically live forever, whereas human beings are bound to short bursts of consciousness while they remain on this plane of existence."

I nodded because different threads of faerie lore showed up in all sorts of books and movies, and I'd heard about it. Of course I'd heard about the humans who were lured into Faerie for what felt like a few weeks, only to return to their own realm and find that they'd overstayed their own lifespans. But even though the faeries in those tales had looked and acted differently from the ones I'd met myself, it was my own fault for not questioning it. For not seeking answers to the queries I was probably too afraid to ask for too many good reasons.

"How long?" I mumbled, swallowing down a gulp of what felt and tasted like a ball of snot. "I've been gone for, what? A couple of months at the most? How long is that in human years?"

Lucais made a small noise in the back of his throat. "That's the problem. I don't..." He trailed off, peering around my mother's motionless frame as if he was searching for a calendar on the wall.

I knew he wouldn't find one. She was never interested in remembering the day of the week—although she'd never been interested in checking the time, either. And yet, suddenly she was the proud owner of an antique grandfather clock. Huge, wooden, and loud, it clashed with almost everything else in her house. The reason why it might suddenly be there circled my mind, but I pushed it away. I could not bear to think about that.

"I'm not sure," Lucais confessed, raking a hand through his light gold hair haphazardly. "Something isn't adding up here. We should hardly be a year into their future, but Brynn was a little girl when we left, and now she looks like—"

"An adult," I finished for him.

Brynn looked like she was fast approaching her eighteenth birthday—if she hadn't already had it. Tears sprang to my eyes again, my face crumpling. I bent to hide my expression against my knees so he couldn't see it while I heaved over a silent sob.

"We'll find out," Lucais promised, crouching down in front of me. "I swear to you that I'll find out what happened." He tugged my hands free from where they were fiercely tangled in my hair and tried to coax my head up. I sucked down a gasp of fresh air, wiping my wet, sticky nose in the crook of my elbow before I obeyed, and then I dragged a hand over my cheeks and upper lip to swipe away the last of the moisture before I met his gaze. "I am so sorry, Aura. Please believe that this was never my intention."

Even if I wanted to be furious with Lucais, I couldn't find the strength within me to do it right at that moment, so I let him haul me to my feet. He proceeded to explain what would happen when he lifted the spell he'd placed upon the world to freeze time—which apparently wasn't placed upon the *whole* world, though it felt very much like it was—and I refrained from sharing any of the mean comments that were in my head about what good it did him to be able to freeze time but not travel through it.

Precariously ducking his head and twisting his torso to fit through the space between my mother and the doorframe, Lucais showed me that we'd need to place ourselves in the right positions to catch up with the passage of time when the spell expired, or else we risked fracturing the veil of reality he'd placed upon the human world in order to make it sustainable without magic. With the townhouse and my family members essentially in suspended animation, I felt like I was walking through a haunted house. We made our way through the low-lit hallway, beneath a globe that used to flicker but was suddenly bright as a star, and into the dead quiet of the kitchen, where not even the hum of a refrigerator brought the room to life.

"At this point, we'd already be inside and finished with the initial greetings," Lucais mused, pulling a chair out for me at the old wooden table I remembered so well.

It was possibly the *only* thing I still remembered well in the house. He pushed me down into it with his large, slender hands on my shoulders.

"She's probably making a pot of tea...so you need a mug," Lucais muttered, glancing around. Just as I was about to point him to the cupboard at the end, he made a satisfied sound and lunged towards it. Lucais pulled out a mug I'd never seen before in my life—but at least I still knew where they were kept. "Here you go." He placed it down in front of me distractedly. "Now. What's missing?"

"Milk?" I offered weakly.

He snapped his fingers and spun on his heels towards the brand-new fridge I'd also never seen before. "Yes, I—" The High King broke off and went still as a statue, except for the very slight tilt of his head as he stared at something on the refrigerator door.

"What is it?" I demanded, fear curdling the contents of my stomach. "*Lucais.* What is it?"

Before he answered me, the spell timed out. I heard the grandfather clock in the hallway begin to tick again, followed by an incessant hum like a swarm of bees above my head. Then the sound of a dozen different televisions each set to a different channel switching on. I shut my eyes as everything came rushing back to the surface of time, and—

"—can't remember the last time I saw the old Ogre since the bookstore closed down, but I'm sure if I give Patty a call, we could set something up. It's so seldom we get you back home, after all," my mother was saying. Her voice was normal and easy as it filtered through the kitchen and filled up all of the vacant, frozen corners, breathing life and substance back into them.

My eyelids fluttered aggressively, trying to acclimate to the scene before me in the weak afternoon light. The townhouse was west-facing, and very little natural illumination came in through the windows after the burst of morning sun at the back doors faded away.

Standing by the stove dressed in a set of pink cotton pyjamas, my mother wore a knitted shawl that had once belonged to my grandmother around her shoulders. I stared at it, feeling the colour draining from my face. Without missing a beat, Lucais reached into the refrigerator and pulled out a carton of longlife milk, setting it down on the table before taking a seat next to me.

The rickety wooden chair creaked beneath his weight. Far too casually, he slung an arm around the back of mine. When I felt a crossbreeze tickling the nape of my neck, I leaned back to peer down the hallway. Finding the front door still open, I elbowed Lucais in the ribs. He followed my line of sight and waved a hand in the air, closing it with magic—right as Brynn strode into the room, scowling down at the two of us like she had witnessed the entire scene and had long outgrown her thing for fairies.

For a moment, I thought back to the three-eyed faerie in the palace and how insurmountably guilty I'd felt when I thought of Brynn finding out. But the way she was staring at Lucais made me second-guess myself, and a low, unsettling feeling took root in my stomach.

What did you see on the fridge? I telepathically demanded of the High King as we carefully and quietly observed my sister's movements around the room.

She sauntered over to the pantry and pulled out a box of dry, sugary cereal, popping pieces of it into her mouth like popcorn as she leaned back against the edge of the counter and stared daggers at me. Somehow, each crunch sounded like a threat. I tried to gauge whether she really was taller than me or if I was just in a state of all-consuming panic.

There are three usual suspects that interrupt the rhythm of time between our worlds, Lucais said through the connection between our minds. *Time passes differently depending on how it's filled. The couple of months you've spent with me shouldn't have equated to more than a year back home under normal circumstances, which means that something major happened while we were away. Huge global events kind of seize the timeline here until it haemorrhages in weeks and years.*

Global events like...?

Generally, it's a world war. He hummed in his mind. *Sometimes, an axis-tilting political election.*

Or? I pressed him because he didn't seem to believe that either of those things were the cause.

A plague.

A plague?

I tried *so* hard to keep the disbelief from showing on my face, but my sister was watching us with eyes like a bird of prey, and she caught the microexpressions before I did. The look on her face darkened. Our mother was oblivious, chatting absentmindedly while she brewed a pot of tea with her back to me at the stove. She talked about all the things that played into John Dante's decision to ultimately close up shop and retire to his derelict cabin out of town with Patricia Farley to keep him company. From the snippets I managed to glean between my sister's staring competition and Lucais's mental telepathy, it sounded like he was putting all of his energy into fighting a million-dollar property development company who wanted to buy up his land and demolish the cabin so they could build a resort.

If I wasn't torn in so many different directions at that moment in time, I would have snorted at how true to character that sounded.

I rubbed at my chest to soothe the pang in my heart.

Shifting uncomfortably in his seat, Lucais tipped his head towards a pamphlet on the refrigerator when I glanced over at him. *They call it a pandemic now. Look at the information sheet pinned up there.* He met my sister's sharp, suspicious gaze and cocked his head to one side as if he was reading her expression like a book. *They went into a full lockdown here and lost months of their normal lives,* he added after a moment. *That's why we've come back so far into the future. It sped up time for them in a catastrophic way.*

Not just for them, I wanted to say. But I kept the thought to myself. The price for abandoning my sister was my cross to bear.

"Grandma's dead," Brynn said flatly. I flinched, blushing furiously, and she scoffed. "Grandpa, too."

"Brynn!" my mother scolded, turning on her. "Don't be so cruel. You know it wasn't Aura's fault that she couldn't make it to the funerals..."

I'm going to be sick.

My father's parents lived overseas, and we rarely heard anything from them, but we'd been close to my mother's family. *I'd* been close to them, but they were moved into residential care on the other side of the country before Brynn was even born. When they stopped being capable of shielding me from the abuse, I'd stopped telling them about it. I couldn't remember the last time I'd visited, but that clock...

"Oh, hush, child. Ignore her." My mother huffed, tucking the shawl a little tighter around a body that suddenly looked much thinner and frailer than I'd even noticed before. "Would you like a cuppa, Luc?" she offered, hesitating before taking her seat across from us.

My eyes grew round. *Luc?*

The High King ignored me, instead opting to flash one of his most charming smiles at her when he replied with, "No, thank you, Mrs. Roberts."

A ball of nausea bobbed up and down in my throat at the title. She'd cheated on the man with a fucking faerie, but never gave up his last name. Even after she had finalised her divorce in the early days, before he came back with a generational pattern for his daughters to break and an entirely different attitude served on the side of addiction. Somehow, the nausea intensified further when I heard her response to the High King's velvet-smooth voice.

"Please," she said, soft and brimming with endearment. "How many times do I have to tell you to call me mama?"

"Why would he call you mama?" I blurted. It took everything in me not to gag right over the sugar bowl. *Why did I think this was a good idea? It's never a good fucking idea. This is worse than Christmas.*

She rolled her watery blue eyes at me and took a sip of her steaming tea. "He's my son-in-law, the father of my future grandbabies. Why wouldn't he call me that? It's better than Mrs. Roberts, like I'm some school teacher."

I realised that she'd poured me a cup of tea while I was fixated on the pamphlet tacked to the fridge, so I forced my hands to wrap around it. The warmth of the ceramic felt too hot, too real.

"Right," I muttered, bringing the mug to my lips. And then, into Lucais's mind, I shouted, *Son-in-law?! You rewrote their memories so they think you're my husband?!*

He covered his surprise with a cough. *Well. "Husband" seemed a lot easier for them to digest than to admit that I'm your Oracle-fated soulmate with whom you might only accept the bond in order to avoid becoming the leader of all things evil. Because then we'd have to tell her the man she had an affair with was actually from the Court of Darkness, which is highly suspicious and borderline depressing. And I thought you wanted this visit to be short and sweet.*

I growled at him inside my head.

"Do you know yet if you're getting time off over the holidays?" my mother was asking.

With some difficulty, I managed to follow her through the conversation, learning bits and pieces of new information about the life that Lucais had fabricated for me in her mind to avoid erasing me altogether. Since time had sped up so much, the enchantment that he'd placed upon her needed to follow the normal progression of human years. And that meant explaining away my prolonged absence with a fancy new job in another city.

In her mind, my father had passed away in hospital after many trips in and out of the rehabilitation facility during the first few years after I was gone. He'd suffered liver failure due to excessive drinking. By that point in time, I'd already fallen in love with the city and pursued a career in investigative journalism.

My obsession with all of those crime books, murder and makeup videos, and the cast of long-standing television shows turned out to be more than just a phase I went through. She presented me with an article I'd written on the pursuit and capture of a serial killer in the country's capital, a proud smile lighting up her eyes.

Lucais and I had married two years earlier, and while my mother's memory of meeting him for the first time was hazy, she loved him and couldn't think of a better match for me. I gleaned most of this from the way she doted upon him, constantly offering to make him a snack or pour him a fresh drink—even though he had barely taken a sip from the first one she'd finally nagged him into accepting. I gathered that we'd been together long enough for children to be expected, but I couldn't determine the number of years that had lapsed from our discourse. It made me uncomfortable.

Not knowing how much time I'd lost with them was like an itch I couldn't scratch. The skin all around it was becoming red and raw as I tried to reach it with the tips of my nails.

The whole time we talked, Brynn stood against the counter behind my mother's chair, slowly chewing on pieces of dry cereal. She didn't take her eyes off us, though they slid back and forth between my face and the face of the High King at different points in the conversation with an almost serpentine gleam. She certainly seemed to know things, like the enchantment hadn't worked on her to its full extent. I wondered if she was somehow part-faerie, too.

Eventually, there was a knock at the front door. I tensed, but Lucais squeezed my knee under the table when my mother stood up to answer it. As soon as she was gone, Brynn pounced.

Throwing the cereal box to the side, she took one long step from the counter to the table and braced her hands flat on the wood, leaning down to speak quietly into the small space between us. Her voice was foreign, even down to the intonation, and the words sounded far too mature for the baby sister I had left behind before she'd even completed her first decade of life.

"I know what you are," she hissed at Lucais, with all of her adult teeth, "and I know what you did."

Blood drained from my face. When I looked over at my companion, he appeared amused by the admonitory edge to her tone. The faintest smirk ghosted across Lucais's lips, but he showed faultless restraint and matched the severity of her stare with his own impenetrable golden eyes. After lingering for a moment to consider the challenge, she switched her merciless glare from his face back to mine.

I expected a many number of things to come out of her mouth, even the profanities she never got the chance to learn from me. Brynn stood over me like a waking nightmare or a vengeful angel—a beautiful, strong young woman held together by the bandages she had been left to apply around her broken bones herself because the sister who swore to stay and protect her had disappeared one night and not returned for...

How many years has it been, Brynn?

But she didn't tell me. She didn't say any of the things I wanted to hear. All she said before she stepped back and sidled up against the counter was, "Amelia was right about you."

My sister fell out of my reach like the wrong end of a lifeline slipping over the side of the ship. I lurched towards her, pushing halfway out of my seat as I tried to swipe her hand from across the table, but it was fruitless.

"How long?" I whispered sharply, my hand still extended between us as if it could mimic an olive branch. "How long has it been?"

Brynn laughed bitterly. "Wow. You really are pathetic."

Her gaze snapped up, her attention snagged by the person my mother had just brought into the house. She stepped between us for the blink of an eye, moving to open the fridge and pull out a drink for her newest guest. I followed Brynn's stare to find her childhood best friend standing in the middle of the room, looking at me like she couldn't believe I was real.

Alice.

Lucais tapped one finger against the top of my knee. *This is the child you wanted me to help?*

I swallowed and gave him a subtle nod. *I didn't anticipate the time jump, obviously.*

The High King regarded her for what felt like an eternity, but it was probably only a few seconds. *She's doing a lot better now. She's saving for surgery,* he informed me, and I began to suspect that he was reading people's minds—or sorting through their memories. It was probably the latter because our mental telepathy was strictly related to the mating bond, and he hadn't been able to do it with Enyd. *The best I can do is bestow a magical inheritance to help her with the costs of that. She has everything else covered, so she doesn't require any type of enchantment—not even a protection spell. Alice has no disillusionment about who she is or who she is going to be.*

I smiled at her softly.

Alice looked healthy, happy, and like the authentic version of herself she'd always dreamed about becoming as she stared at me with round, bug eyes the colour of melting chocolate. They reminded me of

Amelia's eyes—Amelia, who I hadn't seen yet, and who had apparently said something to Brynn about me in the years I had been gone. I wondered if she'd stepped in to help out in the role of an older sister or if they'd simply gossiped about me to conceal their hurt that I hadn't even said goodbye.

Amelia hadn't known that I was leaving at all. I'd left John in charge of explaining that away, considering that he was part of the reason I left in the first place, and I'd taken the coward's way out with Brynn.

"You don't look any different at all." Alice's voice was filled with honest surprise. "Seriously. What the fuck—sorry, Mrs. Roberts," she rushed to add, her voice spiking in pitch. A faint blush touched her cheeks. "Nah, for real, though. Can I get your skincare routine?"

A laugh bubbled up and out of my mouth before I could stop it. "Sure—"

I was interrupted by a knock on the ceiling—a dark, devious sound that spoiled the first moment of actual relief I'd experienced since returning home, and liberated an awful feeling of impending doom that began to leak down my spine. The timing was impeccable.

My gaze slid to Lucais, whose expression had hardened. The only other person in the room who seemed to have heard it was Brynn. While her posture had shifted when the knock sounded, she didn't take her icy eyes away from my face.

Knock, knock, knock, knock.

"I am so very sorry to cut this short, but it's time for us to go," Lucais announced, rising to stand.

"You look well," I rushed out in a gasp, nodding encouragingly to Alice. "Are you well?"

She beamed at me, braces and all, and did a proud twirl to show off her outfit. "I am really well."

"We took public transport into town," Lucais told them, surprising me with a twisty white lie, "and I'm afraid that, at this rate, we might miss our ride back."

Brynn snickered. "Off you trot, then." She wiggled her long, manicured fingers at me in a shooing motion. Flashbacks to days when she had painted half of my fingers pink with the polish she got in preteen magazines streaked across my vision. *Knock, knock, knock, knock.* "See you in another eight years, maybe."

Eight years.

That made her sixteen years old. Alice would be eighteen. *I've lost almost a full decade with her—*

"*Now,*" the High King said firmly, helping me to stand with an ironclad grip on my arm. "Thank you so much for the tea and biscuits." He graciously dipped his head to my mother, who was smiling up at us like she couldn't hear the pounding on the ceiling getting louder as it moved from over the top of our heads, down inside the walls, and towards the front of the house. "We can see ourselves out."

"I'll call you over the weekend, honey," she sang out to me, turning to engage Alice in conversation as if it wasn't the first time she'd seen me in eight years. As if we talked on the phone all the time. As if I wasn't about to walk out of her house and slip back through a portal into an entirely different world.

Nearly tripping over my own two feet as I stumbled behind the High King to the doorway, I called out to them over my shoulder, "I love you! I'm sorry—sorry I have to rush off—"

Lucais yanked me out of the kitchen right as the hideous sound of nails on a chalkboard began to scrape down the front window. I knew it was the caenim, but I didn't understand why they hadn't just broken down the door if they were aware I was inside. The last time it had happened, I'd thought the horrific foreplay was simply to frighten my family.

"They're trying to pierce the shield," the High King groaned. Instead of going back out the way we'd come in, he took a sharp turn down the hallway and dragged me up the staircase, tears racing down my cheeks like my eyes were leaky faucets. "I'm sorry. I thought we'd have a little more time, but the whole lot of them have come straight here, which is extremely irksome. I don't understand why they decided to bypass the trail we left through the main part of town."

As he pulled me past my old bedroom, I stole a brief glance inside. It had been turned into a storage room inclusive of a guest bed and furnished with plain items that had probably been purchased from an opportunity store in my mother's spare time. It didn't seem to have even a single trace of me left behind in it. I had really gone—I had really been gone for eight years.

"I'm not in the mood to unravel this mystery right now," Lucais went on, more to himself than to me. He grunted as he tried to open the window in Brynn's bedroom without shattering the entire window frame. The lock required a key, and it was missing.

Standing back as he forced it to yield, I surveyed the updated interior design. Her bedroom looked so different from the way I remembered. It was natural for a girl growing up through her teenage years, but disturbing for me on such a deep level.

Where soft toys and pretty dolls had once decorated her bed and the shelves on her wall, Brynn instead had a collection of preservation jars filled with strange types of insects and reptiles. The posters of furry native animals, unicorns, and fairies had been replaced by collections of butterflies pinned up behind glass and posters of boy bands I'd never heard about. An array of non-fiction books, covering all different subjects from Greek Mythology to Scottish Folklore, replaced the spots on her bookshelf once reserved for fairytales and look-and-find books. I remembered that pink was her favourite colour once upon a time, but Brynn decorated using different shades of purple and offset the colour against black instead of white.

The only relic of the little girl I had once loved and protected so fiercely before I abandoned her was a stuffed bear sitting in the very corner of the room.

On the old, mirrored dressing table that had been handed down across generations of girls on my mother's side of the family sat a bear I'd had since I was a baby. It had no clothes, and the ribbon around its neck was stained with age and frayed at the ends. But it was preserved on top of a stack of rogue fiction books, and around its torso—

A handmade crown.

Lucais pulled me through the window, the cold air slicing at the tears on my face like razors as we tumbled from the second floor down towards the ground.

Sixteen

My Least Favourite Person in the World

We hit the ground running to the sound of the caenim knocking against the human realm as if Lucais's pliable shield were a wooden front door.

Giving me goosebumps, their razor-sharp nails tapped along the edges of the world with dull, resounding echoes. Once we were out of the townhouse, the sinister touches rattled against the sky and the grass instead of the walls. I felt like I was trapped inside a snow globe they were about to smash through at any given moment. The threat moved with us, eerily shifting from the clouds to the trees, constantly changing.

"Why can't they just"—I clutched my bone-dry throat and sucked a sharp, ragged gasp of air into my lungs as Lucais pulled me across the land, half-running, half-evanescing—"pick a spot and *stick* to it?"

"They're searching for weak spots," the High King replied grimly. A moment later, he tucked my head under his chin and spun us through the air a few hundred metres ahead. He glanced up as another strike of a monstrous fist hit the sky and added, much louder than necessary, "But they won't *find* any!"

When we reached the new industrial estate, my stomach gurgled in disgust for two reasons. First was the reminder that I'd lost close to a decade of my life—and the lives of my mother and sister—in a matter of months, if not weeks. Second was the way the caenim scraped their iron-tipped nails along the steel walls of different buildings, causing them to shudder beneath the phantom touches. The monsters suddenly felt much closer to sinking their claws into us with a thin veil of magic trembling between realms as our only shield—a shield that would become utterly useless as soon as we stepped through the gateway back into Faerie.

Lucais seemed to realise that, too, because he hesitated in the middle of an abandoned lot. Towering around us on all sides were chain-link fences with spirals of barbed wire atop them and hollow, cream-coloured warehouses. All of the workmen seemed to have gone home for the day.

"They're too fast," I said, as Lucais hovered behind me with his back resting lightly against mine, scanning the abandoned lot with clenched fists.

"No, Aura, they're slow." His tone cast suspicion onto everything that encased us, including the very ground beneath our feet. "They're trained on scent. Which means they should have started trying to break through the wards here, when we crossed through the gateway and the first hint of our trail began. But instead, they started at your family's home and followed us back."

An ice-cold itch tickled the hollow of my throat. "What are you trying to say?"

"We've been here less than half an hour," he estimated, scanning the synthetic landscape beyond the fenceline. "At the pace they move, we should've had another thirty minutes before they tracked us to your mother's house." He tipped his head back to slice his golden eyes across the skyline. "It's like they knew exactly where to find us."

"Maybe you're just bad at math," I deadpanned.

Even with our backs pressed together, I still felt him roll his eyes.

"Or maybe it's not the caenim," Lucais countered darkly.

I knew he was probably right. I was no all-star track runner, but I'd still managed to outrun the feral creatures on every occasion. Their forté was endurance; the caenim persisted, wearing down their prey until they'd burned through their energy and lost the will to keep going. They triumphed in numbers, though even that was subjective. I hadn't witnessed any signs that the caenim were intelligent enough to play malevolent games with their victims.

"Wait," I said, holding up a hand, though Lucais wasn't even looking in my direction. "The night we met in the bookstore, I heard someone pretending to read a book." I shivered against the fist of fear gripping my nape as the memory twitched back to life. "It scared the hell out of me."

"I very much doubt that," Lucais muttered, turning around. "You've given me hell every day since then." He folded his arms over his chest expectantly, meeting my heavy stare with one of his own. I stood like a statue, drilling the answers out of him with my eyes. "Fine," he conceded at last. "That obviously wasn't the caenim, but I wasn't *pretending* to read, either. You have no idea how long I had to wait for them to arrive and for you to leave. I was bored, so I sifted through a classic. Sue me."

"What do you mean you *waited*?" I demanded, a blush rising to my cheeks. "How long were you in the bookstore with me?"

The High King might have admitted the severity of his stalking prior to our first introductions, but he might have tried to dance around the truth. I wasn't going to find out standing in the middle of an abandoned gravel parking lot because the Malum were closing in on us from all sides. A precipitous chill in the air derailed our conversation as a heavy cloud drifted across the sun, lingering there like a figure casting a shadow down onto the world. My stomach pinched, and I pressed the palm of my hand into it, trying to counter the plummeting sensation.

Obscuring the light, the silhouettes of the Malum plunged us into a creepy midafternoon gloom, and I knew clouds would never look the same to me if I returned to life in the human world one day.

Soft and low, the High King's voice was a distant wind chime when it reached my ears. "Definitely not the caenim."

The unsettling reply came down against the fabric of his protective wards in a succession of four heavy knocks reminiscent of the fate motif, and I stifled my gasp with one hand. Lucais reached out towards a steel pole on the closest fence and tapped his knuckle against it three times. The resounding noise was a shrill, hollow ring, completing the threat.

"Fuck," he breathed.

I shifted from one foot to the other at his side. "Inside joke?" I enquired, trying to lighten the oppressive mood despite myself. For all I knew, Beethoven was a faerie, too.

"Sure," Lucais agreed dryly, looking down at me with one perfect eyebrow arched. He folded his hands behind his back. "A Malum General walks into a bar and asks for a pitcher of faerie wine. What does the bartender say?"

Suppressing the urge to cringe away from the darkness clouding the edges of his gaze, I rolled my lips together and hummed thoughtfully. "I don't know," I admitted after a moment of serious contemplation. "What *does* the bartender say?"

"Nothing," Lucais quipped, the word swinging out as sharp as a sword. His hands were still tucked away, and he banished some of the distance created by our height difference when he leaned forward and added with menace, "Because the bartender, along with everyone else in the room, is dead."

A quiver spider-walked down my spine, decorating my skin with prickles. My heart throbbed painfully against the inner walls of my chest, but I schooled my expression into a mask of mock amusement.

"Ha." Forcing an eye roll, I steeled myself against the rippling aftershocks as another series of probing knocks rang out across the lot in a new, less ironic symphony. "So we're trapped here?"

"We'll be walking through the gateway straight into an ambush," he confirmed with a sigh. "They can't get in here, so they'll have to wait for us on the other side, which means I'll have approximately one millisecond to evanesce us both out of there and back into the carriage waiting for us in Caeludor. Unless," he added, somewhat reluctantly, "I create a portal."

Vaguely, I recalled the brief lesson he'd given me on the differences between portals and gateways when we first met. But he was so incredibly rude to me back then that I'd focussed more on his bad attitude than I had on any of the magical specifics. My head was swimming with conflicting information every bit as cryptic as the exterior of his palace, like I had fog inside of my brain, concealing a box of answers.

Shaking it off, I said, "So just do that?"

He pinned me to the spot with a searching look. "I have to take down the ward around Belgrave—"

"Definitely don't do that, then."

"—for a split second long enough to create a rip between worlds," he finished, eyes sparkling with the sudden onslaught of unidentified emotion. His face slipped back into that unreadable mask with far too much ease. "You realise we don't have much of a choice here, right?"

I braced myself for an argument, digging my heels into the gravel for support. "You realise I lost eight years with my sister, and I'm not about to let you risk the next eight by giving those bastards even the smallest chance of getting in here?"

He squared his shoulders, facing me fully. "You realise I'm not about to risk *you*?"

My teeth were clenched so hard that my jaw started to hurt. "You realise you don't *own* me?"

"You realise I *warned* you what would happen if we stepped through that gateway, and you agreed to do as I said because I was not—and still am not—prepared to make compromises when it comes to your life?"

"Ugh." I shivered as his words fell over me, serenaded by the maddening tapping of iron nails against the shelter he'd placed on my home. Wrapping my arms around myself, I turned in a slow circle, mulling over our options. The unfortunate reality was that he was correct. I'd agreed to his terms when we came back, not foreshadowing that we might end up trapped. It was his word against mine—his sketchy morals against my broken compass. I released a breath of air with a long, dejected sigh. "You can give it a rest every once in a while, you know."

Lucais slipped his hands into his pockets, but his shoulders tensed slightly. "Give what a rest?"

I gestured vaguely to his looming and overbearing frame. "The whole protective soulmate bit. Even when you're sick of me, you're still so aggressive about keeping me alive. I get it. You take your job seriously. Commendable work ethic and all, but you can tone it down."

A blond brow stretched up into an arch on his forehead, and he rubbed his temple with one hand when he asked, "Are you trying to get yourself killed on purpose?"

"No." I kicked at the gravel beneath my boots. I could admit to making decisions that didn't centre around the preservation of life, but I wasn't suicidal. "Not really."

Groaning, both hands moved to his temples, rubbing small circles on his skin as if he was trying to stave off a headache.

"Why does it always have to be *about* you, Aura? For the love of fuck, I don't have to ask you to marry me—or whatever it is that you humans do—in order to feel guilty if you end up dead," Lucais reminded me wearily, hands sliding into his hair. "For better or worse, you've monopolised my every waking moment since the day we met, and have you ever considered what *I'm* supposed to do if you're suddenly gone? What are you going to leave me with?"

"I'm not leaving," I said, rolling my eyes. "I don't want to die—"

"Then what else do you need to grant me the permission I apparently require to care about your life? Since *I love you* clearly isn't enough—"

I cut him off, incredulous. "You were *poisoned*—"

"I was still perfectly lucid—"

"That's a lie if ever I heard one!"

He dropped his hands from his head and clenched his fists. "I meant it when I said those words to you, damn it!"

"It doesn't matter," I spat back with a little more acid than he probably deserved. "It's not you, and it's not me, and we both know it!"

Lucais looked at me like I'd just hacked off my own nose to spite my face. "Are you dense?" he demanded. "You could be my least favourite person in the world, and still be the only one I'd save if it ended. *That's* what this bond means."

"Exactly my point—"

"No!" he bellowed, cutting a line through the air between us with his hand.

I fell still, watching him like a storm rolling in on the horizon. A vein appeared on his forehead, his jaw locked, and he raised his pointer finger in the air. There was a dark part of me that wanted to lash out and bite it, so I turned my head away with my hands looped around the back of my neck.

"I decided to have these feelings for you all on my own," Lucais vowed. "Trust me, even you yourself had very little to do with it in the end, considering you constantly berate me for saving your *fucking* life!" He stared at me, wild-eyed, chest rising and falling rapidly. "Loving you is its own—"

"Stop it!" I seethed, jerking my hands away from my head. My fingers were so stiff that, for a moment, I worried they'd sprain as his infernal words entwined around my heart like live wires. I'd heard him the first time, and then the second, but I was very deliberately acting as though I had not. "Stop *saying* that!"

"Why?" he challenged me.

"Because I *know*!" I gripped two fistfuls of my hair on either side of my head, my eyes feeling like they were about to explode straight out of my skull. "I know you do. Or you think you do. I heard you! I just don't *want* you to—"

"Oh, for fuck's sake, Aura." Lucais cradled his face in his hands. "Why not?" he implored, lifting his head. "Is it the Oracle? The whole fate thing? The High Mother?" Dropping his arms back to his sides, I caught the roll of his golden eyes as he shook his head at me despairingly. "Who the fuck cares? You want me to summon them and demand they rescind their part in this? Because I'll fucking do it—"

"*No!*"

"Then *what*?" he yelled, so wretchedly I swore the wind changed directions and the empty warehouses shuddered. "What is so wrong with this that you can't let me in for just a single fucking second long enough to show you what's been right in front of your face since we met?"

"*Because!*" I screamed back at him mindlessly. I held no dominion over the weather, so I stomped my feet like a child and kicked up a small cloud of thin grey dust. A few measly stones scattered, clanging against the metal fence.

The High King panted as he watched, waiting for me to elaborate with the kind of patience that could wait out the death of a star. Lucais had waited so long already—he probably thought he had all the time in the world.

"You might love me," I began quietly. The words tasted sour in my mouth. "But you are an *asshole*, Lucais. You think saying sorry is going to erase the fact that you were *horrible* to me when we first met? You think that your good intentions are good enough?"

He watched me, calculating and cool, though his eyes were practically on fire. I stared back at him, shoulders trembling, and devoured the expression on his face that told me he really didn't understand my problem.

"Lucais," I tried again, when my breathing was under control once more. He was pushing me into confessions that would only breed resentment between us, but I had to do it. I had to stop the accursed dance around fate and soulmates.

"I grew up with a man who used to tell me that he loved me when he brought me a stuffed pony to say, *'Sorry I smacked you across the face and sent you to school with a split lip.*'" The admission hung in the air between us, swinging like an axe. "That fucking stuffed toy was wrapped up in good intentions and tied in a strangehold with a bow. But he still gripped me too hard when he was angry," I pointed out carefully, taking a step closer to him.

"He still knocked me into doorframes and the sharp corners of the kitchen bench or the dining table until I bruised when he was upset. Oh," I went on around a quivering lower lip, my voice descending into untempered emotion alongside it, "but he *swore* that he loved me." I paused, letting the words sink in. "That's why I don't know what to do with yours. That's why I don't *want* it."

The High King dragged his hands down his face, leaving momentary streaks of white behind on the flesh where his fingertips had been digging. "Fuck, Aura." He sucked in air through his teeth. "Bookworm, I know."

"You know?" I parroted back, surprised.

"I figured that he was abusive based on your reaction to him," Lucais confided with a measured shrug. "Coupled with the fact that, shortly thereafter, I saw him throw your mother into the caenim, and it was confirmed. Of course, I didn't know the extent of it, but..." He pursed his lips, contemplative.

The way his throat worked around the words meant they were going to be hard for him to say or hard for me to hear. Or both.

"When I brought him to the dungeons in Caeludor, I went through his memories—ah, don't look at me like that, please. I thought he might have known something about your biological father, but it's..." He waved a hand around abstractly as if to emphasise the squiggly lines that took up an angry residence inside my father's mind. "By the Elements, it's a fucking mess inside his head."

"Yeah, it's genetic."

"No, he's..." Lucais trailed off, struggling once more to wrestle the words. "The man barely remembers any of his adult life. It's mostly bits and pieces of his childhood. His parents getting divorced. A drug addiction that started when he was barely an adolescent. And he has some sick, fucking twisted feelings about you festering in the disaster zone inside his head. But none of them were coherent enough for me to pick out any specific instances of what happened, except…" The High King tilted his head regretfully and gestured to my arm, silently asking permission to take my hand in his.

Swallowing the dread anchored in my throat, I gave it to him—limp, but consenting to whatever was going to come next. I had to know, regardless of whether it confirmed my suspicions or threw my entire world into a tailspin.

Gingerly, Lucais brushed his fingertips over my wrist before sliding up the sleeve of my shirt. I realised, absentmindedly, that I'd left my coat behind on my mother's front porch as Lucais delicately traced the trio of circular burn marks on the soft skin in the crease of my elbow. The roughened, healed skin stood out against the thin layer of flesh streaked with the bluish hue of my veins. As a war raged inside of his eyes, I blinked down at the marks impassively, only forming an expression when I realised how close they were to the scar of the iron manacle the High King had left on my arm from our trip through the Forest. The silence dragged on for what felt like days before Lucais spoke again.

"For some reason, he remembers the night he did this to you."

The victimology overwhelmed me, ramming into me like a freight train and crushing all the air out of my lungs. I ripped my arm from Lucais's grip without warning and staggered over to a green wheelie bin a few feet away, barely managing to lift the lid back in time to vomit into it. Groaning as all of the breakfast Wrenlock had piled onto my plate that morning came back up with a vengeance, I heaved every last trace of it out of my stomach and spat the acid in my mouth into the bottom of the bin.

The dry, raw taste burned my throat, lingering there as I coughed and spluttered, trying to dislodge it.

When I noticed that I was inhaling the bin fumes in my eagerness to beat the suffocation of the memories, I stumbled backwards, dropping the lid with a slam. As a sombre silence blanketed the estate, I realised that even the monsters waiting for us in Faerie had stopped knocking on the door to the world that had made my father.

The High King stood a few paces away from me, torment evident on his face. His body was turned mostly to the side as if he wanted to offer me privacy, but his neck was twisted, craning his head back to make sure I hadn't fallen into the bin.

I couldn't have answered his questions even if he'd voiced them.

I didn't know why my father had done that to me. I never understood what had happened that night.

And I didn't want to.

"I am never going to love you like that, Aura."

Tears threatened to pool in my eyes at the sacred vow. I blinked them away. "Then how are you going to love me?" I dared him.

"In whatever way you want to be loved," he whispered. "Even if that means not loving you at all."

Despite the warmth humming around my heart, I couldn't think of anything to say to him in reply. It was all I could do to stand there, watching him, and weigh his words in my mind against everything else that had ever happened to me throughout my whole life.

We might have stood in silence forever if a crack of thunder hadn't broken it. A flash of lightning split the sky, opening a gap wide enough for a swarm of insects to come pouring in like rainfall. I opened my mouth in awe, the question on my lips, but Lucais's thoughts were faster than my words.

Locusts.

Seventeen

You Unbearable Psych Patient

The High King of Faerie had a nasty habit of making split-second decisions. I made a mental note to discuss his narcissistic tendencies with someone who could do something about it before he got himself punched in the face. Or worse.

As if starting a war using the age-old *"because I said so"* approach wasn't controversial enough for him—albeit it was to end slavery, so one point for altruism—the arrogant bastard legitimately wanted to make an irredeemable enemy of his own soulmate. Lucais behaved as though he wanted to flirt with me while I secretly plotted his ultimate demise like it was some twisted kind of foreplay.

Perhaps it *was* a sneaky method of silent abdication—liberating himself of the crown's responsibilities without having to admit to any of his wrongdoings, then laying the blame on a half-breed human girl, who finally snapped on a random Tuesday afternoon and stabbed him with his own apple-peeling poniard.

If vanity was the greatest weakness of the High Fae, then pride was worshipped at their altar.

"I swear to whatever deity can hear us over all of this fucking noise, I will *kill* you if you left any of those Hitchcock nightmares back in Belgrave!" I screamed at him over my shoulder as I ran, covering my ears to shield them from the deafening buzz as thousands of enormous locusts surged around us.

Lucais, as per usual, had decided to lull me into a false sense of security with his misleading words. *Even if it means not loving you at all* in faerie-speak roughly translated into plain English as *I guess that means never listening to anything you ever say again.* And that is exactly what he did when he lowered the shield around my hometown long enough to rip a portal in the fabric between realms—in direct opposition to what I'd asked him to do—enabling an entire army of monster insects to come spilling through the gap like a tear in the side of a bean bag.

If I'd started to doubt my reservations about our pendulum relationship, Lucais's choice to put his own desires over mine certainly swung it back to the opposing end. Again.

The High King had shoved me into the portal he created on the ground before anyone really knew what was happening, myself and the locusts included. Given that the Malum were mentioned every time the subject of those airborne pests was brought up, I started to think they must be keeping them as pets alongside the caenim.

Fortunately, neither Lucais nor the Malum expected me to run for my life as soon as the soles of my shoes touched down on magical soil. The blurriness of the lapsus afforded me a split second of incorporeality to slip my body out of Lucais's grip, and then I bolted like a bat out of hell, shrieking as an onslaught of caenim came into view but not turning back. The foul beasts trudged through the horde of bugs, slow by nature and delayed even further by the creepy-crawly chaos. I took the chance to run for my life across the field, leaving the High King to chase after me, cursing and ranting in an incoherent rage at the back of my head.

The locusts flew in dizzying circles, completely disoriented by the sudden transfer back and forth through the portal. So thick were the clouds of insects that the caenim fell behind within moments of my reappearance in Faerie, and any fast-moving shadows I thought I spied in my peripheral were quickly swallowed up by an angry tornado of wings, pincers, and poisonous spikes.

Thinking he could cheat, Lucais tried to use his magic to catch up with me, evanescing a few paces ahead and reaching out to grab my waist. I expected it from him, so I kept my movements careful and deliberate as I dodged each attempt. I couldn't let him touch me because I knew we'd be back in the carriage in the City of Light in an instant, and then I'd have lost any and all leverage.

"I'm serious!" I yelled at him, manic and wheezy. "Go back there and check!"

"I absolutely will not, you unbearable psych patient!" Lucais shouted back, voice booming over the incessant buzzing of the locusts. He appeared in a whirlpool of black and gold, nearly falling flat on his face when he lunged for me, and I jumped out of reach. "Damn it, Auralie! These things are poisonous!"

"I know! They tried to kill you once," I reminded him. "Why don't you give them a rematch, and I'll go for help?"

I was still shouting and running at the same time. It quickly pushed me to become out of breath, but yelling at him vocally was so much more satisfying than doing it mentally. My lungs burned, and I stumbled on the next few steps as the pattern of approaching caenim forced me into the long grasses on one side of the walking track.

"Because you *are* the help I need," Lucais muttered, appearing directly in front of me. He had anticipated my next move and beat me to it, a step ahead of me, his hands already circling my arms like a vise. "Which is so ironic for someone who—"

Shock ran through me like an electric current when Lucais broke off abruptly, and I caught the look on his face. He was staring at something over my shoulder, but I didn't get the chance to turn around before he pulled me against his chest, and we were slipping away into the next gust of wind.

"I'm not kidding!" I screamed, though my anger was mostly swallowed by the whoosh of the air circling us like a tornado. I tried and failed to pound my fists against his chest as we lingered very briefly inside of a misty white lapsus. Panic was fuelling me, taking the place of oxygen and my beating heart. "I need to know they're safe! I'll never forgive you if even *one* of those creatures becomes locked in their world!"

"Hush," he sniped, his voice breathy and low.

"No. I mean it, Lucais." It dawned on me that we should have already arrived back in Caeludor. He was hesitating, so I grabbed onto it like the fistfuls of his shirt I had snared in both of my hands. "There is no future for us if anything happens to them," I swore, on the brink of tears. "None ever, none at all. We'll be done. I'll be *done*."

The High King must have detected something in my voice that convinced him I was telling the truth because we came to a crashing halt in midair, and he nearly dropped me in the middle of another empty field. Gasping for breath, I stumbled out of his arms with my hands in front of me, poised to break my fall. If I hadn't already regurgitated all of my breakfast, I was sure I would have been violently unwell after that graceless emergency landing.

Bracing my hands on my thighs, I bent over and sucked in air like water, trying to quell the raging storm in my stomach.

We were in a field of long grasses, the pastel colours surrounding us like a pool of water painted by celestial lights. When I felt secure enough to straighten and tip my head back to face the crystalline light sky, I felt a wave of peace wash over me. Guilt quickly followed, engulfing it—for feeling peace when I didn't know if my family was safe, and for liking Faerie's skies better than I'd ever liked the sky in the human world.

Oblivious, Lucais stood near my side, focussed on his hands. He held them as steady as a surgeon might to perform a life-saving operation, and after a long moment embedded with intense concentration, an enormous pulse shot out around us like an ultrasonic wave.

He had cast out a magical net.

In all directions, the bodies of caenim appeared, jerking in the air like fish out of water. Lucais's concentration was absolute, fixated on his hands as the monsters surrounded us on all sides, the scent of their death reek filling my nose and making it crinkle.

Their bodies writhed violently beneath the force of Lucais's power as though they were being electrocuted, and then, all at once, they fell to the ground with a collective, lifeless thump.

Mouth falling open, I watched on in awe as Lucais repeated the motion, a vein visible on his forehead and the throbbing of his pulse in his neck the only signs of exertion as he drew in wave after wave of our stalkers and executed them from afar. The smell rolled over me in cycles—pungent when a group of living caenim appeared, disappearing with barely enough time to clear away entirely before the next group was caught and pulled onto the field. It was the only sign they were truly dead because Lucais didn't spill a single drop of their blood onto the ground.

"We couldn't fight them through the swarm," he explained, voice grave as he lowered his hands. He drew his sword with the resonant slash of steel before extending his hand to me. "It doesn't seem like the Malum are there, but that doesn't mean they aren't hiding and biding their time. Stick close to me," he instructed, his voice devoid of the emotion it had held only a few minutes prior when we were arguing. "And Aura," Lucais added, his gaze cutting to mine, "I *will* kill you myself if you allow them to touch you. You're better off dead than a prisoner."

My blood ran cold at the sincerity in his words, yet I nodded my agreement. He'd mentioned before that they'd do worse things to me than take my life, but I didn't want to contemplate the possibilities. I knew there were more wicked punishments than death—like bearing witness to it, for one.

With my hand in one of his and a sword in the other, the High King of Faerie took us back through the wind to the chaos beside the gateway.

The buzzing was ferociously unbearable, recommencing before we'd even fully touched the solid ground. I let go of Lucais's hand to cover my ears as an angry flurry of locusts swirled around us, so disconcerted that they were unable to fly in a straight line. The frenzy was so intense I could barely see the world beyond them—could hardly catch a glimpse of the field or the sky, let alone the gateway, as if we'd landed in the eye of the storm.

Ducking my head, I squinted up at them, trying to discern their features. The locusts in Faerie were different from any type of insect I'd seen before—enormous, sizes ranging from a medium-sized dog all the way to a large horse, with bulbous black eyes like common flies, and an exoskeleton of plated armour, the colour of purple and blue bubblegum with striking green lines through their midsections. Sharp spikes reminiscent of needles were present around the exterior of their mouths, but I couldn't see the stinger that had dislodged inside of Lucais's waist when we were staying at the House. I couldn't see any limbs on them, either, though they had two pincers on top of their heads shaped like antennae—designed to kill instead of learn.

Lucais didn't hesitate for a moment before he sprang into action, wielding the sword above his head with expert precision, cutting down locust after locust as he took heavy, measured steps through the cluster in what I assumed was the direction of the gateway.

He was a vision of death and steel, each of his movements a piece of choreography rehearsed for the stage. Slicing his sword across the underside of their bellies brought them crashing to the ground. A bubbly, black fluid leaked out beneath my feet as their wings strained to continue beating fast enough to lift their brutalised bodies back into the sky. Following him, I skirted their corpses, my hands fastened to my ears as if they'd been glued there to suppress the noise. When a locust fell, the sound of its buzzing took on a higher pitch as the wings beat against the dirt, and it disturbed my empty stomach.

It wasn't until we'd stepped closer to the gateway that I managed to figure out where the deadly spike was kept. The familiar appendage was tucked beneath it, reminding me of a shrimp in a cocktail glass rather than a bee in a hive. It gave the locust a hidden advantage, allowing the victim to draw closer to it before being stung.

By the time the swarm gathered their wits again and assembled some form of order, Lucais had slain hundreds of them, clearing a layer of wings and pincers away from the tops of our heads. Through the blur of colour and the vibrational beating of their transparent wings, I glimpsed the gateway. I couldn't spy any of the Malum, which meant they'd either retreated or were hiding in the shadows of distant trees. There was no doubt they'd been the ones knocking on the outside of the world when neither of their attack dogs possessed the ability to taunt us like that—

"Duck!" Lucais yelled.

Robotically, I followed his instructions and dropped to my knees without a split second of hesitation. I moved in time for him to pivot, sending a bolt of light flying from his fingertips in the shape of a fatally sharpened dagger. With wide eyes, I watched it soar through the air and pierce through the bodies of at least six targets before evaporating.

Light magic? Lightning?

Whatever it was, he'd sent it to skewer a group of locusts who were a hair's breadth away from gripping me with their pincers and then doing the Oracle knew what with me once they had. As the disorientation cleared away, the rest of the swarm were becoming aware of the High Fae man slicing their comrades into bits of broken shell and wings, and they were assembling into attack formation from all angles around us.

Still kneeling on the ground, I blanched, wishing for a moment that I'd taken up Wrenlock's suggestion to better prepare myself for situations where fighting required more than a few words off the back of a sharp tongue.

Even so, Lucais was a perfect match for the swarm. So skilled, in fact, that I began to wonder how they'd ever managed to sting him in the first place as he balanced a sword in one hand and magic in the other. His fingertips shot out bolts of what I was certain had to be lightning. Honed into lethal edges and a perfect point, they hardly ever missed the soft underside of the locust or a perfect hit directly in one of their eyes. Meanwhile, Lucais continued to slice them into pieces with his sword, aiming for their wings when he couldn't get the angle right to gut them.

I cringed against the ground at his feet, feeling pathetically human and useless. The magic that had spilled dark, soft breaths against my fingers at the House was nowhere to be found. I didn't even think it was watching me from a distance anymore.

Part of me wished I'd accepted it the first time it had presented the offering of its horrors to me, but the rest of me knew I had made the right choice. I needed to build the strength of resistance before I acquiesced to its demands. The alternative would have made me a conduit like it had done in every other situation—and I needed to be the controller or nothing at all.

Even though being *nothing at all* felt like slamming my head into rock bottom repeatedly as I cowered at Lucais's feet like a worm.

When a path through the sky had been cleared away well enough for us to move again, Lucais sheathed his sword and gripped me with a hand. It was the one he'd used to wield magic, and his touch was so hot it hissed against my shirt. Muttering an apology, he wrapped his arm around my waist and hoisted me up. My arms and legs wrapped around him instinctively, and then we were back in front of the wall of glass, staring at our reflections as he cradled me against him like a tired child.

In the mirror image, the vague outline of the swarm took shape again, the reflection growing clearer as the locusts drew closer to our backs. Wriggling, my sense of self-preservation drove me to pull away, but Lucais tightened his one-armed grip on my body and held us in place. All I could do was trust him as I watched the last of the vengeful swarm descend upon us from the sky like a thunderstorm, the buzzing of their wings drowning out even the sound of my own racing heart.

The High King waited, waited, waited.

Panic rose in my chest with the quickening of my pulse until—

Lucais spun around so fast my stomach collided with my lungs. A hand shot out, his palm turned towards the onslaught, and an inferno of light and electricity appeared between us and them. White-hot magic splintered across it as far as the eye could see, a kaleidoscope of murderous colours that acted like an electric fence. Lucais's arm didn't buckle as the locusts flew straight into it, unable to react in time to pull back and escape a barbaric death.

They fell from the sky, and the High King retreated into the human realm before their bodies had stopped twitching on the ground or I even had time to blink.

He evanesced from the portal back to the industrial estate and gingerly let me down. I breathed out a long sigh of relief to find that the world was as it had been when we left, though it was growing darker by the second, a few stars and the ghost of a half-moon already visible in the twilight sky.

Gravel crunched under our feet as we pivoted in slow motion, searching for masked signs of the disturbance caused by the portal. Logically, I knew the Malum's creepy little attack bugs would have been programmed to immediately follow us back into Faerie, but I never would have been able to live with myself if they hadn't—if even one of them had lingered behind.

The High King's golden eyes met mine through the half-light. We exchanged a look of acknowledgement that the humans were safe and completely unaware. When that fear crumbled away, we moved towards each other in unison and linked hands, returning to the gateway with the next gust of wind.

Our silence was companionable, born of necessity as exhaustion took the place of adrenaline, and we let our hands fall apart when we returned to Faerie. The back and forth transfers from the magical realm to the non-magical realm had taken a toll on me. I lifted my gaze to the High King, curious to see if he felt the same dizziness. Sensing my attention, Lucais turned his head, lips parting around a question he never got the chance to ask.

With his eyes trained on me, Lucais didn't see that one of the locusts had managed to drag its injured body towards the gateway.

He didn't see the pincer still twitching atop its head.

He didn't step out of the way in time to avoid the razor-sharp edge of its claw shooting open and slamming closed one last time.

Eighteen

Kiss It Better

Lucais yelled a string of incoherent profanities on either side of a soul-distorting scream. The locust was still clinging to life, though barely. It spent the last of its energy in a final attempt to bring down the High King by slicing his lower limb open.

Hopping away on his uninjured leg, Lucais swore viciously and left the locust to bleed out on the ground. I lingered, staring down at it as the surrounding dirt grew damper with each passing second. The deathly vacant and cold eyes were pitch-black—and yet, I could feel it watching me as the outpouring of its lifeblood slowed to a gradual stop. The field was muddied with their blood, littered with their bodies, and I felt a mindless surge of rage overcome me.

I kicked the locust so hard that its entire body flipped, and then I stomped down on its head as hard as I could manage, crushing both pincers beneath my boots first, followed by the horrifying eyes, and then its skull. The sharp *crunch* as I finally broke through and pulverised it between my boot and the blood-soaked ground was grossly satisfying.

For a brief moment, I almost felt as if the whispering rush of my magic had come flooding back to witness my atrocities, but as soon as I glanced up, the feeling vanished.

"Aura!" Lucais yelled, agitation grating in his voice.

Twisting my head to follow the sound, I found him several hundred paces away from where I stood along the cusp of the battlefield, like he couldn't get away from them fast enough—even in death. I frowned. Despite the fact that it hurt him, Lucais hadn't lifted a finger to retaliate, content to let it succumb to its wounds instead.

"Aura," he called again, a little softer. "Will you please move away from there?"

Brows raised, I threw my hands up in a careless gesture. I couldn't fathom why it was such a big deal for him when they were all very much dead upon the grasses, but I could see the anguish crossing his face even at a distance, so I relented and left the graveyard behind as I walked over to him.

The High King grunted as he lowered himself to sit beneath a tree. Both legs were stretched out in front of him, the knee of the injured one slightly bent. I couldn't withhold my grimace as I peered over at the open wound. The skin had been cleanly sliced straight down the side of his calf, cutting through layers of flesh and muscle almost to the bone.

Blood, red as my own, was trickling out of the wound much slower than I'd have expected from a human body suffering the same injury. For a long moment, the two of us hesitated, dallying in the silence that had fallen over the clearing in the wake of the attack.

"It's not going to heal on its own," he ground out through his teeth at last. "It's not a venom sting, but the fucking locusts have iron-tipped claws."

"Like the caenim," I murmured, watching the feverish rhythm of his chest as it rose and fell. A faint sheen of moisture coated his skin, making it shimmer like body glitter under the strobe of nightclub lights.

"Yes," Lucais whispered, hissing as he tried to straighten his injured leg. His face contorted, beads of sweat forming on his brow. "Exactly like the caenim."

Glancing over my shoulder, I checked to make sure the field was still devoid of life forms. He'd executed the caenim, and I'd stomped the last living locust to death, but the Malum were yet to show their faces. I didn't feel like we were being watched, but I still wondered if we might have been because nothing else really made a lot of sense. They'd been within an arm's reach of us—of *me*—and yet, as soon as opportunity showed favour to them, they'd vanished.

"You can't walk, then," I surmised, tilting my head to the side as I settled into a crouch next to him.

"No, Auralie." Lucais threw me a derisive look. "I can't fucking walk." He glanced pointedly down at his leg, the gaping wound appearing even worse the second time I beheld it. My stomach churned. "We don't have a choice. You'll have to kiss it better," he said.

My stomach flipped again. "I have to do *what*?"

Lucais huffed, a sharp exhale through his nose. I noticed that the light in his eyes was paling ever so slightly, but then he closed them. "Fucking kiss me, Auralie. Do not make me beg."

"I'm not kissing an open wound—"

"On the mouth, you infernal vixen!" he shouted, eyes flying open again. His hand moved in a flash, grabbing my chin and tugging me towards him. I lost my balance, palms slamming into the ground to stop myself from falling over his lap, and gasped as tiny rocks and stones dug into my skin. My lips were in striking distance of his, but Lucais just held me there with a firm grip, his ragged breathing flooding my face with the scent of caged desire and concealed pain.

"Kiss me, please," he breathed, the gold in his eyes swirling like a sunset storm. He was on the verge of begging. "Press your mouth to mine and pretend that you can love me enough to leave it there until I feel better."

In the back of my mind, I was aware that he'd pulled similar tricks on me before. He'd lingered in my bed for days longer than necessary after the last locust attack, milking my sympathy and attention until Morgoya had stormed into the room and blown his cover. Even then, he'd feigned weakness when he'd finally gotten out of bed, waiting until I was seconds away from tearing my wrist open with my own teeth before he burst into laughter and gave up the façade.

Still, Lucais seemed to have some weird thing with locusts, and he'd required my blood to cure him of their poison in the past. Maybe the iron on their claws was more potent, too.

I studied him, the sharp angles of his face softening with the effects of pain, the colour of his eyes simmering down into bland shades of sand and seashells, and the hapless expression that overtook the shape of his mouth when he reluctantly convinced himself that my answer would be no. As he was about to move into position to force himself back onto his feet, I reacted, my hand shooting out to hold him in place.

"Fine," I whispered. "Okay."

Something indecipherable flickered across Lucais's eyes, but he waited patiently for me to close the distance between our lips.

"Because you went back for them," I told him firmly.

I was stubborn, irate, and most of my threats were empty, but I was under no misapprehension that I could *force* the High King to do anything he didn't want to do. Lucais had known the locusts followed us back into Faerie, yet he'd returned to put my mind at ease that my family was not at risk.

An unsteady breath crossed the threshold of my mouth, and then it was pressed against his.

Lucais's lips parted immediately, drawing me in slowly, his tongue skating across my upper lip before dipping into my mouth. Lucais tasted like sunlight and cotton candy, but I was the one melting as he carefully explored me with his tongue, nipping my lower lip when he wanted to drag me closer, tilting his head to achieve a deeper angle. His hands were suddenly in my hair, and I was sliding onto his lap.

He crushed my mouth to his, the elimination of space between us deliberate and measured. Lucais held me with skill and reverence, taking the time to touch each part of my tongue with his, to leave no part of my mouth ignored. A moan formed deep in my throat and escaped unbidden, and Lucais swallowed it greedily, tightening his arms around me until I forgot which parts of my body belonged to me and which parts belonged to him.

I felt my nipples hardening into aching peaks beneath the fabric of my shirt, defying the pressure of our bodies pressed so infinitely close together. Lucais's tongue caressed mine with lazy indulgence, the tips of our noses touching briefly as we swapped angles back and forth—like it was routine, like we'd kissed each other a thousand times and knew exactly how to do it thoroughly and powerfully.

Liquid heat pooled in my lower belly, a sensation like molten lava dripping down my spine with each stroke of his tongue and pull of his lips. When one of his hands slid from the back of my head to rest along my jaw, holding me in place as he bent his head to the side and swiped his tongue along the roof of my mouth, accompanied by a faint rumble deep in his chest, I—

We have to stop. His voice was in my head, his words clear yet distant—and in total opposition to his actions as he continued to kiss me like it was his favourite pastime.

So stop, I replied through the bond, twisting my fingers in his hair as he bent forward to reclaim full control of my mouth, tugging me back to him with my lower lip between his teeth.

I will. He licked the taste of our kiss from the corner of my mouth before sliding his tongue against mine, pushing it deeper, as if he could lure my soul out of my body and imprison it between his jaws. *In a minute.*

Uh-huh.

Shamelessly, I entertained both the kiss and the mental conversation as if they were part of a dream—something that happened that could never be proven because there were no witnesses, and I could probably gaslight myself into thinking that I'd made it all up.

Lucais's taste was exotic, the feel of his mouth exciting in the kind of way that seemed like it was always a long time coming. I lost myself inside him, a slave to the sensation as he devoured me without leaving a crumb leftover for the crows.

With every passing second, with every shift of his body beneath me, my skin was lighting up like a cave of glow worms, each nerve becoming torturously attuned to the way Lucais felt when his skin brushed mine or his muscles flexed. His hands on the side of my face and in my hair felt so permanent—like we were part of a statue breaking free from a spell, coming to life against each other, determined to finish what we'd started when we'd first been hexed.

Visions hit me with every burst of his scent, his taste, the sound of his indulgent moans. Images of us tangled together on the ground, my legs entwined with his, clothes discarded, skin against skin, his body discovering a home deep inside of mine—

He broke the kiss.

I didn't think he was going to, but he did. I scrambled off his lap, feigning desperation to check on the status of his wound to cover the way my skin had caught fire from my hairline to my toes. I sucked in air as I stared at his legs, too breathless and violently aroused to remark on the fact that both of them appeared completely whole and untouched.

Lucais rested his head against the tree, and I stole a glance at him, relieved to find that he was equally out of breath and flushed from head to toe. The bulge beneath his belt suggested that he, too, was violently aroused. But he'd broken the kiss first, so I scooted back and stared at the dirt on my hands, waiting until the distance between us allowed me to come back to my senses. My traitorous heart was a war drum tumbling down a mountainside, beating solely for his attention.

"I healed myself," he said after a moment, his voice huskier than normal. "In case you're wondering." When I didn't respond, he added, "It was much easier to do it with the pleasure of your body to distract me from the pain in mine."

I inclined my head to him, acknowledging the vague thank you. "Are you able to evanesce?"

Nodding, he pushed himself back to his feet and held his hand out to help me up. I pretended I didn't see it and stood up independently.

"Was it that bad?" he taunted, a chuckle slipping past the lips that had been so obsessed with mine only moments earlier. He paused. "Or that good?"

My cheeks were ablaze with a telltale blush, but I swallowed my pride, only to feel incredibly foolish a second later when I realised I had to give him my hand so we could travel back into the city.

"That was intense," I allowed. "But it can never happen again."

He sighed, closing his hand around mine. "Agreed."

It didn't matter what he said.

He was a fucking faerie. He could be agreeing with me, someone he conversed with over a century ago, or a thought he had inside of his own head. The only thing that mattered was what I said and did—which was to vow that it would never happen again because I would be *damned* if I let Lucais Starfire placate me with a stuffed pony, too.

Nineteen

Entomophobia

We collided with Morgoya in the palace hallway as we dragged our weary bodies upstairs. We'd fallen back into the companionable quiet, exhaustion and unreleased erotic tension wreaking havoc on our nervous systems, and neither of us heard her rounding the corner.

"High Mother!" she gasped, a hand flying up to cover her mouth. "You both look awful. Did the Map attack you, or did you attack each other?"

The High Lady was dressed in attire fit for a mystical ball, as per usual. Her gown spilled onto the floor around her feet in elegant waves, hanging off both shoulders to reveal smooth skin and sharp bones, and it was a sparkling silver so bright that it might have been made from crushed diamonds. Her hair was delicately bundled on the top of her head with pearl-encrusted clasps, a few curled strands bouncing around the sides of her face and her neck. She wore black lipstick to complement the silver dusted around both eyes and over her prominent cheekbones.

"We're fine," Lucais groused. "Minor incident with a locust."

The High Lady swore. "Again?"

"I don't want to hear it," he mumbled, waving her away. "I need to take a cold shower."

My cheeks reddened, flaring with heat as if someone had thrown a bucket of scalding water on my face, and there was simply no chance that Morgoya wouldn't notice. Her emerald-green eyes zeroed in on my face as Lucais sauntered off, disappearing around the corner without a backwards glance and leaving me alone to deal with her intruding stare. To divert her attention, I explained what had happened in greater detail from the time we'd left the faerie bookstore, carefully leaving out all of the revelations we'd had when we were with the Map because I imagined that Lucais would want to talk about that himself.

Her catlike eyes were positively alight with an emotion I couldn't place. "They sent both caenim *and* locusts? And he really went back?"

My bones were aching, the muscles in my back screaming for the upstairs water pressure to massage them beneath a hot shower. "Yeah, but he sure as hell didn't want to," I muttered, rubbing my eyes. "I don't know what his deal is with those things. He acts like he *enjoys* fighting the caenim, but—"

"Lucais has orthopterophobia."

I stared at her, blinking in a stupor. "I am exhausted, and I have absolutely no idea what that means."

"It's a form of entomophobia," Morgoya answered kindly. The High Lady put a hand on my shoulder and squeezed gently before turning her head, a wistful gaze trailing after the High King, who had long since disappeared from the hallway. She let out a long breath, shaking her head as if she couldn't quite believe what she was hearing. "Lucais is deathly afraid of locusts and grasshoppers. He has been ever since he was a faeling."

Blankly, I followed the direction of her gaze, staring down the empty hallway. I blinked a few times. I opened my mouth to say something, but closed it when I realised I didn't know what words I wanted to employ.

"Aura?" the High Lady whispered. "You look on the verge of collapse. Are you okay?"

I brushed off her concern. "I wish you hadn't told me that," I grumbled as the room started to lean precariously to one side. The adrenaline crash was hitting hard. "I don't want any more fucking ponies."

I was so tired I felt like I was about to fall in a heap on the stone floor. Before the delirium overtook me completely, I forced my aching feet to continue taking one step after another until I'd trekked back to my bedroom, determined to find somewhere softer to land than the corridor.

As I walked away, I called back to her over my shoulder, "I'll see you at the Court thingy later."

Morgoya didn't reply, and I didn't make it to the hot shower. As soon as I found my bedroom in the palace, I dove onto the bed and fell asleep to the movie my mind played of the kiss beneath the tree and all of the things that very nearly could have followed.

It continued on a loop of unattainable pleasure until Morgoya knocked on my door a few hours later to let me know the *Court thingy* was beginning to assemble downstairs—in case I wanted to wash off all the dirt and unresolved sexual tension first.

Twenty

You'd Look Good with Duct Tape Over Your Mouth

Everybody was staring at us. I felt exposed and fragile, like I was standing in a display cabinet with all of my ugly truths sketched into the wall behind me for the world to bear witness.

Killed a faerie. Abandoned her family. Lied about being slapped by her teacher in the second grade.

A familiar heat grazed the back of my neck before trailing down my spine in a playful caress, and I glanced towards the High King. I was far too deep in my own inner monologue to reprimand him for prodding me with his magic in public, but the words were washed away—one by one scrubbed clean off the walls of my mind like Lucais's attention was a splash of water on fresh ink. I studied his side profile, watching his awareness of my gaze tilt one side of his mouth upwards.

Thank you.

He ignored me, but his lips twitched.

The collapsing palace had a great hall carved into the northern wing. It was a hollow, cavernous space—a ceiling so high I couldn't discern the colour of it with absolute certainty, large white pillars lining the outskirts of the room, and arch windows of stained glass high up on the otherwise bare stone. No wall sconces. No rugs lining the hard, cold floor. No chairs, save for the enormous throne placed in the centre of the dais at the far west end of the room.

Lucais lounged in it, the seat crafted from a substance that mimicked the aesthetic of glass. As far as I was concerned, he had a poor track record with furniture—particularly chairs—and yet the throne was so delicately transparent. After we entered with Morgoya and Wrenlock, he assumed his position at the forefront of the room, and the entire frame lit up with a blazing gold as his light filled the spaces around him.

He was the King of Light. It made perfect sense that he would perch upon a Throne of Light.

Absently, I wondered if it was the same for all of Faerie's rulers. I pictured thrones of darkness, fire, water, earth, and wind—mostly to distract myself from the hundreds of eyes that hadn't left my face even to blink since I'd walked in through the enormous double doors. But for a fleeting moment, I was curious about what sort of throne I might be given if I was to accept the mating bond with Lucais and become his High Queen...

The concept was repulsive from any angle, so it very quickly wilted away and died.

I didn't want a throne. I didn't want a mate. I didn't want a crown.

Lucais wasn't even wearing his crown. Like me, he'd cleaned up after the locust attack and quite possibly taken a power nap, but he'd made a promise to me that the first time I saw him in his crown, he would be wearing absolutely nothing else. He couldn't very well keep to that promise in a situation where so many other faeries had flocked to stare at me while they listened to him speak.

As we stood and waited for the High King to address the room, a niggling sense of pride wormed its way into my chest because I was able to recognise so many different races of faeries.

I spied Eldrick standing near the front of the crowd with a handful of other Hobgoblins. He inclined his head to me deferentially, but I watched his tongue slide out of his mouth to lick his lips when he did, and I cringed inwardly.

Behind him, there was a small group of Vampyrs with skin painted in various tones of death and ebony hair that looked like torn pieces of shadow pulled from the night sky. When I met their reproachful gazes, they bared their extra-long fangs at me and hissed. Lucais silenced them with a single look, but hurt still pooled in my belly when I remembered their sister had been accidentally impaled by one of Enyd's soldiers in the House. Their grief had been a tangible substance that exploded across the room, coating everyone's skin in its ashes.

Many of the High Fae were present, and their gazes were somehow the harshest to bear. Some resembled the familiar humanoid form with accentuated features and elongated ears, but others seemed to have adopted scales, tails, horns, and additional eyes, fingers, or even limbs. Their skin tones embodied every colour of the rainbow in varying pigments.

Elera was standing by the door with two other unicorns, and while I decided not to question it, I did spend a moment wondering what her group's political investment was in Faerie—if they had one.

A group of translucent figures lingered by the door on the opposite side, coming in and out of focus. Instinctively, I thought of them as ghosts, but then I remembered that Lucais had referred to them as Spectres when I'd accidentally killed the maroon-skinned faerie.

I picked out a group of men I might have mistaken as human beings were it not for the considerable amount of extra hair on their bodies and claw marks across their faces—the Wolf-Folk, surely—and opposite them were large creatures bearing a striking resemblance to the caenim, taking up as much space with the two of them as an entire family of Centaurs did.

Lucais immediately reassured me that they were Bogeymen when he sensed my alarm through the bond—and explained that when they come to Court, they were always on their best behaviour, but I'd better steer clear of them in dark alleys lest they feel the need to take over my mind and body for sport. They had eyes and ears where one would expect to find such body parts, but their jaws were much longer and wider, and they had mouths like a baleen whale. Almost as soon as I looked at them, I averted my gaze.

I recognised a Basilisk—and regretted it—as well as the group of Ogres, a pair of Trolls, a lone Cyclops, the group of Elves, a beautiful creature who might have been a Wood Nymph, and a shorter gentleman who bore a striking resemblance to a Leprechaun. I even observed Goblins long enough to mark the differences between them and Eldrick's kinfolk.

Lastly, there were airborne creatures who flew too fast for me to really see them, but I was fairly sure they were the Pixies and the Sprites.

When the doors finally closed at the end of the long walkway between the clusters of faeries, I expected Lucais to begin speaking. Instead, he simply stared ahead at the bare floor between his constituents. My eyes darted back and forth almost a dozen times before I saw them—and recognised them.

The Little Folk.

They were, quite frankly, the smallest creatures I had ever seen before in my life. As a child, I supposed, it was only natural that they had appeared slightly bigger. Otherwise, they looked exactly as I recalled—bobbing heads with large, dark eyes, tiny mouths, soft tufts of wispy white hair, some with long, matching beards. All of them glowed with a bright luminescence that almost surely served as a protective measure. They carried magical satchels with deep pockets, which was where they used to stow the treasures they brought to me in the backyard of our first house.

As they approached to greet their High King, I wondered if they knew who I was—and found it very surprising, yet equally heart-warming, when they skirted the edge of the dais beneath Lucais's throne and came to bow before me instead.

A few sharp gasps echoed between the stonework in the hall. On the other side of the dais, Wrenlock's mouth fell open. But Lucais only smirked with a deep, relaxed, almost feline satisfaction.

I bent down to meet the Little Folk, extending my forefinger for them to climb up onto my hand like they had done when I was a child. Two of them did, the pearly luminosity around them making my eyes water up so close. My palm tingled as they walked across it and began to lay down scraps of bark from their pockets, manipulating their position with magic.

Naturally, I couldn't hear them when they spoke because their lungs were so small and my ears were so large, but treebark messaging was how they had always communicated with me when they wanted to say something they couldn't tell me in any other way.

I waited patiently for them to assemble their pieces the right way up. Once they had, they stepped backwards, tickling me again as they bent their heads to their feet in a bow. Holding my breath, I lifted my hand close enough to read what was scorched into the pieces of bark, mindful not to blow the tiny creatures off my hand with any release of my breath.

Welcome Home, Princess.

It felt like someone had knifed me in the stomach. I nodded my head once, gently returning them to the ground before any surge of emotion had me breathing too forcefully or accidentally drowning them in a falling tear.

I had been a Princess when I was a child. I'd called myself one, so it never struck me as odd that the Little Folk referred to me in the same way. I loved it. I wanted everyone to think I was a Princess. But the idea that they'd known my intended fate the whole time—that I was truly in line for a throne in Faerie through some weird, prophetic twist of fate...

"Auralie," Lucais murmured. "Are you ready to begin?"

My eyes bulged in their sockets, though it wasn't exactly like he could draw much more attention to me than I was already receiving. However, he could have easily spoken the words into my mind, so I had to wonder why he was making a point of checking with *me* on when to start *his* meeting in front of all of those faeries. Unless he was merely trying to embarrass me, to test out how red my cheeks could become before literal sparks started to fly off my flesh.

"Um." I swallowed, blood thrumming in my ears. "Yes?"

Lucais inclined his head to me before turning his gaze onto the assembly, the faces of whom all looked rightfully perplexed by the display. "Greetings," he said, and his voice boomed through the room with a ferocity I had never heard before. It wasn't angry; it was just *powerful*. "I appreciate that all of you have made the effort to present yourselves here today. Please take note that we have representatives from five out of six Courts. Blythe's Court of Darkness is an apology. Again."

I raised a brow at that but held my tongue—both physically and mentally. On the walk down after I'd quickly showered and changed my clothes, Morgoya had briefed me on the developments with the Court of Earth. It appeared that Gregor had gone dark, but his people behaved as if they were unaware, and everything was stuck on a business-as-usual cycle until the High King's spies could obtain sufficient evidence to determine which approach would be wisest.

"I come bearing good news and bad news," the High King went on. "Which would you like to hear first?"

Did he seriously ask them to pick and choose the order in which he delivers updates like pieces of gossip? Who is running this show?

"Bad," someone called out.

"Good," someone else said only a millisecond later.

"Bad was faster," Lucais declared. "So here it is. The caenim are out of control. There have been numerous sightings of them across the realm, which I'm sure you've all heard about. They savaged Sthiara. Multiple casualties and missing faeries. I don't know what their endgame is, but I do know they are probably starving from so many years spent scavenging the Ruins, and they are relentless."

My confusion simmered like a cauldron filled with poisons and potions. He knew their endgame was to retrieve me—to kill me and bring my body to the Malum. At least, that was part of it. He wasn't lying, but he was twisting things again.

What is he doing?

"I did not count how many attacks the Court of Light sustained over the last few months, but it's more than enough to piss me off. I do not expect the number to reduce in the near future," Lucais disclosed. "I advise everyone to exercise caution when travelling in the more regional areas within any of the five accessible Courts. Do not let your guard down even inside the more heavily populated areas. I have secure wards up, and Caeludor is always safe. You are welcome to seek shelter here until the threat is neutralised. Please, tell your friends and family the offer extends to everyone. Unless you're a Banshee or a caenim yourself, Caeludor will welcome you."

"What's the good news, then?" someone asked.

The High King grinned, winking at the crowd as he straightened in his seat. "The good news is that we're having a party. These miserly beasts defy logic, but I have a plan to eradicate the threat that is not reliant on dialectics. So, we may as well celebrate now because we all know my plans are marvellous and usually always work."

He nodded with conviction, like he believed what he was telling them—as if he, Lucais Starfire, the High King of Faerie and King of Light, was *manifesting* the outcome he desired. And maybe he did. Maybe he *was* right. Maybe he needed to appeal to a higher sense of power, above even his own, simply to keep himself in some sort of check.

There were a few questioning murmurs bouncing around the room. Some feet shuffled and hooves clopped. An Ogre coughed, the sound low and throaty. But overall, the crowd remained calm and impassive. I wondered if it had been his plan all along to let them believe a lesser version of the truth so they wouldn't freak out.

Lucais had told me the people in Caeludor would panic if they learned about what happened in the Court of Light, and he wasn't there to calm their fears. I assumed he meant by his words and actions, but rather, it seemed like his very presence was all they required to remain unbothered. I could have sworn he was going to tell them about the

Malum, though. Or was that simply what he wanted me to believe? Faerie was no stranger to the caenim, but the residents did not know to whom they belonged. As far as I could tell, all of Faerie believed the caenim were a lonesome, outcast species—like the Banshees, but the Banshees were a people. Lucais treated the caenim as if they were the faerie equivalent of dogs.

The new development with his plan to *capture* caenim—the result of absolute insanity cogs turning in his deranged mind—was another matter entirely. It was hinged on secrecy to protect his dark truths...

Oh. And I suppose this is, too.

My face fell, the thought dropping from my mind like a star. It landed in the pit of my stomach, a crater burned into the crust of the earth from an alien spaceship of unfortunate realisations.

Lucais was never going to tell them the truth.

He *couldn't.*

They would hate him—

"The carousal begins tonight!" the High King proclaimed, surging to his feet with arms thrown out to the sides proudly. The illumination of his throne went dark as soon as he was no longer upon it, but flares of light and sunbeams shot from his fingertips, igniting the room like a dawn sky.

Everyone in the throne room burst into cheers and applause—the sound musical, a chorus of neighing and growling and chirruping against a symphony of human-like voices. At that exact moment, I knew they loved him.

At least, they had loved him once. Before the Gift War. Before the death of land-dragons. Before he made choices that changed everything—decisions powerful enough to end old worlds and create new ones. And as all of it transpired before my widened eyes, it became glaringly apparent that Lucais wanted to get back to that love more than he wanted anything else in the world.

He wanted to be the man who told a group of faeries they were all likely to die soon and have them cheer and chant his name in reply.

Lu-cais! Lu-cais! Lu-cais!

I heard the ghost of that ancient crowd resounding in his mind as he watched on, hopeful for an encore—a memory I was viewing in his head, whether he intended to share it with me through the bond or not.

"One more thing before you go," he called out, holding a finger up in the air. The crowd instantly settled and hushed. "The Court of Light malfunctioned for a split second there. I'm sure you've all heard about it and would like some explanation. Well"—he lazily extended an arm, directing the point of that finger at me—"you see that redhead over there?"

Collectively, the eyes in the room swung from Lucais's face back to mine. My cheeks burned the colour of beetroot.

"It was her. And she is *mine*," he declared, his voice an ancient growl. "I've brought you back a High Queen, if she so desires. If she does not, that's none of your business. She is still *off-limits* to all of you, and you will treat her with the utmost respect at all times or face the penalty of death." Lucais straightened his coat. "Yes, you've seen her before. In the Oracle. Take a good look at her in the flesh now," he went on, "because she's even prettier when she dresses properly and actually brushes her hair. But I'm afraid she may not like the lot of you ogling her for the rest of the night. And come to think of it...quite frankly, neither do I. So, get out, go away, off you trot—the lot of you." He waved them all away and then grinned like a devil. "I'll see you at the festivities."

My hands were shaking. I was glued to my spot on the ground. *Deep breaths.* Even his quip about my hair and clothes didn't make a mark because I was numb and trembling from head to toe. I couldn't decide if I was more angry, scared, thunderstruck—or something else entirely. I was not *his*. I never would be *his*. I didn't like *him*. We had kissed twice, and he thought he could lay claim on me like a parking spot? Not to mention the fact that I resented the threat he lay upon his own people—as if I needed his protection. As if I *wanted* it.

The pendulum swung again, but the faeries were not fazed.

They offered gestures of goodwill to us before they left. Some looked towards me, others looked at Lucais, but every last one bowed, waved with a flash of their power, inclined their heads, or clapped and whooped one more time before they left the hollow throne room. When only a few stragglers remained—faeries who, I suspected, were members of the palace staff—I spoke to the High King in my mind and tried to unstick the soles of my shoes from where they'd started to grow invisible roots into the stonework.

Why did you lie to them?

I didn't lie. You know I can't lie. He sat back on his throne, the light blazing around him once more. A flicker of exhaustion from our earlier activities scattered across his face once nobody else was looking at him.

You didn't tell them the truth.

The whole truth, he countered. *That's different.*

I thought you were going to tell them about the Malum. And the caenim reports—were you exaggerating the severity or were you keeping things from me in the House?

A beat of hesitation. *I was nearly going to tell them about the Malum, but we've had a change of plans, haven't we, little beast? And the caenim reports were not specific. I didn't count them. I couldn't because I was too busy worrying about you. So, technically, not a lie. If they want to panic, they are free to panic. If they want to get blackout drunk tonight and forget everything I ever said, they can do that, too.*

I snorted. *What sort of a High King are you?*

One without a High Queen.

Ew.

You'd look good in a crown.

You'd look good with duct tape over your mouth.

Ooh, kinky. He picked a stray hair—one of mine, I realised with great horror—from his coat sleeve, and held it up to examine the colour against his light. A smirk slowly spread across his mouth.

Go away.

It's my palace—

Wrenlock appeared at my side, summoned by the look on my face. He stood between us, his tall frame blocking my vision of the High King. "Hey," he said.

"Hey," I said back. My feet were free, so I kicked at the floor with the toe of my boot, trying to suppress the twist in my heart. "How was your day?"

He shrugged. "Busy enough. I was thinking about you, though. Are you coming to the celebrations tonight?"

I peered around him at Lucais, who pulled a face and shrugged as if to say he didn't know what I planned to do, and he didn't care to find out. Wrenlock ducked his head, reclaiming my eyes.

"I'm not sure." I sighed. "Are you trying to ask me something?"

His mouth pulled up into a lopsided grin. "Sort of, yes. I thought maybe—" He broke off, holding up a hand. "I have no expectations, but maybe you and I could go to the carousal in Caeludor together and...hang out."

I couldn't help myself. I burst out laughing at the suggestion, bottling it only when hurt flashed across his face. "I'm sorry," I gasped. "It's only that you said... You want to hang out with me?"

His eyebrows knitted together. "What's wrong with that?"

"It's..." I fumbled for the right word. "Such a human notion," I decided at last, speaking on a light exhale of breath. The conversation reeked of nostalgia, as if he wasn't a High Fae man a few hundred years older than me and I wasn't being held half-a-prisoner in Faerie by an irritating High King. My mouth curved up at the corners. "You know... Hanging out."

"You realise humans descended from the High Fae?"

I rolled my eyes. "Yes, Wrenlock. I know. Faeries came before the chickens *and* the eggs."

A smile touched his eyes, even as he chewed on his lower lip. "Do you not want to? Hang out, that is."

Something inside of my chest fluttered, the sensation triggered by my silent laughter. "Yes, that's fine. We can hang out."

"Good." Wrenlock beamed at me, all warmth and openness and trust. "I'll come by your room at dusk."

"Okay—"

Lucais strode up to us then, pausing on his way towards a side door out of the room like we were an afterthought. He waved that annoying finger between us, and I wished I *had* broken a piece of it off in that cottage illusion or bitten it in the human world.

The memory of the way he pressed that hand up against the side of my face to hold me in place while he explored my mouth with his own streaked through my mind. But the way that he used it to poke and prod at me the rest of the time dulled any of the more pleasant associations.

"Whatever the two of you are going to do," he said, his voice a lazy lilt, "you are not to leave this palace tonight."

"Fine," Wrenlock agreed, though his dark chestnut eyes flashed, and his shoulders tensed.

Lucais lifted a brow and pouted at him, as if he'd been expecting a fight. "Fine."

They turned towards me like they assumed I'd break the tension or referee the back-and-forth idiocy of a situation the two of them had conspired to create all by themselves. Both of them held secrets and promises in their eyes, glimmering with devious intent, settling between us like an invitation.

Shaking my head at them, I simply said, "Fuck off."

Twenty-One

I'm Not Snooping

The plans and preparations for the carousal were well and truly underway by the time I slipped out of a palace side door and braved the encroaching fog.

I knew it was impossible—that it *should* be impossible—for the fog to sense my presence and react to it, but I felt distinctly as though the cloudy mist rushed for me as soon as I stepped onto the damp ground and closed the wooden servant's door behind me. In a matter of seconds, I went from being unable to see three feet in front of myself to being unable to see my own hands at my sides, so I turned to the wall and rested my palms against it.

The fog clung to my clothing like smoke as I worked my way around the edge of the palace, using my hands on the wall to guide me. Dampness clotted in my lungs, each breath coming harder than the last until the texture of the wall finally morphed from smooth to rough. I had a few hours until dusk, though it made very little difference amongst all the white clouds, and I was determined to use the time wisely.

I had a hunch that my eyes did not betray me when I spied the crumbling exterior of the palace, and I only needed to prove that it was happening once.

In the illusionary cottage, Lucais had revealed that he was in a power struggle with some kind of malevolent force inside of the wards around the Court of Darkness—something wrong, something *other*. He was the High King, deemed the most powerful being in all of Faerie, and he certainly possessed enough strength to hold his own in a magic fight. He'd executed an army of caenim without having to take a single step.

So why is the ward a struggle, and why is the city submerged in fog?

The weather in Faerie was attuned to his moods, and yet for some inexplicable reason, Caeludor was the exception. The Court of Light remained as clear and sparkling as it had ever been—even when he was fighting and injured—but the moment we arrived back in the City of Light, we were drenched in the obscure mist once again.

Lucais categorically refused to explain why his city was enveloped in a perpetual blanket of cloud, but if I could prove that a crumbling palace was hiding underneath it, perhaps he would start taking my questions seriously.

Or perhaps I would start asking other people.

Logic told me he was overselling his own abilities or he was leaving bits and pieces out of his story because something didn't add up. Lucais had a history of lying by omission and painting pretty, counterfeit pictures. For that reason alone, I couldn't keep myself from wondering how much of his supposedly unparalleled strength and power had already been expended, and if he was ever able to rest long enough to recoup that energy.

Is magic debt a thing?

Can a High King not have limits?

He does. He must.

I would find them—and soon, because I was running out of time.

A few steps further, and my fingers curled around a chunk of damaged stone. My chest pulled tight, and I hesitated for a single heartbeat, frozen in place against the wall.

When I recovered my hand, dust coated my skin. Tentatively, I poked it with a finger, then gently swept my palm over it. The surface felt abrasive, and when I slid my hand further along, I heard the brittle crunch as the part of the wall I was holding broke off and tumbled to the ground behind me with a heavy, dull thud.

Yelping, I jumped backwards, momentarily confused by the sounds and afraid that something was going to land on my head. It was a reflex born of self-preservation and buried in recklessness. By the time I realised what had happened, it was too late. The fog instantaneously filled the space between the palace and my outstretched hands, and I was completely disconcerted.

Did I twist when I moved away from the wall? Which direction should I be facing now?

I took a cautious step forward, bending at the waist to give more reach to my hands, but there was only air slipping through my fingers. Turning slightly, I repeated the action until I was confident that I'd completed a full circle. Each time, I stepped into empty space, and my hands found a cool grasp on a big handful of absolutely *nothing*.

The beat of my heart was a stutter in my chest, the blood flow bordering on painful as I succumbed to an instinctive wave of panic. All of my senses went onto high alert.

With fog so prevalent, I couldn't study the landscape around the palace. For all I knew, it could be resting on a cliffside, the cusp of a volcano, or surrounded by a moat filled with crocodiles and sharks. My steps were loaded with danger, the pressure of my body weight on the ground like a finger on the trigger of a handgun aimed at my head.

Breathe, I instructed myself.

With great trepidation and measured breaths, I lowered myself to my hands and knees. The ground was so soft my knees sank into it, moisture seeping through my clothes from the grass blades and biting into my skin with an ice-cold touch. Dirt stuffed itself beneath my fingernails as I gripped the ground for stability and began to crawl, feeling ahead with my hands for any hazards.

I imagined that, if the fog miraculously cleared, I would have looked quite the fool.

The fog didn't clear, though.

By the time the ground fell away from my extended hand, I had probably been crawling around for at least ten minutes, and my fingertips were numbed by the icy mud. It threw my judgement well off base. The fear of falling, as my outstretched hands missed the ground, jolted me forwards until suddenly the grass and mud were ripped out from under me like a magic carpet that tipped me down a treacherous rabbit hole.

My stomach flipped and squealed and roiled as I fell, and then—

"*Oof!*"

I landed with a hard thud on an unwelcoming floor, and the breath whooshed out of my lungs with a short, hoarse, unintelligible cry of surprise. Even more surprising than my harsh, abrupt landing was the lack of fog when I opened my eyes. Raising my head to check my surroundings, my eyebrows shot skywards at finding the air clear—although it was dark and flecked with transparent clouds of dust, stirred by my inelegant arrival.

I was inside the palace again, and everything was broken.

Where I sat, the room had been destroyed, its remnants spanning around me like the interior of a crater in the earth. It was as if the hand of the divine had reached down from the sky and scooped everything out—floors, ceilings, walls, and doorways from the ground to the rooftop. Furniture and paintings and broken mirrors lay discarded in uneven pieces around me, coated in dust and cobwebs.

About a floor above me, there was a gaping hole in the wall. It was positioned where a new landing should have been on the remnants of a decomposing staircase. The fog reappeared, plugging the gap as if a doorway had taken physical form out of the clouds lingering outside.

I fell from there.

Some of the mist wafted within the boundary of the damage, a faint whisper of vapour shaped like exceptionally long, wandering fingers gripping onto the roughened stonework collapsing in that part of the palace. As a deep feeling of dread settled in my belly, my eyes skated across the edges of the decrepit wing, searching for another way out. The entire section was corroded, all entry and exit points sealed off as far as my widened eyes could see.

Columns and pillars had collapsed on each other, criss-crossing over the chasm between walls as the cavernous space cascaded up in ruin towards the heavens. The bone-white stonework was holding each empty floor at bay—a skeleton serving to prevent further disintegration against gravity. I couldn't even tell if there was a ceiling left at the very top or simply another makeshift reparation born of fog.

Nothing was secured.

At any moment, part of the structure could come tumbling down, even where I sat stranded in the middle of the floor with chunks and slabs of stone littered around me. If I didn't know any better, I'd have thought perhaps I was in a construction zone, but Lucais wasn't renovating. The entire area was so fragile that it had been cordoned off and condemned.

And guarded.

"The fog is an enchantment," I realised out loud. I was right, but it had never felt so wrong. "*That's* why the palace doesn't have one. It's in the fog!"

"You're not supposed to be down here."

Clamping my hand over my mouth to suppress a scream, I spun around, flipping my position so I was sitting on my knees. "Lucais," I gasped.

He emerged from the shadows and dust like a creature of nightmares. Lucais's blond hair shone nearly white in the grey light, his skin radiating an ethereal glow that put holy artefacts to shame, and the look on his face was one of pure, uninspired devastation. Hands in his pockets, he didn't smile at me—not even with his eyes. I bit back the desire to cringe.

"Are you happy now?"

Carefully, I climbed to my feet, transferring the thick layer of dirt and powder from my hands to the fabric of my pants. "I don't understand what you mean."

He gestured to the damaged space around us as he moved closer, his presence alone enough to cause an atmospheric shift. Debris clattered to the ground somewhere in the hollowed-out chamber, and a fierce shudder gripped the skin between my shoulder blades. I tried to steel myself against it, but it was no use; it rippled through me while Lucais stalked over. I caught the slight narrowing of his gaze as he watched.

"You wouldn't leave well enough alone," he said, and his voice was full of tightly bound restraint. "You wouldn't take my word for it." His steps echoed with dangerous purpose as he approached me. "Now that you have found physical proof that I am not infallible, are you happy? Does this make you feel better about your decision?"

My eyebrows dove to meet each other above the bridge of my nose. "Why would I be happy?" I asked, a little breathless. I didn't truly understand what was going on. "And *what* decision?"

Lucais stopped in front of me and slid his hands from his pockets. Reaching out, he brushed his thumb across my cheekbone from my earlobe to my nose, studying my skin as if it were marred with soot. It probably was, but that didn't explain the chemical reaction his touch left upon my tingling skin in its wake.

"The decision not to be with me," Lucais answered at last, placing his other hand on the small of my back. He gave me a gentle push, guiding me over fallen debris towards the outskirts of the room.

"That's not a decision," I scoffed, twisting my neck to peer up at him. "If there's only one option, do you still call that a choice?"

The question was rhetorical, so the only response he gave me was a small sigh and another gentle nudge to skirt the tangle of curtain strings lying across the floor. I followed his instructions and felt a sliver of relief settle on my shoulders once we were no longer in the middle of the impending crash site.

"We went over this already," I complained, shrugging off his lingering touch like a coat that was suddenly making me feel too hot. I was irritated that he was the one who pulled back—*twice*—yet he acted as though the ball was in my court. Pinning him to the spot with my eyes, I searched his face for answers, daring him to prove me wrong with more than a few pretty throwaway words. "You don't want to be with me any more than I want to be with you."

"No," the High King agreed quietly. He folded his arms over his chest, golden eyes flaring as he stared me down with the power of a thousand suns. "But I also don't go snooping around your bedroom looking for things to absolve me of the guilt of that."

Head rearing back, my spine straightened, and goosebumps crawled over my skin with the gall of a huntsman spider. "I'm not *snooping—*"

In a flash, the High King grabbed my arm and pulled. My body crashed into his with the grace of a runaway shopping trolley, and my face snapped up, ice-blue eyes narrowed with the precision of a sniper as they locked with his galaxies of gold.

The lovely planes of his face reflected the small amount of light surviving in the dense gloom, casting dark shadows on the unforgiving angles and ridges. I was momentarily stunned by his beauty once more—to be staring so closely at the face of someone who had been designed with magic in the forefront of the creator's mind, who could manipulate the fabric of the world with the light that lived and died inside his eyes.

"Little white lies," he interjected, shaking his head.

A ball of saliva gathered at the back of my throat, and I tried my best to swallow it discreetly.

"You were snooping," Lucais insisted. His voice was a seductive purr, coaxing me to admit to my crimes and waive my right for legal representation. "You caught a glimpse of something you shouldn't have seen, and you've been desperate to find out if it's real ever since. Well, here you are." He gripped my shoulders with both hands, long fingers splayed widely across the base of my neck and collarbone, and spun me around to face the collapsing wing of the palace.

I gasped as my back pressed into his chest, and warmth poured into my body from his solid presence in musk-scented waves. My skin prickled with the urge to touch him, to press my flesh into his until the fibres of our souls knitted together.

But why is the fog enchanted, Lucais?

"I am not infallible, Aura," he said slowly. I wasn't quite sure if he was answering my question—if he'd even heard it. "I am a man." His hand slid down my chest a fraction, and embarrassment branded my cheeks a colour that only ever bloomed for him as my human heart cracked against his palm like a thunderstorm in the clouds. "I am…" The High King trailed off, inhaling deeply.

His own heart slammed against my spine as it beat, five times to my two, as if there were a race that neither of us wanted to lose. It provoked a sigh to collect in my chest.

"A man," I finished softly, lowering my gaze to the ground.

"There is a price to pay for everything, and this is how I choose to pay. The palace is older than our history books can determine, and it is part of the job description of any ruler to maintain it." He bent his head down until his nose was nestled between locks of my hair, and a feeling that could consume my entire body in a single wave gathered against my scalp when he spoke again. "It is one thing to possess such copious amounts of power as I do, but it is another matter entirely to actually use it and *more*."

My lower belly clenched at the sound of his voice, a rapid warmth beginning to develop. He spoke softly, but the edge to his tone was practically a weapon, stroking me from my skin down to my soul, sending an uncontrollable torrent of spine-curving shivers dancing across my limbs until my fingers and toes curled involuntarily and my breath turned ragged.

Lucais.

"The amount of power that I am expending on my extracurricular activities, like the wards and all of that nasty business over in the Court of Darkness, is a cost incurred in addition to my usual responsibilities as High King. And it means that something needs to *give*…" His hand slid down my arm until it was curled around my wrist, the pad of his pointer finger against my pulse.

Embers trailed his touch. I felt the vibrations of his voice in my core, setting things on fire.

"This palace—this *city*—is all I have that I am willing to give."

I could not help the carnal sensation that swept over me as he moved his head, tracing the outline of my ear with his nose. The nape of my neck tingled with a delicate and desperate ache. He hummed in response, as if he could sense it, and I gasped. "Lucais."

The profound depth in the sound of his voice was simply unfair. "Yes, bookworm?" he purred.

I was dizzy and distracted.

Focus, I told myself.

"H-how bad is it?" I stammered. My lungs were disconnected. I was suffocating under his touch. Swaying, my body leaned further back against the High King.

His nose skated down the side of my neck. I felt his lips press into my shoulder, kissing the groove inside of my collarbone, and it burned a line of fire all the way down my arm.

"Oh," he groaned, dragging his lips up the side of my neck until he could burn another kiss into my flesh, placing it inside of the hollow beneath my ear. "It's *cataclysmic*."

I felt in his touch, more than heard in his voice, the suggestion that we were no longer talking about the damage to the palace or the price he paid for the use of his powers. We were talking about the two of *us*...

His teeth nipped my earlobe.

I tilted my head back instinctively, but pulled a deep breath into my lungs and gulped down the excess saliva pooling in my mouth. I could do very little about the wetness gathering between my legs, but at least I could stop myself from drooling on him.

"I like it better when you hate me."

"I hate what you do to me," Lucais replied softly, and my stomach flipped. Using the hand wrapped around my wrist, he brought my arm up to rest across my chest and laid his hand out over mine, linking our fingers. His other arm snaked around my waist with the pressure of a constrictor python. When I turned my head to one side, he sank his teeth into my neck hard enough to leave a mark and send a shot of arousal straight to my nipples.

I couldn't help it. I moaned, and the sound echoed through the abandoned wing, amplifying the intensity of every sense and sensation.

"I know that you're a dreadful idea, Aura. But there's this damn *mating bond* telling me that if I bury myself deep enough inside of you that I can never escape, everything else will be okay."

Despite myself, I was tempted to let him. I could hardly breathe, let alone think straight, and there was a strange sense of possession combing through my body. Like it was looking through my genetic makeup and comparing its suitability to his. A stab of fear pierced my heart, momentarily pulling me from the fantasy as I realised it might be all the bond needed to take hold and condemn us both. I didn't know. I wasn't sure. I'd never asked—

"Do it," I whispered. And I could have sworn I heard his heart stop beating for a moment. "If this is how you feel, Lucais, then why don't you stop talking about it and just do it? You're the High King, and you..." I trailed off breathlessly and swallowed the lump rebuilding in my throat. "You've been throwing all of that innuendo at me like a set of daggers ever since I found out the truth. So why don't you just *do* it?"

There was a very long, very charged pause.

I suspected that time itself stood still for the rest of the world as he considered my words.

My offer.

Me.

"No," Lucais said at last, lifting his head from mine like he was waking from a dream. His hands remained on my body, his touch a conflict between two warring realities that might never be resolved.

If it was not for that—the warmth of his skin against mine, and the strange sense of continuity it offered me against all the odds—I might have crumpled beneath the rejection. His dismissal might have stung. Instead, I simply felt validated, so I didn't ask why he put us in such an intimate situation only to turn the offer of intimacy away yet again.

Lucais answered my unspoken thoughts anyway.

"No soulmate is better than a dead soulmate," he whispered darkly.

My blood ran cold, and his arms tightened around me, holding me through the horrified shiver that rolled beneath my skin like an undercurrent. I was so hot and so cold at once, I felt suddenly as though I was coming down with a terrible illness.

Shakily, I asked, "Will you take me back to my room?"

A beat of hesitation pulsed between us like a solar flare.

"Will you invite me into it?"

My heart stuttered and slammed into my chest so hard I flinched. A single, violent pulse throbbed between my legs. "No."

"Then yes."

Twenty-Two

Doesn't She Look Gorgeous in That Dress?

Later that evening, Wrenlock knocked on my bedroom door.

Officially, the carousal didn't begin until the following morning, but there was already a great deal of commotion in Caeludor as faeries far and wide came to get a jump-start on the celebrations that were entirely premature.

I had sensed a deeply rooted insecurity embedded in the recesses of Lucais's mind in the throne room—a fear that he was not enough for what his people needed and wanted him to be anymore. Once upon a time, they had chanted his name and revelled. And then...

Dot, dot, dot.

Truthfully, I still didn't know what had happened next. I didn't know *anything*. I was aware that Lucais believed his feelings for me orbited the determinations of fate instead of existing within them, but who *was* he? What had he done?

Maybe it was the Gift War that disrupted public confidence in his rule, but maybe it was something else. There was tension tightly wound through Caeludor—I could feel it in the air, thick as the fog surrounding the palace—and yet representatives from all over the realm seemed poised and ready to celebrate an outcome he hadn't even delivered. Even those hailing from the Court of Earth—unless all of the smiling faces and revelry I'd witnessed were part of a sickeningly convincing act.

I nearly gagged on the politics of it all.

My stomach gurgled with a mixture of hunger and revulsion, the sensation of sleet shooting a line down my midsection, when I remembered what he was planning.

We need more of those pesky caenim, he'd told me. Because he was going to place them in the outlying towns of Faerie in a bid to encourage everyone to move inland while he dealt with the threats externally. Somehow, that seemed like a better idea to him than being honest about what had happened—and what was likely going to happen.

It was risky. It was stupid. It was irresponsible and not in the least bit regal. Personally, I wanted no part in it. Especially considering the fact that I had no idea how he was planning to actually capture the caenim. Lucais was so chaotic, and it was beginning to chafe.

You're better off dead than a prisoner.

No soulmate is better than a dead soulmate.

His words were the equivalent of a bucket of iced water dumped right on the top of my head. If I wasn't so obsessively aware that he was concealing what were likely to be very morally questionable truths from me, I'd probably go into a shame spiral over the fact that I'd even offered him the chance to have me like that in the first place—let alone on any subsequent occasions.

I didn't know if I would have gone through with it, but we were falling into a dangerous pattern. I was bitterly determined to stick it to the Oracle—until he slid his fingers into my hair or pouted at me, and suddenly, I was the poster girl for prophecies and repetitive life cycles.

How was that any better than my upbringing? I wasn't breaking marriage vows for a faerie like my mother, but I was risking my sanity for one all the same, and it made me feel weak.

"Morgoya sent you a dress," Wrenlock informed me from where he stood in my bedroom doorway. My head snapped up, shoulders seizing because I'd forgotten he was standing there, talking to me while I daydreamed. He pretended not to notice as he held up a shimmering red gown on a very faerie-looking coat hanger carved from a twisted vine. "She said to tell you it's not an apology."

Scowling, I snatched the garment from him. The fabric was so soft, it slipped from the hanger with only the slightest tension.

It is so *an apology.*

And I would accept it. I would. I'd just needed a little bit of extra time to forget that she had known the truth and, instead of encouraging me to uncover it myself, had spent that energy on Lucais, playing some fucked up faerie games to pressure him into revealing it—which, in the end, had not even worked.

"If you can forgive me, then sooner or later, you're going to have to forgive her, too," Wrenlock commented, effortlessly and thoughtlessly striding into the room after me.

I glanced back to find him examining details on the walls, the furniture, the bed. His eyes studiously avoided me while I sighed, stripped naked in the centre of the room, and began to shimmy into the dress.

"When exactly did I forgive you?" I asked, trying to freeze him out with my tone.

It was a failure—something was lodged in my heart, stopping it, and Wrenlock had placed it there.

"Your hatred is beginning to thaw," he murmured, picking up a book from the side table. Wrenlock flipped it open, staring at the pages, apparently unaware that he was holding it upside-down. "Otherwise you would not have agreed to go out with me tonight, and you certainly wouldn't be undressing in front of me."

Craning my neck to peer over a shoulder, I fiddled with the thin spaghetti-strap until it was untwisted and spoke to him vaguely as I did. "You invited yourself into my room after delivering a gown for me to wear," I stated plainly. "Your back is turned. I'm not undressing for you."

"Not this time," he replied under his breath.

Heat flashed in my chest like a flare gun had gone off inside the cavity. It was an amorous feeling in part, but most of it stemmed from the complicated layers of shame I was yet to properly unravel. Because I *had* undressed for him once before—completely and utterly laid bare before him, on the dining table in the House, the first time we had come close to ruining each other entirely.

Even as my face grew hot and my head began to spin in small circles, the ghostly traces of Wrenlock's hands and mouth lingered in certain places on my body. I felt tiny prickles lighting up throughout the network of my nerve endings, as if he'd set a time bomb inside of me that only he could detonate—or disarm.

"Where are we going?" I asked him to distract myself.

The dress, thankfully, did not require any zipping or buttoning. It was a flattering cut, cinched at the waist, hugging my hips, and gathered in a cowl neck with a small chain running between straps at the front. In a dress like that, I was glad faeries didn't believe in underwear because there would be no way to wear it discreetly. I smoothed down the fabric and strode over to him right as he turned around and parted his lips to answer me.

Wrenlock's mouth hung agape for a long moment as he stared at me. His expression fell flat, his eyes unreadable. He remained so for a moment longer than required to make a statement that he found me attractive, and I began to squirm.

Swallowing, I glanced down at myself. "What is it?"

His throat worked as if the muscles were recovering from temporary paralysis, and he blinked a couple of times before his voice managed to free itself. "The colour..." His throat bobbed. "The colour suits you perfectly." Lifting his hand, he gently tugged on one of my curls. "Against your hair..." Quickly reclaiming it, he folded both arms behind his back and bowed his head to me. "Aura, it's perfect. You look like you were made to be worshipped."

I considered him for a heartbeat. Something in my chest yawned and stretched like a cat waking up from an afternoon nap. "Thank you," I whispered.

Wrenlock gestured to my open doorway. "After you," he said, and cleared the thickness audible in his voice. "I thought we could go downstairs. There's a party in the observatory. We can't see the stars through the fog, but there are faelight orbs that provide the same kind of atmospheric benefit. Plus, we can dance."

Smiling as widely as I could manage under the circumstances, I linked my arm with his, remembering that he'd told me he liked to dance. That was one thing about the real Wrenlock that was unique and true to him—and if it was all I could have, I'd gladly take it and use it up. I needed it, even if it was as simple as dancing. I just needed to know one honest thing about him.

"Let's go dancing, then," I agreed. My heartbeat rattled hollowly in my chest, but a warmth began to simmer around it like a gentle fist coaxing it to settle and yield.

It wasn't his fault, said one of the strangers in my head.

The palace was still largely empty as Wrenlock took me down to the courtyard, but I did spy a few different kinds of faeries floating around. Some looked as if they were working, moving things from one place to the next, and others were certainly guests there for the celebrations, wearing elaborate clothing and decked out in crystals and jewels, flowers and foliage. That was the main difference I noticed between the party thrown for the Court of Wind in the House compared to the one happening in Caeludor—the amount of clothing the attendees were wearing, and the botanical and mineral adornments they modelled.

We stepped through a wide doorway embellished with flowing chiffon curtains, and a wash of cool night air swept over me through the open windows and doors on the other side of the observatory. I smelled the sweet scent of frangipanis parading through the gentle breeze.

Music floated across the space. The sound seemed to be coming from the grossly oversized daffodils planted in glass pots in one corner of the room. It was strangely electronic with synth sounds and alternative rock influences. There were both couples and larger groups of faeries clustered together, dancing with vigour or languidly swaying to and fro with their arms linked or locked around one another as orbs of faelight circled them like they were figurines inside a snow globe.

Laid out as a courtyard, the observatory floor was carved from pale white marble, and the light was gloomy, adopting a bluish haze from the orbs bobbing beneath the restriction of the glass rooftop slicing against the low-lying clouds. Vines and overly large leaves partially consumed wooden logs, laid out with faerie food on silver platters and pitchers of faerie wine between red-and-white mushrooms and white daisies, set in a circle along the outskirts.

"Drink?" Wrenlock offered, nodding towards one of the tables.

I nodded and mouthed for him to bring me water instead of risking any of my remaining chances on faerie wine.

When he strode away from me to gather our drinks, I took a deep breath and searched the assembly for any recognisable faces. It appeared that mostly High Fae were attending the party in the observatory, but the High King was not among them. I doubted that I'd see much of him for the rest of the night after our encounter in the destroyed wing of the palace. He'd distracted me with sweet nothings, and I'd let him walk away without answering my questions.

Again.

It was time to start asking other people.

I found Morgoya and Batre on the dance floor together, swaying from side to side with their arms locked around each other. The sight gave me flashbacks to the night in the House when I'd first met Batre. I'd put my foot in my mouth by assuming they were soulmates, and I'd felt guilty about it ever since, but to look at them together and see the way they held one another made it such an easy mistake to make.

They were perfect.

They looked like they were made for each other, and that thought was both exciting and devastating for me to entertain. The stars had stayed out of their relationship, and I wished I could know whether that was the right choice. *What would happen if Batre met her soulmate? Does she have one? Could she ever be happier than she looks right now, on the dance floor swept up in her lover's gaze? Is there any proof that soulmates are promises of happiness?*

I didn't know. I didn't have anyone to ask, and I'd left my copy of *The Sins of Stars* back at the House, so I couldn't even reread certain sections of Livia's storyline to contemplate it in fiction.

As if my watchful gaze had called for them, the two women turned to look at me. Batre smiled widely, and I returned it, making an effort to include Morgoya in the gesture. But the High Lady frowned, a quizzical look crossing her green, feline eyes before she glanced around and pulled back from her dance partner. She tugged Batre off the floor by a single hand, and I squared my shoulders, bracing myself for the interaction.

Unease sent trembles all the way down to my fingertips. We'd interacted pleasantly in the hallway twice earlier in the day, but she looked as if she'd forgotten that, and I didn't know how to forgive someone. I'd never done it before. *Do I just say the words?*

You're forgiven. Please don't do that again because it really hurt.

"Aura?" Morgoya's sweet, lilting voice was brimming with a dubious curiosity, but it reached me at the same time as Wrenlock returned with my water.

"Here you go," he said, handing it over to me. Instinctively, my gaze switched to his face. Wrenlock nodded to the two women who joined us to the side of the dance floor. "Morgoya, Batre. Doesn't she look gorgeous in that dress?"

Batre gave me a look I felt like a physical touch as she nodded in agreement, but Morgoya stared at Wrenlock like he had carried over a bad smell. He ignored her, and within seconds, the creases smoothed out between her eyebrows and she nodded, too.

I tried to catch her eyes, but she averted them. There was an awkwardness in the air as Morgoya stared off into the distance, and I knew it was probably due to my behaviour in the dining room. I also knew I'd need to do more than wear the dress she sent me to communicate that our fight was over, but I'd need to do that in a less crowded space.

Without meaning to, I sighed because I missed my friend.

Morgoya had been the recipient of my unbridled trust, despite her predisposition to dishonesty, and I ached to be able to give that to someone again. I wanted to talk to her about what I'd gone through in the human world, but there was a crack in the floor between us. I had to be careful where I stepped and what I shared because she'd spoken so openly to me in the light of day while keeping me perfectly cloaked in the dark, and that made her more clever and calculated than either of the men had ever been.

I wanted to be part of that with her, but I was hesitant.

Wrenlock took my hand in his.

Batre opened her mouth like she was going to break the ice with it, but the music changed.

"My Queen." Wrenlock raised the hand of mine he held in his own and kissed the top of it, his eyes darting towards the dance floor with a twinkling invitation.

Something in his tone of voice was inherently flattering, as if he could not entertain a scenario in which he did not worship and serve me. It made my cheeks flush, and I inclined my head to acquiesce—and to conceal the colour of my face.

"Excuse us," he said to our silent companions. With a reverence I had never beheld, Wrenlock led me by hand onto the dance floor.

I decided Morgoya could wait, and I wanted to keep Batre out of the whole thing as much as possible.

"Why is the fog enchanted?" I questioned, as we found a space to stand together amongst twirling couples. If I didn't pose the question quickly, I risked being led astray once again.

"It is?" Wrenlock took both of my hands in his and scrunched up his nose. "I've never actually asked about it. He doesn't like to be pressed on certain topics, and I don't like to fight with him if I can help it."

"It's enchanted to guard the palace," I stated plainly. "Aren't you even the least bit curious about it?"

He shook his head. "It makes sense, doesn't it? An extra measure of protection for the most important building in Caeludor, second only to the Temple of All across the whole of Faerie. Especially with the tension between Courts and the Malum sending out hordes of caenim and locusts."

The most important building in Caeludor.

This palace—this city—is all I have that I am willing to give.

Wrenlock didn't know that the palace was crumbling and Lucais was hiding it beneath the fog.

"Do you know about the lapsus?"

His dark gaze snapped back to my face from where it had drifted off over the top of my head, an unreadable expression crossing his own. "Yes," he answered quietly.

Nodding, I chewed on my lower lip. "That's where you both went off to when you left me at the House, isn't it?"

"Yes." The response was immediate, but his voice was wary.

I made a quick mental note to ask Lucais if that was why the House's enchantment had come and gone, leaving me alone with Delia at certain times, even though I had a feeling I already knew the answer. At the time, I had thought the House was shunning me. If my updated theory was correct, Lucais had simply been repurposing his powers to wrestle with the lapsus.

"Do you think it's Blythe?" I pressed, bringing my attention back to the man before me.

"Aura..." Wrenlock clicked his tongue, then sighed. "Do *you* think it's Blythe?"

Peering up at him through my lashes, I said, "How am I supposed to know?"

The music switched to a much softer, romantic melody marked by the flourishing echoes of piano and a low, thrumming base drum. Wrenlock slipped his other hand around my waist as if my body held a mould made only for him, and we began to dance.

The music played without vocals, and the voice in my head sang out in sweet protest as I tensed my muscles in an attempt to resist the familiarity of his touch. *He never meant to hurt you. It wasn't his fault.*

He is not my mate. He was never my mate. It wasn't real. I chanted the words in my mind like a protection spell.

The voice was unmoved. *But you fell in love with him anyway.*

Falling was the right word for it because the action was violent and painful. For both of them.

Even so, I resisted the accusation.

None of this is real.

Wrenlock took the lead in the steps of a dance that vaguely resembled a waltz—quite literally sweeping me off my feet as he glided around the room in a deliberate and wide circle, gripping my waist with one hand as he pressed my body into his own, and holding my posture in the correct form with a strong arm outstretched and hand gripping mine. He moved with the skilled grace of a professional and expert-level speed. I found my body gravitating closer to his for the sake of feeling balanced as he whirled us around the room, between half a dozen other couples who kept stealing glances at the blurry phantoms spinning through time and space like asteroids on a predetermined collision course.

When the song changed, we slowed to match its languorous cadence in one place on the floor, but my head continued to spin.

"You were going to the Forest," Wrenlock murmured softly, tilting his head to speak into my ear above the music. "Weren't you?"

A blissful wave of dizziness rolled over me, blanketing me with a delicious feeling of warmth and safety. I bent to rest my forehead against his shoulder. "How did you know?"

"I pay attention," he said. His words, though whispered, were strong enough to flip my heart. "You're the only thing I pay attention to anymore."

Wrenlock's hand slid an inch lower down my back, and a firestorm of arousal blazed from his fingertips all the way up my spine. It curled into a shiver at the nape of my neck, forcing my head back until I was looking up at him. His own face was tilted towards the floor, his lips barely separated from the top of my scalp. I tasted his breath tangling with mine before I could blink my eyes.

His proximity was startling and relieving at the same time.

"Answer my question," I breathed.

"I don't think it's Blythe."

"Answer it properly."

One side of his mouth pulled up into a grin. "Good girl." He glanced around as if checking to make sure we weren't within earshot of anyone else. "I don't think that the thing in the lapsus is Blythe Darkcloud."

"What *do* you think it is?"

"I think it's a symptom of something else," he replied. "I think he's trying to manage it when he should be trying to find and cure the cause instead."

My eyes narrowed slightly. "Have you told him this?"

"Yes." Wrenlock chuckled. "But do you think he listens?"

I sighed because I didn't, but I knew he eventually would.

The High King was burning through his power on the wards, the lapsuses, and the fog—all of which could be symptoms of a greater problem somewhere in Faerie. I had no choice but to help him find out what it was. I'd already missed eight years of my sister's life. I'd missed the chance to say goodbye to my grandparents. I'd missed countless other milestones and important days in Belgrave, and all of it could be over in the blink of an eye if we didn't act quickly. The longer I stayed in Faerie without them, the more of their lives I missed.

Bringing them with me wasn't an option, either. If I somehow convinced them to come to Faerie with me, that would be sentencing them to the same fate. My mother would probably find it made no difference to her life, but I hadn't gotten the chance to ask Brynn what her life was like—to find out if she had a life that was worth giving up or if she'd even consider leaving it behind. It wasn't fair to ask, anyway. She already hated me enough for what I'd done. For leaving her.

Even if I really wanted to go back to the human world, that was no longer an option. I would live with the sound of those nails knocking against the sky as the creatures from my worst nightmares tried to find a weakness in Lucais's wards, knowing there was a risk that, one day, it would all come tumbling down.

"How were the caenim getting into the Court of Light?" I asked Wrenlock, trying to cover my tone with ignorant curiosity.

He didn't know that I knew about the tunnels with the iron doors beneath each Court—that they had to be opened from the inside—and for Lucais to be surprised by them meant they weren't travelling through the wards or stolen portals. I waited with bated breath to see if he would be honest, hoping the slight acceleration of my heart didn't give me away.

Wrenlock took a deep, thoughtful breath. "They're travelling beneath Faerie through a series of underground tunnels, but they're being helped on both sides," he answered after a moment. "There's a safeguard to prevent the tunnels being used like this, so someone is letting them in. We just don't know who it is."

All of the nervous energy that was twisted and pent-up inside of my bones and ligaments evacuated my body in an instant. I gazed up at Wrenlock with the most genuine smile I'd shown anyone in months. He was taken aback at first, but then his mouth mirrored mine, and a magnetic pull ignited between us.

It was like our souls were stitched together, but our bodies remained separate. I felt him everywhere, all at once—and yet, the only places we were touching was where one of his hands splayed on the small of my back and the other interlocked with mine. My heartbeat was accelerating in a thousand places across time and space with every moment we spent hesitating.

The ferity urged my head towards him until I felt the brush of his nose against mine, and my breath was ripped from my lungs.

Between our lips, the space yawned like a black hole laced with an overdose of desire; the air between us was sucked into oblivion, the pressure like a phantom fist wrapping around our bodies and squeezing to bring us closer together. A flare of absolute need ignited at the back of my throat, swelling behind the hinges of my jaw as the hummingbird thrum of my blood searing within my veins burned every other thought and feeling out of my mind.

I parted my lips and pushed myself up on the tips of my toes as Wrenlock dropped my hand. He threaded his fingers through my hair, and I clutched his bicep as he gripped the back of my head and slammed his mouth against mine.

A burst of power materialised between us—a flicker of magic that caressed our silhouettes before dancing out of reach.

My satisfaction and surprise rolled into one sound—a whimper that was swallowed by his kiss. He slid his tongue into my mouth, and the taste of him took physical form, travelling all the way down my throat, skittering across the muscles in my abdomen like fireworks exploding in a cloud-soaked midnight sky, and finally settling in my core. He was a burning ache, a frantic necessity, an explanation for something I could not put into words.

Wrenlock gathered me against him like a blanket, greedily pulling me closer. I felt the rock-hard erection straining against his pants press into my belly, and my clit throbbed in reply.

The heat building in my core intensified to the point of discomfort as he nipped my lower lip. Using the hand knitted in my hair, fingers pressed with gentle but firm pressure against my scalp, he tilted my head to the side to gain better access to my mouth.

I might have melted.

I was so hot, and I was so wet—

I am fucking melting.

My fingers reached for the waistband of his pants.

"Aura," Wrenlock growled softly, tearing his mouth away. He rested his forehead against mine, panting quietly. I could practically feel the urge to undress me coursing through his body, triggering the tiniest flinch of his muscles or pulse of a vein. "We're in the middle of a very crowded room."

Fuck. My hand froze, and then found a resting place against his hip bone. "Why does this keep happening in the most inappropriate places?"

Slowly, he slid his mouth across my face until his lips brushed the point of my ear. "Because I haven't fucked you yet," he murmured. The bang of my heart hitting my chest was audible. He heard it and sighed. "Baby, I don't think we're going to be able to focus until my cock is buried inside your sweet little cunt and you're sighing foreign curses into my mouth."

There was a glitch in my brain—a momentary malfunction where I could have sworn I blacked out and would have fallen to the floor if it had not been for his arms locked around my waist. *Holy fuck.* My head swam with the heady scent of his cologne and the even headier impact of his words.

He wasn't my soulmate.

But he was honest. He answered my questions. He *apologised.* Wrenlock never held back when he had the choice, and I felt a pull to him strong enough to realign the stars.

Glancing around the room, I saw Batre and Morgoya watching us from the sidelines. They were too far away for me to catch their expressions, but a thought slid into place in my mind, instantly establishing roots.

Do we appear to them as they appeared to me?

They were not fated to be together, but they were perfect, and it was enough to challenge the notion that an Oracle knew our hearts better than we knew them ourselves.

Do I know my heart?

"I need to focus," I whispered shakily. "Take me—take me somewhere else."

His breath hitched. "Aura?"

"*Wrenlock,*" I returned sharply. "Please. Take me somewhere else. Take me outside. I just need to get out of this room."

"Okay." He lifted me into his arms, and—

In a blur of colour and the whoosh of wind, we evanesced.

I pressed my nose into the crook of his shoulder and tried to breathe through the vertigo.

We stopped moving.

The air fell still around us, and the sounds of music and laughter became a distant clink between closed doorways. I opened my eyes, blinking rapidly to correct my eyesight. We were in a large stone hallway illuminated only by moonlight pouring into the palace through tall, arched windows. I could discern nothing more than the shadow of nightfall, which graced the tops of a tree line through the fog coasting by the palace.

Wrenlock moved to release me from his grip, and some raw form of insanity took hold of me. Grabbing his face in my hands, I practically jumped back into his arms, pushing off the ground from the balls of my feet and claiming his mouth in a desperate, clumsy kiss. Stumbling forwards, his arms snaked around me and I fell back against the nearest wall. I felt a twinge against my spine as he opened his mouth to let my tongue explore him again, heard a splintering crack as a picture frame fell and he hitched one of my legs around his waist. Wrenlock released a moan so deep I felt the reverberations of it reach my chest.

He trailed hot kisses adorned with gentle bites and flicks of his tongue all the way along my jaw and down the column of my throat. I tilted my head to the side for ease of access as his mouth brushed my collarbone. One of his canines scraped my shoulder, and the sensation sent a wave of unbridled pleasure rolling out across my body.

Everything that had ever been started and left unfinished came racing to the surface, tackling my nervous system with violence and desperation.

"Please," I found myself saying. *Fuck, I am begging.* "Please, I need you. I can't think straight. I can't take it anymore."

He groaned. "Aura, I don't mind waiting. Until you're ready, until you're sure—"

"I do," I insisted. "I mind. You said that if I had asked a third time..." I took his face in my hands and brought it up to mine again. It was ghosted by moonlight and shadow. We locked gazes. "This is me asking you."

He studied my eyes intently.

"Please," I added after a moment.

"I thought you'd never ask for me again."

Twenty-Three

She Was Obviously Enjoying It

The hallway was cool, quiet, and dark. I was the complete opposite as Wrenlock slowly peeled the dress off my body and replaced the fabric with his hands. My skin was burning, my breath came in heavy gasps, and I was sure there was a light blazing within me brighter than anything I'd ever felt before.

Wrenlock stepped back to let the dress fall away from me. The fabric scarcely had time to pool around my feet before he reclaimed his place against my body. Wedging his arm between us, his hand slid down to my clit, and his mouth claimed mine in an overwhelmingly needy kiss.

My back bowed as his fingers dipped inside of me, but it only lasted for a moment. Wrenlock removed his hand and brought his fingers to my mouth, coated in my arousal.

"Open," he instructed. My eyes flared with shock, but I did as he asked, and his own narrowed with determination as he pushed his fingers into my mouth. Instinctively, I closed my lips around them. "Good girl. Now *suck*."

A small moan built in the back of my throat as I sucked the taste of myself off his fingers.

"You taste that?" he crooned, tilting his head to the side to examine my profile as I swallowed and continued gently sucking. "That's the taste I've had in my mouth for weeks now. Fuck food and drink, Aura. The only thing I've been able to think about since that day on the dining room table in the House has been the way it felt to bury my face between your legs and make you come against my mouth."

He slipped his fingers out from between my lips, and I fell back against the wall, panting wildly. Faeries couldn't lie outwardly, and I couldn't find a loophole in his declaration.

"And the day in the bedroom upstairs?" Wrenlock continued, unbuttoning his shirt. He shrugged it off and cracked his neck. "Fuck. I want you to make a mess all over me, Aura. I want your pussy to make my cock glisten." His hands went to the waistband of his pants, but he paused. "You are sure?"

Biting my lower lip, I nodded eagerly. I was more certain about that than I had been about anything in a long time. It was inevitable—like I had no choice in the matter.

"Words, Aura." He frowned. "I need to hear you say it."

I swallowed. "I'm sure that I want you to fuck me up against this wall, Wrenlock."

He groaned and freed his cock from his pants, pumping it twice in his fist before closing the distance between us with a single step and bending to capture one of my nipples between his lips. Wrenlock's mouth was warm, his tongue soft as it traced circles around the aching peak, and an orgasm started to build in my core from that singular brush of his mouth alone.

I moaned, the sound raw and unrestrained.

Reaching down, he secured one hand around my thigh and hitched my leg around his hip. I felt the tip of his cock nudge me, and I wasn't sure if the wetness I felt slipping between us was from him or from me—

"You might want to pick up that dress," Lucais suggested. "Since you've started killing the servants, it's become increasingly difficult to convince any of the remaining staff to service your bedroom. I think it's unlikely they would be eager to help you wash Wrenlock's ejaculation out of Faerie's finest mulberry silk."

If I wasn't so shocked, I might have screamed, but as it was, I could barely catch my breath.

Wrenlock's shoulders tensed. He looked in the direction of the High King's voice and said, "Lucais—"

"Your presence is requested at the party," the High King interrupted. "You are dismissed. And if you're going to apologise for trying to fuck my mate against a wall in one of my hallways, please don't bother. I've been here the whole time, so I'm aware that it's exactly what she asked you to do, and she was obviously enjoying it."

Wrenlock inhaled sharply through his nose. He bent down to gather up my dress, but the fabric disappeared before his fingers could grasp it. It was back in its place on my body, and Wrenlock's clothing appeared on the floor a few paces further away than where he'd discarded it, beside a broken picture frame that we'd knocked down from the wall. He looked up at me from beneath furrowed brows, an apology and a warning in his gaze.

"It's okay," I whispered.

"Tick-tock," the High King sang from the shadows.

"I'll find you later," Wrenlock promised.

And then he was dressed and striding for the closest doorway. He brushed shoulders with the High King, who emerged from the shadows dressed in black formal attire trimmed with golden thread that sparkled in the moonlight like the stars in his eyes.

Lucais began to walk towards me, but I wasn't in the mood for a discussion. He had no right to be jealous—not after everything he had said and done—and I didn't like thinking about it. I'd lost count of how many times he had wound me up only for Wrenlock to make me come undone. And I didn't want to give any consideration to how much I liked the idea that he had been watching us, or whether he might have continued to watch us under different circumstances.

I brushed past him and veered for the door.

Lucais grabbed me by the arm and pulled me backwards. I felt his chest hit my back as a trickle of arousal spilled down my thigh, and my cheeks burned with self-inflicted mortification.

"You cannot be with him," he hissed.

Oh, he has got to be joking.

"You cannot tell me what to do." I tried to swallow down my ire discreetly, but I could feel Lucais's eyes trained on me like a hawk.

"Yes," he argued with force. "I *can*."

Shaking my head, I pulled my arm free from his grip and spun around to face him. "I thought you didn't care. You said *no*."

"I don't."

"Then why are you wasting your breath?" I demanded, lowering my voice into a cutting whisper and pointing behind me at nothing in particular. "You *made* me do this. At the House, you introduced me to him, *knowing* this could happen—knowing that it was more than likely, given the circumstances *you* designed for us—and even after it started, you *never* tried to stop it—"

He cut me off. "That was at the House, Aura. This is in my city. In *your* city, if you accept the bond—"

"You don't even want me to accept it!" I shouted.

"Because I don't want you to die!"

"Then why do you keep *bringing it up* all the time?"

"Because!" Lucais yelled, raking his hands through his hair. His eyes flared, the tendons in his neck straining. "It's your choice, isn't it? I won't stop you if you decide that this is actually what you want!" He threw his hand out to the side, panting wildly, and I wasn't sure if he was gesturing to the whole of Faerie or to the cryptic fog.

It didn't matter either way.

"How am I to decide when your *fucking* Oracle has already programmed you into the back of my mind?" I spat back at him. "You're my first and last thought, the figure in the corner of my eye, the *creeping, crawling feeling underneath my skin*, and that's not a choice, Lucais. Not when we were meticulously designed for each other by a couple of bored deities. They call that fate!"

He yanked at the roots of his hair. "Some people should be so fucking lucky, Auralie!"

"Luck is different!"

"Oh, fuck this." He chuckled without a whisper of humour. "It's not some crystal ball sending the blood rushing to my cock when we fight like this, Aura. It's you. I *want* you—so bad I think it might actually break me—and I will defend your place at my side until my dying breath, but I'm not about to let you walk all over a fucking *minefield* of caenim with a massive target flashing on your back in order to get to me."

My mouth fell open, and I blinked at him, utterly gobsmacked. "You're insane."

"You *make* me insane." His chest heaved in a despairing rhythm.

"Then we're at an impasse, aren't we?" I smacked the palms of my hands against my face and groaned, dragging my fingers through my hair. "Fuck! Lucais, please. I need you to let it go. This is bad. *We* are bad for each other."

"No," he shot back. "I will not let this go. If you're happy, I don't care what you do when there are not a thousand eyes upon us and the survival of my people doesn't depend on it. But here, that is not the case. We are in the public eye almost constantly, and *you* were in the middle of a very public event. I'll respect your free will when you're not fucking using it *against* me."

I giggled bitterly, a bit like a maniac. "Oh, so what Wrenlock and I *leave* the party to do is too troublesome for you, but what *you* did with those Vampyr girls in front of both your Court and Enyd's—and right up on top of a *podium*—is not?"

His shoulders trembled, and he waggled his finger in the air between us, swiping his tongue across his top teeth. "I was waiting for you to bring that up."

"No, forget it." I rolled my eyes and waved a hand at him dismissively. "Forget I mentioned it. I don't care."

His gaze zeroed in on my mouth, the gold flaring. "Oh, really?"

"Yes, really."

"You don't care." Lucais folded his arms over his chest, a brow flicking up above narrowing eyes.

"No."

"So I can do it again."

I ground my teeth together. "You can do whatever you want, Lucais. And I can do *Wrenlock* whenever I want." My hands curled into fists at my sides, and I exhaled sharply through my nose. "You and I can't be together. We so *obviously* cannot be together that we don't even need to argue about deciding if we want to be, so it makes no difference if the attention I have for you ends up going to him instead. This"—I gestured between us wildly—"is making us *weak*, Lucais. You're haemorrhaging power all over the place because of me, and I'm becoming my fucking mother because of you. Wrenlock *fixes* that, if you'd just let him—"

He grabbed my arm, on the verge of shaking me. "No. Little beast, heed my warning because I am not inclined to repeat myself. If he so much as *looks* at you when we're out in public, I'll have you put in the dungeons with your father."

I shook him off me again. "Bite me."

"*Let me.*"

"You don't even like redheads," I retorted.

His eyes grew wide, as if it was a grenade that I was throwing at him rather than a harmless recollection from the first day we'd met. Eventually, he said, "No, I don't. So what a joke that the universe gives me you as my mate." Lucais snickered, shaking his head at the ground before pinning me to the spot with his eyes. "You will be the first and only redhead I ever bed."

"I will be?" I fought down the rising sense of pleasure, then decided to mask it when fighting the feeling didn't work. "That's so on-brand for you. You're so fucking presumptuous!"

Lucais gave me a withering look. "You know as well as I do that it's only a matter of time. I can't stand it for much longer, Aura." Throwing a hand out towards the ground between us, pointer finger extended, he sighed deeply. "The way that your existence grates against mine. The way the very ground beneath your feet calls to me as if I should be standing in their place and you should be in my arms. The way that parts of me come alive whenever you are near and the way they all die an agonising death whenever you are not."

In the frozen shadows paralysing time as it strained to tick over the empty hallway, I stared at the High King of Faerie. His eyes flared pure gold. The sound of his voice reached out to stroke the inner chambers of my soul, entirely unhinged, the vocals of desperation caressing me with an intensity that brought warmth flooding back through all of my senses.

Tick-tock.

Brushing it off, I pulled free from his hold—the mental one—and turned away. I made it a few steps towards the doorway before he decided to speak again.

"I mean it, Auralie. I just announced to the whole of Faerie that you're the intended High Queen. Don't make me regret doing that."

With a furious breath, I stopped. Turned. Met the gold beacons of his eyes with mine and beat down the urge to get on my knees to worship the power inside of them. Looking into them was nearly a religious experience, like he was tricking me into a confessional.

"Why don't you just tell them you lied?" I suggested with a shrug. "You're so *good* at that."

Spinning away from him, I strode for the doorway, determined that I was going to leave and would not be tempted back into a pointless dialogue with him. He had the chance to apologise to me, but instead he chained me up. He had the chance to tell me the truth, but he left me coated in more half-truths and mystery. And he had nearly been given the chance to *have* me on more than one occasion, but he said no.

"Because I am in love with you," he called after me.

Truth rang out between us like a clock toll.

Midnight. Time to go home before the spell is undone.

"Because I am so desperately in love with you that it's made me sick and reckless, Auralie Roberts. If I somehow managed to convince the whole of Faerie that you are not my fated mate, even after witnessing all of that, then they would expect me to find them a replacement as the Oracle predicted. And I know you don't want to hear any of this, but do you think I can look at other women since I met you? I can barely tell the difference between individual faces anymore. All I know is there is the face that is yours, and then there are the faces that are not."

A single tear slipped down my cheek as I stood in the doorway. I was paralysed, like his words had broken my bones. Out of everything that he had ever said to me, those words were by far the worst.

The cruelest.

"I can lie about a lot of things, Aura. I can twirl and curtsy my way around and in between languages to trick anyone into believing things that are not true—anything but the fact that I am in love with you. That's so obvious, I'm almost ready to give up the notion that rejecting you will protect you if I fail."

His truth was cutting me to ribbons. I was suddenly remorseful that I had ever reprimanded him for the lies. *I liked them so much better, so much better than this.*

It was hurting me. Causing physical pain.

I love you. Snap. *But I cannot have you.* Crack.

"I've said it thrice now," Lucais murmured, coming to stand behind me. His fingers lightly stroked down a curl of my hair, and my heart stuttered in reply. "Don't make me say it again. And don't let them see you with him."

Wiping a tear from my cheek, I turned around—to do what, I had no idea—but I didn't get the opportunity to start figuring it out because the sound of an alarm rang out through the midnight darkness and broke the spell.

"Fuck," the High King cursed, a frantic look in his eyes as he stared out the window. "There are Malum trying to breach the wards around the city."

Twenty-Four

You're Not Heavy, But You Are Annoying

The sirens echoed like a haunting song throughout the palace as Lucais swiped my hand and spun me into his chest. The motion was so fluid and intimate, we could have been dancing the waltz in the observatory, but instead, he was crushing me into his body and evanescing to the border of the palace gates.

A violet-tainted cloud of fog parted for our arrival, the mist scattering into the recesses of the shadows like intruders who had been caught, and two of the High King's sentries rushed forward to pull the enormous gates open for us. Beyond them, Caeludor's streets were coated in the darkest sheen of night. No glowing lanterns lined the downwards slope from the palace into the lower town, and the mist made visibility even worse.

My head was spinning, my pulse sprinting a hundred miles a minute, and my knees locked. I almost tripped and fell flat on my face on the cobblestone when Lucais tugged on my hand.

"Wait!" I called, panting. "What about Wren and Morgoya—"

The High King whirled on me, his expression tortured. "Bookworm," he pleaded, beckoning me with his free arm. His other hand still had an ironclad grip around mine. "There's no *time*."

Blinking furiously, I moved my head—though whether it was a shake or a nod, I had no idea—and stumbled forwards into his expectant embrace. He laid one hand flat on my back, gently but hurriedly pushing me out through the gates and into the darkness beyond. As soon as we had crossed the invisible threshold of the palace's particularly strict wards, Lucais's arm snaked around my waist and we were spinning through the city's streets together.

I hated evanescing from Point A to Point B, but it was even worse when the journey was broken up by frequent stops. My stomach absolutely roared its disgust at me as Lucais pulled me in and out of a cyclonic torrent of wind that had us tumbling into the lower town, one frenzied stop at a time.

Every few blocks down the winding city roads, there were faeries rushing through their front doors, calling out to one another over the sound of the alarm and trying to wrangle clumsy children who were still rubbing the sleep from their eyes. It took me a few stops to realise that Lucais was throwing out orbs of faelight for them—golden orbs, glowing with an ethereal shine like they'd been scooped out of the core of the sun. I wanted to ask why he couldn't have done that remotely, but as soon as the question formed in my mind, I understood.

The Malum were attacking the wards.

His wards.

The thing in the lapsus had attacked him—was still attacking him, as far as I knew—and the effort of holding it back and fighting it off had weakened him ever so slightly, as had the battle with the locusts and the assault on the ward defending Belgrave. Combined with a direct attack so close to home, Lucais probably didn't have the strength to light the entire city back up with his faelight in one hit.

He never displayed the enormity of his power outwardly before—everything was subtle because he didn't need to prove himself when his very existence brought light and storms to the skies above—so to watch him desperately wielding magic to achieve the same things that had once been as simple as breathing for him was terrifying.

I couldn't remember with absolute certainty, but I was fairly sure the city's footpaths were lined with lanterns holding faelight orbs when Wrenlock and I had first walked into town. Considering that Lucais was the city's power source, the Malum's attack must have been quite brutal for it to cause all of the lights to go out.

Or maybe part of it was what I'd said.

Burying my face in the crook of his neck, I inhaled his scent of ink and musk before pressing my lips against his skin. He was warm. His pulse beat in a steady rhythm against my mouth, and I tasted the faintest hint of sweat mixed with notes of sweetness on his skin, like caramel popcorn. I held myself against him like that for the duration of a kiss. It wasn't quite the same thing, but it was all I could offer him.

We landed on a new street.

As the High King dropped one arm from around my waist and threw it out in a wide swing once more, sending dozens of golden orbs spinning from his fingertips, I brushed the hair from my face and looked up at his profile.

The tendons in his neck were visible—a tightness that stretched between the throbbing veins disappearing beneath the collar of his shirt. I saw the difficulty as he swallowed, his throat bobbing with a slight hitch halfway through the action, and my eyes caught the trickle of sweat beading on his temple.

"Lucais—" I started to say, but he was already securing his other hand to my waist again, and then we were spinning. "*Lucais,*" I tried again, though the sound of the wind and the world moving away from us at an alarming speed almost swallowed my voice. "Lucais—"

"Aura," he replied tersely. His tone was not irritated; he was having trouble vocalising.

My stomach dropped. *How many Malum could cause this much of a struggle?*

I don't know.

Even though I should have been expecting it, I blinked in surprise at the sound of his voice in my mind, like a honey-sweet tea calming the stiffness in my throat. And then my cheeks burst into flames because I believed I'd kept the thought private.

Is there any way to find out? I asked as we spun through the aether.

We came to a sudden halt, but he stumbled a few steps when his feet touched the ground. He almost dropped me, and the sensation of falling caused the toes of my own shoes to snag on the cobblestone as I fought to find solid ground, which in turn sent me toppling into him. Lucais threw out an arm for balance and faelight orbs scattered from his fingertips with no direct path. They ricocheted off the cobblestone and spun off into the mist-filled sky above us.

Fuck, I heard him think.

"I'm sorry," I gasped. I staggered backwards, my hands curling around the edges of a wooden flower planter decorating the curb outside a small cottage. Firelight smouldered through the window behind me, the only light left in the entire street. "Leave me here and go ahead."

The sirens continued to blare in the distance—a chilling omen.

Panting, Lucais bent over and braced his hands on his knees. Then, he looked up at me with disgust etched into his features. "Why?" he demanded, his voice hoarse.

I raised my eyebrows at him. "Because I'm heavy, and I'm distracting you, and you're..." My tongue came out to wet my lower lip, and then I bit down on it, hesitating. "You look exhausted."

He rolled his eyes at me. "You're not heavy, but you are annoying."

My shoulders slumped forwards, and I sat back on the edge of the planter. "Finish lighting the city and come back for me," I suggested.

"I'm done." He blew out a long breath and straightened, swiping a hand through his wind-tousled hair. It was like starlight, illuminated in the glow of the firelight radiating behind me and the few faelight orbs that had returned from where they'd scattered into the fog. "Morgoya can cover the rest of the city. I need to get to the wards."

Shock robbed me of the colour on my face. "You're not—"

"I am." Having caught his breath, he strode towards me. "And I'm not leaving you here."

Despite the warmth in his conviction, I found myself gripping onto the flower planter a little harder as he approached. "You're not going to offer me up to broker a peace treaty, are you?"

Lucais curled both hands around my hips with a raw, possessive force and tugged me against him hard enough to knock the breath from my lungs. The hard planes of his chest pressed into my breasts, his fingers digging into my skin, and my heart began beating without rhyme or reason. Heat curled and expanded between my legs. Gazing up at him, his sheer height forcing me to tilt my head all the way back, I found that he seemed to have regained at least a bit of his strength alongside *all* of his usual attitude.

"It depends on how annoying you are between now and when we arrive," he taunted.

And then we were spinning again.

The city fell out from under our feet like Lucais's powers were taking us on a magic carpet ride, and I felt a distinct shift in him. It was a deliberate, carefully held composure, as if he was trying to prove that I didn't exhaust him physically—and neither did the Malum or the thing in the lapsus. Mental exhaustion was another story entirely, and I promised myself that I would be more mindful of it in the future. I would remember that he had so many things coming at him from all sides, and I…

Will I stop being one of them? Could I?

The voice in my head was silent.

The next time we evanesced, it took longer, and when we finally stopped, it was on the top of a hill in a completely new part of the city.

I could tell that we were on the opposite side of Caeludor to the Court of Water by the way the mountains stood over the valley of fog. When we had entered the city, there had been a very harmless entryway paved for us over a sloping hillside—as opposed to the adamant barricade of the Metal Mountains that loomed from every other angle.

Like the one towering above us as we found our footing and Lucais let go of my waist.

Squeezing my eyes closed, I quickly brought up a memory of the Map of Faerie in my mind. Based on what I could recall, the Court of Earth was closest to us. There were passes beneath the land that allowed the caenim to get through, and Gregor was the High Lord of the Court of Earth...

...and suspected of high treason.

The contents of my stomach turned ice-cold.

I guess this proves it.

There was a narrow pathway that looked to have been created almost by accident leading down from the top of the hill. It was lined by the wear and tear of footsteps and the wheels of carts or carriages, following the slope as it rose up and then disappeared into a low-lying cloud of fog that had settled at the base of the Metal Mountains.

Dark, smoky shadows congregated in the mist, obscuring my vision of whatever lay ahead of us, but Lucais was staring directly at it. He had paled. His face was bone-white, like he was seeing a ghost.

I glanced down to find that his hands were trembling at his sides.

Wait here, Lucais said into my mind. His voice, at least, was steady.

Before I had a chance to react, the air in front of us began to ripple and distort, and I could see the two of us standing together in the reflection of what looked similar to the wall of glass from my dreams. Except it was not all-consuming like a gateway; it was smaller, like a full-body sized mirror.

Another portal?

I won't be long.

Why—

I didn't finish the thought because the ripples increased in severity, like larger stones were being dropped into a still lake, and Lucais took a step forward, and—

At the very last possible second, I snatched the High King's hand and fell through the portal with him.

He twisted to push me back, but it was too late.

Entering felt like stepping through mud, whereas the gateway and the portal in the Court of Light had been more like a clear body of water, and I could have sworn part of it stuck to me even after we cleared the boundaries. Not like a physical layer of something—but a magical one.

Lucais moved to send me back to the other side, but it was to no avail. There was nothing there. Panic flashed across his beautiful face, and then he swallowed me with his arms.

The High King fit me tightly against his chest, holding me so close I felt like I could split in half, his heart beating like a wild racehorse fresh out of the gates. I didn't regret following him through it, but an irrefutable sense of dread reached out to caress me, coming directly from the shadows—a touch he tried to shield me from, but could not completely ward off.

He pressed his lips to the top of my head. "Fortune's fool."

"Lucais."

The voice that spoke his name was not mine. It was not familiar to me at all. He had pinned me to his body with such a tight grip that I couldn't move to find the speaker, yet I wriggled against him in vain. I was aching to see, to know. It was such a human voice, such a friendly voice. He'd said that it was Malum—

"Mama," he answered quietly.

And then he very slowly turned around.

Lucais tried his best to keep me concealed, though I was determined to look. Craning my neck as far as it would stretch, I peered around his arm to see the speaker. *Did I hear him correctly? Did he say the word* mama*?*

But then I saw her stepping out of the mist.

She was angelic in her beauty. Incredibly thin, like she was made of starlight strung together with papery skin and completely straight, white-blonde hair that stopped at her shoulders. Pitch-black eyes were framed with extremely long lashes, and her mouth was heart-shaped and blood-red. Her features were sharp and angular; everything was pointed or elongated from the tip of her nose down to her fingernails. The resemblance she bore to her son was uncanny, though his complexion was far darker.

"How are you appearing like this?" he asked. "Are you an apparition?"

"Not an apparition, my Lucais."

Her voice was so sweet and melodious, like a siren song. I found myself stepping out of Lucais's grip to stand at his side and glean a better view of the woman who had created him. He let me, but kept me tightly in his reach with his hand around mine.

"As it turns out," she continued, "we simply had not been consuming enough magic to maintain our true forms. And I have recently been fed." Daintily, she tipped her head to one side and cast a brief look over her shoulder.

We both followed the direction she was indicating, and it took all of my willpower—and a firm squeeze from Lucais's hand around mine—for me to remain motionless and quiet as the sight of dozens of dead faeries in a bloodied pile of broken bones and ink black veins came into focus a few yards behind her.

The colour on her lips...

It was like the body in the courtyard all over again, but magnified to be so much worse. I was sick to my stomach thinking about how long they had suffered. The deaths weren't instantaneous. Not when the Malum were involved. Enyd's sentry had stumbled all the way from beyond the House's wards into the dining room, trying to make his way back to his High Lady before he'd finally succumbed to his injuries.

They're not getting stronger. Lucais spoke directly into my mind again, correcting a previous assumption he'd made about the Malum and their diabolical plans. *They're getting smarter.*

I didn't know if he was really speaking to me or just thinking loud enough for me to hear it, but I found myself poised to reply nonetheless. My lips parted, and then his mother turned towards me, as if the motion had caught her attention.

The movement was not humanlike. It wasn't even faerielike. The way that she moved her head reminded me of the laughing clowns at the Belgrave Carnival I used to take Brynn to visit once a year. Her gaze was positively serpentine—dead, yet still occupied. I could feel the danger in it, as if direct eye contact broke whatever spell made her appear so angelic and holy from afar.

"Aura," she said.

Lucais used the fist he had closed around my hand to pull me firmer against his body. The chaos emanating from him was enough to send a building collapsing onto its side. I sensed fury and devastation growing inside of him like a wave poised to drown an entire civilisation.

"I always wanted someone like you for him," his mother admitted in a low voice.

My eyes widened. *She knows.*

She dropped her gaze for a moment, and the illusion that she was friend rather than foe returned. She looked so much younger than I had imagined, and I briefly wondered if her appearance was true to the woman who had died and turned Malum, or if the way she presented herself to us after feeding on innocent faeries was simply a preference. Not that it mattered, in the grand scheme of things.

"If only I had the power required to change things around for you now," she went on softly, raising her scrutinising gaze from the ground beneath my feet.

"What..." My voice faltered. I cleared my throat as delicately as I could manage with all of the fear his mother provoked slipping down it. "What do you mean?"

She gave me a sympathetic look that was somehow extremely condescending at the same time. "He has to be with Margot."

Margot. Wrenlock's sister.

"I will never marry her," Lucais cut in, his voice firm. He was vehemently shaking his head. "No."

The lady made from moonlight and murder simply shrugged. "Fine. I like Aura," she said sweetly. Extending one long, bony arm towards me, she beckoned me with her hand. "Give her to me, and I will send her back to you once her transition is complete, my child."

My stomach flipped, and though I tried to stop them, my eyes flew back to the pile of dead faeries behind her. That wasn't a queue of High Fae waiting to transition into Malum. It was plain old murder—borderline cannibalism, surely—and she was a certifiable lunatic if she thought I'd fall for it.

"Transition? How many human girls did you have killed before you found me, exactly?"

She pursed her lips, levelling a thoughtful stare on me. "You know things." Glancing at Lucais, she sighed deeply. "Fine. We were going to kill you," she agreed, a haughty look in her eyes. "But it does not matter which woman the High King takes as his bride as long as she is Malum. If his choice is you, then I shall make you Malum, and you shall be the new High Queen." She lifted a shoulder in a delicate shrug. "If the transition is successful, nobody will mind. Not even Margot."

My forehead creased, and I opened my mouth to reply, but no words came out. She had rendered me utterly speechless.

Lucais inched forward. "You will touch her over my dead body, and then you will fight my ghost to take her."

His mother gave him a withering look before rolling her eyes. "*Mating bonds.*"

Lucais made a strangled noise in the back of his throat and gestured between us with the hand that was not holding mine a prisoner. "*Mother-in-laws,*" he retaliated bitterly.

Her head reared back, a look of disbelief passing over her eyes. "What on Faerie is that supposed to mean?"

Lucais sneered, but I felt the effort in his façade through the bond. "The first time you meet Aura, mother, you threaten to kill her."

"I did no such thing."

"You want to turn her into Malum."

His mother lifted her chin. "That's not the same thing." She had the audacity—I might have even dared to call it *humanity*—to look genuinely offended. "I am not *dead*, you know."

"You may as well be!"

Hurt flashed across her eyes—the first true sign of life I'd witnessed in her since she'd stepped out of the mist.

"Where's father?" Lucais enquired, his voice suddenly thick and unsteady. Hatred trembled beneath the surface, a burn in his throat so strong I could almost hear it crackling.

She shook her head at him gently, and a tiny shard of broken-off maternal love hovered in the atmosphere between them. I recognised the glint to it, the way its edges were shaped, even without proper light.

"Where is he, mama?" the High King pressed. "Why did he not come to see me with you?"

"Lucais, your father knows you do not wish to see him," she proclaimed in hushed tones.

Tears welled up in my eyes as I watched the exchange. I'd heard it a million times before—the excuses, the softening of a voice to try to compensate for the physical and emotional blows, the bitterness and disappointment.

The fucking *blame.*

He knows you were angry with him, Aura. That's why he left the last time. I don't think your father believes you want him to come back yet, so he's taken a job away from us for a while.

Five years or five *hundred* years old—it did not matter. The lashings of parental blame were equally painful.

"Wrong!" Lucais laughed bitterly, casting his eyes around the hillside behind her as if there was an audience I couldn't see. "He's scared, mama. He is absolutely petrified that I might change my mind about letting his crimes go unpunished. And rightly so!" he added, shouting the last part into the distance with a hand cupped around his mouth. Oblivion surrounded us in the portal, but Lucais glared into the darkness as if the darkness might glare back. The sound of his dejection boomed for miles. "For what he did—to the Witches, to Margot, to *you*..." Breathing heavily, the High King stared at his mother with hard eyes, though moisture lined his lower lids. "And for what he plans to do to the woman I love."

Letting out a weary sigh, his mother raised her hands, palms turned up towards the sky. "It is not so bad now that we understand how to maintain our true selves—"

"You're *murderers*!" he bellowed, and his voice broke halfway through the accusation. With his free hand, he pointed to the pile of corpses behind his mother; and suddenly, *I* was holding on to *him* with a protective death grip, hellbent on keeping him in place at my side. "Look what you've done to my people. They are *my* people, mama. My subjects! I took a solemn oath to protect them!"

"It is a necessary unpleasantness," she bartered, "and we are your *family*—"

"Not anymore, you aren't," he snapped.

Anger flashed in her black eyes. "Who will take our place?" she challenged.

"I have no place for you anymore."

"A boy needs a family, Lucais, even once he grows to be High King. Don't you recall when you needed us? Don't you remember what we had to do? Who will replace us—*Aura*?" she jeered, nodding her head to me with sudden disdain. "She won't accept the mating bond. She doesn't even know if she's genuinely in love with you or if her feelings have been falsified by the Oracle, not to mention the fact that she positively reeks of another man."

I blanched, but Lucais was unmoved.

"Trust me," she implored. "She won't stand at your side and fight your enemies—not your true enemies, of which you have *many*, my child. You need someone who loves the ones you love, and who hates the ones who would bring your downfall. Not the other way around." His mother's cool, calculating gaze landed on me. I felt like she was stripping my skin from my bones with nothing but the jealousy in her eyes. "Give her to me, or Faerie will burn."

Lucais was already shaking his head. "You will have to kill me, I fucking swear it to the High Mother. You. Will. Have. To. *Kill.* Me."

"You're wrong."

But he was already turning us back towards the portal, which had reappeared, rippling behind us with an ethereal cerulean glow around the edges.

"Wait—" she started.

"No," he interrupted firmly.

The portal shimmered like the surface of a lake as we approached, much clearer from the Malum's side than it had been when we had entered earlier. We stepped—

"I love you, Lucais," she called out softly. Her voice was suddenly worlds away, like we were underwater and she was above the surface, but the words were as clear as if she'd whispered them in his ear.

The High King of Faerie paused a single step away from whisking me back through the portal. I felt its pull like a magnetic force battling his restraint as he hesitated for a split second, holding us there. Filled with suspense, my heart was shattering against my sternum.

Lucais lifted his head and turned it to the side, but didn't quite look back over his shoulder as he spoke, his voice breaking on a whisper. "I love you, too, mama."

Twenty-Five

Auralie Starfire

We stepped out of the portal into pouring rain.

Cringing, I ducked my head beneath my hand and flicked my gaze towards the sky. Freezing cold droplets of heavy rain pelted against my shoulders and the top of my head, seeping into my scalp and trickling down the back of my neck. In an instant, my dress was saturated, clinging to my body like plastic wrap.

There wasn't a huge difference between the swarms of fog and the clusters of rainclouds—bar the excessive precipitation—and the typical sounds of a storm were absent. No warning thunder, no incandescent lightning. It hadn't been raining when we slipped through the portal, which meant it wasn't a normal storm.

Something cold and slippery dropped from my chest down into my stomach, triggering a ripple effect of disquiet to scatter across my insides. *His mood swings.*

Searching for a place in the muddied earth, I staggered a few steps forward while gravity settled around me like a second skin. The portal's magic felt tacky and dirty, but the rain couldn't wash it away.

It couldn't cleanse the touch or the lingering taste of the Malum who had created it by syphoning evanescent power from the gateways into Faerie—not the haunted glint in her shallow eyes, not the imprint of her words upon my brain.

Give her to me, or Faerie will burn.

A full-body shudder was halfway through assaulting my skeleton when Lucais tossed his coat over the top of my head, startling me into stillness. The interior lining was slightly damp, but the outer layer of his coat was resistant to the torrential rain and provided some degree of shelter, allowing me to fully open my eyes without raindrops blurring my vision. Parting my lips to speak, I twisted towards him, but all I accomplished was to obtain a mouth half-full of the water slipping down my cheeks from my soaked hair.

The High King put one of his hands on each of my arms and abruptly walked me backwards by three steps before shoving me away from him—

—and straight into Wrenlock's waiting arms.

The force he used was armed with purposeful restraint and care, but the action was so unexpected and completed with such speed that my heart took a swan dive inside my chest. I almost choked on my next gasp of air as the breath lodged in my throat like a stone.

Wrenlock was already turning me around to face him, fingers gripping me tightly, but I scrambled back, spinning like a top as I pushed him away and searched for Lucais's luminescent hair in the darkness and pouring rain. Hands reaching for him, the coat he'd given me slipped from my head as I skipped a few clumsy steps forward, and I barely caught the last trace of him in a glance as he evanesced from the hillside in a fit of tumultuous, heartbroken shadow and fog.

Lucais!

My call was futile, even mind-to-mind.

He was gone.

Coat in hand, Wrenlock stepped towards me. The material was soaked through and covered in mud, but I took it from him regardless and clutched the garment to my chest as the Hand to the High King wrapped me in his burning hot embrace and whisked me out of the unrelenting downpour.

I didn't know why, but I had expected—no, I had *hoped*—to find Lucais in the palace when we arrived back there. Even so, part of me was not surprised at all to discover that he was nowhere to be found.

Morgoya and Batre were waiting for us by the fireplace in the dining room. It wasn't until I noticed their damp hair that I realised they had been standing on the hillside with Wrenlock when Lucais and I exited the portal.

Concern was slathered over their features. Morgoya locked eyes with me; the green of her irises shone like a coral reef beneath tears she hadn't blinked free yet. A sob hitched in my throat, finally breaking away from my chest when I rushed into her open arms. She squeezed me tightly, very softly patting the back of my rain-flattened hair as tears spilled down my cheeks.

"He's at the bank," she murmured.

Choking down my escalating horror, I forced my mind into the present. "The bank?"

"The Memory Bank," she clarified for me.

Jerking my head back, I frowned and muttered, "What?"

Batre appeared at our side with a fluffy white towel in hand. Smiling sympathetically, she gestured to my hair and began dabbing at the ends, which were curling around my collarbone and leaking rainwater like a faucet that hadn't been turned off properly. Angling my head for her, I quickly realised that I had run straight to Morgoya as if all was forgiven.

And she'd let me.

I chewed on my lower lip.

Maybe it is forgiven. Can it be that simple?

"You'll notice that faeries don't trade in currency the way that you're used to doing in the human world," Batre explained. "Money—at least, the way that you know it—is a concept that was created after the Gift War as a way for humans to continue trading without their access to magic. Here, in Faerie, we use memories."

Blinking rapidly, I reached up to take ownership of the towel and continued to dry certain parts of my hair and dress that were creating puddles on the floor around my feet.

Wrenlock knelt in front of the roaring hearth, the fire crackling and spitting at him like it recognised his proximity, and warmed his hands by it. He shook off the excess water in his curly hair before he looked up at me, bracing a forearm across one knee. "A memory in its purest form is too much for a human to bear," he began. There was a grave, foreboding edge to his voice that disturbed something deep inside of me. He took a long breath. "You can tolerate magic in very small doses—mostly in myth, legend, stories—but it is not compatible with your minds and bodies by default." His mouth twisted in a grimace, and he quickly added, "No offence. I know it wasn't *you* specifically who relinquished your claim to magic during the war, but the consequences remain the same. You reject magic, and magic starts to reject you."

Iron in the blood, I thought as I nodded to convey my understanding.

Morgoya took the damp towel from my hands and offered me a thick, woollen blanket in its place. I accepted it, wrapping the length around myself as Batre nudged me towards a plush armchair near the fire.

"The faces on your financial notes are a glamour of your Kings and Queens to cover up the faces you are really trading in," Morgoya elaborated. "Memories hold a great deal of power, so with each transaction, that is the true value being exchanged."

My eyebrows, still slightly damp, rose towards the ceiling. "I don't think I understand a word of what you just said. You cannot possibly deal in memories. *We* cannot possibly deal in memories. They're *memories.*"

The High Lady gave a blasé shrug. "Where do all the memories go, Aura? The ones you can't recall but surely must have because you lived a life full of infinite moments. Once you forget about them, where do they go?"

"I..." My lips parted, closed, and then split apart again. "They disappear, don't they?" I glanced between the three High Fae, trying to discern the likelihood of the conversation being a joke or some new type of faerie trick. Their expressions were dispassionate—and, worse than that, they were *patient* as they waited for me to process and accept what was surely a fable.

"Impossible," Batre informed me softly. "They don't disappear. They don't die. Haven't you ever remembered something that someone else forgot? Or misremembered something?"

My mouth twisted. "Like the Mandela Effect?"

"That's a good example." Morgoya perched on the arm of the couch directly opposite the fireplace. "It's the phenomenon created when a person accidentally trades with their own memory more than once, or when a widely remembered event is traded off by too many people, effectively distorting it."

"You can trade in other people's memories?" I started to shake my head. "That's insane. Isn't that unethical—"

"People share memories of things all the time, Aura," the High Lady interjected. "We do so quite harmlessly in passing, which in turn creates duplicates, and once we run out of space in our own heads—and when we've inevitably created new memories upon which we place a greater value—the other memories are deposited in the Memory Bank.

"You might call it forgetting because humans no longer have access to the magical properties required to trade in these things with mindful intent and purpose," she went on, "but the High Fae retain a sense of awareness that certain moments have been stored away in the Memory Bank. Perhaps we recall the time of the event, but the details have been banked. As High Fae, we rarely need to complete trades like this because we have magic where you require money, but if we do so happen to require the use of a particularly powerful memory, we can make a withdrawal."

"What about people who forget? Amnesia? Alzheimer's? You can't tell me they do that on purpose."

Morgoya winced. "No. They don't. In cases like that, the memories are stolen—but how and by whom is a whole other conversation entirely."

My head was spinning.

It wasn't simply the cold chill from becoming soaked with rainwater under a sudden downpour—or even the harrowing threats from conversing with Lucais's mother inside of a portal trying to break through the High King's wards—that made me begin to shiver. The revelation that we traded in memories without realising it was perplexing, scary, and almost comprehendible.

Children always seemed to remember things adults had forgotten. Brynn constantly reminded me of promises I'd made that I hadn't yet fulfilled, and sometimes, it frustrated me to no end because she delivered her reminders with absolutely no consideration for the burden of monetary value and adult responsibilities. My irritation was unwarranted. I'd tried to shield her from all financial matters in our household as much as possible, so of course she didn't know.

But children remember.

And adults recall things differently.

The manifestation of memories in notes and coins was such a strange concept that I turned to Wrenlock for clarification with a dubious scrunch of my nose. "So you're saying that memories of lesser value would be coins, and higher value would be notes, correct?"

I watched the microexpressions flitting across his face as he considered my question.

"Think of it more like a credit card," he suggested at last. "Humans just like to hoard things—so you created notes and coins. But it is highly subjective, and I think that's why you're always running into issues because you really don't have any idea what you're doing. A trip to the supermarket the day that the freezer section had run out of frozen broccoli florets may not be an important memory for someone who wasn't planning to make a stir fry noodle dish that same night, but it will take a higher precedence for someone who was. Unless they're really singularly disturbed by the event, it will be the first memory they try to offer up for their next transaction over a set period of time, ergo becoming the most valuable until they deplete its worth or bank it."

Stir fry noodle dish.

Rolling my lips together, I tried to keep my expression composed and my mind on track. The dark, broody, ethereal High Fae man crouched down in front of me with long, pointed ears and muscles that were carved from one of Michelangelo's wet dreams had just looked me dead in the eyes and made a reference to a stir fry noodle dish with broccoli florets.

And I tried, but I couldn't keep it together.

"You eat—" I broke off as an unwelcome laugh bubbled out of my mouth, causing me to choke on my words. Coughing, I did my best to reign in my expression, but the upwards curve of my lips was solidified like concrete. "You eat broccoli florets?" I laughed. "Have you ever been to a supermarket?"

He frowned, rising to his feet, but a grin slowly spread across his face as he approached me. "Oh, now you're mocking me?" he teased.

A sequence of giggles floated out of my mouth. "Yes," I admitted, beaming up at him. "I am."

Why is it so hilarious?

Wrenlock's smile made him look handsome in a much more boyish way than his usual charm, and he perched on the arm of my chair, reaching out to cup my cheek with one of his hands. His thumb brushed the last droplet of water from the corner of my nose as he sighed my name. "Aura, I hate broccoli. If I was human and the stores ran out of it, I'd rejoice."

Gazing up at him, my grin softened into a comfortable smile, and my breathing started to even out into a rhythm that matched the calm motions of his chest as it rose and fell. Falling into his eyes and landing on the warm surface of his steady chestnut irises felt like coming home in a way that was still indescribable to me, but with his hand on my cheek, a flood of warmth that could not be replicated by anyone or anything else began to flow through my limbs. I could've sworn some of the water left in my hair began to evaporate.

Someone cleared their throat. I couldn't tell if it was Morgoya or Batre, but I inhaled a sharp gasp of air and broke the stare with the High King's Hand. He dropped his touch from my face to my shoulder as I turned towards the two women.

Whoever it was, they were right. On the hillside, I was ready to dive through portals of unknown origins and land in dangerous, faraway places simply to remain by Lucais's side; but by the fireplace, I was daydreaming about supermarket trips and dinner plans with Wrenlock.

I needed to pull myself together.

"Think about it like this," Batre chimed in. "What determines the value of money? It's not the paper it's printed on. It's what the owner of the memory—or the money, in your case—is willing to trade it for."

"Because you could, theoretically, trade one very important memory of your own life for something worth several less important memories to others and appear to be quite well off financially," Morgoya stated. "When in actual fact you've lost a great deal more than you realise. It's quite nuanced," she added, "but this is the basis of the concept. Our currency is memories, and we have a place in Faerie called the Memory Bank. That is where your soulmate has gone."

A flash of shock crossed my face before I could stop it. Morgoya had decided to forgo subtlety in order to make a point, and I felt a wave of heat emanate from Wrenlock's hand in reply, still resting atop my shoulder. Because he was seated behind me, I couldn't see his expression, and neither of the women met his gaze.

My throat grew tight so I tried to clear it as I readjusted my position, folding my legs beneath me, and settled back into my chair. "His mother was on the other side of the ward," I confessed, although I was pretty certain they already knew. "Do you think he's trading in the memory of his mother tonight, or banking it?"

"Neither of those things," Morgoya uttered quietly, looking down at her hands folded against her waist. "I think he's gone to make a withdrawal."

Give her to me, or Faerie will burn.

It's a necessary unpleasantness.

I love you, Lucais.

"What was her name?" I found myself asking.

"Raella," Wrenlock said. I turned and caught a glimpse of his side profile above me as he stared down into the fireplace, but the distance was audible in the echoes of his voice. He was falling worlds away, deep into the past. "His mother's name is Raella. His father's name is Gage. He's an only child."

Raella and Gage Starfire, I thought.

Auralie Starfire, a voice taunted back to me in my own head. It was Lucais, his bickering humour barely a whisper in his tone.

I didn't have time to evaluate the feeling that coursed through me like a display of fireworks at the sound of his voice returning to my mind or his presence emanating from a nearby location once again. I didn't want to categorise it, or name it, or...potentially scare it away.

"He's back," I said under my breath, standing from the armchair. The blanket slid to the ground behind me the same way Wrenlock's hand fell away when I turned towards the door just in time to see the High King appear in a flash, albeit dimly lit, of grey and gold.

Leaning against the doorframe as if he was bone-weary, his expression was full of determination, and his eyes glowed with the force of a thousand suns when he looked at me and smiled wickedly. "Change of plans, little beast. We're going to the lapsus tonight."

Twenty-Six

The Textbooks

The storm outside barely let up as the High King led the four of us through the palace's empty halls, the sound of the pouring rain dulling the echo of the sirens as they blared on and on in warning of the threat outside of the wards. Lucais walked with purpose, almost feverish in his desire to keep moving, like a man possessed.

I couldn't help wondering what memory he had retrieved from the bank. The way he'd said *mama* could break my heart into a million tiny pieces—and I knew that it would if I let it do so, if I wasn't more careful. A shudder tempted me, but I repressed it because there were things jumping out at me from the darkest corners of my mind, and I wanted them to leave me in peace. I couldn't allow them to see that I was spooked.

Wrenlock chipped away at the ice that had frozen over my heart after their betrayal, but I was suddenly extremely fearful that Lucais would simply melt it—and I wouldn't know until it was gone and there was nothing left between us.

My eyes coasted across his strong back, his broad shoulders, the slightly damp locks of his blond hair, and his arms—the corded muscle I knew was disguised beneath his long sleeves—as he stalked a few paces ahead of everyone else. Shaking my head out of the trance that staring at his physique seemed to put me in, I redirected my thoughts to the portal on the hillside near the Court of Earth, to the frightful encounter with his mother.

Were they close before the war? Why hadn't he tried to save her?

He did try to save them, I reminded myself. He had tried to save his parents and Wrenlock's sister. The High King had gone against the advice from his inner circle and attempted to give them their magic back once the Banshees were banished to the Ruins. Wrenlock had told me he almost succeeded.

Lucais was so powerful that he could control the wards all over Faerie. Single-handedly, he held the vicious and unnamed threats at bay without letting a flicker of his struggles with them show. Lucais shielded me, shielded Sthiara, and shielded Belgrave. *Why couldn't he return the magic to the rebels after their nefarious plans went wrong? How close had he come to succeeding? What made him give it up?*

"Lucais," Morgoya beseeched from where she trailed a few steps behind me.

The High King continued his determined march towards the staircase, leading us to a part of the palace I'd never seen before. I tried to piece together the sections I'd visited—the foyer, the museum, the floor of my bedroom, the dining room, the observatory, the hallway with tall arched windows, the throne room, and the destroyed wing—but I was completely lost. My mind grew hazier with every attempt.

"Lucais," the High Lady tried again. He began to jog down the stairs, ignoring her. "Lucais, you're not thinking clearly."

He leapt from halfway down the stairs, landing nimbly on the next landing, and his head snapped up. "On the contrary," he shot back, pausing for only a second before he sat on the railing and slipped down the next flight of stairs, sailing along the banister. "I am thinking with more clarity than I have in a very long time."

I snorted. *I'd believe that.*

Arriving at the end of the staircase, he jumped to his feet and turned to gaze up at me. His eyes were on fire again in the way that made me feel nervous and disorderly. The look on his face was fiendish, but brimming with temptation. I wondered if he made everyone feel that way or if it was a side effect of the Oracle's prophecy.

"The thing in the lapsus needs to be dealt with, one way or another," Lucais decided. "If Blythe is alive, this is our best chance at recruiting her to our side—and we *want* Blythe on our side. We have Enyd, but we know Gregor is with the Malum now. That leaves us with Owain and Ulyssa. Even if we get both of them, Blythe being on the enemy's side will render all of our efforts useless."

"How come?" I asked, huffing as I finally met him at the bottom of the stairs. Internally, I cursed my weak human body and the pitiful capacity of my lungs. My sense of gravity and balance, too. "I thought Gregor was the most powerful."

"He is," Morgoya replied, stopping beside me. "But it's not about the power."

"I'm sorry?" My gaze bounced between them, brow furrowing. "Then what is it about?"

The High King tilted his head to the side, snaring my eyes in his golden glow. He pursed his full, pink lips, and then sighed in resignation. "Blythe is Unseelie."

"Un...what?"

"Unseelie," he repeated. "It's not about balancing power in situations like this. It's about balancing faith."

"Faith?" My eyes narrowed into slits.

"Adjacent to the High King is the High Court," he informed me blandly. "It's an establishment made up of the Seelie Court and the Unseelie Court. They preach about protecting the image of the High Mother and claim to have established linkages to the Otherworld, but they're categorically useless for all legitimate purposes." He waved a hand through the air like he was shooing a fly away. "During the Gift War, the whole damned lot of them went into hiding. They claim neutrality but stand decidedly on the other side of everything corporeal. It's *so* annoying."

"It's a little more nuanced than that," Morgoya interjected. "They're not the equivalent of Heaven and Hell—"

"Oh, yes, they are," Lucais argued under his breath. He threw a disparaging glance at her. "That's what I based it off when I rewrote a little bit of our history into your world," he told me. "The idea of God and Lucifer came from the High Court, but if they asked me, I would categorically deny it."

Morgoya let out a long-suffering sigh behind me, and he grinned shamelessly at her.

"So Seelie and Unseelie are good and bad faeries," I said.

"No," Morgoya answered at the exact same time as the High King replied with, "Yes."

Feeling the effects of whiplash setting in, I looked to Wrenlock for support. He pulled a face at me as if to say that he didn't know and he didn't wish to get involved.

"Basically," the High King elaborated, "the Seelie faeries believe that all life forms should be protected and cherished. They're bleeding hearts. They developed a particular soft spot for humans when the Gift War ended and it was safe for them to come out of their little hidey-holes. On the other hand, the Unseelie faeries believe that certain life forms should be used for entertainment or hunted for sport because everyone can fend for themselves. Survival of the fittest type of mindset. There was an Unseelie ruler in the Aboveworld during the Dragon War and that's how we ended up with a whole lot of dead dragons. They also just so happen to be the ones who used to throw humans into portals with monsters for bets."

I shivered. "What are you?"

He shook his head. "I haven't made up my mind."

My eyes flicked to Wrenlock. "You?"

"Seelie," he answered quietly.

"Batre?"

"Seelie."

"And you?" I probed, my brow creasing as I turned my head towards Morgoya.

There was hesitation etched into the High Lady's face. She bit her lip, and I knew. "Unseelie."

My surprise arrived with bags fully packed, ready for a long stay. I tried not to let it show, but something shifted inside of her emerald-green eyes, and I knew she had marked the emotions swirling through me.

"It's a belief system," she mumbled beseechingly, wringing her hands. "It's merely a religion like any other. You don't always know someone's alignment, especially if they don't practice all the elements of their faith. I would like to be part of the Unseelie Court in my afterlife, but I don't throw humans away, Aura. I never did."

That was somewhat reassuring, but I was ashamed to admit that I could suddenly picture it if she had done such things. Her razor-sharp features, dark hair and feline eyes, the flawless alabaster skin that stretched without a single blemish from her hairline to her long, pointed, crimson nails beneath silky gowns—all the marks of an ethereal being, enchanting and deadly, depicted in history books and fairytales as the unassuming and fatal temptress over the ages. She could probably convince me to step into a portal, if she so desired.

I could have sworn that I'd seen her before, and I was appalled at myself for not noticing the darkness around her sooner. But that was the point. In the fairytales, the humans seldom see it coming.

"The point is"—Lucais quite literally snapped my attention back to him with the click of his fingers in front of my face, and I wanted to bite them—"that Morgoya and Gregor are Unseelie, but everyone else is Seelie except for Blythe. If we don't hold the majority favour with the Unseelie Court, we risk a huge disadvantage if the Seelie Court decides to vote for neutrality against the Malum—or worse."

I fought back the cold, sinking feeling in my stomach at his last words. Surely no faerie in their right mind would vote to allow the Malum back into the High King's inner circle, but the way that Lucais was glowering at Morgoya made me less confident in my assumption with every second that passed.

"Couldn't you just make a choice?" I questioned. "And throw it to the Unseelie Court?"

He shook his head. "No, that would piss them off because they'd know I was being disingenuous. It's part of the reason I haven't been pestered to make a choice already. They can tell if you're not truly of that belief in your heart, and they know that I'm on the fence. I'd tell the whole lot of them to sink to the bottom of the Underworld if I didn't think Maraja would send them all right back up."

"Maraja is Queen of the Underworld," Wrenlock advised me, before I had to pose the question myself. He looked between the High King and the High Lady wearily. "This little history lesson is wonderful, but can we refocus on the urgent projects before we delve further into the flow chart of faerie politics?"

Lucais nodded fervently and, pinching the bridge of his nose between his thumb and forefinger, closed his eyes and waved everyone ahead of him. Batre, Morgoya, and Wrenlock continued their walk through the palace towards some unspecified destination and the High King waited for me to spur back into motion before he fell into step beside me. I bristled at the warmth emanating from him, at the way my heart stuttered like a stupid little school girl at the notion that he wanted to walk with me.

The feeling was short-lived.

"You didn't know about the Seelie and the Unseelie?" he asked, screwing his face up as he lifted his elbow to peer at me below his arm. He dropped his hand from where it was holding his nose. "Really?"

"Oh my God." I came to a sudden stop, rolling my eyes skyward.

He copied me, and I spun to face him head-on, narrowing my gaze. The High King cocked an eyebrow expectantly, looking down at me exactly like he had when we first met in Dante's Bookstore before I'd slapped him across the face.

"How many times since we met have you told me I need to read more fantasy books?" I demanded. I held my hands up with air quotes, lowering the decibels of my voice in a mocking and admittedly poor attempt at imitating him. "*Aura,*" I growled, pushing the corners of my mouth down into a scowl. "*You work in a bookstore and read too many books.* Wait, no. *Aura,*" I tried again, bobbing my head from side to side. "*You don't read enough books because you don't know anything about magic and portals and demon creatures with funny eyes. Read more books about faeries, Aura. Read more books* written *by faeries, Aura. Brush up on your faerie history and put the hockey porn down.*" I threw my hands up, rolling my eyes again.

The High King had folded his arms over his chest at some point during my rant and was watching me with amusement glittering across his eyes, his mouth turned up at the corners in the most exquisitely attractive smirk. I dragged a deep, ragged breath into my lungs as he waited patiently for me to deliver my closing argument.

"Look, I'm sorry that I'd rather sit down and read a smutty sports romance with a cup of tea at the end of a long day, Lucais. But some of us are just more comfortable relaxing into the idea of cheering your athlete boyfriend on from the bleachers, before he takes you over the rooftop balcony at the grand final afterparty, than we are with the idea of balancing on top of a unicorn bareback with our fated mate after just having fought a *fucking* Banshee off with our bare hands two kilometres out from a settlement of Goblins!" I finished, my lungs tight and screaming for breath.

The High King stared at me, nostrils flaring, for a long moment before he reached out to swipe the pads of his fore and middle fingers down the side of my face. The touch was so gentle that the thought behind the gesture itself made more of an impact upon me than the physical caress. I wanted to lean into it, into him.

"I am not this athlete you speak of," he murmured, "but if you wish to be taken over the side of a rooftop balcony, bookworm, then you need only ask."

I ground my teeth together as a pulse of heat and desire throbbed between my legs. "In my head," I grit out. My defiance was waning beneath a strong flood of blush colouring my cheeks. "I want to do these things in my head."

"Perfect," he purred, flashing a devastating smile at me. "Because I want to do them in mine, too. Let's practice in our minds and then get together to compare notes."

I could have swatted him over the head with the nearest object, but we were standing in the middle of a very large and open walkway, and I suddenly remembered that three of our companions were hovering at the end of it, observing us from afar. Lucais seemed to realise, too. He inhaled deeply through his nose, seeming to weigh up his options, and then eventually sighed, resuming his long strides to join his friends.

"At least you're learning about the real fantasy worlds now," he stated plainly, squaring his shoulders as we approached the group. "Some people learn better on the job than they do from the textbooks, anyway."

I rolled my eyes at his back as he pushed on a side door that opened into a courtyard. The fog was considerably thinner, and as we walked across the bailey towards the stables, it was an effort to keep my head down and my feet in a steady rhythm. Because all I could think about was whether there actually was a rooftop with a balcony anywhere on the palace grounds.

Twenty-Seven

You Sound Surprised, Bookworm

As if travelling through thin air on the magic of the wind was not discomfiting enough alone, the High Fae simply had to insist upon doing it on horseback, too.

While I had suspected that it was a practice they implemented, it was no less disturbing to experience it for myself.

Elera whinnied gleefully as she evanesced to a completely different section of Faerie, her hooves slamming into the hard dirt with loud clomps, kicking up a small cloud of dust in her wake. The impact jolted me with such force that I would have gone flying from her back if Lucais didn't have one arm firmly secured around my waist, holding me against him with the power of an airlock seal.

Gasping for breath, I choked on a mouthful of powdered dirt as the horned horse trotted in a circle, shaking her head and snorting while she waited for the others to join us.

There had been no debate over with whom I'd ride. Elera had made that decision for us by coming to stand directly at my side at the stables while Lucais and I waited for Wrenlock, Morgoya, and Batre to lead out their own animals. She had nudged my arm with her soft, furry muzzle in a borderline aggressive manner until Lucais hoisted me onto her back and swung up behind me.

It felt strangely comforting to ride her again, though I trusted her about as much as I did her High Fae companion.

In the human world, I'd spent a lot of time with horses at the farm my grandparents owned. My mother used to send me there for week-long stays whenever my father came back—at least, before they sold it and moved into a retirement village across the country, closer to my mother's half-brother—and I'd found comfort in the calm and steady presence of the horses.

Elera and I hadn't gotten off on the right foot or the right hoof.

Admittedly, her horns had startled me, and the High King's joke about devouring me didn't help, either. Nor did the fact that, while I'd spent a lot of time around horses, learning how to care for them when I was much younger, I'd never spent much time learning to ride them for fear of falling. But Elera had exchanged a look with me when I tumbled out of the High King's carriage on the outskirts of the city, and that look was part of the reason I decided to stay.

It was steeped in knowledge and forgiveness, and I didn't argue at all when Lucais helped me climb onto her back.

Wrenlock and I hadn't yet found the time—or privacy—to talk about what had happened in the hallway, and Lucais and I had been interrupted by the warning sirens before I had the chance to form a proper response to his demands and that ridiculously emboldened declaration of love. Truthfully, I didn't mind waiting to talk about it. Mostly because I didn't know what I was going to say or how I was going to phrase it, but also because I knew that neither of them were going to like it no matter what.

One way or another, it was temporary.

My time in Faerie was always going to be short-lived. I tried to rationalise my way around it, but I couldn't outrun my responsibilities. I was delaying the inevitable the longer I stayed at the palace with Lucais and Wrenlock in Caeludor—and, deep down, I'd known all along that it wouldn't last. It couldn't. From every possible angle, I still had a feeling tightly woven around my heart, a pressure on my chest reminding me that I was trapped inside an hourglass, and the only way to survive would be to turn everything on its head.

Again and again and again.

Like I had been doing all of my life.

Lucais wouldn't understand that, but Wrenlock might.

As if on cue, he appeared atop an absolutely beautiful black stallion who met the ground with grace as he landed, holding his head up high as he walked to stand near Elera. His eyes were wide and bright, and one met mine with a youthful sense of curiosity before he hastily turned his head. The two restless males were mirror images of one another—large, strong, and darkly handsome. When Wrenlock reached down to stroke his neck, the stallion's flesh quivered beneath the touch, and I noticed that he had no horns. None at all.

Morgoya and Batre materialised next, the former riding a palomino mare with two straight horns in the middle of her head, and the latter on a roan stallion with a single horn protruding from his forehead like the depiction of traditional unicorns I had seen pictures of as a child. His colouring was an ashy blue-grey, but clear patches of pure grey formed around his eyes, horn, and muzzle.

As he walked beside Morgoya's mare, an eye met mine like the much younger stallion's had, but his gaze was filled with the wariness of a wise creature rather than the curiosity of a new one.

"What's his name?" I called to Wrenlock, nodding to the proud black male beneath him.

"Ace," he sang back, beaming as he patted the stallion's neck again. He gestured to Morgoya's horse as she came up beside him. "That's Shande, and that old trooper is Lucky."

The roan stallion beneath Batre snorted at the word *old*.

"When will Ace's horns come in?" I wondered. He was obviously the youngest of all the horses. *Unless...* "Is he a unicorn too?"

I could have sworn Elera sighed. A heavy silence fell over our group. The mood plummeted like a boulder down a cliffside, and I was quite obviously the person who had pushed it.

"There are no horses in Faerie," Lucais informed me in a soft voice. He clicked his tongue in a signal to Elera, and she began to walk.

Glancing back, I saw the others fall into step behind us in single file, their heads hanging heavy with dolorous expressions. I faced the front and wracked my brain to determine what I'd said or done wrong.

Bookworm. The High King's voice was in my mind as we rode on, his tone gentle and brimming with warmth. I immediately felt him all over me, from my head to my toes, and from the inside out. *Here's another textbook history lesson for you. Faerie only has unicorns, but Acey boy won't grow any horns because he was born after the end of the Gift War.*

Why? I dared to ask, though as soon as he had mentioned the war, I felt a sudden pinch in my stomach, suggesting it was better not to know.

Unicorn means one horn in the old language, he said. *The horn of a unicorn is filled with an extremely potent type of magic. It has healing and regeneration properties, amongst other things, but they cannot be transferred. A unicorn cannot use the power within their horn to heal others, only themselves—or whoever has possession of the horn. So, during the Gift War, the humans realised they could harness those powers organically if they baked them into pills and stirred them into potions. It allowed them to continue fighting against us, to take bold risks and chances, knowing they could heal their own if they made any fatal mistakes. But they had to saw off the horns from the unicorns to do so. And so that's exactly what they did.*

My gaze became unseeing, locked in a straight line ahead of us. I felt the blood draining from my cheeks, and I clamped my lips together firmly as a mouthful of bile shot up the back of my throat. *No.*

They killed very few of them, considering the numbers, he went on. *The unicorns were kept awake and alert, restrained with ropes and chains because the horns had to be taken without any type of anesthetic, and then they were usually left alive. Those who survived eventually grew their horns back. As a defence mechanism, we think, the unicorns who were captured and maimed grew back an extra horn. And then again, when those were stolen, until some became so deformed that there is no telling where one horn begins and another ends.*

Sickly glimpses of the six unicorns pulling the High King's carriage flashed before my eyes, their wildly tangled horns growing like sets of brambles. Sharp blinks of pain stabbed at my stomach as my mind cycled through the numbers, trying to reconcile with how many times each of those horses—those *unicorns*—must have been tortured for their horns to grow back in such a state.

And Elera...

We cut her horns off twice? The thought was out of my head and burrowing into Lucais's mind through the bond before I could stop it.

Not you, but yes. You sound surprised, bookworm. But that was only the beginning for human beings, wasn't it?

The truth was a cruel mistress. I cringed, but the action only pressed me further back into the hard and unforgiving planes of the High King's chest. Anger blazed beneath the surface of my skin, disgust as thick as ipecac, an emotion that became lodged in my throat because my heart did not want to digest it. A world like mine—a world turned by the cogs of timeless and nescient regret, operated by a group of people who had given up their magic, only to spend the rest of eternity trying to replicate it in barbaric, bloodthirsty ways. Shaking my head with nearly imperceptible movements, I forced myself to swallow it down. I'd been swallowing it down my whole life, after all. *Why stop now?*

Lucais stroked a reassuring thumb across my upper thigh, but an intrusive thought bloomed in my mind like a pitcher plant, and I wished that he would put his hand around my throat and squeeze until I blacked out. Just until I fell into a sleep deep enough to forget the horrific truth I'd uncovered.

"No," he whispered in my ear. His breath was a heady temptation, a sinful caress. "When I put my hand around your throat, you're going to remember everything I'm doing to you while it's there."

"Get out of my head," I commanded under my breath, digging my elbows into his arms for emphasis.

"You get out of mine first."

"Pfft." I shot a reproachful glance at him over my shoulder. "As if you'd let me," I muttered. "I bet you keep me locked away in there like some sort of pet."

"I think you mean *pest*," Lucais corrected, grinding his knuckles into my side. His voice adopted a lighter tone, as though driving his fist into my rib cage like a screwdriver released some tension. Knowing him, it probably did. "I have tried to evict you from my mind, Auralie, but short of dousing you in pesticides, I've run out of ideas. You're an itch I can't scratch."

I gave you the choice, and you said no, I reminded him, switching back to our mental telepathy. We were well ahead of the others, but the mention of what had transpired between us in the palace's ruined wing felt like something that should be kept between the two of us—and not only because the destroyed section of the palace was a secret. I needed to balance my priorities, at least until I could figure out what to tell Wrenlock.

And by refusing you, I continue to give you choices, Lucais replied matter-of-factly. Even when he spoke into my mind, he was annoying. The cryptic messages he knew damn well I didn't fully understand were becoming tiresome.

"What does that even mean?" I mumbled aloud.

"Let's circle back," the High King replied, clearing his throat as Elera slowed to a stop near a copse of dead trees. The trunks were husks, hollow and flaky, and small, brittle branches poked out in abstract shapes, all of them needle-thin and sharp. Elera was undeterred as she leaned over and tore a piece of bark from one, chewing patiently as she waited for the other unicorns and their riders to catch up. "I was telling you about the unicorns before you distracted me with your witchery."

I blew out a harsh breath through my mouth, but waved my hand in signal for him to resume the process of cleaving my feelings into bite-sized pieces with his history lesson.

"Ultimately, the result of the torture inflicted upon them seemed to change their genetic makeup in some intrinsic, irreversible way." Reaching around me, Lucais gently touched the tips of his pointer and middle fingers to the base of the twisted horn placed on the very top of Elera's head. She nickered in reply. "Foals born after the Gift War ended were born without horns at all, and while we waited for many years to see if they might develop, they've actually stopped producing them completely." He pulled his hand back. "There's nothing we can do about it but care for the horned unicorns who are left, most of whom look like Elera or Shande, and treat the new ones the same as we always have. They're unicorns regardless; they still own their heritage, they're entitled to it. And I believe they still have the same magic. It's just not as easy to take from them now."

Tears pricked at my eyes, triggered by shame and horror as I ran my fingers through Elera's mane. It was coarser than her coat, but it slipped through my fingers with ease. *Lucky wasn't always named Lucky, was he?*

Lucais merely squeezed my knee with his free hand.

Desperately, I wanted to be surprised. I wanted to feel shock nipping at my fingertips, increasing the speed of my heart as it beat within my chest, but it never came. It never would.

The revelation that the first generation of humans had maimed and slaughtered thousands upon thousands of beautiful, innocent creatures like Elera so they could steal their magic for themselves was the first act of what would ultimately snowball into an entire history of tragedy, greed, and hypocrisy. It didn't surprise me, but it made me feel sick to discover new evidence of our inferiority in the midst of a completely alternate realm of shunned possibilities.

"Try not to dwell," the High King murmured in my ear, sliding his hand a little higher up my thigh as his fingers splayed out across the too-thin fabric of my pants. "Think about that rooftop balcony instead."

"There are no rooftops balconies," I hissed, trying to put out the fire that blazed underneath my skin at his words, at the sensual stroke that was his voice. Quite frankly, I'd have preferred the hand around my throat and a bottomless pit of sleep, but I would take whatever mental redirection he was offering, given the only other option. "And even if there are, we'd never find it. You've got the whole place submerged in fog as dense as a lake."

"I'll make you one," Lucais suggested lightly. His lips brushed the shell of my ear, but he dipped his head no lower. "Would that make you happy, bookworm?"

A beat of warmth and longing pulsed in my core, lighting up the nerve endings that spanned from the main switch between my legs all the way down to the very tips of my fingers. He could touch the ends of my hair, and I'd feel it resonating in my clit.

"We've been over this," I reminded him, trying to shift away from the pressure adding fuel to the fire. He kept his hand in place, his thumb angled precariously inwards. "You can't make me happy. You can't do anything. No soulmate is better than a dead soulmate, remember?"

"Killjoy," Lucais accused, but he straightened behind me, removed his hand, and said no more.

Without the distraction of the High King's velvety voice in my mind or his scorching touch on my body, all of my other senses quickly came back to me. A bit like walking out of a movie theatre and finding that the sun had already set, I found myself slowly coordinating the realisation that we were no longer bathed in an endless sea of impenetrable white fog. All around us, the air was clear and free, and I could see miles ahead of us, across a land that reminded me of the outback during a tropical storm.

Rainclouds the colour of molten silver and indigo rolled over us, looking like the High Mother was exhaling the smoke from a pipe and blowing it across the sky. Instead of the cool crispness I'd felt encasing me in Caeludor, I was enveloped in a balmy breeze, and it stirred the tendrils of my hair that had fallen out of the silk ribbon Lucais had used to tie it back before we left the stables. I let my eyes rove over the scenery as a magenta sunset was chased beneath the horizon by the approaching storm. Flecks of surviving light sparkled above us in certain places, almost like constellations in the night sky back in the human world, but not quite the same.

Before I risked rekindling any dialogue with my ill-fated mate by asking about his skies or his secrets, I cast my eyes around the landscape behind us, trying to discern where we had landed on the Map of Faerie when the unicorns evanesced. The ground was rock-hard beneath Elera's hooves, the impact duller yet louder than it had been even through Sthiara with each step, and it was totally barren. Every now and then, a cloud of dust was disturbed by a rogue torrent of wind, but there was no flora. I couldn't even see weeds surviving between any of the deep cracks in the dry, red dirt, let alone anything planted with intent or nativity. My mind immediately recalled a barren landscape Lucais had once mentioned to me—the Opiate Desert—but that was inside the Court of Wind, and I knew we needed to get as close to Blythe's homeland as possible to see the lapsus.

Reckless as he was, it was very unlikely that Lucais would permit us to travel through Gregor's land, given the current political climate. But if we couldn't access the Court of Darkness itself, that meant we were in... *The Ruins.*

"Tell me we are not here to catch a caenim," I insisted quietly.

"We are not here to catch a caenim, little beast."

Before the relief could wash over me, a flash of lightning split the sky, and Elera reared back, squealing. My stomach hit my throat before crashing back down with an almighty splash of queasiness.

"Down, girl," Lucais murmured, stroking her mane reassuringly. His other arm was still holding me against his body like I was an extension of him. "Good girl. It's okay."

The muscles in my core tightened at his voice.

"We're almost there." Wrenlock clicked his tongue somewhere behind us, and Ace trotted to catch up, pulling against the grip Wrenlock had on his mane as they stepped into line at our side. Ace's ears were flattened and pinned back. "Should we leave them here with the tree bark and trek the rest of the distance on foot?"

The High King nodded, gently patting Elera's mane. She peeled another piece of bark off the tree and began to chew noisily. Lucais dismounted first, then extended his arms to help me down. My eyes must have been filled with panic because he flicked my chin affectionately before joining the others, and the action pulled my anxious attention back down from the sky—which was being repeatedly split apart by ultraviolet streaks of lightning that very nearly mimicked the shape of a dark grin slicing across a face of dark storm clouds—to the ground and the High Fae standing around me.

"The storm is a side effect of the Court being in a full lockdown," the High King explained.

He was addressing the group, huddled in a circular formation as the unicorns gathered around the trees a few paces away from us, but I had a feeling the briefing was mostly for my benefit. I knew that Wrenlock and Lucais had been visiting the lapsus while I was at the House, and it wasn't a far cry to assume that Morgoya, at least, had joined them once or twice.

"It's harmless, static electricity from the wards alerting me to the fact that they're sealed off when ordinarily, they wouldn't be, and it's magnetised by the malignant energy inside the lapsus. It gets worse the closer we get, which is how we'll know when we've caught up to the"—the High King waved a flippant hand at the storm ahead and scrunched his nose—"*thing* inside it."

"Have you decided what you're actually going to *do* with it?" Batre asked, eyeing him as if she thought he was well and truly falling off his rocker. I liked her more than ever for the expression on her face.

"No, but I can't keep playing footsies with this fucking thing any longer," Lucais replied indolently.

Morgoya wrapped a reassuring arm around her girlfriend but remained silent. I chewed on the inside of my cheek, torn between reprimanding him for his tone and chasing away the creases from his brow with my fingertips.

Heaving a sigh, Lucais dragged a hand down his face. "I'm sorry. The Malum have been feeding on faeries. I saw Raella in the portal, and she was Raella again—thanks to the lives of about sixteen assorted faeries she'd opened like a box of fucking party chocolates and dumped like wrappers on the hillside. She said it gives them the power to maintain the illusion of their High Fae forms, which means that's what they've been experimenting with, and all of the faeries they've stolen from townships like Sthiara are already dead."

Anxiety shot out across my body with a reluctant twitch of my shoulder. It was more than the High Fae around me displayed, but I could feel it in the air. The devastation. The concern. And the High King's suffocating guilt.

"I don't know what else that man is doing. I don't know how much stronger they're becoming, and I don't know if they've managed to syphon magic to utilise themselves or not. If we're lucky, it extends as far as their image," he declared, shaking his head. "But if they manage to overcome the Banshee's anti-magic curse and regain power to utilise as weapons or as defence, then I don't know if we'll be able to prevent another full-blown war if they decide to storm the city and take it by force. Especially not with Gregor's help, the fucking bastard."

"Did she propose again?" Wrenlock queried. His throat bobbed when I glanced at him, and he met my eyes for a moment before looking back towards the High King.

"Margot wasn't there." Lucais's tongue swiped across his bottom lip. He hesitated before divulging the remainder of the conversation. "Raella offered me Aura instead, though. She said that I could take her as my bride and all would be well—if I allowed them to turn her into Malum first."

"Damn it. *Fuck*," Wrenlock hissed, spinning away with one hand splayed across his mouth and the other on his hip. Morgoya and Batre echoed his sentiments.

"This needs to end," Lucais insisted, nodding to the deepening shadows in the distance. His voice was wavering, the whispers of exhaustion slipping through. I wasn't convinced that it was purely physical, either. "The Malum are still throwing things at the wards around Caeludor simply to annoy the fuck out of me. Blythe's either in there or she's not, but we can't wait any longer. And I can't let it grow more powerful than it already is. I left the Malum alone for too long. I can't risk making the same mistake here."

"What exactly is your plan?" Morgoya questioned apprehensively.

Lucais grinned like a fiend. "I'm going to make one hell of a scene."

Twenty-Eight

Extraordinarily Long and Unorthodox Foreplay

"I thought you told me that we aren't here to catch a caenim," I said through my teeth. "If you make a scene in the middle of the Ruins, what else do you think is going to happen?"

The High King winked at me. "That's because *we* are *not* catching a caenim, little beast. *You* are going to lure the caenim *out* by being here with me, but Wrenlock and I will do the catching. We can't have a repeat of that day in the clearing where..." He trailed off, dislodging a lump in his throat with a cough. "Well."

"Well?" I prompted, crossing my arms over my chest obstinately. I hoped the fire in my throat was reflected in my eyes as they pinned him to the spot with an unyielding glower.

Lucais's warm, honey-coloured gaze softened as he coated me with it from head to toe. *Where you not only had to think twice about saving my life, but you hesitated before saving your own, too.*

A hot, loud heartbeat hit me in the throat, but I rolled my eyes at him and scoffed. "You're insufferable," I accused.

"Yet you keep suffering," he returned with a sigh, but another devilish grin lit up his face in spite of it.

Amusement glittered in Lucais's eyes when he gave a quick shake of his head and returned his attention to our companions. Taking a measured breath, he brushed a hand down the front of his shirt and composed his expression.

"I don't know whether they'll come from the north or the south, but I am certain that a horde of the Malum's delightful little friends will come out to greet us if we muck around with the lapsus for too long. Ideally, we need to capture them all so we can use them later on. Kill them if absolutely necessary, but the fewer trips we need to take out for this, the better."

"I've never faced one of these creatures head-on," Batre mumbled from where she stood at Morgoya's side, their arms around each other to ward off the chill in the air. "Are you sure this is the only option?"

The High King almost looked remorseful. "Yes. We've already been out here about a hundred times over the last few months, but I can never break through the exterior wall of shadows to catch even a glimpse of the creature inside the lapsus. We're running out of time," he went on, throwing me a sidelong glance. "And unless the Malum's visit was only intended to scare everyone, we can't shrink Faerie. Gregor can let them in and out, but they'll get trapped on the wrong side of the border if I realign the external wards while they're knocking on Caeludor's front door like salespeople."

I cringed away from the thought, and Batre's round, pink-tinged cheeks rapidly drained of colour.

"We nab the caenim in case Raella leaves," the High King went on. He gave a cursory glance to Morgoya. "I need you both to stay with Aura. The last time she was around these creatures, she was too busy drooling all over the gloriousness of my violence while I slaughtered them all to notice the one that nearly ripped her spinal cord out from behind her."

A northerly breeze brought a precipitous chill over us, and the cold instantly burrowed down into my flesh, burying itself beneath the layers of my coat.

"So you keep saying," I grumbled. Throwing my hands up in the air to conceal a shiver, I groaned. "What am I even doing out here this time, then?"

Lucais regarded me quizzically, the faintest of smiles playing across his full, pink lips. "You're the cheese," he said at last.

Morgoya finally turned away with an exasperated sound and joined Wrenlock by the unicorns.

"The cheese?" I repeated, glaring at him.

"Like the cheese you lay out for rodents and the beasts inside dark and wonky little places." He pursed his lips and hastened to hold up a finger in the air between us. "Before you get snippy with me again, I'll have you know that I think very fondly of cheese."

Dumbfounded, I stared at Batre, but the poor woman was unable to offer me anything but a sympathetic half-smile. I slid my carefully expressionless gaze back to Lucais, who smiled sweetly at me with all of his teeth.

"It is not surprising at all that you didn't have a girlfriend when I met you," I groused, dropping my eyes to my feet and rubbing my left brow bone to stave off the brewing headache.

"Oh, Auralie." The High King tutted at me like a scolding adult as we began to walk back to the copse of trees. "If I did have a girlfriend when we met, I would have left her immediately."

Even though I knew that he was absolutely serious, I could not refrain from biting.

"They would have sent me a thank you note," I sniped, coming to an abrupt stop.

The storm rumbled in the clouds above, and Batre wisely continued on without us. A crease had formed between my eyebrows, and I couldn't smooth it out before seeking clarity. We'd talked about shrinking Faerie, catching caenim, and visiting the lapsus—but only very briefly, and never with self-sacrifice as a key point of our strategy.

"You seriously brought me all the way out here as bait? For the caenim *and* the lapsus?"

Lucais made a conflicted sound in his throat, twisting his mouth as he considered how best to respond. "It is your scent they're trained on," he bargained at last. "And the lapsus is a gamble. Absolutely nothing might happen, or something very interesting might happen. It might help if you think of it from a productivity perspective. Two beasts, one soulmate?"

My mouth flattened into a hard line.

"Help me out here, bookworm. I'm desperate."

I arched a brow at him. "And what happens if I die?"

"I'll let you kiss me one more time before we get started just in case you do."

It was absurd and childish, but I couldn't get the retort out of my mouth. The sound of a loud slap yanked our attention over to our companions, standing a few feet away from us. Batre's eyes were widening by the second as she stared down at Morgoya's hand, laid flat against her stomach as if she'd just hit her with the back of it.

"I fucking *knew* it!" the High Lady hissed.

Batre bit down hard on a smile. Their feelings were clear—from the moment Batre had approached me at the House to enquire about our bond all the way through to when Morgoya had snubbed Wrenlock not once, but twice, in the palace. Even Lucais communicated his feelings well enough for me to feel confident in my understanding of them. At first, he'd accepted the way I felt about his best friend. Part of me was inclined to hold on to that even through recent times, when the High

King's opinion seemed to sway back to the other end of the scale. I didn't know that he felt jealous so much as excluded. But Wrenlock...

His chestnut eyes wandered across the sky—a little disbelievingly, to be honest—merely in an effort to avoid mine. A pang of guilt slid down the back of my throat. I really needed to talk to him later.

After I dealt with the antics of the High King as he spiralled into a fit of madness.

"You," I accused, swinging my gaze back to Lucais. Guilt for a lot of different things was piled up so high against my spine that I felt like I might start to choke if I didn't shift some of the blame onto someone else, and he was the best candidate.

His full lips twitched into a feline pout that had my heartbeat tripping over itself. "Me."

"You mean to tell me that you brought me all the way out here to play the part of smelly rat cheese so you can play catch and release with a bunch of flesh-eating monsters that are going to ravage the towns across the outskirts of your own kingdom?" I pointed towards the horizon for emphasis, and he nodded with mock solemnity. "You do this simply to force people into enough of a panic that they'll flee into the citadel. All so you can then move on to playing whack-a-mole with the wards and lapsuses around Faerie without anyone finding out that you might have *accidentally-on-purpose* sentenced an entire Court of faeries to a fate worse than death?"

Lucais's eyes twinkled as he mulled over my words, nodding vaguely. "Yes," he agreed with an exceptionally pleasant smile.

My hands balled into fists. "This is the stupidest and most selfish plan I have ever heard anyone concoct in my entire life," I declared, shaking my head with incredulity. Why I had thought he might attempt to vindicate himself from the very specific, very awful accusation was beyond me. "You are horrible for doing this—for expecting *me* to do this!" I crossed my arms, eyes crinkling at the corners. "You should feel terrible right now."

The High King rolled his eyes skyward and took a firm step towards me, the gold in his irises solidifying as they narrowed on me. "What exactly is it about me that gave you the impression that I'm a golden retriever boyfriend?" he enquired impatiently. "Please do let me know so I can take the necessary steps to correct the dreadful misapprehension you've apparently been under this whole time."

"You keep saving my life," I seethed, "and then complaining about it. Forgive me for being a little bit surprised that you're now willingly throwing me out into the middle of the Ruins to lure caenim and other miscellaneous beasts for yet another one of your harebrained schemes."

He held my glare unflinchingly. "I will never ask you to do something that you're not perfectly capable of doing."

"Oh, yeah, like fall in love with you?" I made to turn away, but he snatched my chin with one hand and used it to pull my face back to his.

Inches away, Lucais's breath settled over me like nitrous oxide. I was slightly taken aback to discover that, despite my mockery, his expression was the portrait of calm. He spoke very carefully and very slowly. "I double...dog...dare you."

For a long moment, I stared at him, breathing heavily. I knew we had an audience, but there was a part of my soul—sick with interference from the stars, and twisted almost irrevocably around his—that wanted to ask for that kiss. I knew he'd give it to me. I knew that pulling back from him and clearing my throat as if it would push the lustful haze from my head would be my one regret if something did go fatally wrong, but I did it anyway.

"If the two of you are quite finished with your extraordinarily long and unorthodox foreplay," Morgoya called, coming to meet us, "we're near the border of the Court of Earth and the Court of Darkness. A few miles ahead, Aura, you'll start to feel a shift in the atmosphere, even though we're technically on the other side of the wards. It gets rather cold and gloomy."

Nodding, I mouthed an apology at her once the High King had turned away from us. She shook her head at me, eyes flaring as if to say she was enjoying every second of it. But even I knew the tension between Lucais and me was dangerous. It was so thick it would eventually suffocate one of us or snap and decapitate the other. We didn't have much time before something had to give, and I was well aware that I would be the one giving.

I just didn't think it would be the thing that was expected of me.

Only a week or so into my time in Caeludor, and I was already getting comfortable. Reacquainting myself with my emotions, letting little human fantasies peek through the surface of the depths of my mind. Allowing myself to forget that I'd done things that were so much worse than anything the High Fae around me could claim. That was part of the problem. I felt so at home with Lucais and Wrenlock because, no matter what they did to me, I knew I could beat them in a challenge of wickedness if I admitted to my crimes.

Trailing behind the group, I took the opportunity of the quiet to reorient myself.

The Ruins spanned over a much larger space than I had originally thought because we began to head west, as if Elera had evanesced further out of Faerie's normal boundaries than I'd expected. While the dead ground didn't change much as we walked, stepping over jagged rocks and deep splits in the red clay dirt, the temperature did begin to drop, and the darkness swallowing up the horizon began to take a much more physical shape. What I had originally thought was nothing more than a symptom of nightfall colouring the sky turned out to be the shadows of the Court of Darkness—an opaque black fog to rival the one Lucais had placed around Caeludor in its density.

My mind immediately spiralled into comparisons as it tried to understand the Court of Darkness's blight. *An enchantment, perhaps, if the fog was anything like it was in the city. But is it enchanted to hide something? And if so, what?*

The dark, smoky clouds stuck to the boundary line almost rigidly, a wall spanning from the hellish ground beneath my feet towards the heavens high above me. The colour and texture matched what I'd witnessed on the Map of Faerie, though I didn't have the same bird's eye view from the Ruins. It stood, not quite like the wall of glass, but rather like an enormous, inky hedge maze crafted from shadows and nightmares.

In a trice, I was a child again, dwarfed by something sinister.

Once we had drawn near enough for our movements to disturb the shadows, I peeked over my shoulder at the Court of Earth. The dark wall split the two Courts apart neatly and followed the natural boundary lines. As far as my mortal eyes could see, Blythe's land was completely swallowed by the unrelenting mist. Gregor's Court, on the other hand, didn't look affected by its neighbour's ailment.

The Metal Mountains were visible in the distance, miniscule from where we stood at the cusp of Faerie—like the shape of a cargo ship on a horizon that was initially mistaken for dry land. In the south, I couldn't discern any major landmark features like The Watch as it was depicted on the Map, but the rest of the Court looked fairly normal. At least, in line with my expectations of it under normal circumstances. No tumbleweeds, no inky black lines poisoning the soil, and no rebel soldiers pointing at us.

There was nobody at all, actually.

I didn't see any townships or standalone buildings in the vicinity—only wildlife and natural scenery. Barely a few paces away from the shadows at the border, there was a flowery bush in bloom, rooted in healthy dirt beside a small pond. Toads jumped in and out of the water to a symphony of croaks and clicking noises.

Giving one last longing glance towards the Court of Earth, I turned and hastened to catch up with the High Fae. They were less enamoured with different parts of Faerie than I was and had already begun to march up towards the worst of the storm.

I guessed that it was mostly due to the fact that the Court of Earth were traitors to the crown, but even with that knowledge in the forefront of my mind, there was something beautiful about it. Like my world, but laced with magic. For the very first time, I was gazing upon Faerie with my eyes open—and not too distracted fighting through fog or trying to forget my own existence to properly notice it.

Keeping about an arm's length of distance between myself and the dark wall, I followed the High Fae in a straight line a few paces behind Wrenlock. Ahead of him, the High King was deep in a low-toned conversation with Morgoya, and Batre—High Mother bless her—lingered behind to remain near my side.

Only a step or two ahead of me, the rosy-cheeked woman offered me a kind, dimpled smile over her shoulder as we walked, the ends of her twin braids bouncing against her back with each of her long steps.

When she turned away, I glanced down at my feet, and that's when I noticed it.

The darkness.

Clouding around my feet like low-lying mist, the shadows from Blythe's Court had slithered out to greet me. I faltered a step, though the shadows presented no resistance, and the motion of my boots kicked up a flurry of darkness. Some of the shadows scattered for a split second, but they quickly dispersed in the air, and a new wave of them rolled over my ankles. I twisted to one side, then the other, and on both occasions found that they were pooling behind me.

I swallowed a tight lump in my throat, heart pounding wildly in my chest in its insistent but futile demand to be let out and freed. When I sidestepped, I pulled the darkness with me, like a magnetic force was tying us together. A cold sweat trickled down my spine, falling from the spot on the back of my neck where I felt the brief touch of a hand.

"Bat..." I tried to say her name, but my lungs were heavy with damp, useless air. Drawing in a ragged, wet gasp, I tried again. "Batre," I rasped.

She turned, and her face paled. It might have been the gloom, but I'd seen redness on her cheeks a moment prior. Her eyes grew round, head rearing back as if she was about to fire questions at me, but I was already shaking my head to convey that I had no fucking idea.

I stepped sideways again to demonstrate that it wasn't me drifting too close to the wall—it was the darkness coming out to me. The shadows flowed around my feet, following my every movement. When I continued on in a straight line, they were gently dispelled with each stride, like I was splashing through the tide on an evening walk along the shoreline.

"Aura..." Batre's voice was quietly alarmed. "Aura, are you okay?"

Hearing the question, all three of the High Fae walking ahead of us abruptly stopped and whirled around. Feeling embarrassment warm my skin beneath my heavy coat, I watched as Morgoya's eyebrows hit her hairline. Wrenlock opened his mouth in the shape of an *O*, and Lucais did a double-take. However, none of them met my eyes. All of them—even Batre—were fixated on something over my shoulder, positioned in my blind spot. I didn't want to look, but my head began to turn on its own volition to follow their line of sight.

Batre's hand flew up to stop me.

"Wait!" she cried, glancing at the High King. I gave him a beseeching look, my chest feeling like it was about to fall apart into a three-hundred-piece puzzle. "I think... I think you'd better hold still for a moment, don't you?"

My toes curled in my boots, but I did as she advised and held very still while the High King approached me with the caution normally reserved for a wild horse. Flaring my eyes, I sent a silent demand for him to tell me what he was staring at behind me. His gaze flicked to mine for a heartbeat, but it conveyed nothing more than uncertainty and apprehension. The shadows were still spilling out around my feet, though they reared back, drawing closer to my ankles and climbing up my calves towards my knees as he approached.

"What?" I implored when nobody said anything. "What is it?"

The High King waved over his shoulder for the others to approach before he dropped into a half-crouch, bracing his hands on his thighs as he cocked his head to the side like he was appreciating the curve of my ass. He was transfixed by *something*.

"Aura," Morgoya remarked softly. "You've got a shadow."

My brows knitted together. There was no sun. It was overcast and gloomy. None of them had a shadow.

"Not just any shadow," the High King murmured. He turned his head to the other side and let out a low, haunting whistle. "It looks like it's attached to her."

"What?" I exclaimed. It was redundant, and I knew that, but panic had taken over the control system in my brain, and hysteria was riding the clutch. "What's attached to me?"

"The shadow..."

I saw him reach a hand out, felt him coast it down along my back. The motion made me stiffen, every muscle in my body straining to pull taut. A flicker of electricity sparked out across the muscles in my shoulders and lower back at his near touch, but there was something else in there, too. Something dimming it.

"Hmm," he murmured. "That's rather fascinating indeed. It doesn't separate from her body, but my hand slips straight through it."

"But that is Aura," Wrenlock contended. He drew a swirly line in the air with his pointer finger, one eye squeezed shut as he scrutinised me. "Look at it. The same height, the same curves of her figure, the same posture—even down to the curls in her hair."

"It's hanging off her." Batre's voice was a ghostly undertone. "Like—"

"A shadow," Morgoya finished, squaring her shoulders. "By the Elements, she looks like Blythe."

The High King straightened. "Indeed."

I opened my mouth to ask them how in the hell I could possibly look like Blythe, but as soon as I did, my teeth started to chatter violently. The trembles swept all the way down to my fingertips, and suddenly, all of my energy was sucked into the endeavour of maintaining self-possession. My teeth and the hinges of my jaw ached with the effort. I felt hysteria brewing a pot of uncontrollable sobs at the bottom of my throat, sprinkling in a dash of blood-curdling screams and a pinch of sudden onset nyctophobia.

"Wasn't this your theory?" Wrenlock questioned, putting a hand on the High King's shoulder. "You said that you believed Aura to be the heir to the Court of Darkness, did you not?"

"I did," Lucais admitted, stroking the light sprinkling of stubble on his chin with one hand. At long last, he looked at me properly—held me with his eyes. The trembles subsided, but barely. "I tasted dark magic in your blood, Aura. I stand by that theory, and I'm honestly inclined to take this as confirmation." Arching his brows, he pointed to my feet. "This is the third time the darkness has reacted to you in strange ways, and right now, it's treating you like a familiar."

"The third time?" somebody asked. I thought it was Batre, but I was too deep inside my consternation vortex to hear it properly, and I didn't dare break away from Lucais's eyes lest it swallow me completely.

He nodded, gaze still locked with mine as he lifted a fist and raised one finger. "The dark magic in her blood"—a second finger—"the shadows on the Map of Faerie"—a third—"and now this."

"Are you sug-suggesting that my father lied to m-my mother?" I stammered. *God, it's hard to hold still. Pull yourself together.* "Because sh-she was sure he was from the Court of Li-Light."

The High King held his palm up to me, exchanging the steady presence of his gaze for his hand so he could break eye contact and watch the shadows at my back while he approached me. He treated the darkness like a snake, poised ready to strike, and I trembled so violently I thought I'd be sick. Still, I accepted the gesture gratefully. I focussed on his palm, tracing the lines on his skin, counting the silver rings on his fingers. When Lucais was close enough to touch me, he gave me that hand.

"Here's the thing about faeries, bookworm," he drawled, threading his fingers through mine. A shot of warmth trickled over me, starting from where our knuckles touched and palms rested against each other. "We can get away with murder if we say the right things. He may have told your mother he was from the Court of Light, but that doesn't mean he was born there. Maybe he travelled into your world through the Court of Light's portal."

"But the ma-magic—"

"Light manipulates the darkness, darkness manipulates the light." His warmth reached my shoulder blades, and they slumped forward ever so slightly. The tightness in my chest relinquished an inch. "Rumour has it there were once just three Courts in Faerie, back in the very beginning of time. The dark and light faeries were the first, the wind and fire faeries were the second, and the earth and water faeries the third. People who believe this lean heavily into the idea that those elements cannot exist without each other, which is partly true, but there's no substantial evidence to back up the claim. Even so, if he was clever—and I'd wager he is, having met his daughter—he could have pulled a few parlour tricks out of his sleeve to make it look like he was using the light. An untrained eye most likely wouldn't be able to tell the difference."

Great. As if I need another reason to hate him. I shuddered as Lucais's warmth brought full motion and feeling back to my legs. He was undoing the fear paralysis meticulously, using both his words and his magic to achieve a seamless result.

"Is he in there right now?"

The High King's gaze strayed to the shadow maze contemplatively. "Maybe. He could be anywhere in Faerie, but if he lived in the Court of Darkness, he'd be there now. I know all of the dark faeries who were away from home when the wards were sealed shut, and none of them fit the description of your biological father."

"Then let's leave him," I muttered, letting go of Lucais's hand. I wrapped my arms tightly around my shoulders and ducked my head to warm my nose in the crook of one elbow. "I've already been damaged and disappointed by one father. I really don't need to go through that again with a new one."

Lucais's expression softened. He started to shrug, but his High Lady interrupted him.

"It's inconceivable," she averred. "It can't be, can it? There's never been a human heir to any of the Courts."

"There's never been a human heir to the throne, either," Batre offered neutrally.

"That's true," Lucais mused. "She's already broken many of our standards—the High King's soulmate, a human with no prior history of wielding magic doing it well enough to kill a Banshee—but so have I, and she was designed to be my equal."

"You said the whole Banshee thing was light magic," I reminded him. "So how can I have used light magic and still be the heir to the Court of Darkness? You said yourself that you'd have to be clever to manipulate it like that, and I have no idea what I'm doing."

"Okay," he allowed. "That's fair. But how else do you explain this? If you were a light faerie, the shadows would shy away from you, not hitch a ride on your back."

There was silence for long moments.

Finally, Morgoya broke it. "I never would have guessed that Aura would be your soulmate, but I don't doubt it now. I'm just not convinced that she's Blythe's heir because—I mean—" She huffed, looking at me with a desperate gleam in her eye. The dark-haired beauty was reaching for something—all of us were, and we were becoming increasingly frustrated when we didn't grasp onto anything with enough substance to stick. "How old were you when Blythe disappeared?"

"Uh..." I pulled a face at Lucais. "What, like, fourteen?"

He grimaced. "Yeah."

Age gap.

Shut up.

"See?" Morgoya persisted. "I just cannot accept the idea that a human girl who never even knew she had magic was that powerful at the age of fourteen. No offence, Aura."

"None taken."

"But that's assuming that Blythe did disappear seven years ago," Wrenlock added. "What if it was later than that?"

"My point would still stand," Morgoya replied, shaking her head. "A teenage human girl who doesn't even know she has a claim to magic being strong enough to force out an existing High Lady who is four hundred years her senior? It just doesn't seem like the right explanation." She scrutinised me, her red-painted mouth twisting. "Does it?"

"Yeah, if we were in a book," I muttered. Lucais snorted obnoxiously, and I pulled a face at him before turning back to the High Lady. Sighing, I pinched my brows together. "When was the Oracle's prophecy?"

"Five, maybe six months ago?"

My spine relaxed, and I shook my head dejectedly. *That was not related, then.*

Lucais waved both hands like he could clear the clouds of confusion away. "Look. I am sorry we don't have anything more concrete to go on yet, but you didn't see the way the shadows on the Map reacted to her presence. They've been clouding Blythe's Court for so many years, resistant to even my light, and yet one touch from Aura's hand made them scatter into the aether. Unless she put them there herself and then forgot about them, what other explanation could there be?"

Everyone stared into the void lingering between us.

"Because I'm human?" I suggested dubiously. It was all I had to offer to the conversation. I switched my gaze to Wrenlock's calm, handsome face. "Because when you reject magic, magic starts to reject you, right?"

The tall, dark man smiled at me, but it didn't reach those beautiful brown eyes.

With his entire hand, Lucais gestured regally to the shadows still wafting around my feet. "Then explain that," he said with a sigh.

I grunted, annoyed, and let my head fall back. When I opened my eyes, the storm was still swirling above us, reminding me of our original purpose in coming to the Ruins and the Court of Darkness. Lucais must have been on the same train of thought because he instructed us to bench the topic for another day in a less creepy location, and then led the group onwards.

A cold chill seeped through to the bone as the shadows danced around my feet. I couldn't feel the shadow behind me, but I could see darkness collecting at my back in my peripheral vision. I considered asking Lucais or Morgoya to send it packing with a blast of their light magic, but the closer we got to the lapsus, the less the shadows bothered me. They didn't feel foreboding or dangerous anymore. I had a weird sense of the slate being wiped clean with back and forth strokes that matched the pace of my footsteps as our group drew closer to the storm.

Lightning flashed above us, and rumbles of thunder broke out into a brawl on top of our heads, steadily increasing in volume. Nobody said anything, and I wasn't quite sure what else to look for aside from signs of environmental disruptions, so it took me by surprise when a thread of the shadows in the Court reached out to greet me like a hand.

The sound of my sharp intake of breath was swallowed by a boom of thunder.

The shadow hand poked me with a long, jagged finger. It wasn't like the mindless dark swirling around my feet; it presented itself to me with purpose and intent at eye level. I froze, my muscles tensing and joints locking into place as I waited for a sensation to follow. A tickle or a searing pain. Something.

I felt nothing, and it poked me again.

What the fuck.

A shiver zigzagged down my body as a second hand reached out to join. And then a third. And a fourth.

This is getting ridiculous.

"Hello," I hissed, skirting the outstretched hands to continue following my friends. "Now, go away."

The damn things were undeterred. Shrugging off their attempts to prod me with shadowy fingers and dodging as new upper limbs formed out of the darkness ultimately gained me nothing—they wouldn't let me through.

They encircled me, backing me up against the border of the Court of Darkness.

It was at that moment I realised how dangerous something could be even when it couldn't be tangibly felt. I tried to swipe the hands away. My flesh and bones fell straight through the wrists made from shadows, but they took a moment to reform. Wildly, I started swinging at them, flapping my arms around in disjointed movements as I attempted to bat away the hands that extended towards me long enough to slip out of their reach.

It was like mopping up a spill in the ocean.

I made a noise in the back of my throat, and saw Lucais turn back for me right before the unholy mother of all shadow hands rose up from the dark maze like a wave, rolling straight towards my face. Without thinking, I jumped backwards—

And fell straight into the darkness at my back.

A guttural scream ripped from my lungs as the shadows sank their teeth into me.

In a torrent of wind, I was ripped in half and stitched back together in the dark.

Wrenlock had been right. It fit me perfectly. Every curve along my body and every strand of my hair was swiftly and seamlessly engulfed in darkness, but it was like falling into a pool of jelly. I couldn't swim away. I couldn't run and hide. The more I struggled, the more disturbed the shadows became, the more it hurt, the louder I shrieked, and the deeper into their grasp I fell.

I held my breath to starve my lungs of the fuel they needed to scream, and met the High King's shell-shocked gaze with my own.

A gale raged around me, whipping at my clothes, but the shadows were static. Pain built and built with the momentum of boulders rolling down a hill inside my chest, but I bit down on it, clamping my teeth together to foil the screams.

With one look, I could see the panic in the High King's eyes as he assessed the situation—that he couldn't tell where my body ended and the shadows began as the Court of Darkness devoured me.

Lucais lifted a hand, his golden eyes blazing with power, and shot a steady stream of searching light towards the shadows. But the darkness anticipated his move and yanked me backwards, forcing me deeper into the abyss. Sparks flew as the shadows rose up to form a shield, blocking his light from reaching me. The High King's power hit the darkness like molten lava crashing down the side of a volcano during an eruption, and the shadows only pulled me tighter into their ranks.

A veil of black and white fell between us, ripping colour from my vision. Straining my eyes before they could adjust, I searched for any of the High Fae standing along the cusp of the Ruins. Relief crashed into me when I found them again, but it was a momentary glimpse through a murky film—and only long enough to see the end.

I smelled them coming.

The shadows tightened their grip on me, pinching another shout of pain out of my mouth that quickly snowballed into a cry of warning as an enormous caenim flew past me from the clouds of darkness at my back. The beast lunged out of the gaping hole the shadows had made to hold me as their prisoner of the dark, and it went straight for the High King of Faerie.

Twenty-Nine

Get It Off Me

An entire horde of caenim flew out of the abyss behind me.

My inner child had been right to fear the wall of shadows because it held a terrifying, hidden reality inside. The Court of Darkness was possessed by a true maze—shadows that carved a labyrinth of walkways throughout the land, reducing the light to almost nothing and disorienting anyone trapped inside it.

A sob tore through my chest as I watched the caenim disappearing through the veil of shadow along the border of Blythe's Court. Tumbling out of the darkness like nightmares coming to life, they landed on the unforgiving red dirt of the Ruins with their teeth, tongues, and claws poised to slash my friends to ribbons—my friends, who were still reeling from watching me being pulled inside the dark maze by the smoky clouds.

It was like an old movie playing on a screen bigger than my mortal eyes could conceive—a black-and-white silent film with special effects that were difficult to follow through the grainy quality of the imagery.

There were hundreds of caenim. Maybe thousands.

The shadows were teeming with them. Each time a new beast leapt past me, the magic on the other side of the darkness splintered, tugged in new directions until all I could see was a white-hot fireworks display of power shooting out across the Ruins.

Another caenim leapt out of the shadows, and Batre screamed. Loud enough to shatter the sound barrier between us. Loud enough to bring everything back to full speed. Loud enough to distort the darkness for a moment that lasted only as long as was required for me to see the caenim with its ghoulish, iron-tipped claws around Morgoya's throat. The darkness rallied and swarmed between us once more.

No!

I shrieked with enough power to rip my head free from the confines of the shadow's body mould, violently thrashing from side to side as I put everything inside me into yanking my arms and legs out of its grip.

The figments of darkness hadn't felt like anything too familiar when they initially touched me, but the longer I stayed inside their cocoon, the more reminiscent of the portal they felt. I was being plied with tacky and dirty magic until I couldn't take it anymore, stuffed full of it like a roasted chicken.

It was everywhere—a violation of my mind, body, and soul. My heart was beating violently as if the effort would bring me any closer to Morgoya and Lucais, but my mind was being ripped in half, the continued assault of the darkness serving to distract me from what was occurring in the Ruins. Though I tried to hold onto that devastating connection, it soon slipped from my grasp, the clamour of battle following suit, and then I was alone with the sound of my lungs straining once more.

The dark had teeth and knew how to bite.

With every snap of a shadow against my flesh, I was overcome with a sensation of wrongness flooding my veins. It was underneath my skin and fingernails, between the curls whipping around my face, coating the raised hairs on my arms and the back of my neck, inside every last one of my pores, filling the wrinkles of my skin and fingerprints, and between my toes. The filthy, unnatural darkness was the moisture on my eyes, the breath in my lungs, the clenching and unclenching of my heart, and the poisoned fluid it was pumping through me.

It was me, and I was it, and there was no escape.

There never had been, and there never would be.

Reunited or split apart—

The pitch of my scream, rising through the chaos like a ribbon stolen by a hurricane, hit such a new height that I didn't recognise it anymore. The shrill, keening sound shot out of me like the wailing noise from a stovetop kettle as I threw my head back, escalating with every slice of darkness into my skin, leaving a trail of scalding tingles down the column of my throat.

Wretched and cross, I tried to fight it off because desperately—so, so desperately—I wanted to win. But it was futile, and part of me knew that. Had *always* known that. I couldn't ward off the darkness when all I had to offer up in its place was more darkness.

Nevertheless, I still felt like I might die from overexposure as nausea gurgled in my stomach, and everything that was wrong in the world filled me to bursting point.

Flashes of light danced across my vision through the other side of the maze, searing the veil like a hot poker dragging its tip down a curtain. Sparks ricocheted for miles—an explosion that could have been an atomic bomb as easily as it could have been Lucais.

It was powerful enough to rival Batre's scream, ferociously tearing down the sound barrier until bits and pieces of the battle came flooding through to my ears, but I couldn't see or hear Morgoya. The only sounds were of the caenim—grunts, growls, and woeful moans, like an orgy of death and destruction—as they continued to whoosh past me and wage an attack on my closest friends.

Feeling dizzy and confused, I started to think about the storm again. It had either gone quiet, or the dark cloud covering me was so thick that it prevented any signs of it from peeking through. It was too hard for me to tell whether the flashes of light and vibrations on the ground beneath my feet were the storm or the High King lashing out at the universe from the Ruins, but if I had to place a bet with my life as the collateral, I'd be betting it on Lucais.

I wondered what he was doing and what he was thinking, but our mental connection had been jammed by the veil between us. It was still there, and I could pick it up like a receiver in my mental hand, but there was no dial tone because all of the phone lines were down. I called him, but I knew he couldn't hear me. I knew it because he didn't answer, and yet I could still feel him like a hand around my wrist—like he was also holding the receiver in his mind even though silence was the only connection stretching through the line.

Using that feeling to spur myself on, I wrestled with the shadows, pushing forwards only to spring back like I was fighting with an elastic band. When I managed to get one of my arms free, it was only ever for a nanosecond before the shadows swallowed me up again.

Everything ached.

Cramps seized my muscles and invisible cuts decorated my skin like tattoos that couldn't be seen—only felt.

Frustration shot out of my mouth in a noise that started as a yell but quickly escalated into another howl that dragged itself out of my throat like a morning star.

What do you want? What do you want from me?

My mental cry was full of anguish, and the shadows in the Court of Darkness rejoiced. Like a key unlocking a door, the answers to my questions came flooding in so hard and fast that I thought my head might explode. They rammed into me, one after the other, relentlessly battering me until I lost the strength to hold my own head up, and I had to rely on the presence of my copycat shadow to do it for me.

Tears streaming down my face, I hung limply in the air, the darkness cradling me like a martyr while it drained the last ounces of self-possession from my bones. Even then, my body struggled with the transition, rejecting the caress of darkness the same way I'd recoil from a burning hot oven tray.

My reflexes were on overdrive, desperately trying to shake me free from the hideous touches slicing into my back, tickling my spine with knife-sharp claws, and pulling at my fingernails and hair. I had no control over it—

Try harder try harder try harder try harder try harder try harder—

My throat was shredded raw by my screams as I flailed, kicking my feet and turning my head so hard I thought my neck might break.

Break break break break break break break—

Something hot and wet dripped out of my nose, pooling on the plump curve of my upper lip before tracing the outline of my mouth and spilling down my chin. At first, I thought it was from tears, but then I tasted the wicked metallic tang infiltrating my mouth as the other nostril began to bleed, too.

Let me go, I begged. *Please, let me go.*

Flashes of blood, weaponry, and warfare filled my mind. Each vision came at me like a monster out of my closet, lunging as soon as I opened the door, or a bullet train I couldn't dodge. Every time I flinched away, the shadows spun me around, and another horror rushed out of the maze to take its place.

My head lolled back, the force of each pull and tug enough to dislodge it from the rest of my body. In truth, I wasn't sure why it hadn't. Unless—

See.

Images that had to have been from the Gift War tore me to shreds.

Visions of burning buildings, decimated cities and towns, empty playgrounds with merry-go-rounds covered in scorch marks that had melted half of the structures into the ground, black stillwater inside houses with their roofs ripped clean away, and fields of bodies in shining armour coated with blood and gore.

As I peered closer with my mind's eye, my blood turned ice-cold in my veins because—

Men. Women. Children. Bloodied, bruised, and broken bodies. Piles of them clad in bloodstained clothes covered the fields around the decaying Forest. Smoke burned, billowing up from a space hidden deep inside, followed by the gradual collapse of trees as they lost their fight and crashed onto the floor.

Wet with blood and coated in dirt, the pieces of the lifeless faeries who had bled out onto the ground lay between the burial piles—hearts, lungs, intestines. Dead crows lay scattered between the corpses, lured in by the rotting organs of the fallen before something had killed them, too. Some were mid-feast on a soldier's open wound. One had its beak stuck inside a rib cage, their smooth, feathered neck lax and their wings splayed out to the sides. Visions of a great stone wall replaced the field, bodies slung over the battlement as if the men and women had been on watch when it struck them. Weapons were stacked neatly against walls, and there wasn't a single trace of blood or gore to be found. Those people hadn't seen it coming.

A town at the base of a volcano, melted by the lava that had been stopped by something only halfway through burning up the last remnants of its victims clothing and shoes before it cooled and set.

A lake with faeries face-down, floating in the water—

"STOP IT!" I screeched. "*Stop* it! *Stop* it! *Stop* it!"

Uncontrollable sobs took over, and I was no longer able to plead with the shadows. Saliva dripped out of the corners of my mouth as I wailed, mixing with the blood that had started to dry on my chin, and a sickly-sweet burn gathered in my chest—the kind of feeling that convinced me I was about to die and be glad of it.

Because the visions weren't of a battlefield from the Gift War. The world I had been shown wasn't from the past. It was in the future—a war that hadn't started yet.

Mercifully, the darkness pulled back the most confronting aspects of its mental beating, but only so it could show me the worst. The feeling overcame me first—the precursory sense of danger that hollowed out new depths to the pit in my stomach before fleeing to hide from whatever was coming next—

And then I saw it.

But it wasn't the dark.

It killed off the darkness, too.

It killed off...*everything.*

Try harder try harder try harder—

"No! No, I won't!" I shouted hysterically. I squeezed my eyes shut as tightly as I could, desperate to force spots and lines onto the backs of my eyelids. My soul-deep craving for a flicker of light and colour was overwhelming. I needed to see something—anything. "I won't! Get off me! Get off me!" I heaved in an enormously deep breath, preparing for spontaneous combustion if that's what it would take to end the torment. "*Get it off me!*"

Something firm wrapped around my ankles like large, rough hands, but they lacked the warmth and softness of a human being or a faerie, and a scream coiled in my throat. It ripped out of my chest when the placebo hands tightened their grip and pulled me, hard and fast, like I'd imagined the monsters beneath my bed would do if I let my foot dangle over the side as a child. It happened so quickly that it didn't give me or the shadows in Blythe's Court a fighting chance.

Cold air rushed down my throat completely out of order, leaving me gasping for breath when I fell out of the shadow prison and onto the solid ground with a thud.

Immediately, I rolled onto my side so I could heave everything up and out of my stomach.

Liquid flooded my throat, pouring out of my mouth, thin and watery like cordial but with a distinctly rotten and sickly taste. I opened my eyes to find black water pooling on the red dirt, which was so dry and hard that it initially resisted the presence of moisture. Pathetically, I wailed again, flipping onto my back so fast that my head slammed into a rock I didn't see behind me. My eyes slammed shut, and I saw stars murdering each other—

"Get off me!" I yelled. Through the roaring in my head, I could hear my voice becoming weaker and rougher as I wore my voice box down to gravel and dust. "Get it off me! Stop it! Let me go! Please, please, God, let me go..."

I felt hands on my face. Soft hands, small fingers. Warmth. "Aura."

My body jerked away from the touch—a reflex reaction, defending itself. "It's not me," I cried, my voice shattering on the final word. "They don't want me! It's not me. It's not me..."

"Aura!" A hand touched my eyelids, soft fingers tipped with something hard and pointy.

Morgoya.

My eyes cracked open, stinging and hindered by tears. Mouth watering and throat tight, I pressed a hand to my heart and tried to regulate something—my breathing, my heartbeat, my emotions. Anything.

"I..." The sound of my voice was beyond croaky. It was barely there, barely recognisable.

"Shh," the blurry-faced High Lady crooned. I recoiled, highly suspicious. "It's okay. You're with us. You're out."

I noticed that she didn't tell me I was safe.

Thirty

Wrathful Sorrow

I stared up at the Court of Darkness in a fit of silent rage.

Hatred filled my lungs with every breath. I was so angry with it for being incorporeal. For not being something I could punch or hit with things.

Feverish gasps filled my lungs with the smell of dusty red clay and the moisture gathering in the atmosphere from the electrical storm raging on above me. The dark maze had gone back to the way it was when we first arrived, the wisps of shadow sticking to the boundary line of the Court, a solid wall swaying only gently in the light, frosty breeze. I wanted to kill the shadows. I wanted to chase them and hold them down while I beat the living fuck out of them for what they'd shown me, for what they'd put me through, for even *dragging* me in there in the first place—

Before I knew what I was doing, I released an almighty scream at the Court of Darkness, pouring my rage out into the space between us.

When my lungs ran out of air, the sound turned into a quiet sob that wracked my chest with sharp, tight flashes of pain as my body called out for oxygen again. I hauled a gasp of air into my mouth and swallowed it down painfully, my shoulders rocking with each silent cry of wrathful sorrow. I let it run its course, the shadows watching me from afar like they would deny everything and take their sins to their graves, and then I turned my back on them.

Blythe and the Court of Darkness can burn in hell.

Lucais and Wrenlock were executing caenim. Their movements were less urgent and more routine as they combed through the Ruins a mile or so away from us.

Chunks of black and grey littered the ground—a graveyard of dead beasts. There were so many carcasses heaped on top of one another in piles, reminding me of the grisly visions I'd been forced to watch of the world dying against my will.

The smell was putrid, but faint, dwindling as life was violently wrested out of the very last of their kin. I couldn't count how many were left, let alone how many had been killed, but my estimate was high.

I felt a pinch in my stomach when I thought of Lucais being forced into committing so much violence on the same day. He must have been exhausted.

"Are you hurt?"

Gazing up into the High Lady's malachite-splattered face, I tried to search for my voice to reply, but it had shredded my throat, and I couldn't get the words out. I simply shook my head at her instead.

Morgoya tucked a strand of her dark hair behind one ear, dripping with fresh red blood from where her earlobe had been sliced in half. There was a deep cut across the side of her neck that extended down to her collarbone. It was already clotting, but dark bruises had formed on her ghostly white skin across her throat and on her temple. Indentations like human bite marks were present as if the creature had bitten her with the teeth in its eyes. She was missing an earring; her hair was matted to the top of her head and the sides of her face with dirt and gore.

Noticing the panic flaring in my eyes, she shrugged delicately—and then winced as if the movement hurt her.

"Close call," she told me softly. "Batre pulled it off me before it could do any real damage. I'll see a healer, and they'll put me back to rights."

In a daze, I looked around for Batre and found that she was lying on her side near me. She was awake, alert, and appeared to be unharmed, but visibly exhausted.

Panting wildly, her chest heaved, her cleavage nearly spilling out of her dress with each breath. While the High Lady had worn a set of fighting leathers, her girlfriend hadn't changed out of her usual green velvet dress, complete with a petticoat beneath her skirt and a waist trainer around her bodice. Accentuating her large, round curves, it matched both the colour of Morgoya's eyes and the ribbons in the long twin braids that Batre wore in her hair. But it was even more ill-fitted for battling caenim than my simple loose pants, shirt, and overcoat.

"Are you alright?" I mouthed to her. My lips felt dry and cracked, my tongue and the roof of my mouth like cotton.

She nodded. Dirt was smeared all across her face. "You?" she mouthed back.

I hesitated. If Batre was okay after fighting the caenim head-on and rescuing the love of her life before a missing earlobe became a missing head, then it didn't seem fair for me to be anything other than fine myself. Except that I wasn't okay. I wasn't even close to being okay. After what I had just been through, I didn't think I'd ever truly be okay again.

All going well, I'd die long before the world was brought to its knees and executed by the end of everything, but I didn't know how I could be expected to survive the sight of it. The *knowledge*. The *blame*.

A sharp twinge in my back caused me to whimper as I struggled to right myself and sit up. Morgoya reached out to help me, her thin arms possessing a considerable amount of strength as she supported my spine—which felt like it had been turned to jelly.

Tears sprang to my eyes again, blotting out my vision as I held each of my arms in front of me and pushed back my sleeves to examine my skin for cuts and bite marks left by the sinister forces inside the maze.

"What are you looking at?" Morgoya murmured.

My mouth watered, filled with a sour taste, and my head swam as I tried to choke the words up. It felt like someone had fixed a lasso around my lungs, and even the slightest effort to bring in and dispel fresh air became a mammoth task with variable success rates. The burn in my throat was horrific.

"Proof," I said, though I wasn't sure I'd managed to actually utter a single sound.

Scrubbing the tears away from my eyes with my hands, I glimpsed my clear, pale skin before my arms dropped back to my sides, and my gaze landed on the vines wrapped around my ankles. Before I could react, Morgoya stroked a soothing hand down my back.

"It's okay," she whispered. "Batre pulled you out."

Batre was the one who yanked me out of the maze?

Grunting, she pushed herself up into a sitting position as well, and I turned in time to catch her curl one hand into a fist. In synchrony, the vines unfurled from my ankles before withdrawing into Batre's sleeves.

"How the fuck did you do that?" I asked, not even caring how rude it sounded. I hadn't meant to lose my manners, but they were snowed in under the shock on my face. The feeling sizzled beneath my skin, sick and uneasy, because frankly—

How in the fuck had she done that?

"I'm from the Court of Earth," she admitted in a low voice. Her smile was flat. "I was born there. Most of my family still lives there, actually. I'm one of fifteen children who were born into a long-standing bloodline of earth faeries." When my jaw fell open with an audible click, she shrugged. "My parents are soulmates, and they're very old. Truthfully, most earth faeries are quite old." Brushing dust from her palms, she grunted softly, and I couldn't discern the meaning behind her inflection when she added, "They're an *old, proud* nation."

I blinked in stupefaction, but with a main city called *Immorta*, I supposed it wasn't surprising.

"I don't..." I trailed off, eyes straying to where Lucais and Wrenlock were visible in the distance.

They were disposing of the caenim executioner-style; the latter held the beasts up while the former swiped his sword in a sideways motion that made it look very much like he was slitting their throats. I had the momentary thought that they had managed to maim all of their attackers during the fight, and since it had calmed down, they were going back and ensuring that all of them were actually dead.

I still felt Lucais's mental hand around mine, the dial tone beeping quietly again on the phone line between us, waiting for someone to punch in the right numbers.

"You live in the Court of Light."

"I will live wherever Morgoya lives," Batre replied simply, and then she smiled in earnest. "You don't have to live in your own Court. Many High Fae travel, work, and live in different Courts. It's just not as common as it is in Caeludor, for example."

"Right." My head was throbbing, the pulse in my brain enough to drive a psychiatrist insane. "I didn't know that." I cleared my throat, meeting her eyes despite the raw, skull-penetrating ache that was begging me to close my eyelids and allow them to coax me into an eternal sleep. Or as close to it as I could reasonably get. "Thank you for saving my life."

Batre's long, thin lashes fluttered. "I would do it again and again, Aura. I'm just glad that I *could* pull you out. Lucais was trying everything." She looked over to the High King and his Hand. "I almost thought he would end up tearing into the dark like it was a real, living thing with his bare hands. He rained light down on the shadows like bullets from a machine gun and sent waves of it crashing into the wall. He even sent something like a sky-dragon at it. It was made of light and breathing light like fire. I've never seen anything quite like it before, but the shadows predicted every move he made and deflected as if it were light fighting light. It was so..."

"Strange," Morgoya finished for her, drawing my attention back to her face. The wound on her ear had clotted, but she'd definitely need to see a healer and take a long, hot bath to clear off the caenim gunk that had coated her from head to toe. "It's more than being two sides of the same coin. That wall is totally resistant to light. It played with the sky-dragon like it was a puppy."

I swallowed. "Which means I'm not a light faerie. Which means that my father definitely isn't a light faerie, either."

The High Lady studied me, her catlike eyes narrowing, causing a delicate crease to form on her brow. The movement cracked a line through some of the dried beast blood on her face, and a strand of her dark hair sprang free from where it had been plastered onto her temple. "I suppose," she began slowly, "you are correct."

I held her gaze, brimming with questions.

"I never did believe him when he told me you used light magic to kill that Banshee."

A miserable laugh drifted up through my chest, popping like a bubble at the base of my throat. "I never did believe him when he told me I killed it."

In a whir of black and gold, the High King appeared before me, kneeling on the ground. His hair was dishevelled, splattered with green and black blood, and his face was covered with dirt, soot, and a look of exhaustion. The colour in his eyes had dimmed to a barely noticeable yellow, like the sun through a thin sheet of cloud.

"Bookworm—"

Lucais didn't get to finish his sentence because, a second later, Wrenlock appeared in a furious gust of air a few steps away, and then he lunged at the High King. He tackled him to the ground, and I barely had the time to pull my legs back so they didn't get caught up in their tussle. Wrenlock pinned Lucais beneath him, and the High King stared up at him with an expression of confusion and disgust reshaping his features moments before the Hand punched the look off his face.

"What the fuck?" Wrenlock shouted, gripping him by the collar of his tattered and bloodstained shirt. "You save her! You *always* save her!"

The High King shoved Wrenlock onto the ground with a grunt of revulsion and sat up, wiping saliva and blood from where it had dripped down from his nose and mouth onto his chin. He didn't even spare his friend a glance before he looked directly at me, resting his elbows on his knees, feet flat on the ground, breathing heavily.

Look. The fucking bastard was cornered by a hundred caenim from all different angles, he informed me through our mental bond.

I stifled a sigh of relief that it was well and truly still intact.

They'd only just finished pouring out of the shadows. At least a dozen were at his throat, many more at his back... I was having flashbacks to you in that field, honestly. I figured that I'd probably regret it if I let him die, and even if I didn't regret it on account of myself, then you were going to make me regret it if I pulled you out of there and you found your lover boy with his heart cut out on the ground behind me.

I rolled my eyes at him to conceal the way I gagged at the thought of Wrenlock—of any of them—being one of the bodies with missing organs on the ground.

I took a single eye off you for a split second, he went on, *and blasted the damned things back to the pit of evil they'd crawled out of before they did as much to him. But I had a hand on you at all times, and if I'd lost that, I would have gone in after you. They couldn't possibly fight me off forever, little beast. I would have ripped them apart and followed you inside their remains.* He held my stare, weighing my reaction heavily. *Nothing would have kept me out.*

Swallowing the lump in my throat, I nodded because I knew he was telling the truth. I'd felt the phantom of his hand on me at all times while I was inside of the maze. I'd leaned on it for all of its strength as I'd tried to fight my way back out. Between the two of us, I had no doubt we would have eventually met each other somewhere inside of the dark.

I glanced at Wrenlock, who was crouched down and glaring at us like he hoped I was shouting profanities at the High King through our bond, but he didn't believe that I was. "It's okay," I told him. His expression tightened. "I'm okay."

I wasn't, but it was not because of Lucais.

Wrenlock turned his head away to release an almighty breath and rose to stand. Gesturing to the necropolis, he said, "The fuck are we going to do with all of this?"

Morgoya patted my shoulder gently before doing the same thing. "Well," she said with a grunt, "I think maybe a fire..."

I heard you shouting, the High King whispered into my mind while our three companions debated the best course of action for cleaning up the disaster we'd created. I was surprised they were even considering tidying it up, given the mess was inside a place they'd aptly named the Ruins. *What did you mean when you said it's not you?*

A flash of death, destruction, and devastation assaulted my mind. I dropped my eyes to my hands, folded in my lap, and showed it to him to the best of my abilities. To my surprise, the pictures were murky and vague, like memories of a dream, though I'd only recently had the very real experience firsthand.

I don't think they want me to rule them. The Court of Darkness isn't coming back from this. They want to be destroyed. They want to find the thing more permanent than the dark, more final than death. Nothingness. The end of creation. I think they want me to let them out. I don't think they want me to save them.

But they do want *you.*

Yes.

Then they're not going to stop until they take you from me. Regardless of whether they mean for you to save them or destroy them, the call of power from one of the Elements and its Court is impossible to resist.

I won't answer it, I insisted. *I have no business there. I never want to go back again.*

Wrenlock theorised that the lapsus was a symptom of a much bigger problem, and I knew without a doubt that he was right. The lapsus was a symptom of the world ending. Faerie was dying, and the malediction started in the heart of Blythe's Court.

The High King climbed to his feet and walked over to me, helping me rise with his hands underneath my arms. He kept one hand there while he slipped the other behind my knees, lifting me into his arms and holding me tightly against his chest. Without a backwards glance at our friends and the fires they were trying to start, Lucais began to carry me to where the unicorns were waiting for us near the copse of trees with flaky bark.

Elera trotted over to us as soon as she noticed our approach, and I didn't have the energy to shrug her off when she began to use her large, hot tongue to clean up the blood, sweat, and dirt on my face. As thoroughly disgusting as it was for me, I knew it was a gesture of kindness from her.

We'll see, bookworm. The High King's grave reply was significantly delayed. *We'll see.*

Thirty-One

Tommy

The Malum had retreated from the city's wards by the time we returned and the High King tucked me into bed, which I had to think was an incredibly creepy coincidence. It was a relief for both the High King and the people of Caeludor, though, because it meant the faelight would be back up and running in the city automatically, and Lucais could get some rest. At least one of us had to—and after what I'd seen, it certainly was not going to be me.

Initially, I did try to get some sleep, but as soon as I shut my eyes, I was plagued with visions from the Court of Darkness. They came back to me in fragments, and I wasn't sure if I should feel relieved that I couldn't seem to remember them with clarity—or concerned.

The bits and pieces I was able to put together painted a picture that aligned with all of our darkest fears combined. The Court of Darkness was, in fact, being controlled by the Malum. There was not a sliver of doubt in my mind after experiencing the feeling of its magic—the feeling that had been so like the magic fuelling Raella's portal—and even if that wasn't enough to convince me, I had a mountain of evidence piling up in the very back corners of my brain.

From the unique colour of the maze's interior shadows to the low visibility in my mind when I tried to recall my mental pictures of things that had once been so clear.

It was like my dreams of the man in the dungeon—of Lucais in the dungeon, bathed in shadows so dark they made a moonless night look like a rainy afternoon, as flickering images of a body covered in burn marks and tattoos came rising to the surface before new waves of darkness dispelled the illusion and washed everything away. I was swimming underwater in a murky river without the faintest idea of which way was up, and my recollection of the dream—and my time inside of the Court of Darkness's wards—was a bull shark I didn't see until it was right in front of me, its jaws spread wide open, coming for me at high speed.

It swallowed me whole, and we began anew.

I never stood a chance.

So, instead of sleeping, I went into the bathroom and sat in the shower until I lost track of time. Even though I knew it didn't work the way I wanted it to, I couldn't bear to do anything else until I'd tried to soak off the lingering touch of wrongness that had been left upon my skin. I sat there, staring at the steam fogging up the glass until my back became so numb I had to turn off the cold tap completely just to feel something again.

Eventually, the hot water ran out because the palace was not the House, and there was nobody—and no one—looking over me. I stayed beneath the stream of water as its temperature rapidly dropped from scalding to freezing, and I didn't move until the shower head started to sputter.

When I turned the tap off and crawled out of there at long last, I didn't have the energy to dress. Exhaustion clawed at my eyes, begging them to close.

Barely wrapping a soft black towel around my chest, I stumbled back into the main bedroom and fell onto the enormous trunk sitting at the foot of the bed. The room was mostly dark, save for a single faelight orb Lucais had left on my bedside table, and I shuddered to see the shadows dancing on the walls from the sparse trees well beyond my window. The fog concealed most of the moonlight trying to be witnessed in the night sky, and I was once again alone with my thoughts in a bedroom that never truly belonged to me.

I didn't know when I fell asleep or for how long I was unconscious, but I woke with a start during daylight hours, lying sprawled out on the lower half of the bed. I'd kicked at the towel on top of me until it went flying onto the floor nearby because I'd been dreaming of the lapsus and the towel had felt like its sticky magic.

Groaning, I leaned over the edge of the bed and pried the trunk open just far enough that I could yank an item of clothing out of it to cover myself.

A wrinkled grey shirt fought me every step of the way, but eventually slipped out of the gap. As I buttoned it, I thought back to my dilemma with my memories and everything else in my life that was wrong, damaged, or outright broken.

The dreams. The lapsus. The darkness in my veins.

My father, a prisoner of the dungeon. My other father, trapped inside the Court of Darkness. My mother and sister, living their lives in the human world, the former oblivious to everything that had happened to me since the day the caenim crashed through the front window of our little downtrodden townhouse, and the latter oddly suspicious.

The magic that had abandoned me. The magic that had destroyed me. The bond with Lucais, and the pull to Wrenlock, and—

"Fuck, it's crowded in here. No wonder you don't sleep well."

I jumped in my skin, my fingers slipping on the second last button and ripping it clean off the garment. My heart was in my throat, but that was beginning to feel normal, and my throat was still scarring over from all of the screaming I did inside of the lapsus, so I didn't make a sound as I looked straight into the three eyes of the maroon-skinned faerie I had killed in the palace's hallway.

Fuck, it's crowded in here?

I stared at him, then stared at all of the empty space around him as he stood in the middle of the floor at the foot of my bed. He was corporeal, but there was a paleness to his complexion that hadn't been there when the sword I was wielding went through his chest.

And then it hit me.

"You're not real," I deadpanned. "You're in my head."

He took a step forward.

In the gloomy daylight, there wasn't very much of my bedroom that was in a position to lay claim to a shadow, and he certainly didn't.

Up close, he was strangely handsome and youthful. If I didn't know that the odds were stacked against me in Faerie, I would have guessed he was around my age. His third eye was slightly smaller than the two fairly standard eyes sitting below it and seemed to blink twice as slowly. He had long, seductive lashes on his two main eyes and none at all on the third. I thought his irises were black, but it might have been the poor lighting.

Mouth turned up into an iniquitous smirk, his full lips were smooth and a shade or two darker than the rest of his body, and his teeth were alarmingly white and razor-sharp when he parted them to speak.

"Atta girl," he muttered, his voice husky yet a pitch higher than I was expecting. It was also very familiar, which, like most things in Faerie and the forsaken palace, made me feel exceptionally uncomfortable.

"I killed you."

One of his thin brows curled upwards. "How considerate of you to remember."

"I didn't mean to kill you," I said slowly. Part of my head felt like it was being stuffed with cotton candy, and I was growing more and more distrustful of myself and my perception of reality. Still, it was only polite to err on the side of caution and apologise. "Oh," I rushed to add, "I'm sorry."

He pressed his lips together to subdue his smile. It was amused, but far from friendly. "You're getting better at apologising. Props to you for that." He made a motion to tip his hat to me, though he wasn't wearing one. His hair was thick, plentiful, and dark red. I noticed that his ears were elongated and pointy, but I wasn't convinced he was High Fae.

I frowned. "Do you accept?"

"No." His smile flattened, but the deadly charm still danced in his eyes. "That was an apology, not the magic words to undo your careless erasure of my life."

"Okay." I blinked up at him, lost for words. If he wasn't alive, but he was standing in front of me, and he'd spoken into my mind after his death on not one but two separate occasions, that meant he was a—

"Spectre," he finished for me. "Oh, come now. Don't look so surprised, Auralie. I told you that I'm in your head—which, by the way, is at capacity and should really have had the vacancy sign turned over long before now."

Considering he'd died at my hands, I was willing to overlook his commentary on the state of affairs inside my head. Lucais had mentioned Spectres, but in my horror at what had transpired, I hadn't even thought to ask him what he meant by it.

"I've been...Marked?" I asked softly. "Are you—"

"Haunting you?" he interjected, slipping his hands into the pockets of his black trousers.

I studied them, trying to remember if he'd been wearing the same black velvet waistcoat and crisp white shirt when he died—and, hearing me, the Spectre made a disgruntled sound in his throat and removed his hands from his pockets. Rolling his eyes, he unbuttoned his waistcoat to reveal a bloodstain on the shirt beneath it in approximately the same spot that the sword would have entered his body.

"Ah." I cleared my throat. "I am sorry about that, too. That's a...nice shirt."

He gave me an incredulous look while he buttoned himself up again. "As I was saying," he continued, smoothing down the fabric at his front before replacing his hands in his pockets. "I *would* be haunting you if you were anyone else. You took my life, so the usual recourse is for me to stalk you through the rest of your life in the name of revenge. And don't get me wrong, Auralie, I'd love to drive you mad, but unfortunately, it seems like someone beat me to it a long time ago." His brow creased as he stared down at me with an intensity to make me cringe, and I thought I detected a flicker of genuine concern cross his eyes, but he blinked it away.

I straightened my spine and said, "So you've come back to insult me to death instead?"

"That wasn't an insult, sweetheart."

"I'd hate to be on the receiving end of a compliment, then."

"Better than the receiving end of one of your swords."

My face flushed bright red, and the heat spread all the way down my throat, reminding me that I was dressed in nothing but a grey shirt with two buttons undone. I balled both hands into fists and used them to shove the excess fabric of the shirt all the way down the gap between my crossed legs. "Sorry."

He sighed. "Look, my name is Tommy. We're stuck together until I can figure out a way to claim the repentance I need from you to move on in my afterlife, and I only showed myself to you today because I can't get what I need from you if you die." Tommy pinned me to the spot with a stern look. "You've been through some shit, Auralie, and from the looks of things upstairs, it's only going to get worse."

The corners of my eyes crinkled. "What does that mean?"

Tommy's shoulders slumped, and he lifted his chin, shaking his head at me. "You know I can't say."

I lifted one hand and pinched the bridge of my nose, squeezing my eyes shut. "Right. I didn't know that, but sure."

"I've come to ask you not to do things like run through fields of locusts or sit at the bottom of the shower until the water gets so cold it could give you hypothermia. If your death isn't caused by my haunting,

I'll be trapped here forever, Auralie. You killed me. You took my life, and I know you didn't mean to, but that doesn't matter. So, I've come here to beg you to remember that. If you don't want to damn me eternally, you cannot die at anyone's hands other than mine before I've found what I need to move on. Then, when I have discovered what I need, you'll help me get it so *nobody* has to die or be damned."

"I..." I shook my head, my mouth hanging open, no words able to come out. I stared at the wall beyond his shoulder, at the shadows lingering in the tiny gap between the bookcase and the stonework. I could have sworn I felt them staring back. "I'm not...suicidal."

Tommy's head bobbed dubiously. "So we're in agreement? Because if we aren't, I'll have to reevaluate my options, and those include the people close to you."

Blinking furiously at the wall and feeling very much like I was being interrogated by my therapist in the human world again, I made a small, uncertain noise on an exhale of breath, and eventually nodded to signal agreement. "Yeah, we're..." I peered up at him quizzically. "We're in agreement."

"Good." Tommy stepped up to me, bending down until his face was within two inches of my own. I could see the flaws in his presentation up so close—the slight wavering of his features as though he wasn't really there, the way his proximity lacked any warmth or scent, and the way that no breath entered or escaped his lungs when he spoke. "I'll hold you to this, sweetheart. I'll be back when I've found what I need. Until then, stay the fuck alive for me please, and say my name three times if you think you're going to die."

A thick, painful throb hit my chest. "Why three times?" I asked breathlessly.

"It invokes the power of the bargain between us."

"What bargain?" I exclaimed. My head reared back so fast that my whole body tilted, and I had to fling a hand out behind me to catch myself before I fell backwards onto the bed.

"The one we just made." Tommy winked at me and straightened, smoothing down the front of his waistcoat like it was a nervous tic, and my heart dropped from my throat to the floor beneath the bed, where it immediately became coated in dust and cobwebs, and the spiders started to make nests inside the arteries.

"No..."

Tommy tutted at me. "Trust me, it's a better deal than I would've given anyone else." His dark eyes drifted over the front of my shirt to where I still had one hand holding the fabric in place to cover the space between my legs. "Now, sweetheart, you had better get dressed. I'll be seeing you."

The Spectre tipped his invisible hat to me again—

And then he was gone.

Thirty-Two

My Nightmares and Demons

When a knock came at the door later on, my heart lurched with anticipation.

It was all so silly.

I lifted my head from the tear-stained pillow, unable to even call out an invitation to enter, and waited for the High King of Faerie to open the door and slip inside. When he didn't, my heart dropped like a bungee jumper again, but I forced a small smile onto my face as Wrenlock softly closed it behind him and crossed the room.

He didn't hesitate. He came straight over to the bed and lay down behind me, wrapping me up in his tight, warm embrace with the kind of strength that would give my nightmares and demons a run for their money. One arm fit around my waist as the other slid underneath my head, and he pressed his lips to the top of my hair.

"The caenim are dead, and the Malum have left the wards outside the city," he murmured in a voice as smooth as bourbon. I already knew that, but I let him continue to comfort me. "You *never* have to go back there, Aura, I swear it to you. You don't ever have to go back. I will never make you go back. I won't let you."

A new tide of tears washed up on my cheeks, wetting the shirtsleeve of the arm he had tucked underneath my head. I felt bad for him; it must have been uncomfortable to keep his arm sandwiched between the wetness on my face and the wetness on my pillow, but he didn't flinch. Wrenlock held me in steady warmth and quiet, the soft sound of his even breathing white noise in the background as I fell into an internal debate over whether sleep was too risky or worth it.

I knew, deep down, that Lucais wouldn't come up to check on me. I knew it, and yet I'd hoped for it, anyway. He set up the platform for my dive into disappointment at great heights, and he helped me climb up there, but I was the only person who could make myself fall from it. I was the only one responsible for whether or not I jumped. And I'd been standing on it, curiously peering over the edge since the very first day I met him...

Until the first time I'd seriously considered taking the leap.

But that day had come and gone. It was a new day, and it was Wrenlock who had come up to check on me. It was Wrenlock who promised that I'd never be forced to return to face my nightmares. It was

Wrenlock who held me against him without having to cry, beg, or fight about it back and forth.

Lucais was a part of me I would never be able to get rid of, despite having tried over the course of many months. I was finally ready to admit to myself that it was because I didn't truly want to be free of him. But the platform was incredibly high in the air, and he wouldn't tell me what was waiting for me at the bottom, so I didn't move. A trust fall was suicide in a place like Faerie.

So, I waited instead, knowing full well that we'd likely wait on each other forever.

I wriggled back against Wrenlock, nuzzling my head into the crook of his arm and breathing in his heady scent of warm sunlight and smoke from the fires. I knew there was something I'd been planning to speak to him about, something I had wanted to tell him or explain...

But by the time I drifted off to sleep, I'd forgotten what it was.

Thirty-Three

The Caenim in the Throne Room

It invokes the power of the bargain between us.

With the Spectre's words ringing in my ears for the next few hours, I tossed and turned between the sheets as I dreamed up all the worst-case scenarios in which he could use it against me. Eventually, I fell into a blissful state of oblivion, and I slept for as long as I possibly could.

When I woke up, I was alone, and my head felt heavy and sore. Tommy had tricked me into making a bargain with him, and my nervous system was too frazzled for me to be able to think in a straight and sensible line. I hadn't heeded Lucais's warnings about the wording that faeries used to fool humans, and it landed me in the web of another man's trickery and bullshit—which was just fucking *perfect*.

By the time my stomach pains began, I was willing to relent my desire for sleep and wander downstairs to find some food.

I followed the general direction that Wrenlock had taken me the couple of times he'd escorted me downstairs from my bedroom, but I barely made it to the staircase before a familiar voice sang out my name.

A tentative smile curled my lips as I turned around to face the High Lady of the Court of Wind.

"Enyd," I greeted her. My voice held more cheer than it ought to, considering everything that had happened since we'd last seen each other. I tried to snag the emotion between my mental fingernails and hold it back, but I found myself drifting towards her with some bizarre semblance of joy alight in my eyes. I liked Enyd, and I was happy to see her. "When did you arrive?"

"Three days ago." The High Lady beamed at me. "Nobody was home, but—" She paused in front of me, sighed, and leaned forward to capture me in a warm hug. "Oh, it's so good to see you again, Aura!"

Enyd was considerably smaller than me—shorter by at least two feet, lean and finely muscular, with pixie-like ears that were pinned back by the strip of grey fabric she wore around her head—so she stood on her tiptoes to reach me. When she pulled back, she flicked her eyes up and down my body as if checking for injuries. They were dark and suspicious, taupe in colour to match her short-cut hair.

"Are you well?"

"I'm…" I trailed off uneasily. *I can still lie….*

She waved a hand at me. "That was a stupid question. I'm sorry. Have you come to invite me to dinner? That mate of yours is one of the worst hosts in the entire realm, and I'm starving for both food and decent company." One side of her mouth twitched upwards as she linked her elbow with mine and nudged me in the side. "He's lucky to have you."

"Thanks," I muttered. I didn't know what else to say.

He doesn't have me? His best friend has me? Nobody has me, and I'm actually leaving—oh, wait. No, I'm not. Every corner of the world is under attack, actually, and I'm a walking heat signal for it. Plus, I'm being haunted by a dead faerie who would be immensely pissed off if I just abandoned him to eternal damnation. By the way, what race of faeries have maroon skin and three eyes—and how worried should I be that I just struck up a sketchily worded bargain with one?

None of that was appropriate to dump all over an acquaintance who wasn't even there to see me personally, but rather to visit with the High King, who was officially the last person in the world whom I wanted to find out about the Spectre. I didn't know what he'd do or how much worse he'd make it if he tried to get involved. We'd made a bargain ourselves when he brought me into Faerie, and all he'd asked for in return for the safety of my family was my panties.

I'd wait to tell him about Tommy until I knew what the faerie man was going to demand.

Between the two of us, Enyd and I seemed to possess enough knowledge of the palace's layout to find our way into the cosy dining room without issue. We chatted about insanely normal things as we walked—like the shopfronts in the lower town, where the best pastries could be found, and what kind of live music we enjoyed listening to in public houses. When we finally walked into the dining room and we unlinked arms to take our respective seats, I felt like I was stepping out of a fever dream.

Lucais was sitting at the head of the table, which was neatly laid out with hot tea and biscuits, staring across the room into the roaring fire in the hearth, most of the gold shining in his eyes once more. He must have slept more than I had, which was a good thing, considering I had been locked away in my room for days. I hadn't counted, but my veins had the sluggish feel of hibernation.

That realisation made Tommy's appearance and accompanying request somewhat more reasonable—maybe I *was* acting a little bit depressed. It still didn't mean I was suicidal, but if my death would sentence him to a life of solitude as a lonely Spectre, then he was well within his rights to ask me to help him. I owed him that at least.

"You look happy to see me," Enyd said under her breath, pulling out a chair at the other end of the table and staring daggers at the High King as she sat down. "You weren't even here to greet me when I arrived."

I hesitated in the doorway for a moment before the High King rose to his feet, albeit somewhat begrudgingly—or perhaps he was just as tired and sore as I was—and pulled the chair out next to him. Taking the hint, I scurried over and smoothed down the back of my long, grey shirt as I lowered myself into the seat. In my apathy, I'd pulled on a pair of loose pants, but I didn't bother to change my shirt with the broken buttons before I'd left my bedroom.

The High King sat back down and slouched against his chair, resting one elbow on the table as he spun a butter knife around on a napkin. "You were two days late," he stated calmly.

Two days late.

I did the math quickly. If Enyd was granted a week to mourn her dead soldiers at home, but was two days late coming into Caeludor, then it had been nine or ten days since we'd left the House. I'd spent three or four days in the palace at the most, which meant I had been unconscious for almost a week before I awoke in the carriage. Taking a sip of water from my pre-filled glass, I suppressed a shudder.

"Well, you'll have to forgive me," the High Lady of the Court of Wind quipped. "We had trouble finding the place."

He pulled a sardonic face at her.

"Really, Lucais," Enyd persisted, waving a hand towards the window. "I would have thought you'd have done something about all of this dastardly fog by now."

The High King took a long swig of a deep purple liquid that smelled far too strong to be tea, went to put it down, but thought twice and drained the glass to the dregs. He made a refreshing *ahh* sound as he carefully placed his empty glass back down. "I've been busy."

Enyd's gaze flitted to my face for the briefest moment. "Mmhmm."

Lucais's own eyes narrowed with derision. "Classy, Enyd. Really classy—"

"Stop it, you two," Morgoya snapped.

I might have sagged in relief. I'd never been so grateful to see the High Lady glide into the room—because she was bathed, mostly healed, and back in her usual good spirits. And also because whatever was going on between Lucais and Enyd felt like something that would drain the last surviving drops of my energy if someone didn't tactfully diffuse it.

"Enyd, we're very sorry about the lack of fanfare upon your arrival," Morgoya went on. She sounded sincere, but I had my doubts. "As I'm sure you would have heard, we had some uninvited guests show up during the start of the carousal whom required our immediate attention. I trust you have made yourself at home—and I *know* your men have made the most of the free wine at the public houses in town regardless."

Enyd shifted in her seat, but she gave the other High Lady a reluctant nod. "Indeed they have."

While Lucais and Morgoya briefed Enyd on the latest Malum updates, taking great care to avoid any mention of my suspected heritage and unfortunate experience being attacked by the shadows at the lapsus, I ate the plate of food that appeared in front of me in silence. I didn't ask where Wrenlock and Batre were, but I had plans to find them both after dinner to express my gratitude for the kindness of the former and check on the welfare of the latter.

The fireplace crackled and popped behind me, the heat coasting over my back giving some relief to the parts of my body that felt bruised after the invisible attack of the shadows.

At some point, I found myself looking over my shoulder at the way the flames danced, casting shadows on the brickwork. I couldn't remember if that was normal for fireplaces, given that we'd never been able to afford to live in a house with one of them, but the dance of the flames was enchanting, and the way the shadows moved with them...

"...and if you were ever going to warn me about the caenim in the throne room?"

Enyd's question snagged my attention, and I twisted back to the table, frantically glancing between the High King at my side and the two women who sat with an empty chair between them at the other end of the table.

Lucais placed his hand over mine and patted it gently. "We did kill most of them, but I was able to capture a few of the beasts," he reassured me. "I couldn't put them in the dungeons, so they're caged up using magic in the throne room." He gave me a meaningful look, and I understood. They would likely become ten times more feral than they already were if they were locked downstairs with Hanson and my father, and if they managed to escape with the strength of their bloodlust...

Well, that wouldn't be so bad, but still.

"Okay," I mumbled. I flipped my hand beneath his so I could wrap my fingers around him and squeeze, signifying that I understood the parts he couldn't say in front of our guest. Then I turned back to watch the fire dance.

The High King continued fielding questions from the High Lady of the Court of Wind, which I felt she was more than justified to ask, given that she'd only just discovered he'd been keeping an enormous, universe-altering secret from her for the High Mother knew how long, and it had ultimately cost her the lives of many good men when she visited the House. I was thinking about all of that, and the method that he believed he was applying to his madness, when I shut my eyes to ease the sting of staring at a source of light for too long. And when I opened them again—

"*Aura!*"

Lucais pushed me to the ground, landing directly on top of me with one of his hands around the back of my head to soften the impact. He stared down at me with an expression of unbridled panic and horror manipulating his face. We were both gasping for breath, and I felt his heart slamming into my sternum as if it was trying to merge with my own. Blinking rapidly, I felt around for my tongue, parting my mouth to let the question fly free.

"What—" I started to say, but then I felt it.

Pain.

Lifting my hand from the floor, my eyes slowly moved from Lucais's stricken face to the red, swollen burn on my fingers and the palm of my hand. Tiny little blisters and bumps had already formed, the skin a combination of pallid white and dusky pink. My eyes drifted to Lucais, who was staring at me as if he couldn't comprehend my reaction, and then to my hand.

"It's already healing," I commented. My voice sounded foreign and far away, and I knew it was the most bizarre thing for me to say given the circumstances, but it was like I had lost control.

"Bookworm, what were you *doing*?" he demanded.

"I..." I shook my head, and Lucais gently removed his hand from underneath it. I relaxed against the plush carpet while he stroked a finger down my cheekbone, leaning into the touch ever so slightly. "I was just looking at the shadows..." I made to turn my head towards the fireplace again, but the High King seized my chin and forced my head back into place, locking my gaze with his.

"No," he said firmly. "Aura, you put your bare hand inside the fire. Your bare, *human* hand. It's healing—and I'll be damned if I even fully understand *why*—but if it had been a chopping block, or a pot of acid..." Lucais shook his head, a few blond locks falling across his face. "This is what I was afraid of."

"Forgive my ignorance," Enyd called from where she stood behind the High King, peering over his shoulder on the tips of her toes. "I seem to be missing something rather critical again."

Lucais squeezed his eyes shut, groaning softly. He rested his forehead against mine for a moment before he pulled back and rose to his feet, helping me to follow with my uninjured hand. He looked Enyd square in the eye and threw an atomic bomb to the wind as he said, "Aura is the heir to the Court of Darkness."

Enyd's eyes went round, her voice filled with surprise and a tinge of borderline supercilious admiration as she murmured, "Is she?"

"Oh, no," I cut in, shaking my head and waving my uninjured hand in the air. "No, no. I'm not going to accept it, even if I am." I laughed nervously when they all turned to look at me as if I were insane. "I'm not...interested...in that. Uh." I swallowed audibly. "Sorry, I guess?"

Lucais pinned me to the spot with a dour look. "You don't get a choice," he informed me seriously. "This is just the start. The magic will force you into it, Aura. It recognises you. It knows who you are now better than ever before, and if you don't accept the title…" He trailed off, the outlines of torture taking shape on his breathtakingly handsome and gut-wrenchingly forlorn face.

"What?" I questioned, flicking my eyes between all of them. "I'll say the words," I avowed. "I'll formally reject it, or whatever it is that I need to because I don't want it." None of them looked affected by my words. "I'm serious," I insisted, sounding a little more hysterical with every passing second. I took a step back from the High King, letting his hand drop. "I don't *want* it. I reject it!"

"Aura." Lucais stepped forward, seizing me by the shoulders. "It's not a mating bond. It doesn't work like that. The Court of Darkness will only be able to seek out a replacement for you when someone with stronger dark power than you is born—"

"No," I gasped. "No! There has to be a loophole. Lucais, tell me there's a loophole."

The corners of his eyes crinkled despairingly. "They'll look for the second most powerful dark faerie once you die."

Tears welled up in my eyes, the liquid in the back of my throat thickening. "What are you saying?"

"It's going to do one of two things to you, bookworm. It's going to convince you to come back to it"—his throat bobbed—"and if you don't, it's going to pursue you to your death."

No. NO.

I couldn't go back. I could never go back. I wouldn't survive it again. I barely survived the first time.

My vision went blurry, drifting over Lucais's shoulder. When my eyes refocussed, they landed on Tommy.

The handsome, sharp-eyed Spectre stood with his brows raised and arms folded across his chest, leaning against the doorframe. Tommy didn't look smug, but his expression wasn't comforting, either. When his dark gaze met mine, he tipped his nonexistent hat to me, and I felt myself beginning to free-fall.

Tommy parted his lips and mouthed the words, "I told you so."

Thirty-Four

Don't Ask Such Infuriating Questions

I always knew I would die before my time.

I had a midlife crisis when I was ten—or at least, it had felt like a midlife crisis. It was definitely some kind of crisis, and if I hadn't made it to my twentieth birthday, I wouldn't have been the least bit surprised.

My father made us a statistic, increasing our chances of early and unexpected death according to the studies I'd read, and my anger towards him made me reckless and volatile. Belgrave was a quiet, uneventful town filled with nosy people, but we got a lot of tourists. It was always at the back of my mind that a random driver passing through on their way into the city might see me sitting down at the docks alone, willing myself to stow away on the next boat, and kidnap me. It was just a thought. But even then, sometimes, I wondered if it could qualify as a desire. The deep, dark kind. Maybe that was why I kept going back despite the fact that I was never going to get on a boat.

Even at the age of ten, I knew that was fucked up—knew *I* was fucked up. But the darkness inside of me had never felt like power. It was not a call so much as it was a warning—the persistent echo of an enigmatic impending doom.

Something bad is going to happen. Maybe it already has.

It left me riddled with paranoia, weakening me like I had been ingesting poison since birth. Deep down in the cobweb-covered recesses of my mind, I kept a truth under lock and key—the unshakeable feeling that all of it was my birthright. I'd always assumed it was my father because that would make perfect sense to anyone who had the displeasure of knowing him well.

The fact that both nature *and* nurture were set against me from the very beginning made me sick to my stomach.

I'd known that, too, though. My shadow on the ground didn't follow me everywhere I went in the light of day because it had to, but because it *wanted* to know where I was going.

Subconsciously, I'd always felt it there—larger than life and darker than night, stalking me through my childhood and growing alongside me like a toxic vine that had its roots buried underneath my skin. Feeding off me. Intertwining with me. Becoming me.

If Faerie was telling me the truth, I *had* been born with it. The dark magic was a seed when I was a toddler—something mild that occasionally made me kick my legs and wriggle in an unknowing effort to dislodge it from my body—but the magic fed off every bad thing that had ever happened to me, so it burst into full-bloom and consumed me when I turned eleven.

The Court of Darkness was my punishment.

I was set to inherit a damned Faerie Court, barely functional and populated by dark faeries who had either been traumatised beyond the point of salvation or condemned for their sins inside of it since the moment I'd shown up in Lucais's life. The irony was nauseating—that I was the reason he had shunned them, and yet, they were supposed to be my responsibility.

"If I go back there, will I ever be allowed out?" I wondered aloud as Lucais stomped through the palace, his hand tightly wound around mine like a vise. "Can I still visit Brynn, or will it be too dangerous?" I paused, gnawing on my lower lip. The next question I needed to ask started hurting before I'd even gotten it out. "Will *I* be too dangerous?"

The High King shoved at a heavy oak side door with his free hand and sent it flying off its hinges with a loud crash. Splinters of wood ricocheted off the ground as it bounced across the cobblestone outside like a rock skipping across a lake, each subsequent bang dropping in volume until the door skidded across the ground, only stopping when it hit the other side of the palace's exterior.

There was a damp chill in the air outside, perpetuated by the lack of light in the sky beneath the city's thick layers of fog. Over the courtyard, it hovered well above the ground, somewhat reminiscent of a ceiling. It allowed me to glimpse parts of the palace that hadn't been destroyed, though the gloom coated it like an accelerant for the sparks of Lucais's moods and made me feel very unstable.

As he dragged me across the open space by my hand, I gazed up at the palace's untouched exterior towering over us, the mist wafting between the turrets akin to the water in a river skirting large rocks as it flowed downstream.

"You're not fucking going back there," he growled, yanking me across the bailey. "Don't ask such infuriating questions."

I dropped my gaze back to the ground and sneered. "You'd rather I die. Got it."

In the middle of the courtyard, Lucais came to a screeching halt and whirled on me with an expression that had me almost stumbling over my own two feet. His face was contorted with negative emotion—pain, rage, or hatred, I wasn't sure. But then he spoke, and it became perfectly clear.

"When are you going to drop the *fucking* act, bookworm?"

Rage. His golden eyes were glowing with the power of a thousand suns across a thousand different galaxies. But there wasn't even a glimmer of hatred in a single one, and the emotion was so strong it left no room for pain to share space in that moment.

For once, I didn't debase him by asking what he meant.

I sucked in a deep breath through my mouth, letting his hand fall out of mine as I lifted my arms and wrapped them both around my torso in a feeble act of self-comfort. "I can't."

"You can't?"

My shoulders rose and fell with enough force to send a twinge shooting down my spine. Heart pounding steadily in my chest, I met Lucais's eyes and resisted the urge to fall into them and burn myself alive. "It won't matter either way now. I can't be both the High Lady of the Court of Darkness and the High Queen of Faerie, can I?"

I knew the answer was no. He knew that, too. Morgoya was in charge of the Court of Light, which meant that even Lucais himself couldn't claim both roles. The High Mother wouldn't allow it. Regardless, I needed to say it out loud, and he needed to acknowledge that he heard it.

Lucais hesitated, resisting something, and then seemed to decide it was inevitable, so he shook his head grimly. "No. No, you cannot."

Mouth pressed into a hard line, I shrugged expectantly. "Then there really isn't any point in hurting both of us by pretending we could even have a future together."

The High King's eyes were conflicted. After a moment, he said, "You could just be the High Queen." I must have looked as confused as I felt because he added, "The crown supersedes everything else. If you accepted the mating bond and the throne beside mine, the Court of

Darkness would—or at least it should, under normal circumstances—be forced to leave you alone and look for your replacement amongst the other dark faeries."

The crown supersedes everything else.

"Lucais..." My brows twitched, head swimming with a sudden heat that intensified my puzzlement and that tiny little bit of hope I felt pulsing inside of my chest. I squashed it beneath my mental boot, because if the Court of Darkness didn't kill me, that emotion certainly would. Blinking through my disorientation, I said, "But this means that Blythe is dead, doesn't it? Whatever is in the lapsus killed her and consumed the rest of the Court."

And then showed me what it wanted me to let loose upon the rest of the unsuspecting world.

"Yes," Lucais said slowly. He didn't have to literally read my mind to understand where it was headed. "The second most powerful dark faerie is a gamble, but it's worth taking if it means that you stay here."

"I don't think you understand." I bit my lip, feeling very much like the pot calling the kettle black. "There is no way a sane individual is walking out of that Court. You'll have a wildcard on your hands, and there's no guarantee you'll win favour with the Unseelie Court."

The High King made a very handsome portrait of denial personified.

"It's a maze, Lucais. A literal maze filled with nightmares at every turn. I've been on horror trains and haunted houses at theme parks that seem like a baby animal petting zoo compared to what's happening in there. You said that the thing in the lapsus is reliving the same moment in time over and over again. Like it's being repeatedly shocked by electricity. I *felt* like that when I was inside it, but it pulled me beyond the lapsus. I was *inside* the Court, and it's filled with..." I trailed off, my skin prickling as it turned ice-cold.

The visions and memories from the time I spent as a prisoner of the shadows were still murky, but they'd left me with an empty, hollow feeling and the remnants of fear so profuse it was leaching into my bones.

"Caenim," he finished for me gently. A severe, kindred warmth blazed in his eyes as they bore into mine. "And monsters that do terrible things. I know, my love." Lucais took a step towards me and softly cupped my face in his hands. The expression on his own face ran through me, piercing my soul. "I heard you screaming. I think some of the splinters of those screams are still lodged in my heart." His throat bobbed. "One day, I am going to butcher every single one of the abominations inside of that Court who dared to reveal their ghastly selves to you. But you don't have to go back for that."

My chest pulled against a flare of desperation. "What if I don't even want *you* to go back for that?"

He shrugged, a smile ghosting his lips. "No matter. I'll drag them from your nightmares and execute them here in the bailey for you instead."

Tears burned at the backs of my eyes, but they didn't spring to life. I was choking on emotion, utterly devastated by the look on his face. My bottom lip wobbled as my mouth opened to speak, heart flipping while I watched Lucais tracking the movement, concern and desire flaring in the golden oasis of his eyes. He was giving up the charade, letting the game play out to a deadlock, and I couldn't stand it. It would destroy me, and that would then ultimately destroy him. If I had any sense at all—

When he moved to close the last sliver of distance between us, I jumped backwards, ripping myself out of his touch as though I were a frightened animal. Irritation crossed over his face like a cloud chased by resolve, and I tripped over my voice as I hastened to interrupt him.

"I need you to be mean again," I blurted, holding a hand up between us for pause. If he reached me, the game was over, and the both of us would surely lose.

He faltered a step. "I'm sorry?"

"Tell me..." I glanced around hopelessly for support, but we were alone in the courtyard. "Tell me I'm not your type," I implored. "I have too much meat on my bones. Say that I'm stupid, and half-brained, and..."

The tears that wouldn't fall burned like a house fire inside of my skull, the smoke clouding my mind and strangling my throat. I wracked my brain for all of the horrible, vicious insults he had hurled at me since we met, but none of them stood a chance against the way he was looking at me inside the cocoon of that moment.

"Why?"

My knees trembled. "Because," I whined, my voice cracking. "That was all I had, Lucais. In the bookstore. That cabin in the Court of Light. At the House." I swept my tongue against the roof of my mouth, throat clenching as I forced down the lump in it. The truth truly *caned*. "That was all there was between us, and without it, I'm—" I broke off.

His head twitched ever so slightly to one side. "You're what?"

"Tell me you hate me," I demanded, taking another step back.

"I hate you."

For a moment, surprise overtook my desire to drive a wedge between us because I hadn't really expected him to be capable of fulfilling my request. And he had done it so easily. My grasp on the nuances in the High Fae's take on language was dangerously weak even after all of the time I'd spent dancing around it with them.

"How can you say that?" I asked, curiosity purifying my tone.

The High King took another step, twice the length of mine. He gazed down at me, the scent of home rushing over me in waves tall enough to drown the mountains. "You just asked me to."

"I know, but you're so close to me, and you can't lie. That means it's true."

"I hate a lot of things about you, little beast," Lucais replied, snatching my hand and placing it on his heart. It beat rapidly inside his firm chest—a hummingbird trapped inside a cage of marble. "I hate what you've done to me." He moved my hand down his chest, trailing it over his stomach with painstaking slowness. "I hate what you're *doing* to me." With his hand over mine, I grazed the buckle of his belt, and then he pushed my palm onto the thick, granite-hard erection straining against his pants.

A flood of heat coursed through my body from my mouth straight down to my core, and I gasped at the way Lucais's cock flexed in my hand. I itched to feel it bare, to press my palm into the heat of his soft, sensitive skin, and curl my fingers around his girth as far as they would go. Without breaking eye contact, I pushed the heel of my palm against him once, twice, until his hips rocked into me, trapping my hand between our bodies as he banished all of the unnecessary space to damnation. My heartbeat pulsed twice as strong between my legs, and the scent of sex permeated the air around us.

The mating bond.

Lucais gently freed my arm, bringing the hand that had just been grinding against his erection up to his face. He placed a delicate kiss on my knuckles, eyes fluttering closed. "I hate that you take so much from me and give me nothing in return," he went on, and my heart dipped. The High King brushed his mouth against my wrist. "My mind is yours. My body is yours. You could slit my throat and I'd beg you to use my corpse as a shield or keep me for spare parts." His bright eyes opened to mine, sunlight dancing with the waves on the ocean. "My soul is woven together with auburn-coloured thread, Aura. My kingdom is yours. My crown is yours. And if you want more than that? I'll break the treaty with the Underworld and steal the crown from the grave of the last known Dragon Master who had it." Lucais bent his head, lavishing a kiss on the sensitive skin in the crease of my elbow.

"Even if it means I have to hold my breath for a hundred years or patch up my broken wings with steel bars," he vowed, carefully lowering my arm back to my side. His voice was sombre, velvet-smooth, and as familiar as my own. "I hate that—all of that—about you, but not because it's *you*. It's never been because of you."

Lifting a hand, Lucais caressed the side of my face, and I leaned into the touch. Tingles spread down my spine like the brush of a fern frond and a warm, midsummer breeze on my bare skin.

Threading his hands through my hair, he tugged gently to fasten his grip and stared firmly into my eyes as he said, "I am, and always have been, the problem. I am the High King of Faerie, and I am fully prepared to enforce the most ridiculous laws upon the people of this kingdom to make them dance like puppets purely for your entertainment."

I forced myself to swallow.

His eyes darkened, shadows creeping in from the edges, and the distance between us—distance that was anything but physical, and therefore took an extreme amount of work to close—reared up again to rejoice. "And I don't know what that makes me. A bad High King, that's certain. Unseelie, even?" He sighed in resignation. "Perhaps."

I felt like I was drifting through the clouds, as light as a feather and free as a bird—and headed right towards a storm, too enamoured with the sky to care.

"I hate that I love you, Aura. Because I hate that my love for you is going to hurt people. That it could hurt *you*."

My heart was on fire, and I'd only ever kissed him.

My soul was uncovered, and I'd never even bared it to him.

He simply knew it, like I knew his.

From the day in Dante's Bookstore where he'd saved my life and told me to run—spoken straight into my mind, his thoughts taking their rightful place beside my own—I'd come back to him despite all rhyme and reason. I'd walked into the bookstore and landed face-first in the ironclad gaze of my soulmate, and he hadn't let me out of it for a moment. A touch that could burn through the veil of reality was our first hello, and I'd been on fire with it ever since. The knowledge that he was everything. Everything I'd been reading about and waiting for my whole life.

My anomalously short human life.

The truth was a coin worth the price of the universe, and it had two very important sides. The first side was that I loved him with all of the broken, brittle parts of me—loved him enough to want to heal them so they would never cut him, loved him enough that I could let it go if he said he wanted to see those parts of me, too.

But the second side...

"Lucais."

"Yes, bookworm?"

"I'm going to break your heart."

"Auralie?"

"Yes, Your Highness?"

"I'm going to let you."

Thirty-Five

You Don't Have to Touch It

"Why does your heart beat five times instead of three?"

Lucais held the door to one of the palace's drawing rooms open for me, which seemed like an unnecessarily gallant gesture considering he could have opened it with a single wave of his hand. "Your average High Fae beats once for mind, twice for body, and thrice for soul. As High King, mine beats once for mind, twice for body, and thrice for soul—and then once more for kingdom, and once again for crown."

My eyebrows shot up with intrigue. "What will happen to mine when I accept the bond?"

Lucais's expression tightened. "We need to talk about that," he replied curtly.

"Oh, for the love of fuck," I muttered, trailing into the room behind him with my head hanging low. After everything we'd just exposed to each other in the courtyard, we were still stuck in the same frustrating place.

That is a more accurate statement than you might realise, he uttered into my mind.

Before I had a chance to ask what he meant, I heard the quiet slam of a book being closed, and my head whipped up to find Wrenlock sitting at the head of a long, polished wooden table. The room was fairly empty compared to the space we usually dined in together, with colourful oil paintings hanging on the xanthous walls and not a whole lot of anything else. The table had matching chairs, simple wood carvings without adornment or cushions, and a large silver candle holder sat in the middle. It was empty. I peeked at the title of Wrenlock's book and was quietly shocked to find he was reading a fiction novel written for pleasure. He didn't like reading—or at least, he hadn't.

"Aura has decided she wants to accept the bond," Lucais declared like it was the most unexpected breaking news in the world. Maybe it was. He swung his arm out like a pendulum blade between us, and didn't sound excited or even remotely happy about it, which irked me beyond belief. "I don't know what you think we should do, but I'd rather have it out in the open now."

Oh, I'm going to throttle him. Why does Wrenlock have to do anything?

"I can make up my own mind," I cut in, shooting daggers at the High King. "I don't have much of a choice in any case, so I'd really love it if you could refrain from trying to turn me off the idea until it's all been said and done."

Lucais's eyes flared with something I couldn't decipher, and he said, "That's the thing, bookworm. You don't know what it is that has to be done."

Flabbergasted, I flung my hands up in the air and tossed a beseeching look towards Wrenlock. When all else failed, I could usually count on him to speak plainly with me if he was able to do so.

But his mouth was tight as he looked up at me from beneath dark, furrowed brows. "The mating bond requires a ceremony of sorts," he began quietly.

I rolled my eyes, but I was willing to accept a ceremony if that's all it took. "Fine. The sooner I put the whole horrible ordeal behind me, the better."

Lucais let out a strangled laugh. "Oh, bookworm."

"Stop playing cat-and-mouse with her," Wrenlock chastised.

The High King shot him a chilly look. "Fine," he bit out. Taking a deep breath, he turned to me. "The traditional law states that the mating bond cannot take effect until the relevant parties have"—his tone wavered, and I could have sworn I saw Lucais's body swaying slightly from side to side as he wiggled the fingers on one hand in the air between us awkwardly—"consummated...the...bond."

His hand stopped moving. I stopped breathing. Wrenlock stopped sitting behind the table and rose to stand, walking around the side until he stood between us, his hands clasped in front of him and an expression of concern etched into his features.

"Aura?" he probed.

I stared wordlessly at the shiny surface of the table visible between them, its dark wood stain reflecting the yellow light from the faelight orbs that bobbed against the ceiling, and suddenly it all made sense. Wrenlock's awkwardness whenever I'd asked him about the High Fae's intimate practices and his refusal to go all the way with me at the House, my lack of informed consent aside. Morgoya's fascination with whether or not we'd done it yet. Lucais's gentle rejection—which felt like it had happened on more than one occasion, even if I wasn't fully aware of it at the time.

Dozens of memories came flooding back to me, moments I was glimpsing through a different lens where we *could* have fallen into each other in that way but never did, despite the ever-present ache of escalating desire. In his bedroom at the House after he rescued me from the field of caenim. The day he'd antagonised me with his harsh words and soft touches in the armoury. When he'd kissed me with enough passion to overthrow Eros in the dungeon and then violently threw himself back against the opposing wall. All those times he'd wiped away those lingering remnants of my lips and skin. He had touched me like he wanted to devour me, but then he always pulled back. And the whole time, I had thought it was because he was toying with me.

No soulmate is better than a dead soulmate, he had told me. Because if I became the High Queen, my fate with the Malum would be sealed. They would *have* to kill me in order to fulfil their desire for a Malum Queen to rule Faerie at his side, and it would no longer matter whether Raella's offer to turn me had been genuine at the time she had made it, or if Lucais could find a way out of it for me.

My bewildered gaze drifted up to the High King's face, his eyes the homing beacon for mine. His mouth was half-open, the words of whatever he wanted to say caught in his throat, and he shook his head at me slightly. Lucais looked hopeless, the image of someone who had tried everything.

I swallowed hard.

The realisation washed all of my bitterness away. Lucais had wholeheartedly believed that giving in to his desires would kill me, so he held himself back the entire time. Let me work the burning, pent-up frustration and desire that his very presence stirred inside of me out with Wrenlock to avoid being backed into a corner if I'd ever decided to throw caution to the wind and be even more direct about it than I'd been in the crumbling wing of the palace.

"Why didn't you tell me sooner?" I whispered softly.

"I was too scared to mention the outstanding decision of our mating bond to you again in case it prompted you to reject it." His voice was thick with tension. "The first time didn't work because the person you were rejecting was wrong, but once you know who your soulmate is, the rejection is permanent. I never would have been able to win you back if you did it properly."

I took a shaky step forward. "Lucais—"

You don't want this, he murmured into my mind, halting me in place. The expression on his face was an interesting mix of being afraid, sad, and outrageously turned on. *I know that. I tried to avoid it, Aura. I really did.*

How do you know what I want? I whispered back, and a thrill went through me at the instant flare of his raging arousal that pulsed through the bond.

Fine, he conceded, his voice rough even in my mind. *But I never wanted it to happen because you have no other choice. So now we're definitely fucked, and not in the way either of us prefers to be.*

There was an extended, charged pause. How could we turn it into our own choice, instead of our first time being a last resort?

At the exact same time, we both gradually turned our heads towards Wrenlock, who was still standing there, a brow arched at our silent conversation with clear agitation. A nagging feeling pulled at the back of my mind that there was something I'd been meaning to tell him, but for the life of me, I couldn't recall what it was.

"No," Lucais said with audible disbelief, seeing the awareness alight in my eyes. "You have got to be kidding."

"I didn't say anything," I breathed, my tone adopting a defensive edge. But I knew what he was talking about because I clocked the same light in his own eyes.

"You get even more insane by the day, I swear to the Oracle." He dragged a hand through his tousled blond hair, gripping the back of his neck. "It's nothing personal, believe me," he said to Wrenlock, gesturing to him with his free hand turned palm-up towards the ceiling. "But that's really not my thing."

Wrenlock blinked—and then caught on like a grassfire. I watched his face contort as he flipped his gaze between us, eyes widening and then narrowing, mouth opening and closing. Finally, he pinned Lucais with a glare and said, "You're not my first choice, either, you know."

The High King gave him a withering look. "It's not about you," he snapped back, affronted. "It's about what you"—he waved a hand towards Wrenlock's crotch—"currently have on offer."

Wrenlock's stare was patronising. "You don't have to touch it."

"I'm not going to touch it."

"I don't want you to touch it."

"Oh my God!" I exclaimed, tossing my hands up in the air and taking a determined step in between them. "This is absolute lunacy. Forget about it, please."

"Wrong deity," Wrenlock said wryly.

"Wrong name," Lucais muttered.

"This is the dumbest idea any of us have had yet. And that's saying something, considering some of the plans you've concocted," I added for Lucais's benefit. "I don't even know whose idea this was in the first place, but there is no way all three of us are going to be satisfied in an arrangement like that."

Lucais cleared his throat suggestively as Wrenlock drawled, "I think the end goal in something like this is really just for *you* to be satisfied, Auralie."

"It won't work," I argued pointlessly, but I could have melted into the floor at the thought of it. Images rushed forward from my most private fantasies, stored behind doors that were bolted closed with so many locks even my conscious mind couldn't reach them. "It won't..."

"It could if we all make stipulations," Wrenlock proffered, his voice taking on a dangerously seductive edge.

"Can mine be that you're not there?" the High King asked him hopefully. I knew it was a joke, but it further solidified my very sensible belief that the whole thing was a terrible suggestion.

Even so...

Arousal was blazing underneath my skin hot enough to melt my very bones, and the pink tinge that brightened my cheeks was impossible to hide. The High King tilted his head to the side with fascination, which only made the colour deepen as it spread from my hairline to my collarbone.

You really are interested in this, he realised through the bond. *Aren't you?*

I gulped, but my mind immediately flashed back to the way it had felt to know that he'd been watching when it was only Wrenlock and I in the hallway during the start of the carousal, and I couldn't quell the spike of arousal evident in the way my heart raced and my skin flushed. *I don't know.*

Bookworm, he crooned. *Tell me you want this. Tell me how badly you want me to fuck you with Wrenlock in the room. Do you want him to watch? Do you want him to touch you while I make you come?*

A wash of dizziness hit me like a speeding truck, and I swayed, falling forward to brace myself on the edge of the table. My head was so hot it was drying out my mouth, and I couldn't think in a straight line. I'd never done anything like that before. I'd never even seen something like it happening on a screen. I'd only ever read about it in books.

And yet...

"Fine," Lucais said abruptly. He must have found his answer somewhere on my face. "Go on, Wrenlock. Tell us how we're all going to fuck each other without causing irreparable damage to our relationships and psyches. Aura's intrigued, so I'm listening."

Wrenlock made a low scoffing sound before folding his arms over his chest and answering the question in earnest. "Aura and I have already explored some intimacy, and the two of you have a mating bond, so I don't think it's going to be all that difficult." He made a good show of sounding convinced despite the fact that he didn't look it when I glanced at him over my shoulder. "You don't want to touch me," he said to Lucais. "Do you also prefer that I don't touch you?"

I could have sworn my eyes bulged out of my head like a cartoon cat at the implication, but there was nothing comical about the flood of arousal that began to drip down between my legs. I tried to resist, but I was compelled by hypercharged interest to turn to the High King and gauge his reaction. He looked gobsmacked.

"I..." He glanced at me as if he was seeking my advice, and it was honestly a nice change of pace for the two of us.

I merely shrugged. "You are a free agent."

Lucais scrunched his nose up at me, but said to Wrenlock, "I suppose I don't mind. I've never really thought about it. Are you saying you want my—"

"I'm saying you should stop being an idiot long enough for us to set some safe boundaries, if you really want to do this for Aura."

The High King sneered. "You know I'll ruin you for other men."

"Should I leave?" I interjected, trying to sprinkle some humour into the mix to diffuse the extremely potent tension that seemed to have a dozen different traceable causes.

Wrenlock raised an eyebrow at me. "I literally have no boundaries," he announced, which surprised me a little bit. "Aura?"

I gaped, and Lucais smirked at me. "I..." I mumbled. "Well, I..."

Truthfully, I'd never thought we'd get to that point. I wasn't foolish enough to think that hooking up with Wrenlock when I was fated to be with Lucais was going to come without its complications. But they didn't seem all that intricate when the line between love and hate was skewed in favour of the latter.

I looked between the two of them. Light and dark, night and day—and for reasons that had absolutely nothing to do with their physical appearances. I felt an undeniable pull to both men, a sensitivity that only they could access, and the longer I stared back at them, the less insane the idea began to seem.

"Uh...no, you're right." I nodded once in Wrenlock's direction. "We've kind of already been together, and you..." I trailed off, meeting the High King's hot, assessing stare. "We've been on the brink of it for months."

A flash of satisfaction lit up his eyes, but I caught myself checking Wrenlock for signs of jealousy or hurt. I found none, which was strangely validating.

"So...no real boundaries then," I concluded. The group activity that the three of us were proposing to do was really the only thing coming to mind that I'd never done or considered doing before.

Lucais leaned forward, scrutinising me with an extremely sexy half-smile on his face. "But what about other things?" he asked. "What do you dislike? What do you *love*?"

I had an intensifying feeling that he'd be the reason I discovered the full extent of both of those things, but I didn't dare say it aloud. Instead, I thought back frantically to all of the books I'd read after Dante's closed for the day. Short of providing them with an extensive list of ticks and crosses...

"I like the way you kiss me," I told Lucais. He was an expert with his mouth. "And I like the way you talk to me," I added, glancing up at Wrenlock. "I'm open to most things, I think."

"Well, that settles it," the dark-haired man said under his breath.

A jolt shot through my heart, crash-landing like a meteor between my legs.

Indignantly, Lucais exclaimed, "Excuse me, what about my boundaries?"

"You already told us," Wrenlock said flatly. "How many boundaries can you, of all people in the world, possibly have?"

"Not mine." The High King pointed to me with his eyes. "Hers."

"Mine?" I asked at the same time as Wrenlock echoed, "Hers?"

"Yes." Lucais's tone was petulant. "Forgive me for making an already complicated situation even more complicated, but I'd really like to make just one more request."

"Fine." I waved a hand, but he stared directly at Wrenlock when he spoke. I didn't miss the way his tone iced over with the hint of warning.

"Her mouth is mine."

He stared at the High King impassively. "What in the—"

"I don't care about whatever has already happened between the two of you," Lucais interrupted. "I don't want to know the details, but I would like to request that, while the three of us are together, Aura's mouth and the sharp and nasty tongue that comes with it belong to me."

"You've literally watched us kissing," he argued.

Lucais raised one devilish eyebrow. "You know very well that is *not* what I'm talking about."

Wrenlock frowned, but deferred to me with a look.

Aura's mouth and the sharp and nasty tongue that comes with it belong to me.

His comment sent me spinning backwards in time to a moment where I had looked the blond fiend dead in the eyes, fully convinced that he hated me. He stood on the staircase in the House and joked that the Court of Darkness—my destined place in his world, though we hadn't a clue about it back then—was formerly called the Court of Pretty Little Human Things With Sharp and Nasty Tongues.

Because he thought I was pretty. Because he thought that I was as pretty as a lochgrub, one of the most well-known aesthetic wonders in all of Faerie. He thought about my mouth and what it might be capable of doing beyond insulting him and trying to scare him off by hurting his feelings.

I blinked at him, borderline tearful, and unfathomably wonderstruck. *This whole time?*

He inclined his head to me. *It is one of your many exceedingly redeeming qualities.*

I was floored. Completely and utterly spellbound. There was no question in my mind, so the enthusiasm came rushing out like the dam that finally broke.

It's yours. My mouth is yours.

The arch of one blond brow twitched as he fought off a smile. *Are you going to tell him that?*

Our silence was broken by my sharp intake of breath as I turned to Wrenlock and said, "Okay. Lucais won't touch you, and you won't touch my mouth, and I won't..."

"You won't do this if you don't want to," the High King offered in the silence of my uncertainty. "Even if you feel like you have no other choice. Because you tell us to start looking for another option, and we'll start looking."

Wrenlock nodded his enthusiastic agreement with the sentiment, and my heart warmed at their attempts to soothe me when we all knew perfectly well that there was nothing left to search for outside the palace walls.

"I won't do this if I don't want to," I repeated. A bizarre thought struck me that the repetition of those words was as close to wedding vows as we were ever likely to have. I had to stifle a maniacal laugh. "Even if I feel like I have no other choice."

"Then we're all agreed."

"Agreed."

"Agreed."

Fuck.

Thirty-Six

We'll Be Friends Tomorrow

We met in the High King's bedroom a little while later.

I'd hyperventilated in the shower for a good ten minutes before I decided to pull myself together.

The choices, despite anything the two men might insist, presented an impossible scenario. If I did not accept the mating bond with Lucais and formally become his High Queen, it was likely that the Court of Darkness would continue to haunt me, either driving me into the shadows again, or to my death.

Even if I didn't want to believe anything that Wrenlock and Lucais were telling me, the Spectre who visited me the last time I was in my own room had already warned me about it. Simultaneously, he had been very clear that he did not have my best interests at heart, and then he'd proceeded to trick me into making a bargain with him over it. Maybe it was the result of my childhood trauma, but I was more likely to trust the words of people who never pretended to care about me.

Besides, I couldn't die at anyone else's hands, or Tommy would spend eternity trapped in solitary confinement because the person he needed to haunt had become a ghost herself. Considering what I had done to him, that was reason enough for me to remain alive.

On the other hand, though, there was absolutely no way that I would willingly give myself over to the Court of Darkness. No way at all. I'd sooner die, but then I'd be breaking promises to both humans and faeries alike—the Spectre and Brynn.

None of that even mattered when I was being completely honest with myself in the mirror, though. When I stared at my reflection, remembering the way that Lucais had smudged the makeup on my face so he could still see the wine-coloured birthmark that spilled across my left eyebrow, and took several deep breaths before permitting the thoughts to take centre stage in my mind.

For better or worse, I wanted to be with Lucais.

The flood gates had opened. He was a craving I'd likely regret satisfying during the lulls, but I couldn't get him out of my head during the peak of my hunger. I was worn down from trying to piece together the fragments of reasons to avoid our fate, and I was scared to admit that I was capable of being so outwardly selfish. The fuse was there, and I was holding the match, so all I had left to do was strike it and embrace the rapturous feeling of blowing my entire reality into smithereens.

If it imploded his world at the same time, he would have to shoulder the blame. He would have to take an equal share of the responsibility for the catastrophic consequences we faced—and I would have to find a way to let him—which was something he seemed very much prepared to do when I walked into his room and found the entire space alight with faelight orbs and burning candles.

The High King of Faerie's bedroom in the palace was considerably grander than his dishevelled room at the House had been. It was large enough to rival the great hall where the throne sat, and carved from rough-textured grey stone, broken up by numerous rectangular windows, each covered by white chiffon curtains that gathered in ruffles at the top.

His furniture was lavish but simple—a mirrored dressing table beside a matching set of drawers constructed from heavy red oak, a set of six bookcases that increased in height like steps towards the high coffered ceiling, a large desk and simple wooden chair, and finally a second, much longer bureau.

In the middle of the room, an enormous sheer canopy bed sat like an island of fluffy pillows, silky sheets, and thick blankets. A trunk identical to the one in my bedroom was placed at the foot, and Wrenlock sat perched upon it in a sleeveless dark grey tunic and pants, his elbow resting on his knee, his head bent to prop his chin up on his fist. He looked devastatingly handsome in the firelight, the warm undertones of his deep brown skin set aglow by the flames. When he saw me, his depthless eyes brightened, and he lifted his head, giving me a small smile.

Lucais stood at the dresser behind him, clad in black—a pair of loose pants and a button-up shirt that hung open, revealing the smooth, perfect planes of his chest and stomach. The definition of his muscles made my mouth water as I traced the lines with my eyes, from the tight set of his abdominals all the way down to the sharp cut of his hips dipping below the waistband of his pants.

To further deepen the contoured ridges on his body, he was decorated with tattoos. They were etched onto his skin with dark ink, but they almost surely held some type of magical properties, like they might shift colour or change shape when nobody was looking at them. I made a mental note to ask him about them later—along with all of the many other questions I had stored somewhere in my head, saved for a time we could talk without snapping at one another or making heartfelt declarations of love.

I was aching to follow the lines vanishing beneath his shirt, eager to map all of them out and commit the landscape of his body to memory. My recollections of the nightmares were growing foggier by the day to the point where I felt as though I was seeing the High King's body for the very first time as he lingered by the dressing table. The back of his shirt was reflected in the mirror as he stood there, a drink in one hand, rubbing the fingers of his other hand against his palm and thumb as he watched me step into the room and close the door behind me.

I hesitated on the threshold, trying to still my wild heart.

If I took a step further into the room, there was no question about it being a choice. The Court and Oracle be damned—because nobody suggested or prophesised that I should sleep with both of them on the same day, let alone at the same *time*. It was all our own doing, our very own decision, our way of rewriting the star-told story for which we had been destined.

His blond hair shone like the sun in the combined illumination of light and fire, and I knew in an instant that Lucais standing there, looking at me like that, was the most beautiful sight I would ever see. And I needed it desperately after seeing so much horror.

I stepped into the room.

"I didn't think there were any candles in the palace," I said quietly. "At least, not any that were still usable."

He lifted a shoulder. "We keep relics from previous rulers in a separate part of the palace. I figured that this was a human sort of notion, and the occasion called for it."

"That was sweet of you."

The High King swallowed, the motion visible even from where I stood across the room, and dragged his gaze away from mine with visible reluctance. "Would you like a drink?" he offered, gesturing to a large crystal bottle filled with dark red liquid on the top of his drawers.

Biting my lip, I weighed my options. I'd never consumed faerie wine before because it never ended well for humans in all of the fables, but if there was ever a time to start...

"One glass will have a moderate effect on you, I'd assume," he added, ducking his head. "But it's your choice."

Moderate effect.

At least he was being honest.

"I'll have half a glass, then, please."

The High King nodded and busied himself pouring me a drink.

We crossed the room at the same time, meeting each other in the middle. The atmosphere was thick, the air perfumed with the scent of frangipanis, musk, and the ink between the pages of an old book. When he passed me the glass, our fingers brushed, and an illicit thrill ran through me. I lost control of my breathing pattern and the rush went straight to my head, making me feel suddenly light on my feet. I hadn't even sipped the fucking faerie wine yet, and all he'd done was touch my hand, yet my heart felt like it was hurtling down a steep incline with faulty brakes and there was a hot, pulsating tension building in my core.

I downed the entire half glass of thin, sugary liquid in one go.

"That was... Uh, okay. Easy now." Lucais took the glass back from me and returned it to the crystal tray on the top of his dresser, pausing to give me a strange look over his shoulder before he put it down. It could have been admiration as easily as it might have been disapproval.

The wine was delicious—a heady taste that carried a lovely sharpness once it was swallowed. I immediately wanted more, but I refrained and started to wonder if the stories of humans losing all of their wits at the hands of the drink were less about the liquid's potency and more about the consumer's gluttony. In any case, it was already going to my head, magnifying the light, airy feeling I was falling victim to simply from being in the room with the two of them and all of the candles.

My hand brushed Wrenlock's shoulder when I extended it out to the side for balance. Gripping my arm, he pulled me towards him, and I found myself settling into his lap. His scent of sweet candied fruit and bonfire smoke filled my senses, momentarily distracting me from the presence of the High King, who hovered by his dressing table like he was scared to move lest he spooked me.

"Hi," Wrenlock purred, his voice low and soft.

"Hi," I said back. A glimmer of self-consciousness broke through as he bent his head to capture my mouth with his own.

The kiss was searing, his touch a brand straight from the crucible. I relished the taste of his mouth, sweet from having downed a glass or two of wine himself. I didn't protest when his large hands secured themselves around my waist, urging me to shift onto his lap until I was straddling him. We kissed each other in a comfortable, familiar way despite the fact that we'd only done it a few times. The feel of his strong shoulders and torso beneath me chased away the loneliness in my bones until all that was left was a vast expanse of possibility.

I couldn't explain it.

Wrenlock felt like coming home, but so did Lucais.

The very notion that I would fall in love and come to belong with two men from the Court of Light clashed so severely with my inheritance of the Court of Darkness, but it had been an undeniable factor of the pull between us since the first day we'd met.

Maybe I needed both of them to pull me back from the brink of my inevitable darkness.

I felt Wrenlock harden beneath me as we kissed, felt the pulse of arousal shudder through him as his cock jerked in his pants, and then I heard a soft collection of clinks—like stones hitting the bottom of an empty fishbowl.

Pulling back from his mouth, I turned to see Lucais removing the silver rings from his fingers, dropping them into a small, decorative bowl on the edge of the dresser beside him. My mouth watered at the subtle but unmistakable intimation, and I had to force myself to swallow. He met my stare, a gentle curiosity sparkling in his own, respectfully challenging me to react.

Slowly, I rose from Wrenlock's lap and took three steps towards the High King.

Eyes on me, he removed the last silver ring with a soft clink that rang out through the air with extended finality, and then he matched my steps until we were standing so close together I felt his breath hitting my skin as he stared down at me.

"So..." I breathed.

The touch of a smile fell upon his mouth at the shaky undercurrent in my voice. He cocked his head to the side, speaking very softly, "So."

"Do I have to say the magic words?"

His smile broke through the surface. "Yes. Something like… *I, Auralie Roberts, am so fortunate to take you, Lucais Starfire, as my Oracle-fated mate* should do quite nicely, I think."

"I, Auralie Roberts, take you, Lucais Starfire, as my Oracle-fated pain in the ass…"

He let out a delighted laugh, tipping his head back. I watched the way his throat flexed and felt a nearly overwhelming urge to press a series of quick but indulgent kisses across it. "I suppose I could be in a short while, if you asked me nicely enough."

The humour left my eyes in a blink. "Oh." I glanced between them, apprehension pricking me like a thorn in my side. "Actually, I'm glad we brought that up because it's going to be a *no thank you* on that from me."

Lucais snickered with the wicked glee of getting the last word, but Wrenlock simply shrugged as if to say that he wouldn't be bothered either way.

"You don't need to say anything, bookworm." The High King tucked my curls behind my ear. "There are stories of some not even realising that there's a mating bond at play until after sleeping together, once it clicks into place." He sighed, golden eyes roving over my face. "I do need you to be certain, though. You cannot take its acceptance back any easier than you can its rejection."

Nervous energy skittered across my skin, but I steeled myself and tilted my head back so that I could look at his face fully.

For maybe the first time ever, he looked at me like he was someone I could trust. I hoped that my expression was brave, even though I didn't feel much like it at all. Lifting my shaking hands, I tugged at the open collar of his shirt to warn him of what I was about to do before I raised my arms higher and pushed it back from his shoulders. He angled his arms behind his back, letting it slip effortlessly onto the floor.

I'd seen Lucais completely shirtless before, but it was no less striking to see him like that again—and even more so with the glamour removed. My chest felt so tight, I wasn't sure that my heart was still beating.

"Sure, I'm certain," I drawled, attempting a nonchalant shrug. It turned into a loosening of my shoulders, rolling them back against the budding tension. My voice was shaky. "What's a mating bond between friends?"

The High King's eyes warmed, and his voice dropped to a husky whisper as he asked, "Are we friends, bookworm?"

I wet my lips with my tongue and swallowed hard. "We'll be friends tomorrow," I said.

He dipped his head, his gaze transfixed by the shine on my mouth, a satisfied smirk curling on his own that made him look younger, lighter, and freer than I'd ever seen him before. Except for that day on the staircase in the House, perhaps, when he'd stood underneath a halo of light and I'd compared him to an angel in my head. That was the Lucais who grinned down at me with softness and joy decorating his expression, and it eased something inside of my soul to bear witness to it again in the moments right before we sealed our fates.

"We'll be friends tomorrow," he agreed, his voice a soft murmur as he nodded gently but enthusiastically and bent to kiss me.

It was soft and lazy, the caress of his lips on mine so patient and revering. He brushed his mouth against me with only enough force to flick my bottom lip, allowing me to taste the faintest hint of him again. I pushed up on the tips of my toes to meet his mouth, parting my lips to capture his kiss, and our tongues collided with a hot, all-consuming sensation that sparked something deep inside my brain before travelling through the rest of my body like a switch lighting up the mainframe.

The silken caress of his tongue tangling with mine sent a harsh shot of arousal straight to my nipples. They hardened into painfully tight peaks, squeezing a low, burning ache that radiated pulses of electricity out of my core.

I was wearing a modest indigo silk chemise that went all the way to the floor with thin, lacy straps, baring most of the skin from my breastbone and up. Lucais's hands slid up to grip my face as he deepened the kiss, and the collision of his skin against mine sent a second jolt of liquid heat through both of us.

He pressed into me, the warmth from his chest searing through the fabric of my gown, and a light ache coiled in my nipples, my breasts feeling heavy and full, the burn of need simmering beneath my skin all too much.

A small sound vibrated in the back of my throat as Lucais angled his head for better access to my mouth, and we both staggered a step to the side, lost in the sensation of trying to crawl inside of each other. Hands still firmly secured on the sides of my face, he walked me backwards in a rush to find stability, and we hit the nearest bedpost with a bump.

I felt a spike of arousal flood the space between my legs and begin to drip down my thighs, the ball of nerves between them tingling with a static warmth. The tension expanded from my core until it was at my waist and behind my hips, and the muscles in my legs were clenching.

Lucais's hands were trembling ever so slightly as he slid them down the sides of my neck and curled them around the thin lace straps on my shoulders. Panting wildly, he broke the kiss long enough to open his eyes into mine, searching for something that I assumed was reassurance or permission to pull the straps off me. My gaze darted to Wrenlock, who remained seated on the chest beside us, his eyes alight with desire and a hand draped across his mouth, one finger clamped between his teeth.

When he met my eyes, Wrenlock dropped his hand and rose to stand. The two men shared a glance, wordlessly reaching an agreement on something that had me wondering if it was actually their first time, and I found myself trying not to breathe too loudly as they moved to either side of me and each grasped one of my straps.

I was going to die. I was going to die because they were going to kill me, and they weren't even trying to commit a felony.

Slowly, they pulled the lace from my shoulders, and the ache in my breasts intensified as the fabric slipped over them in what felt like slow motion before it abandoned my body and pooled onto the ground around my feet.

Lucais inhaled deeply. It wasn't his first time glimpsing me without clothing on, but still, he breathed out a low, "*Fuck.*"

I pressed the back of my skull against the wooden bedpost and closed my eyes, choking down air with as much finesse as I could manage, given the fact that I could feel their breaths caressing my skin as they bent their heads to my chest.

My eyes fluttered open, and with a sharp mental curse, they immediately clamped shut again. I was at risk of spontaneous combustion either way, but I couldn't bear to meet their gentle eyes as they ravished me with them.

The heat of their gazes was already more than enough on its own. I'd been admired before, and complimented by the few people I'd been intimate with, but never like that. Never by someone who looked like they'd kill to keep me—who *had* killed to keep me—and never more than one person at the same time. The sensation of being adored by both of them at once was thick and intense, a form of pleasurable mental strangulation through which I needed to keep my lungs breathing deeply and evenly, or else I would actually pass out.

Wrenlock kissed the side of my breast first, leaning with one hand on the bedpost above my head, while Lucais's lips coasted across the soft skin of my stomach as he lowered himself onto his knees before me.

I writhed against the bedpost, desperate for the missing friction that my fallen gown had provided, and felt a set of sharp teeth close around one of my nipples in reply. The other side was quickly subjected to the same excruciatingly torturous pleasure, and when their tongues came out to sweep over the sharpness of their bites, I moaned so loudly that I was instantly embarrassed. The whole palace could probably hear us. Although, there were so few occupants, it surely sounded worse in my mind than what it really was.

With my eyes firmly shut, I let my head loll back against the bedpost, locking my knees to keep myself standing upright as they worked a series of sharper, quieter moans out of my mouth.

They sucked and pulled and bit me, dragging my nipples with their tongues and teeth, both of my breasts screaming with ecstatic pleasure as they were worked in unison. I felt the heat in my core tightening with every stroke and nip, with every slight bob of a head against my breasts, and with every last whispering sound that joined the three of us in the room. The tension pulsed in the semblance of a steady bass rhythm, and I let out a broken whimper when I realised they were bringing me to the edge of an orgasm with their mouths on my breasts alone.

Their hands hadn't even touched me yet, the wetness between my thighs undiscovered.

In the white-hot, lust-filled haze of my mind, I barely knew what I was doing when I finally moved my arms from my sides and brought my hands up to twist into their hair. Lucais's soft locks were against the crease of my arm as he knelt before me, and his moan sent a bolt of satisfaction coursing through me when I tugged softly on his roots. Wrenlock's head was higher, his neck bent as he leaned on the bedpost with me, his hand cupping and squeezing my breast from underneath, and his teeth grazed my nipple as he sucked it into his mouth, pulling hard against gravity until it was bouncing gently between my body and his face.

Digging my fingers into their hair, I held their faces to me, riding the growing waves until the tension between my legs was blistering and on the verge of bursting, and that was when Wrenlock slipped his hand down between my thighs.

I was so wet that his fingers parted me with ease, and he pressed the pads of his fore and middle fingers against my clit with gentle pressure. Groaning, I rocked my hips against him, and then I felt another hand brush the side of my leg. Lucais's hand caressed the sensitive skin on the backs of my knees, coasting up and down with a featherlight touch. His fingertips sparked shivers through my flesh that caught ablaze with Wrenlock's ministrations as he rubbed slow, firm circles over my clit.

When Wrenlock's mouth released my breast, Lucais's other hand took its place, twisting my nipple in perfect synchronicity with his own mouth. I shattered into a million pieces as soon as Wrenlock placed a soft, teasing kiss in the detonation zone on the side of my neck, just below my ear, and chased it with a euphoric bite hard enough to leave a mark.

I felt a shudder ripple through Lucais as I cried out. My release rolled across my body, crashing into parts of me I had forgotten about—a balloon that had been filled by so many weeks of fighting and flirting, finally let go inside of a room of precious artefacts. My back arched as I moaned, and then I collapsed into the aftershocks, Wrenlock and Lucais supporting me against the bedpost with their arms until my legs stopped shaking.

Lucais trailed delicate kisses up the side of my leg, over my hip, and across my rib cage as he rose to stand. I couldn't bear to look at him, but I forced myself to do it anyway. His eyes were filled with soft, warm emotions that reached out to greet me with open arms and wide smiles.

"That was..." I found myself unable to complete the sentence and find the right words. "Did it work?" I asked him instead, breathing unevenly.

A dark, carnal look gleamed in his eyes. "Oh, no, bookworm," he purred, a wicked crease forming between his brows as he reached up to brush my hair back from my face and then leaned in to kiss the side of my jaw. "That wasn't it."

I'd finally regained the ability to regulate my breathing, but his words made it catch in my throat. Lucais's face was the picture of sinful satisfaction as he observed the widening of my eyes, so I glanced at Wrenlock.

He placed a slow, sweet kiss against my temple and removed his hand from where it was still cupping me between my legs. His fingers glistened with my arousal, and my eyes turned into saucers as he lifted his fingers up towards his mouth.

Wrenlock had the audacity to wink at me as he said, "That was just us warming you up, baby."

I watched, my lips parted around a silent gasp, as Lucais's hand shot out to capture Wrenlock's wrist, stopping him before his fingers reached his mouth. They exchanged a heated look as Lucais guided that hand in the opposite direction, their arms crossing over me. And then, right in front of my face, the High King of Faerie sucked the taste of my orgasm off Wrenlock's fingers.

Thirty-Seven

Switch Places With Me

Heat scorched my skin as Lucais dragged his knuckles up and down my arm while we watched Wrenlock undress. The shirt came over the top of his head first, landing on the floor like a silent splash of ink, and then he began to work his belt free. When his pants dropped with a soft clang of the metal clip against the stone, my mouth ran dry.

We were really doing it.

Lucais's golden eyes sought out mine. "Would you like to do the honours?"

With a gulp, I looked between the High King's face and the buckle on his pants. My hands were shaking as I reached for him. It took a lot of effort to keep them steady enough to work everything loose, and once I had, he bent down and slowly lowered them to the floor, keeping his molten gold eyes trained on mine the entire time. I swallowed again.

Wrenlock came to stand behind me, the press of his naked flesh into mine sending a ripple of shivers across my body. He kissed my neck while I watched Lucais straighten up again, which forced me to take half a step back—about as far as I could get before I stepped fully into the solid wall of Wrenlock's warm body and there was nowhere left for me to go. The High King was *huge*.

Is it a height thing?

I didn't think so, but I was suddenly driven to find out what gave a man a right to be so...so...

Lucais wrapped one hand around himself almost self-consciously while I stood there and gaped at him like an idiot. Seeing it and feeling it through his pants simply hadn't been enough warning. The clothes he wore didn't do him any justice whatsoever compared to the bare image, and I was suddenly less aroused and more frightened.

Wrenlock, on the other hand, was a good size—a nice, steady length, a thickness that looked as though it could fill me to the point of instant gratification without renovating my insides—and I thought that was more than enough considering my experiences with human men. My modest subject pool consisted of one thing or the other—length or girth. There never seemed to be both, and there was certainly never an excess of both elements at the same time.

Even so, liquid heat pooled in my lower belly as I watched Lucais stroke his length up and down in spite of my hesitancy.

"Bookworm," he whispered. "Breathe."

I'd stopped and I hadn't even realised. Wrenlock lifted his head from my neck and let out a loose chuckle when he clicked onto what was going on.

"I can't fit that inside of me," I lamented. Somebody needed to point it out. "I'm human."

"So what if you're human?"

"It..." My eyes flared. "It will rearrange my internal organs. I'll end up in a hospital, which is—wait, do you even *have* hospitals in Faerie?"

"Auralie, I'm not going to hurt you—not if you aren't going to enjoy it." His eyes warmed as if to strengthen the sincerity of his vow, the gold deepening into amber, and a thrill ran through me despite myself. "I am not going to damage you in ways I cannot fix. I'm sure it's impossible, in any case. Fated mates and all of that, if you recall?"

I sucked in a deep breath, filling my starving lungs, and then returned to sizing Lucais up. He made a valid point. When I angled my head to the side like I had been while Wrenlock was kissing me, Lucais's cock looked like an impossible task, but with my head sitting straight on the top of my shoulders...

I bit my lower lip. *Maybe.*

"Do you want to try him first?" Wrenlock whispered in my ear, trailing his hands down my arms. It probably seemed that way when my eyes had been transfixed on Lucais ever since he'd taken off his clothes, but the debate in my mind was ongoing. "It's okay, baby. I've got you."

Lucais softly kicked the trunk at the foot of the bed out of the way—kicked it like it was a balloon and not an extremely heavy wooden storage container—and sat down on the end of the bed. Legs bent with his feet flat on the ground, he presented me with a perfectly enticing invitation to sit on his lap, sidling up to the thick erection resting against his stomach.

He watched me, expression heated, as I pushed my shoulders back and stepped over to him.

Holding his hands out, Lucais let me step willingly into his embrace before he wrapped them around my hips and pulled me close. He was warm and soft as I climbed onto his lap until I was straddling him. A hum vibrated beneath my skin at the contact, inimitable energy zinging between us, and I felt my core tighten with a sharp stab of expectant pleasure.

Wrenlock spat into his palm and reached that hand between us, coating my already slick entrance with his saliva. Then, he placed his hands on my shoulders, gently kneading the tension out of them as I locked eyes with Lucais and we exchanged a small nod.

I rose on my knees as high as I could while he gripped the base of his cock to position himself underneath me, but I fell short. My legs weren't long enough, and his length was an inch or so too much. We both hesitated, taken aback by the immediate technical problems we were facing until Wrenlock slid his hands beneath my arms and lifted me in the air high enough for Lucais to get himself into position.

My fingernails dug into his shoulders as I stared down at the space between us, totally consumed by thoughts of what we were about to do and whether I'd even be able to do it.

"You can take him, baby," Wrenlock promised me. "Just go nice and slow."

He supported me while I lowered myself onto Lucais. I stopped when I felt his tip nudge my entrance, my joints locking into place, muscles seizing up.

Fuck. Fuck—

"Nice and slow," Wrenlock purred in my ear.

I sought comfort inside of a pair of golden eyes.

Lucais held my gaze, his evident desire mingling with concern as I lowered myself down until the tip of his cock was inside of me.

The warmth was instant and overwhelming. Sparks began to fly at the base of my spine, a reckless heat growing inside my core, desperate to be coaxed into an uncontrollable explosion. In an instant, my fear switched sides. I was no longer afraid of being hurt as much as I was afraid that if I sank all the way down onto him I might never be able to get him back out.

Visions from the field of the two of us trapped in an eternity as one erotic statue circled my mind again.

"That's a good girl," Wrenlock encouraged, removing his hands from beneath my arms and resting them on top of my shoulders again. The excess inch or two that hadn't been able to fit between us before was inside of me, and I could hold myself up again as even as the mutual hesitation was prolonged. "You can take some more of him, baby. I know you can."

With my hands on the High King's shoulders and his palms resting against my hips, I lowered myself down until his erection was an inch deeper, groaning when I felt the pressure building as his girth coaxed me to open up and allow him to stretch me. Lucais was taking shallow breaths, his pulse dancing at the base of his throat. I could tell that it was taking most of his strength to stop himself from seizing control of the situation.

"Relax, bookworm," he murmured. I felt his fingertips twitch against my waist, tempted but restrained. "We were made for this. We were made for each other."

My heartbeat sped up. His words triggered a small wave of hot arousal to pool between my legs, so I nodded and slid down on another inch of his cock. And then another. Another. *Another.*

The feeling that bloomed in my core was euphoric. The tip of his erection pressed into a part of me that triggered countless sparks of pleasure to roll out across my body from the blazing heat between my hips all the way out to the very ends of my fingertips and my hair. It bolstered my confidence, urging me to move my hips again.

The motion dragged a long, loud moan from both of us in unison as I sank the rest of the way down until Lucais's cock was buried inside me, all the way to the hilt.

My lower belly tightened as I clenched around him.

Neither of us dared to move a muscle, but the *fulfilment*...

The sensation of unrivalled ecstasy rolled over me in small waves, lapping up against every last pleasure centre in my body as hot as a summer sun. We'd barely started, and yet I felt as if I might come apart at the seams if he so much as breathed on me. Feeling the same thing despite the lack of friction, Lucais moaned, the sound so small and rough I knew he'd tried to silence it.

He filled me, completing me, and I could have stayed there forever. We would never have had to move. The feeling of him being wedged so deeply inside of such an intimate part of me was enough. The look on his face as his starcore eyes dissolved into mine, heated and swirling with adoration, was enough. We found nirvana inside of each other, so pure that time had no choice but to stand still and bear witness.

Wrenlock's fingers flexed on my shoulders, massaging my aching muscles, driving pleasure down through my spine, and the pressure caused me to move my hips on Lucais. So quickly that I could scarcely take in a gasp of breath, the little waves built to a crescendo—a tidal wave that would crash over us and wash me away. I felt him everywhere, inside and around an orgasm that was about to destroy me from within, and though it was the only truly painful part of what we were doing, I used my hands on his shoulders to propel myself backwards until we were separated again.

Lucais's erection slapped against his stomach, glistening in the candlelight with my arousal.

I fell back into Wrenlock's arms, panting wildly. The ache in between my legs screamed, empty and lost, begging for him to return and fill me again.

I pressed my mouth into a tight line and made a sharp sound of denial. "Mm-hm. I can't. That..."

The High King was staring at me like he was every bit as afraid of me as I was of him—like he'd felt the same wild abandon taking over his mind, body, and soul. Before Wrenlock could ask a question we wouldn't be able to answer using real words, Lucais swallowed, reaching for my hand and squeezing.

"Let's take it slow," he suggested, voice thick and fragile. He glanced up at Wrenlock and then back to me. "Switch places with me," he ordered.

With gentle hands, Wrenlock placed me down on the bed where Lucais had been perched, laying me back until my head was nestled against the blankets and my hair fanned out around my face. I felt electrifyingly exposed as a burst of cool air swept over me, prickling my skin and forcing my nipples to harden into tight, pink peaks on my bare chest. The High King knelt at the end of the bed, gently urging my legs apart, and began to trail his mouth up along my thigh, leaving a line of searing kisses from the inner corner of my knee all the way up to my hip bone.

"We have all the time in the world," he promised, his voice low and husky. My pussy clenched as his breath caressed my skin when he bent his head to me, whispering, "I'll give you whatever you want from me for as long as you need it."

Lucais's tongue swept over my entrance, circling my clit, and I instinctively writhed, bucking my hips against him as the sheer heat of his mouth overwhelmed me. I hadn't realised that he'd hooked both arms around me until he used them to hold me in place, his hands on my hips, his head buried between my thighs. Wrenlock lounged on the bed at my side, his mouth switching between teasing my breasts and indulging my mouth in slow kisses that rivalled the patience of the High King kneeling between my legs.

As promised, Lucais took his tasting of me slowly, leisurely stroking my clit with his tongue before fucking me with it, the only sense of urgency showing in the way his hands gripped my hips and tugged me further down the bed until I was sure that he couldn't breathe. In the back of my mind, I was keenly aware of that, though I was floating back and forth from coherence as his ministrations coaxed shallow breaths and moans from my chest. However, after a few minutes without Lucais resurfacing for air, I shifted away from him, trying to offer him a reprieve as I wriggled up towards the pillows.

Lucais lifted his head from where he was sucking on my clit, his eyes foggy with pleasure, his blond hair a mess across his forehead, and frowned up at me. "Don't tell me you're not enjoying this as much as I am," he implored.

I bit my lower lip, glancing at Wrenlock for some kind of affirmation, but the dark-haired man was sporting an amused smile as he ran his fingers over one of my erect nipples and then the other. He bent his head to my chest, sucking on one side, clearly demonstrating that he had no intention of getting involved with my interruption of the High King's indulgence.

"I don't want you to not be able to breathe," I muttered, falling back onto the bed as Wrenlock's mouth triggered a soft moan to escape from my mouth.

Lucais shook his head, brushing the hair back from his face as he rose to stand. "By the Elements, I never thought I'd hear you say those words to me." He reached down to clasp both of his hands around each of mine, pulling me into his arms. Wrenlock rolled off the mattress, and Lucais turned, lying back on the bed and positioning me so that I was sitting on his chest. "Aura, I am the High fucking King of Faerie. I don't need to *breathe air*. I need you to sit on my face. Right. Now."

Before I could say or do anything in reply, he tugged me forwards, positioning my thighs on either side of his head, and then his mouth was against my centre. I watched, transfixed, as his tongue pushed up against my clit, massaging it gently before he moaned against me, staring up at me the entire time. The sight was so unbelievably erotic that I nearly came all over his face right at that moment, but the lingering whisper of self-doubt and the absolute terror I felt at the thought of solidifying the bond with him once and for all held me back.

Lucais didn't seem to mind. In fact, he seemed to prefer that I took my time so he could take his.

Shortly thereafter, though, my orgasm was inevitable. I felt it building to unalterable heights as I began to rock my hips, grinding against Lucais's face, and I started to relax in the kind of way that touched more than simply my muscles.

Leaning back with my hands on his hips, I rode his face. He moaned so loudly that I felt the reverberations all the way up to my nipples. For a split second, I jerked out of our rhythm, struck by the sudden realisation that I didn't know where Wrenlock had gone. But I was riding the waves of euphoria so close to a climax that it only threw me off for a moment.

Tipping my head back, I looked towards the floor where all of our clothes were discarded, and my orgasm came splintering over me with a force strong enough to rip my lungs straight out of my body when I found Wrenlock kneeling between Lucais's legs at the end of the bed, his dark hair bobbing up and down as he sucked on Lucais's furiously hard cock. As I watched, one of Lucais's hands slipped from my hip, across the sheets, and fisted in Wrenlock's curls. He held on with a demanding grip, pushing his erection deeper into Wrenlock's mouth with the next motion. A set of dark brown eyes flicked up to meet mine with heat and temptation emanating from their burning cores.

Wrenlock's cheeks lifted only by a fraction as he smiled at me around Lucais's cock, and I was undone.

The sound I made probably would have had numerous calls placed to local authorities if we had neighbours—and if I wasn't currently fucking the highest ranking authorities in the entire realm.

The sight of Wrenlock blowing Lucais while I rode his face was enough to destroy me. I came so hard that I couldn't quite tell when it started and where it stopped, only that it ricocheted through me until unimaginable pleasure turned into borderline pain. I was shaking so hard that I practically threw myself into the pillows on the bed beside Lucais so I wouldn't collapse on top of him or fall onto the ground.

Curling up around a pillow, I buried my face in the linen and inhaled a few deep breaths, accompanied with the High King's sweet scent of musk and sunlight.

Four hands found me moments later, stroking my hair back from my face and massaging my backside and thighs. The two men spoke in hushed, gentle tones as they doted on me with whispers of praise and reassurance, but I couldn't identify and separate their voices through the aftershocks of my orgasm and the world-tilting repercussions.

"Shh, perfect girl. It's alright. You did so fucking well. So fucking perfect for me."

"That's it, baby. Atta girl. Take a few deep breaths for us."

One of them pulled the blankets over me, and as I settled underneath the warm fabric and all of their soft touches and sweet words, I must have found the desire to sleep inside their safety.

Thirty-Eight

A Mind-Reading Spell

I awoke to the smell of freshly made coffee somewhere close to my head. My entire body was abuzz with feeling. I was sore, I was fulfilled, and above all I was exhausted. I felt like half of my soul had been scooped out of my body and given to someone else—Lucais, probably. In exchange for it, he'd given me one of his white shirts to wear overnight. I felt the buttery soft material shift against my skin as I rolled over, surfing the waves of his natural cologne.

When I opened my eyes and sat upright, I searched the room and found him standing by the large arched window closest to me. The daylight was bright enough to confirm that it was morning, although I had no way of knowing the precise time.

The window was almost floor to ceiling in height and about as wide as his shoulders. The chiffon curtains had been pulled back, though it made very little difference when the only view he had was of the endless and impenetrable fog. Even so, he stared out of it as if he could see through the mist to whatever corner of his realm lay beyond; and, for all I knew, maybe he could.

"How are you feeling?" he asked without turning around. The High King's voice, though tender, startled me. As he circled back to study me, he brought a mug of steaming hot liquid to his mouth and nodded towards something over my shoulder.

I glanced behind myself to find an identical mug waiting for me, levitating in thin air as if it had been placed on top of an invisible table. Propping myself up on the pillows and bringing my knees to my chest, I claimed it, shivering as the warmth spread from my fingertips all the way through to my toes. The enlivening aroma made my mouth water, so I took a sip of the coffee while I pondered how best to answer his question.

"I feel strange," I said at last. "Because I still feel like me, and I kind of expected that I wouldn't anymore."

Lucais padded over to me barefoot. He was shirtless, wearing only a pair of loose grey pants that hung low around his hips, and the bed dipped as he sat down as close to me as possible on the edge of it. I had half a thought to find Wrenlock, certain that I'd felt warmth from both men throughout the night, but he wasn't in the room with us.

"He's coming back," the High King assured me. "As for feeling different..." One side of his mouth pulled up in a roguish smile, but there was a touch of bashfulness in his golden eyes. "You remember how we said we'd be friends today?"

I nodded slowly, taking another sip of coffee.

He cocked his head to the side, biting his lower lip. "How do you feel about tomorrow instead?"

"What do you mean?"

"I mean..." Lucais's soft laugh was unsteady. "I'm afraid that you fell asleep quite early. That was our fault," he hastened to add. "We wore you out before you and I were able to fulfil the requirements of the mating bond."

Forgetting that I was holding a mug full of hot coffee, I dropped my hands into my lap, and half of my drink splashed over the side. In an instant, Lucais waved his fingers in the air, and the caramel coloured liquid froze like an ice statue before it could splash all over the blankets across my lap. He followed it with a circular motion of his wrist, reversing the entire accident. I watched in awe as it splashed back *into* the mug, and he gingerly reached over to take it from me before setting it back atop the invisible side table.

I blinked up at him, heart racing. He was slowly but surely letting me see more of his magic at work, and it was mesmerising. More than that, even. It was humbling. And terror-inducing.

"What do you mean?" I questioned faintly. "I know that I didn't imagine last night happening. I'm sure I have at least a hickey to prove it—"

The High King laughed and reached out to stroke a finger down the side of my neck, lingering over the spot where Wrenlock had bitten me hard enough to leave a mark. "Bookworm," he crooned. "We certainly engaged in an array of very pleasurable activities last night, but there was one particular thing that we didn't do, and that one thing just so happens to be quite essential if we want the mating bond to take effect."

Understanding washed over me with the flush of pink that touched my cheeks. "You didn't..." I trailed off awkwardly, staring down at his crotch. Beneath the light fabric of his pants, I saw the immediate twitch of his cock springing to life at my attention, and the colour on my cheeks deepened.

"Oh, no, I did." He grinned like a fiend when he saw the expression on my face. "Around the same time as you, actually."

My heart skipped a beat, sparing one for the space between my legs that throbbed once at the imagery of Wrenlock getting Lucais off while I came apart on top of him. "But not...with me," I hedged, uncertain.

His smile was coy. "Not exactly, no."

I took a few deep breaths, weighing up my options.

If the bond hadn't been solidified, that meant there was still time for me to change my mind if that's what I wanted to do. But if I didn't want to back out, then we had to start it all over again, and I wasn't sure I'd survive it.

The way Lucais had felt inside of me was all-consuming and lethal. It was hard enough to look him in the eye after he'd fucked me with his tongue and pulled me apart at the seams, so to lose myself completely with him would surely feel a million times more intense—and a million times more unforgettable and inescapable.

"How many times does it need to happen?"

"Just once. Each. Together. Preferably around the same time."

I pushed my shoulders back and straightened my spine, letting my knees fall to the sides so I was cross-legged beneath the blankets. "Okay, then," I agreed. "We'll be friends tomorrow, and we'll finish this today."

One night to get it over and done with would have been ideal, but one entire day wasn't the worst thing in the world. Steeling myself, I untangled my legs from the blankets and moved towards him.

"Down, girl." Lucais laughed. He took the hand that was reaching for his erection and brought it up to his mouth, placing a kiss over my knuckles. "You just woke up. Your safety net hasn't come back yet. And you need something a bit stronger than coffee to replenish your strength."

I rolled my eyes, but I fell back onto the pillows and conceded.

The High King didn't ask me what I wanted to eat. Much like he had done with the coffee and tea, he simply took it upon himself to make it—and make it bizarrely accurate to my tastes.

He summoned a large tray of food so close to the breakfast spread the House used to send into my bedroom. It was filled with pancakes, waffles, assorted fruits, and golden syrup; there was a plate with thick slices of toast, paperdove eggs, sticks of butter, jam, and another pot of perfectly brewed coffee, complete with a pitcher of milk and cubes of sugar. Lucais sat with his legs crossed on the other side of the bed, facing me across the breakfast tray. My eyes bounced back and forth between the food and his unreadable expression while I tried to untangle specific memories from the haze in my brain.

"You..." I began after a few moments of his expectant silence. I extended a finger in the air between us, then hesitated, biting my lip. "I don't know if this sounds unhinged, but"—I frowned at the food, then flicked my eyes up to meet his curious gaze—"you were sending me food at the House."

The High King's mouth twitched, evidently against his will. He reached for a sprig of grapes and popped three into his mouth in quick succession, chewing thoroughly before he responded. "Was I?"

My brow creased. "Weren't you?"

"It's possible."

"I thought that it was the House. This whole time..." I trailed off, staring blindly at the foggy window over his shoulder.

He shrugged, bringing my vision back into focus. "A strong enchantment can absolutely take on a life of its own," the High King told me. "I enchanted the House, but over time, it's become far more independent. It has a mind of its own." He buttered and cut a slice of toast, handing one half to me. I took it, my mind still reeling. "The House takes most of my suggestions on board, and it wouldn't survive for long without me, but I don't have total control of it."

I shook my head slightly as I recalled that the House had locked my bedroom doors but still allowed him to come in through the balcony, which I'd thought was absolutely preposterous behaviour at the time.

"For example," Lucais went on around a bite of toast, "the interior design. The House alters its own décor and layout to suit the guests. Did you notice that your bedroom bore a striking resemblance to your bookstore? I certainly did—because I had nothing to do with it. That was the enchantment, observing you and adjusting the House's layout to suit the parts of your identity it was able to perceive. The problem is that it changes the *entire* building to fit the new design." He rolled his eyes. "The whole time you were there with me, I couldn't find a single fucking thing in my own bedroom."

I stifled a laugh. "And the Forest?"

"The Forest," Lucais said tightly, a scowl overcoming his face, "is a perfect example of a faulty spell."

I put a hand over my mouth to conceal a smile. "So what went wrong then?"

"You're better off asking what went *right*. And the answer to that would be absolutely nothing." He dusted breadcrumbs off his fingers over the empty plate, and I took the opportunity to take my first bite of toast, chewing patiently as I waited for him to speak.

"I was young and experimental," he divulged at last. "My family's cottage—the one you saw replicated to host the Map—was located in the Forest of Eyes and Ears before it was destroyed in the war. We had to move to Caeludor when I became the High King, which happened much earlier than anyone had expected, so we would occasionally travel back there for long weekends. I hadn't actually lived there long enough to form a solid attachment to the cottage myself, but I knew my parents missed their home. My father, most of all, because his inventions and experiments were housed there, and there was plenty of space for him to work." Lucais stopped long enough to make up a fresh cup of coffee. He took a sip before offering it to me, which I took gratefully.

"The Forest, on the other hand, I was obsessed with," he went on. "I was in a bad mood one weekend. My parents had been arguing more often because of all the stress they were under and I knew it was my fault, so I foolishly decided that if I could create a spell strong enough to make it seem that I had disappeared, then the crown might find someone else and all of our problems would be resolved."

Lucais's words hit a very familiar nerve. I pinched the skin on one of my knuckles inconspicuously to counteract the sting.

"The Forest was large, dense, and glorious even before the enchantment," he continued, leaning back on his hands. "I spelled it to cover my tracks, concealing me from any*one* or any*thing* that might come looking for me. For example, the crown—or my mother. But I mixed it up terribly. Instead of spelling it so that *I* couldn't be found, the incantation made it so that *she* couldn't be found. In the end, I had to mix a mind-reading spell in with the cloaking hex, which was an awful concoction. The combining or layering of spells and hexes is a terrible idea and should be avoided at all costs, by the way," he added, giving me a severe look. "It's a dangerous business and almost always means that something in one of the spells is bound to go terribly wrong. In this instance, the thing that went terribly wrong was that the Forest became sentient, gained the ability to read minds, feels justified in moving things around to manipulate travellers, and resents me for the rest of eternity."

"But you found your mother?"

"Yeah." Lucais exhaled in a light huff. "She was pissed."

I remembered the way the Forest had gone straight for his throat when we originally travelled through it, and I couldn't help the laugh that bubbled up and out of my lips, though I probably didn't try as hard as I could to keep it down. The boyish, good-humoured look on his face sent me into a fit of giggles so contagious that even Lucais couldn't hold back a snort of amusement.

That only made the whole thing even funnier, and soon my waist was cramping. I clutched at it, tilting to one side as uncontrollable laughter spilled out of me until my eyes were wet and I couldn't breathe. The tray of dishes clinked with the movement on the bed, and Lucais waved it away before he went down, too.

We switched from laughing at his anecdote to laughing at each other in an instant. Even as my mouth went dry and the chuckling subsided, I couldn't wipe the smile from my face as I stared at him, his head resting on the pillow next to mine, his hair as gold as his eyes, his smile as hopeful and fragile as mine.

"I sent the food to your room," Lucais admitted after a long stretch of companionable silence. He dipped his head. "I treated you poorly. I said some terrible things to you—truthful things, but I let them get twisted out of context, knowing they could hurt you that way. I was so scared that you would feel the things I felt. And, admittedly, I was furious that I was even feeling them there for a while, too, but I kicked myself afterwards. Every single time. I sent the food and coffee up to your room and drew your baths so that you'd feel..."

Loved.

He didn't finish the sentence, and he didn't need to. I knew exactly what he was telling me, because I'd felt loved by the House. Cherished. Valued. Protected. It had cared for me through moments when I was on the brink of giving up on caring for myself. It had shown me a sense of belonging that I'd never felt before in my life and didn't think I'd ever feel again—

Until that exact moment.

"Thank you," I whispered, dropping my gaze.

Lucais nodded curtly, staring at where our fingers had found each other in the space between our bodies. His knuckles were soft as they brushed up against mine, but the underside was roughened by calluses from his training. I knew he left them there intentionally because he could so easily spell them away. It reminded me of something he'd said in passing that I had filed away for later exploration.

"I have a question."

Lucais's eyes narrowed almost imperceptibly. "Yes, bookworm?"

"You said something downstairs about broken wings."

His fingertips stopped in the act of stroking circles over the palm of my hand. I could feel the immediate tension rolling off him, though there was very little change to his demeanour otherwise. For a moment, I weathered a stroke of regret for daring to ask about such a sensitive issue, but we were taking so many baby steps forward.

"I noticed that there are faeries in Caeludor who do have wings," I ventured, warily. "But I've never seen yours."

His throat worked around a hard swallow. "Those faeries are much younger than I am."

"But what does that mean?"

Lucais hesitated, pulling a long breath into his lungs, and threaded his fingers through mine, squeezing once before he recoiled and rose from the bed. "My wings were irreparably damaged during the war."

In the blink of an eye, I had a flashback to the gnarled mess of horns on top of the unicorns who pulled Lucais's carriage and the glinting steel of unclaimed weaponry scattered across the mountain range, and a dark chill rippled through me. As Lucais walked towards the dresser against the wall, I watched the muscles rippling across his back, following the shadows of the tattoos that dipped and flowed over the ridges of his strong shoulders and arms.

For a war veteran who maintained the wear and tear on his hands deliberately, it was odd that he had no scars anywhere else.

"I was only one of many soldiers who were wounded, but most were able to repair themselves or seek the attention of a healer in time," Lucais explained. His voice was distant, though he remained so close. "It's not often that faeries suffer long-lasting injuries. You need a significant trauma to occur first, and then there has to be a substantial delay in obtaining the necessary care. Most of the time, we can heal ourselves. Other times, like the time I was stung by a locust, we rely on others because we are unable to do it ourselves."

I wrapped my arms around myself tightly, recalling the panic I'd felt searching for a healer in the House the day that he was stung.

Most of the faeries downstairs had laughed it off because they thought I was talking about the real Wrenlock instead of the actual High King. I'd wanted to throttle every last one of them—except for the small girl who had stepped forward to help me, the faerie who had saved his life with my blood.

"The damage is sometimes invisible," he continued. "There are some severe psychological impacts amongst the faeries who served with me, and there are some physical injuries that persist against the test of time because they weren't able to be fully healed. The symptoms come and go for them. For me..." Lucais trailed off as he poured himself a glass of wine from the crystal drinking set on his drawers and downed it in one gulp. "There are very few like me who could not be healed at all. My wings were permanently broken during the *Battle of Burning Waters* outside of Caeludor. The humans who shot me out of the sky had a short period of time alone with me before the rest of my company could get there and intervene, but it was enough time for them to make sure I'd never fly again."

Suddenly, I remembered the day he'd left me behind in the Court of Light, and it made so much more sense. Elera and Lucais had gone through so much together. They'd *lost* so much together. He'd delayed our travel arrangements on purpose, choosing to walk instead of evanescing in order to spend more time with me alone, but it had made him agitated. I'd never understood why. Not until the moment he told me that he was born with wings and the war had broken them.

Elera and I needed to feel the wind on our faces.

It was the closest they'd come to it again.

My eyes fell shut of their own volition. "What happened to them?"

"The humans?" He chuckled bleakly. "Nothing. I let them go free, but it was only a matter of weeks before I banished the whole lot of them into a non-magical realm and ended the war."

When I opened my eyes, I had the bones of an apology on my tongue, ready to assemble them and offer it to him whole. I'd spent a great deal of my life feeling guilty for things, so it was easy to assume a sense of responsibility for the horrors that had been inflicted upon Lucais and the other faeries, but I found him standing in front of the window again and lost my ability to speak.

His silhouette was dark against a halo of bright light, bleached through the fog, and two enormous wings had appeared on either side of his body. They were tucked in close to his shoulders, barely spanning past the sides of the window though the apex of each wing surpassed the top of the arch, and I realised that it was because he couldn't stretch them out any further.

Built like an angel in their outline, they were translucent as a dragonfly and delicate as the winged faelings I'd watched flitting up and down the main city streets when I arrived. I found myself crawling off the edge of the bed and wandering over to him, entranced by the seamless way they'd appeared, the way they melded with his flesh as easily as his arms. He was silent and patient as I approached, marvelling.

Up close, I could see the damage. The light flooding in through the window made it difficult to tell from afar, but the membrane had been torn to shreds until hardly any of it was left between the thin veins and digits that crossed over the entire surface area. Only the outer margins survived intact, though barely. Every second or third digit had sustained what looked like fractures or breaks—very small cracks and abnormalities to their structure, resulting in a deformation of the overall wing that hadn't been obvious at first.

"Can I touch them?"

In the thick, heavy silence, I heard him swallow. "You can try."

With a featherlight touch, I traced the sturdy outline of Lucais's outer wing—

They disappeared.

As easily as they'd appeared, they vanished. I blinked a few times to adjust to the change as he slowly turned back around, pulling a plain white cotton shirt over his head. The action ruffled his hair, and he swept it back from his forehead before speaking again.

"It's not you," he promised, reaching for another glass of wine. "It was a reflex. They're never exposed to the open air these days, let alone a woman's touch. I have a permanent glamour over them to help reduce some of the pain and put an end to all the pitiful fucking looks." He swallowed the entire contents of the glass in one gulp again, looked at the perplexity written all over my face, and then let out a resigned sigh.

"You don't have to—"

"In High Fae culture, I am considered disabled," he interrupted quickly. "Amongst my people, our wings are a point of pride, and the ability to fly has always been as standard as walking is for yours. To have lost that is devastating. Some people who hold onto the old ways too tightly still think it's shameful, weak, disgraced. Nobody dares to fly around me anymore, not even Wrenlock and Morgoya. They think it's respect, but I think it's pity. I can still rule and live a perfectly normal life with some alterations, such as evanescing, which didn't become popular until my wings were butchered by the fucking humans and I decided to make it look like fun."

A sharp pain stabbed me right in the heart.

I knew he wasn't talking about me. It wasn't about me at all. Still, I wanted to cry for him.

"Alright." Lucais placed his glass back down with a loud clang and smiled, though it didn't quite reach his eyes. "We've officially shot the mood to the pits. Do you want to share your deepest, darkest, most shameful secret with me now, and then we can move on?"

I tried to smile back at him, but I thought about it. I seriously considered it.

Could I tell him about the worst thing that had ever happened to me? Could I admit to it, knowing that it hadn't even happened to *me*? Because that was the truth of the matter—my greatest shame was hidden inside the fact that the worst thing that had ever happened to me, the horror that kept me up at night and completely altered my brain chemistry, had not even happened to me.

I'd only witnessed it. I'd only *been there* for it. I'd only contributed to the reason it had happened in the first place.

I didn't even own my own fucking trauma.

"I can't."

Sighing morosely, Lucais took both of my hands in one of his. "Aura, I hate to bring this up right now, but I really need you to think about this. The mating bond is not a fix-all solution. We are still going to enact it, so you don't need to look at me like a jilted bride, but it's not going to protect you from the Malum." He pointed to the fog beyond the windowpane. "It's not going to shield you from the caenim and the locusts. It may not even completely solve your pending issues with the Court of Darkness, if I'm completely honest. You're going to need to rely on yourself more than you have in the past, which means dismantling the block in your head preventing you from using your magic."

I shook my head. "No."

Dismantling patriarchal belief systems that had been ingrained into me since birth? Yes.

Dismantling magic blocks designed to suppress catastrophic powers for my own protection? No.

"Aura," he said again firmly. "I lost my wings because I was distracted for a split second in the middle of a war. What happens if this escalates to that point again? What if, next time, there are soldiers as well as caenim and locusts? What if my father has been breeding an army of Malum this whole time, and I am too busy looking at you to see them coming?"

Pulling my hands out of his, I turned around, snatching the first pair of pants I could see lying on the floor. They weren't mine, so I pulled the drawstring extra tight around my waist and then fixed it in a double knot so that they would stay up. The length would be an issue if I didn't walk carefully, so I walked over to the chest of drawers and rifled through them until I found a pair of socks. Bending over, I pulled them on until they were almost up at my knees, and then I tucked the excess length of the pants into them. I hadn't worn shoes to his bedroom the previous night, so I resolved to leave without them.

"I get it," I said, running my hands through my hair as I straightened up. "This was a bad idea. You said it from the start—it's dangerous. We are dangerous and a very bad idea, so let's just thank Lady Luck we didn't get quite that far, and then we'll call it a day."

I moved to open his bedroom door.

"Bookworm, stop. That's not what I'm saying, and you know it."

"No, Lucais, I don't." My voice trembled, so I pushed my feet to move faster. *One after the other.* The voices in my head told me to keep running. Always, always running. "I think that's exactly what you're saying. I think that's what you've been saying this whole time, and you're just too afraid to admit it."

I heard his footsteps padding along the stone floor and felt his brooding presence following me as I found a staircase and began to descend it, though I didn't know where I was going—only that I had to leave. I had to keep moving, keep walking, because I couldn't do what he was asking me to do. What he *kept* asking me to do. Even thinking about it was messy and painful. Attempting it was even worse. If I succeeded at unleashing the magic again, it would only cause more destruction.

"Have you forgotten what happened last time?" I muttered, loud enough for him to hear it. My voice rose in pitch and volume as I plowed onwards, picking up the pace until I was nearly jogging down the stairs. "I took the light out of your sky. You hexed a whole Forest to turn against you. My father was a dark faerie, and I'm being summoned to lord over a realm that wants to watch the world die in deafening silence. What if I do something like *that* next time?"

"So we'll be prepared for it," Lucais returned, still trailing me. His voice was annoyingly even and calm. "You can't do much damage in a place like this anyway."

"You have *no idea* what I'm capable of," I seethed. Heat was accumulating in my chest, making my pulse feel weak and thready.

"*You* have no idea what you're capable of," he shot back.

At the bottom of the staircase, I found a side door and shoved it open, secretly hoping that it would slam closed on his face as I stalked out into the freezing morning air. The stonework was so cold that it sliced through the socks and bit into the soles of my feet, icy and resolute.

The door fell closed with a resounding slam, but the High King was right on my heels. "You already know you could be the answer to all of this!"

Halfway across the courtyard, I whirled so fast I almost slipped over and fell onto my ass. "Yes," I shouted, "and I *don't* care!"

"What the fuck, Aura?" Lucais's brow creased as he threw his hands out to the sides. "Why the fuck not?"

I was burning up from the inside out, despite the glacial temperature of the ground beneath my feet and the air in my lungs. Breathing took more effort than it should have. My heart was running so fast that it was no longer even beating; it felt like one long, constant pressure in my chest.

He'd finally done it.

He'd pushed me too far.

The confession was poison on the tip of my tongue, and it was self-preservation to spit it out.

"Because when I care, Lucais, people *die*."

"What?"

"Lucais!" I shouted his name into the bitter atmosphere mindlessly, stamping my freezing foot into the cobblestone. "I am not right. I am not right in my head"—with both hands, I pointed to my brain—"or in my heart"—I mimicked the motion of stabbing myself in the chest—"or in any part of me. I mean, *look* at me!" I waved both of my hands up and down my body as if he wasn't looking properly and required directions. "I can't control magic, but I can't absorb iron. What the *fuck* is that about? I am anathema, and you're honestly lucky that you're finding out now before you're mated to me for the rest of your—"

"Will you *stop*?" Lucais had a wild look in his eyes, and a strong breeze picked up in the courtyard that probably had something to do with it. "There is literally nothing about you that doesn't look or feel right to me, you infernal fucking woman!"

"You don't even know me!" I shrieked.

"What more do I need to know?" he shouted back, the deep tone echoing against the stonework. "For fuck's sake, Aura, I've already seen the worst parts of you. I think we're going to be just fine!"

I tipped my head back and glared up into the fog, swirling like storm clouds against the wind stirred by Lucais's upheaval of emotion. When I finally said the words into the mist—when I *screamed* the words with all the might of my lungs—they were as much for me as they were for him, because I'd never uttered them out loud before. Ever.

"*I had a brother!*"

Silence accompanied the stilling of the clouds.

Silence that had once been my closest friend.

Silence that was going to devour me whole and spit out my bones if someone didn't break it.

"What happened to him?" Lucais asked once the mist had finally settled around us again.

It solidified until we were encased in a protective cage of grey fog, so opaque and firm I might have been convinced it was soundproof, too. Like it was determined to shelter my secrets alongside my body.

But I'd kept it for far too long.

It demanded to be known.

So I confessed my sins to the High King of Faerie and prepared to face his judgement.

"I think I killed him before he was born."

Thirty-Nine

Never Eleven

Wisps of thin, white cloud drifted across the space between us, mingling with the condensation in every whisper of our breath. The chilly quiet was forbearing while the gruesome truth settled in, digging claws into our flesh and latching onto the stonework like a weed ready to burrow in between the cracks and make a home somewhere it didn't belong.

Lucais was a pale statue in the gloom. His hair was nearly white, like the light was draining from his body, and his eyes were hardened. I didn't blame him. The truth was stuck to me, sticky as blood, and he didn't deserve to be splattered with it.

His voice entered my mind, cool and even toned.

Tell me everything.

"It happened before Brynn was born," I said, starting at the beginning because I had no other choice. "My mother was pregnant with a baby boy, and he died. Ten years ago. Stillborn. It was my fault." The admission tumbled out of me, despite the fact that tears pricked my eyes with needlelike precision, and each word felt like I was choking rocks down my throat. My hands shook so hard at my sides that I had to clutch the oversized sleeves of his shirt in my fists to keep some semblance of control. "They only wanted to have that baby because of me—because I wasn't his child, so they tried to have one of their own to save their marriage."

Lucais arched a brow as if to question my sources.

"She told me so herself without really saying it out loud," I croaked. "She said my little brother was going to fix our family. I didn't know that she'd cheated until I'd already met you, and then, all of it made so much sense. He was conceived because of me, and he died because of me."

I swallowed, hard.

"My father—the man in your dungeon—was blind drunk one night, and I got angry with him. I was sick of the way that he behaved, the way he treated me when he thought she wasn't looking, and I started to feel so pathetic and weak for *taking* it all the time. I decided to stand up to him, even though he was so much bigger than me. It was stupid, but the voices in my head convinced me that I had no other choice. They told me that I was going to die if I didn't do something to prove that I wanted to live, and they said that they would help me, and honestly… I believed them."

A howling cut into the air as furious wind tore through the obstacle course of palace spires high above us. But Lucais lifted a hand, and the wailing sound was immediately muted.

"I couldn't control it," I blurted. His steadfast attention spurred me on. "I often felt something trailing me, lingering around my hands like some kind of immaterial bracelet, and I heard it speaking to me whenever I needed someone the most. It was always there if I was lonely, but I never really acknowledged it, even when I felt like it was asking me to let it go free, and I shouldn't have given in to it that night.

"As soon as I unhooked it, the voices took over. He started verbally, like he always did, and for the first time in my life, I yelled back at him instead of cowering under the blankets or the table. I screamed at him and told him that he needed to pull himself together. I asked him what gave him the right to bring another child into a miserable home like ours. How would a baby sleep soundly when he was always shouting at me?

"He was livid. He roared at me like some kind of monster, saying I had no right to speak to him that way, and that if I pushed him any further he'd send me packing to a boarding school and I'd never be allowed to come home, and that he wouldn't give a fuck what my mother said about it. He'd do it when she wasn't around to stop him.

"It escalated so quickly from that point on that I can't remember what happened next, but suddenly, he couldn't breathe. He was choking. And even though I wasn't touching him, I knew I was the one doing it. I was strangling him to death, and there were objects lifting into the air all throughout the room—the television remote, coasters, books, lamps—but my hands weren't touching a single thing.

"I thought about trying to stop it, but it didn't *feel* like the right thing to do, so I just stood there and watched. I just watched him fighting for a gasp of air until he collapsed, but he fell forwards, which put my feet within his reach, and he pulled me down to the ground with him before I could step back. He managed to hit me hard enough to break whatever trance was happening, leaving me alone and undefended.

"At the time, I thought that the force of his fist had momentarily disabled the powers I had, but I realised a few weeks later that it wasn't him at all. My power wasn't good for anyone—not even me—and I couldn't control it no matter what was happening."

I shivered, recalling the next occurrence of that night, and suddenly a tasselled blanket was wrapped around my shoulders and my feet were in my boots. Lucais hadn't moved a muscle, though. He stood there, his face a mask of impenetrable concentration as he watched and waited for me to complete my confession.

"He started to beat me like he never had before," I whispered, throat tightening. "Only once across my face, which was the hardest, and the rest on less obvious parts of my body. By the time my mother heard me screaming and came running out of the shower, he was scrambling to secure his hands around my throat. I was kicking him as hard as I could with the one leg I'd managed to pull free from underneath him.

"My mother intervened, but he was in such a blind rage that he didn't process the change when my face became hers. He didn't even care that her belly was round with his own child. I left and ran to the neighbour's house to get help, but I'm pretty certain he kept beating the absolute fuck out of her until he heard the shouting at the door because she was unconscious when I came back.

"For the longest time, I thought I had something to do with what happened to her pregnancy—like the voices had sought her out when they left me alone with my father in the living room, and maybe they tried to hurt the baby or something. It was my fault, no matter which way you look at it, but the thing that followed me around devoured all of the light. It was quiet most of the time like a shadow or an imaginary friend, which made perfect sense because the mood in the house was always so fucking dark," I told Lucais.

And then I took a deep breath, bracing myself for the conclusion I'd been at all by myself for the last ten years.

"That baby was the only bright thing that had ever existed in that family...and I'm so sure that I accidentally snuffed it out."

The tears were streaming freely down my cheeks. I scrubbed them away, and my breath caught in my throat when my eyes came back into focus and I realised that Lucais's face was wet, too. As soon as our eyes met, he staggered a few steps to the side, falling against a nearby post as he wiped the bottom of his nose with his shirt and glanced around at the fog like he expected to find some kind of explanation inside it.

"You're telling me that you..." Lucais's voice shattered. He dug the heels of his palms into his eyes and made a small, broken noise in his throat before he met my tearful stare again. "You're telling me that you spent more than half of your life thinking you killed the baby inside your mother's womb?"

I could feel the hysteria brimming the way it used to when I was in therapy, but I was well practiced with holding it back, because I'd never allowed myself to talk openly about anything that had happened that night. I had only ever talked about the dreams—or at least, that's what I had tried to do.

"He had me convinced that there was something wrong with me," I said. "And he didn't even know about the shadows or the voices. He used to make comments that I'd be jealous about the new baby. That maybe I should stay with my grandparents after he was born so I wouldn't cause an issue." I tucked my hands beneath my arms to ward off a soul-deep shudder, pulling the blanket tighter around myself and staring at the ground. "I didn't *feel* jealous. I didn't really want the baby, but I never wanted to hurt him. I thought maybe I'd done it by accident, though. Like I hadn't been careful enough, and I'd spilled the poison someone had put inside of me, and somehow it touched him."

"Your mother never thought to tell you otherwise?" Lucais's tone was low but hard, and edged with something so menacing that it caused my head to jerk up in surprise.

"I never told her how I felt," I confessed. "And she wasn't capable of talking about it, so she never brought it up."

His frown was as sharp as knives. "And-and-and—there weren't doctors?" he stammered, pointing at the ground like it was the guilty party while he glared at me. "There weren't any nurses? Surely, she went to hospital?" Lucais demanded. He waited for me to nod. "None of them determined that it had been caused by the fact someone three times your size had attacked her? None of them fucking *reported* him?"

Lucais's expression was incandescent, an unstable blend of being both furious and flabbergasted at once, and I realised that my father had no working memory of what had happened to my brother or else the High King would have already glimpsed it. I'd suspected as much, because Brynn had changed everything for them, but something inside of my stomach reared up with claws and teeth to have it confirmed.

"She went to hospital and told them she'd been in a car accident," I explained as calmly as possible. "My mother never pressed charges against him for the assault—for any of the assaults—and she hadn't been far enough along in her pregnancy for my brother's life to have been considered separately to hers even if he'd survived until birth. We respect women's rights and autonomy where I'm from, but there is a law that requires a baby to be born alive before it is entitled to any legal protection even in a wanted pregnancy. Her lack of cooperation meant that the police were disinclined to pursue legal repercussions on their own."

"What about the people who came when you went for help?"

"The neighbours were too scared to speak up, and I wasn't questioned. One of the nurses at the hospital saw my face and reported it, but by the time anyone came to check on me from child services, he was long gone and the bruises had faded."

"And they never thought to check if she was actually *in* a car accident? The police never thought to check that a car—"

"He drove her car into the neighbour's garage shortly after the incident," I cut in, lifting my shoulders. "I don't know if it was to threaten them into staying quiet or simply to corroborate their story. It was all within a couple of hours of it happening, before the police arrived. Back then, nobody had home security cameras to prove it was faked." I exhaled in a torturously long sigh.

"My mother said that she missed the brakes and hit the accelerator instead when she was parking the car after going to the shops, and that she'd already unclipped her seatbelt. They didn't check or they would have seen that there was no shopping in the car—there wasn't even any fucking food in the house." I shook my head, relaxing my arms. "Everyone *knew* what really happened, but as long as she was unwilling to cooperate, they wouldn't do anything about it. They said they couldn't."

Lucais clutched his head with both hands and walked around in a tight circle, hissing, "What the *fuck...*"

I swallowed. "There's more."

He halted and gave me a beseeching look.

"She was in hospital for about a week, and they wouldn't let me stay with her because I was supposed to have had a perfectly capable and loving father to look after me at home," I went on, suddenly feeling emboldened to see the story through to its bitter end. "He didn't visit her—probably citing fatherly duties or some other kind of bullshit—so that meant I couldn't, either. He drank himself to sleep by midafternoon most days, though there were two days when he was simply...gone. He went out and didn't come back until he had to pick her up from the hospital. She came home, but the baby didn't, and so...she went to bed."

I let my gaze drift away with the mist as I amassed the courage to admit to the last of it. Lucais waited patiently, but I had begun to feel the tension rolling off him.

"She went straight to bed, and then she didn't get up. For four and a half months," I divulged. My voice was flat. "My father stuck around for three weeks."

Lucais was in front of me a second later. His hands were in my hair, his eyes feverishly searching for an anchor within mine. When he spoke, his voice was raw and uneven. "Auralie, what are you saying?"

Tears welled up again as I blabbered at him.

"I'm saying that I didn't grow up like you, Lucais." I pointed nonspecifically at the enormous palace behind him. "I didn't have family dinners in a cosy dining room. I didn't have friends come over after school. I didn't have food in the fridge or the pantry or parents to help me with my homework. I went into Dante's Bookstore to escape, but most of the time I was looking after her. He stayed...and I-I don't know why he bothered because he didn't help," I stuttered.

My head was shaking uncontrollably against Lucais's firm but gentle grip. "I-I washed her sheets. I brought her painkillers. I brought her food and then took it away when she refused to eat. I filled up her water bottle and went to the corner store to buy bread and milk with the money I stole out of his wallet when he was fast asleep on the couch."

Lucais was slowly shrinking in height as I rambled and sobbed, but my eyes were so blurry I couldn't get them to focus long enough to figure out why.

"I tried so hard to keep the peace, but we had another fight because she didn't have any clean fucking sheets. I was so tired of rinsing out the bloodstains." I groaned, feeling the burn at the base of my throat, and my hands balled into fists. "She just... She *refused* to get out of bed unless she absolutely had to, and by then, she'd usually soaked through everything. And I tried to be understanding. I did. She was depressed because she had the baby that week she was in hospital, and then they took him away. I-I don't know what they did with his body, but she came home like a woman who'd had a baby. Except she didn't *have* her baby. I know she had every right to be depressed, but she was bleeding for weeks and she just *wouldn't* get up!"

I wiped away the moisture that was dripping from my nose, a sob hitching in my throat. The horror of reliving it was offset by the sheer relief I felt easing the weight off my shoulders as I recounted the way it had made me feel. Righteously or not.

"She didn't change her pads until she'd bled through the sheets and fucking blankets and mattress protectors," I moaned. "I had to change them because she wouldn't, and he claimed he didn't know how to, and I thought she might die if I didn't because that's how she was acting and Lucais... Lucais, there was so much blood." My voice wobbled, so I clutched my throat and felt a scream gathering there, ready to tear me to ribbons.

"There was so much fucking blood, Lucais, and I'd never seen so much of it before. I hadn't even had my first period yet. So I asked him to get some fresh linen for her, but he refused because he was drunk and I-I guess he didn't want to drive or something. I was so angry because it was our fault. Everything that had happened was his fault, and it was my fault, but he wouldn't fucking *help* me...

"I hated him," I cried. "God, I fucking hated him. I yelled at him, and then it happened all over again, but this time, I was like a grenade. I think I literally blew up the house because I was so upset and I'd let the voices off the leash that first day when I shouldn't have. One minute, he was standing in the doorway, and then the next, he was laying on the floor and there was a fire in the sink. I passed out, I guess, and I must have hallucinated because I honestly thought he was dead.

"But when I woke up, my mother's sheets had been changed, and he was gone. I-I-I thought I'd had a psychotic break and killed him and covered it up and then forgot. But eventually, he came back, so many months later, and that's..." I sucked in a final breath of air that filled my lungs to bursting point, letting the rest of my body fall still as I focussed on the sharp tension running from the base of my throat to the top of my stomach. *Exhale.* "That's when they started trying for Brynn."

A few heartbeats thumped inside of my chest while my darkest secrets melted into the fog.

"Aura." The muffled voice of the High King came from below me. I glanced down to find him on his knees at my feet, arms around the back of my legs, face pressed against my stomach. "I am so violently sorry."

The realisation of everything that I had confessed slapped me across the face like an icy cold rag, and I shivered to break the spell. Carefully, I took a series of measured breaths until I felt centred and grounded again, and then I gave Lucais the standard response to an apology like that by reaffirming that an apology was unnecessary because none of it had anything to do with him.

"No," he said, pulling his head back from me. His eyes were molten gold, the colour stronger and more breathtaking than I'd ever seen. "When we met, you should have felt safe with me. I should have been someone you could trust, and not because you'd never had that before, but because that was *my* responsibility. It only makes my actions more deplorable to discover that I was one of many individuals who assassinated the right to possess your faith. I failed you"—he swallowed—"and for that, I am so immeasurably sorry. I was wrong, Auralie. I was so, so wrong."

A problem I'd faced for most of my life was rooted in the fact that I was raised by people who didn't mean any of their apologies, so I'd never bothered to learn how to mimic them. I also didn't know how to genuinely accept them—and to do so because I wanted to, not because it was expected of me, although I had made some strides in that area with Morgoya.

So, I stroked the High King's hair instead, letting the swirling mist tempt me into a daydream that made the rest of the world cease to exist for a while.

"I still don't know that I didn't do it," I said eventually. "Literally, I mean." My actions had caused it one way or another, but that was the difference between the first and third degree.

"Aura, you were eleven years old."

"I was never eleven years old," I mused. "I was never really eleven."

Sighing, Lucais rested his face against my stomach again. "We really are made in each other's image. I was High King when I was eleven, and you were fighting real world monsters."

"What?" I spat, surprise sharpening my tone. Wrenlock had mentioned that Lucais was the youngest High King in Faerie's history, but he hadn't given me an exact age. "When was your coronation?"

"Oh, that's a damning question." He forced a humourless laugh. "Auralie, I can tell you with complete certainty that you are not responsible for the tragedy that took your brother's life—magically or otherwise—because I *am* responsible for the tragedy that took the life of the High King before me. I know what it looks like to be the guilty party and you are not it."

"Wrenlock mentioned you were a boy when you came into your full power."

Lucais snickered. "A boy, sure. I was born the day that my predecessor was crowned High King—I believe it was *during* the ceremony, in fact—and the thing about our hierarchy is that the existing ruler *feels* the moment that their successor is born." His tone was scathing, a rollercoaster of animation and cynicism wrapped in a velvet voice. "We're supposed to know, like some kind of psychic link triggers a countdown to your approaching expiry date. The minute the poor bastard was crowned, he felt my presence and knew that his time in power was severely limited. He spent his entire year ruling Faerie marking off the hours until I was ready to take his place."

"So you really have been pissing people off since birth," I muttered.

He bit my hip bone playfully. "Rulers in Faerie generally die at the end of their reign, which makes it so much worse. It's a pride thing as much as anything, but the severance of our connection to the land is said to be so intense that it strips us of the will to live. There are not many ancient rulers left, if the myths are true and any survived at all, because they either died in extenuating circumstances or they were dethroned and decided to fade away in some distant corner of the world."

"So what happened to the last High King?"

He hummed against my waist, and the vibrations warmed me from head to toe, warding off the chill that had numbed the better part of my body since we'd stormed out into the courtyard. "Well, he spent his year in power keeping us out of the Dragon War, so I inherited a realm of peace and prosperity—at least, on the surface—but he only made it until I was about eighteen months old. I was a baby when my parents had to move us into the palace in Caeludor because the pull of the crown was so strong."

"Like me and the Court of Darkness?" I questioned, cringing as I tried to refrain from picturing the crown luring a child into an open fireplace.

"Very much so," he agreed. "The problem is that you can't publicly crown a fucking toddler as the High King of Faerie, so my parents and the old High King conspired to hide it until I was deemed old enough. Apparently, the crown didn't like that idea. It started to reject him, and no matter where they hid it, or how they guarded it, or what they did to keep me away from it—I guess they thought it was for my safety, because an infant High King is a very vulnerable High King—they never succeeded in keeping us apart. Every time they lost sight of me, they knew they would find me in the same room as the crown, playing with it like a fucking toy."

"So then what happened?" I pressed, intrigued and a little bit terrified.

"Well, bookworm, I suppose that you could say I killed him."

I rolled my eyes. "You did not."

"At the very least, I drove him to suicide," he insisted. "The three of them worked extremely hard to keep up appearances in front of the realm, but they suffered through years of lies and secrecy and near misses. The whole time, the old High King was being actively rejected by a power that my people believe comes directly from the High Mother herself, and he was fighting the natural urge to give up. I was barely able to walk when he died. Then, it was all over."

"That's it?" I asked, squinting into the mist. "He dropped dead?"

"He hanged himself from the chandelier in the palace entryway," Lucais informed me. A chill snaked down my spine, vicious and slippery. "He did his best for as long as he could, but then he left me on my own when it became too much, giving everyone who knew the truth no choice but to reveal it to the rest of Faerie and face the consequences without him. Even though the circumstances were very different, I suppose I was never eleven either."

"That is so morbid..." I felt the splatters of his confession the same way he had felt mine, a sticky and dark residue that may never wash off once it had been shared. "Who *was* the old High King? Was he from the Court of Light, too?"

Lucais shook his head, burrowing his nose beneath my shirt and brushing it against my skin. "No. Last rule belonged to the Court of Fire. His name was Hugo. There's a portrait of him somewhere in the palace, along with all of the others."

I frowned. "Is that why all of the candles in the palace have had their wicks pulled out?"

"They have?" The High King's head reared back, and he gave me an eccentric look as he rose to stand, keeping his hands on my hips. "I didn't realise. I never need to look at them." Lucais shrugged one shoulder, gaze drifting beyond me as he mulled it over. "Maybe it was one of the staff marking his death or my transition to power." He pushed his lower lip out, thoughtful. "Maybe Hugo did it before he died."

"It's only the ones that were left behind in each room," I clarified. "Because the candles you used last night from the storage room were perfectly normal."

Lucais arched one golden eyebrow skeptically. "In that case, it was probably my mother," he muttered. "She was overprotective like that. You know, before she became a deranged killer."

Snaking my arms around his waist, I leaned into him, resting my head against his chest and letting a breath of calm wash over me in his embrace. Lucais adjusted his arms so he was cradling my head with one hand and firmly pressing my torso against his with the other. We stayed like that for a long time, surrendering to each other in the courtyard, hidden within the fog.

Eventually, I spoke again. "What are we going to do about your mother?"

I felt him smile against my hair as he pressed a kiss to the top of my head. "What are we going to do about that block in your head?"

I groaned into his chest. "I have to kill it, don't I?"

He hummed his agreement against my hair, and I realised that he'd figure it out on his own. I wanted to ask if he'd sifted through my memories to find it, but I decided that it wasn't worth offending him with the question when I preferred not to know the answer.

"Fine," I grumbled. "I'll do it."

I'll kill the loudest voice inside of my head.

The High King made a low, satisfied sound in the back of his throat and peppered the top of my head with kisses. "That's my perfect girl."

When we disentangled our arms from each other and he stepped back from me, the devilish grin on his face could have sent me to my knees. His eyes were positively glowing with pride and I became aware that I wasn't getting through it without some of his theatrics.

As if on cue, Lucais bowed, and the fog began to clear away from the courtyard, revealing a grand design of silvery grey stonework with carvings of gargoyles and sharp turrets. I squinted at the sky and found little flags with the Court of Light's insignia flapping in the breeze high above us, too far up to be witnessed through the usual settlement of fog. The post Lucais had leaned up against was a flagpole, but the flag hadn't been raised.

I surveyed the courtyard as a whole, open space, and found that it was larger than I'd initially thought. We were dwarfed by the palace heights, encompassed by a curtain wall with high-placed windows. Turning around in a slow circle, I watched Lucais's power chase the last of the fog away from the corners of our space, like we were in the middle of a snowglobe. The white clouds met along the outskirts, remaining in place a few metres above our heads and the rest of the palace.

"Why do you—" I started to ask, but my question snapped in half when my eyes fell upon the last of the retreating clouds.

The mist cleared around my father, bound and gagged, on his knees in the middle of the bailey.

Forty

The Mad High King

My violent fantasies used to make me question myself.

Is this psychopathy? What if nobody can fix what's broken inside of my head?

I would argue against my own anger until I felt guilty for being angry in the first place, until I was torn in half between feeling righteous and sinful on any given day, and until I was the perfect canvas for a man like my father to play pretend at being powerful.

He wasn't powerful anymore.

And yet, I still wanted to kill him.

The man on his knees before me lifted his head as if summoned by my train of thought. His face was creased with frown lines, smeared with dirt and grime, but his blue eyes were as cool and clear as I'd always remembered. I had spent weeks of my childhood staring into them with fabricated love, desperately trying to convince myself that we were the same, that I saw something alive in them when he stared back at me.

I hadn't. I never did, I never would, and part of me had always known it wasn't my fault—but that part of me had been hanging on by a thread for a very long time.

"He's weakened and unarmed," I said, looking up at Lucais.

The High King was leaning against the flagpole, casually watching on as I circled my father like a shark and weighed up my options. When I spoke, he arched one brow and replied, "So?"

"So isn't it a little redundant now? He can't hurt me anymore."

Catching on to the situation he was in at long last, my father began to squirm, and a series of alarmed noises came from his mouth, muffled by the gag. I glanced down to shush him harshly and caught the flash of hatred in his eyes when I did—which didn't help his case.

Lucais pushed off the flagpole and sauntered over to us, completely ignoring my father and his pointless, incoherent pleas for assistance. Placing his hands on either side of my head with his fingertips on my temples, he bent down until we were eye to eye. "Can't he?" he disputed. "Isn't it harder to heal the damage when the bastard who caused it is still alive and *actively* kicking you?"

My father screamed into the gag.

"For the love of—" I broke off with a sigh and tore my eyes away from the High King, reaching down to undo the dirty fabric that was stuffed into my father's mouth and tied tightly around the back of his head. "What could you possibly have to say right now?" I demanded, wincing as I helped him spit out the rest of the linen, wet with his saliva.

"You fucking *bitch*—"

In a split second, my father's head smacked into the cobblestone with a sound that made my stomach somersault. Blood trickled from his temple inside of a large, red welt as he lay on his back with Lucais's boot pressing down on his throat, though I'd hardly caught the flash of his movements.

"That was the wrong thing to say," the High King snarled. He must have increased the pressure of his foot because my father's face began to turn bright red all over, and a hissing sound escaped from his otherwise silent, open mouth. "Mind your fucking manners when you speak to her, or the next thing that comes out of your mouth will be the laces of the boot I jam down your throat."

My father remained deathly quiet, and Lucais glanced towards me for permission to let him go.

Head spinning, I nodded slowly.

My father coughed and spluttered, rolling onto his side as if that would help clear his airways. Wheezing, he gazed up at me, and the hatred in his eyes was replaced by something I'd never seen before. I would have liked it to have looked more like regret, but that wasn't even close, and I was so disappointed that my shoulders slumped.

Even disarmed on the ground before me, the man who had raised me to withdraw into myself and cower from him still had the power to leech all the feeling and strength from my bones with a single word or a look. I shook my head, stumbling backwards.

"I can't do it."

"Yes, you can."

"I can't."

"Are you weak, too?" Lucais's voice was soft in my ear as he moved to stand behind me. "Weak men make it their mission to force you into feeling small so they can feel powerful. They confuse being bigger with being better. Do you want this world to keep happening to you, or do you want to start happening to *it*?" He held me firmly in place with his chest pressed into my back and his chin resting over my shoulder. "You can do it, Aura. You can do anything you want." His lips grazed the shell of my ear. "You happened to me without even trying. You've *destroyed* me without so much as a conscious thought, and I'll never get over it. I haven't been the same since the day I learned your name, since you branded yourself on me and I became your possession."

A shiver skittered down my nape as Lucais tucked a loose strand of my hair behind my ear and slipped his free hand into mine, dangling limply at my side. I felt the outline of something cool and hard like steel warming between our fingers, but I was too mesmerised by my father's snakelike gaze to look down and see what it was.

"You *own* me, Aura." The High King's voice was low and rough, stoking a fire in places that had never felt warmth. "Mind." He trailed his lips up the side of my neck. "Body." He kissed the corner of my jaw. "Soul." His nose brushed the hollow beneath my ear. "Kingdom." He pressed his mouth against my temple. "Crown."

Be still my beating heart.

My fingers curled around the item between our hands involuntarily as Lucais urged me to take possession of it, and I felt some of my strength returning as I clutched the weapon like a liferope.

"I will never be rid of the imprint of you," he went on in a husky murmur. "You think you can do that to the most powerful man in the entire world—to the High King of Faerie—but not the spineless, pathetic louse who bullied you for your entire life?" Lucais gently lifted my arm, placing his mouth against the bare skin of my wrist. He angled the hand I was using to clutch the dagger into position to stab the blade in a downwards thrust over my shoulder.

I was clay in his hands, totally under his spell as he moulded me into a weapon, but I started to tremble as he guided my body through the action, moving us in slow motion with his hand over mine.

"Open your eyes, bookworm. Your nightmares are over. You never need to hold back or hide again."

A half-laugh, half-sob tumbled out of my chest as we paused with the dagger pointed down at my father's body, lying stiffly on the ground, glaring up at us.

I'd shown Lucais all of my weaknesses, and he was still standing behind me. He was still seeking out my touch, stroking his fingers up and down my free arm, the fabric of his shirt on my body soft and thin between us. He wasn't ashamed or scared—

"Wait." I swallowed, trying to suppress the unsteadiness in my voice. "I need you to clear something up once and for all, please."

His voice was a whisper, his breath sweet and heady. "Anything."

"The fog."

"I already told you about the fog."

"It's concealing the damage to the palace, I know." Twisting around in his arms until he released me, I stepped away, the weapon in a tentative grasp at my side. "But you cleared it away from the courtyard, so you're obviously in control of it. Why submerge the entire city?"

Lucais's mouth pulled to one side as he debated, little creases forming around the corners of his eyes. He clicked his tongue. "You remember when I told you that the thing in the lapsus was using me as some kind of conduit?"

"Yes."

He pulled a sheepish face and scratched the back of his neck. "Well, it's been poisoning the city in its free time. I'm not a willing participant, but I can't seem to stop it, either. The most I've been able to do is to reduce the severity of the impact and slow the progression."

"The palace is dying?" I gasped, glancing ruefully towards the grey stonework and towering spires behind him.

"Not the palace." The High King's throat bobbed. "It's the whole of Caeludor. I'm masking it with a very strong glamour at the moment, redirecting the worst of the damage back into the palace, which is...why the fog has to be all-consuming."

I blinked into the empty space between us. "What if you stopped masking it? How much of the palace would be left?"

"I won't."

"But if you did?"

Lucais grimaced, wrestling with his natural urge to conceal the truth. I wasn't sure if he was being more open with his expressions around me or if I was getting better at reading them. "The entire city would fall to pieces," he admitted in a hollow voice, waving at it half-heartedly. "Buildings would collapse. Homes and businesses would disappear. Playgrounds would crumble. That sort of thing."

My eyebrows shoved together. I'd been through the city multiple times, and it was always full of faeries living, working, and playing. The palace, on the other hand, was devoid of life more often than not, so it made sense that nobody had really noticed the crumbling wing. But for the city to be disintegrating...

"How do they not know something is wrong?"

"Oh, they do. Everyone thinks that the fog is part of the Oracle's prophecy," he revealed, dropping his eyes to the ground between us. "They think that it's mood related, that I've been pining for you since I first glimpsed you inside of the Oracle."

The puzzle pieces came crashing down in front of me like bricks falling from a disintegrating wall, and my stomach dropped with them. "*That's* why you glamoured me?"

"Yes, so you'd best get a wriggle on with dismantling your block." Lucais gave me a pointed look, nodding his head towards his prisoner, and then chased it with a handsome grin.

"How long has the city been submerged in fog?"

"Mmm. What is it, like, four or five months now?"

A memory tugged at the corners of my mind, but I couldn't grasp it. Every time I extended my mental hand, it darted out of my reach like a kite caught in the winds of a cyclone. I shook my head, forcing myself back into the present moment.

"It's only a matter of days or weeks now before my people realise that it's been a ruse the entire time and they start to panic in earnest," Lucais pointed out. "I have no intention of relinquishing the enchantment over the city, but I'd say mass hysteria might pose a bit of an issue on that front."

I pressed the heel of my palms into my eyes, dagger pointing towards the heavens, and began to pace, dodging the legs of my father, who was still lying on the ground with his hands and feet bound, probably hoping that we'd forgotten about him. "Why did you do it then?" I demanded, spiralling through pitfalls in my head. Lucais had kept the secret from everyone—his best friends, his Hand and High Lady, and me—at great personal risk for months, only to blow the lid off the primary cover on a whim one afternoon. "Why take the glamour off me when you knew it would destroy the illusion you've been fighting so hard to keep? When you knew your city might fall into ruin?"

He held my stare in his unflinching gaze and spoke very slowly when he gave his reply. "Because you wanted to be seen."

Although my stomach couldn't help but flutter with the endearment, my head was still spinning. I never would have asked him to do that if I'd known what was really going on. I never would have complained about it in the first place. I *never* would have asked him to put my feelings above the lives of his people.

"Are you mad?"

"I might be." Lucais shrugged nonchalantly. "The Mad High King has a nice ring to it."

"It does not."

A crushing smile bloomed over his mouth. "Bookworm," he purred, stepping towards me. He touched my cheekbone and chin with gentle fingertips—a steady calm in a sea of chaos. "You'll have to forgive the clumsiness in my handling of our relationship. I'm sick with obsession. It's been extremely inconvenient, actually."

I shook my head, trying to shake free of the infatuation that his words were going to pull me into.

His sweetness was a vortex, and those revelations were proof that avoiding the acknowledgement of any feelings was the right decision, though I was afraid we'd already taken it too far. His eyes simmered as his gaze fell into mine, enveloping me in an entrancement that felt unyielding and forever—even if it cost him the world.

"At what point do you decide it doesn't matter anymore?" I whispered, trying to inject some acidity back into our dialogue. It was too soft, too sweet for all the damage we were doing. "What's your tipping point? Where do you draw the line?"

Lucais gazed at me for a long moment before he answered. His eyes traced the features of my face as if he were memorising the lines of a poem. "I don't," he said at last. "You draw all of the lines, Auralie. I merely enforce them."

Feeling the blade in my hand again through the haze of my emotions, I inhaled deeply and turned back towards my father. I was heartbreakingly aware that I had to put an end to it once and for all because Lucais needed to know that I was capable. He needed to see the line being drawn in the sand, though it zig-zagged in an awful pattern between right and wrong and the undefined spaces in between.

There was no other way.

If his eyes were on me, everyone's lives were in danger. His death would kill the enchantment holding the city together like it would the House and Forest—and my death might kill him. By the time new leaders emerged from the Court of Darkness and Caeludor, there was every chance it would be too late, and the heart of Faerie would have already been condemned. The Oracle prophecy would come to pass, and the Courts of Light and Darkness would be unified at the cost of everything I had witnessed inside of the lapsus—a total eclipse of silence and erasure.

Staring down at my father, I signalled for Lucais to pull him back up to his knees, and then I lifted the blade in the air, examining the glint of steel in the gloomy light. My hands knew what they wanted to do, but the magic wasn't speaking to me. It hadn't returned since I'd left the House, but I pushed back against the self-doubt and pulled on my focus. I was going to draw the line with or without magic. I was going to be brave. I was going to kill the loudest voice inside my head.

The voice of my father.

Angling the blade above his chest, I walked around in a half-circle to stand behind him. Closing my eyes, I felt the pull between the blade's razor-sharp point and the dead space inside him where a heart might have once rented out a room.

There was nothing there, and I didn't have the upper body strength to try to find it, so I moved the cool kiss of the blade to his throat. I felt completely human as I pressed the tip of the dagger against his skin, wondering if Lucais's power was preventing him from squirming as the blade pierced through the first layer of my father's flesh, and a trickle of blood spilled onto his stained, ripped shirt.

I pictured the end result in my mind's eye—my father's body, blue eyes alien and lifeless, as the end was dealt to a lifetime of misery and suffering through which I'd begged for answers that could be given but never would.

If I had been different, would it have made a difference?

Why couldn't you love me anyway?

Did you ever want me at all?

Were you sorry?

Why?

"You wouldn't." The dark voice of the man on his knees sent wicked chills down my spine, though it was no more than a hoarse whisper. "You wouldn't kill your own father."

I laughed once without humour. "I'm well aware by now that you are not my real father."

Surprise lit his eyes for a brief moment. "No," he declared, not even pretending to sound disappointed. "But I am Brynn's father." He coughed, the sound a wet rasp. "You wouldn't do that to her."

At the mention of my sister, guilt crawled over my skin like ants, and I hung my head. "No," I breathed, fighting back the onslaught of emotion. *Eight years.* "But I would do it *for* her. For my brother, too."

From a few paces away, Lucais posed a quiet question. "What was his name?"

"I don't know. They never told me, and I was too scared to ask." I gripped a fistful of my father's hair and forced his head back to look him in the eye, though he refused to meet my gaze. My hands were shaking, and I knew he could feel it. Disgust rose up in my throat with demands that I stopped touching him and moved far away. "What *was* his name? Do you remember?"

"I'm never telling you." He hacked up a ball of spit and phlegm. "Because you don't deserve to know, Auralie. You weren't even his real sister. You're the brat of some dumb fuck who used your bitch mother as a cumrag—"

I couldn't name the feeling that came over me, but I snapped back at him. For the last time in my life, I bit him back, and it was fatal.

The wet heat of tears rolling down my face matched the sticky warmth I felt sliding between my fingers as I held the blade over the open wound in his throat, closing my eyes as if that could block out the gurgling sounds he made as he bled out on the cobblestone.

He'd killed my brother. He'd tried to kill *me*. He'd abused my mother and Brynn. I could have spent the rest of my life trying to understand, but not anymore.

Not anymore.

He had finally answered for the things he'd done, for the cruelty he had placed on me when I was too young to know the difference from love, for the torment he inflicted upon me, and all of that useless shame. He answered in the only way he ever could, the only way he understood—

With violence.

The body slumped over, hitting the ground with a dull thump.

"Bring me Hanson," I breathed, the exhale of air clouding in wisps in front of my face.

I was so hot, positively burning up from the inside out, but I couldn't move. I was paralysed, glued to the spot with a death grip on the hilt of the blade, and I knew that I needed to seize the moment of clarity before the wind changed directions and I became lost inside the smoke again.

Through the bond, I could sense Lucais's uncertainty, but he did exactly as I asked without question, and a moment later, Hanson appeared in the courtyard beside my father's lifeless body.

Hanson was in as poor condition as I recalled. Worse, even. Far worse than my father had been, likely due to some kind of spell suppressing his cognitive functions, based on what I'd witnessed when he was in the dungeon. Hanson was given no such privileges—his lack of awareness was due to pure exhaustion. Swaying on his knees, he struggled to remain upright, and his eyes were barely able to split open wide enough to look at his surroundings. I had a feeling that he was too far gone to register anything even if he had.

My throat immediately tightened up, but I pushed through the encroaching panic attack and stepped towards him with the blade in my hand. Blood from my father's corpse leaked across the stones, red as a rose. It soaked into the fabric of Hanson's pants and trickled beneath my shoes—the only colour I could see in the gloomy morning.

I didn't hesitate, though my stomach churned, and a pinch in my chest squeezed a small sound of abhorrence from my mouth as I placed the blade against the paper-thin skin of Hanson's pallid throat and ripped it across from left to right.

When he collapsed, it barely made a sound because the impact was so light. Even the overflow of his lifeblood rushing out of the new opening in his throat was weak compared to my father's. Hanson had been left to slowly leak magic and blood in the dungeon for months, malnourished and atrophied—until the moment I'd ended it for him.

I sucked in a ragged breath and dropped the blade with a clang, staggering a few steps back. Willing my racing heart to quiet, I turned and found Lucais's golden eyes trained on me in a curious, evaluating stare. Swallowing tightly, I nodded and started to make my way back towards the palace, wrapping the blanket tightly around myself. Lucais lingered behind without a word, either to piece the picture together or to clean up the mess. Either way, I knew he could see it—*the line*.

Killing my father was justice.

Killing Hanson was mercy.

Forty-One

You Should See Yourself From My Point of View

I showered in Lucais's bathroom.

We still had a fate to seal of our own, though the bloodshed in the courtyard wasn't much of a turn on for me. I would have liked to wear something nicer than the blood of the men who had harmed me when the High King and I bared our souls to each other and damned them to an eternity of servitude in Faerie, but there was a thin layer of blood around my nails that I couldn't scrub away.

I was still trying when Wrenlock came back. Striding straight into the bathroom, he went to wash his hands in the marble sink and didn't glance up at me until he reached for a towel to dry them. Finding me immediately, his dark eyes settled on my reflection in the large mirror spanning the entire length of the wall. When he turned around, Wrenlock leaned back against the counter, tossing the towel aside before his gaze snagged on my hands.

"What did he do now?" he asked, his tone clipped but weary.

Abandoning my endeavours, I tilted my face up towards the shower spray and let the warm water massage it as I considered how to reply. Wrenlock didn't know even half as much about Lucais or me as I'd originally thought. He had no idea about the prisoners in the dungeon or the extent of my childhood trauma, and I was reaffirming my belief that some things might be better left buried, so I simply sighed and shook my head at him.

"You have dirt on your face," I said.

Eyes widening, Wrenlock immediately began the process of blindly scrubbing at random places on his face and then checking his hands in an effort to remove it.

I laughed gently. "You'd better get in the shower."

"Are you sure?" Wrenlock paused with his fingers smoothing over the bridge of his nose. His eyes skimmed the bathroom as he took a step forward and slowly dropped his hands. "We haven't had a chance to talk about last night."

"I'm fine. Last night was great." I hoped he didn't think the lack of animation in my voice was reflective of my feelings about it. The post-murder adrenaline was a very different bodily experience to post-sex adrenaline. "You know we have to do it again, though." I bit my lower lip. "Well, *we* don't, but we...can."

Steam rose from the hot stone floor as I waited patiently for Wrenlock to peel his clothes off and step into the shower with me, the heat radiating from his body almost hotter than the water. He made quick work of washing away the lingering traces of dirt and dust. I considered asking him where he'd been, but ultimately decided against it because I didn't want to prompt him to ask me about the blood on my hands again.

When he was clean, Wrenlock opened his arms for me, and I gladly stepped into his wordless embrace. The bare, warm skin of his body provided a welcome comfort, and I relaxed against him even as I felt certain parts of his anatomy beginning to stiffen. With a light sigh, I slid my hand down his side, tentatively exploring the lean, hard muscles of his abdomen as his dick twitched against me.

The sound of footsteps and a door slamming echoed in the main bedroom. It wasn't like the time the High King had interrupted us in the hallway. Neither of us jumped out of our skin or even made a move to disrupt the intimate peace we had crafted against each other. We simply held one another under the water and waited for him to join us.

"Don't stall on my account," Lucais declared, striding into the room with his shirt already halfway over his head. He splashed his face with water at the sink. "Enyd cornered me," he went on, bracing his hands on either side of the counter and staring down at the drain. "She's got trust issues like you wouldn't believe." He made a pinched face in the mirror and began to mimic her with a squeaky tone of voice I felt was actually kind of unjust. "'*Why are there caenim in the throne room, Lucais? Why didn't you tell me Aura hadn't accepted the bond yet? Are those statues in the courtyard new?*' Fucking Elements, I wish she wasn't our closest ally so I could send her home."

"If you scare her off with your bad attitude, I am going to hurt you," Wrenlock stated calmly, arms still draped around my shoulders as we stood halfway beneath the steady stream of water. "You need someone like her on your side."

Lucais scoffed, turning to face us. "Oh, relax. I'm well aware—" He broke off abruptly. His golden eyes heated as they drifted over my body, lingering on the curve of my ass, the cascade of wet hair falling down my back. A smile took shape on his mouth around the same time as his posture softened, and all of his political frustrations were forgotten. "Bookworm."

"I hate it when you look at me like that," I lied.

"I hate it when you shower naked with my best friend," he lied back. I could see the outline of his erection through his pants, so there was clearly a missing stipulation somewhere in his words, enabling it. "Do you want to do this in the shower?"

I shook my head.

"The bed?"

I nodded because his room didn't have a balcony.

Lucais showered while Wrenlock and I dried ourselves. I was busy repeatedly scrunching my hair, trying to drain the water out so that I didn't dampen all of the pillows, when Wrenlock came over to me and took the towel from my hands. His eyes held a warm smile, though his face remained smooth and impassive as he ran his fingers through my hair, gently massaging my scalp. The pressure felt so good that my eyes fluttered closed. I didn't open them until I heard the shower shut off, and that was when I discovered that my hair was completely dry.

I looked up at him in the mirror and smiled. "That is so cool," I whispered.

Wrenlock smiled softly as he fluffed a few of my curls. "Isn't it?"

Lucais's blond hair, darkened by the water, came into view in my peripheral vision. I glanced towards him as Wrenlock's hands trailed over me, cupping my face, and I watched on as the High King dropped his towel. My eyes roved over him eagerly, taking in the full view of his naked body and finding things I hadn't the night before.

I began at the towel, noticing a tattoo of patterns and markings curled around his ankle like a serpent as heat stirred in my core at the sight of his bare skin, and followed the ink as it drifted up and around his leg. The space between my own legs pulsated with need when my eyes landed on his impressive and still somewhat intimidating erection, heavy and thick with a large vein on the underside. I caressed his stomach with my eyes, tracing the dip of his hips and the ridges of his abdominal muscles, emphasised by the ink of his tattoos as the continuous design stretched upwards, over his chest and collarbone to the sharply defined column of his throat and the edge of his jaw.

The High King ran a hand over his face, wiping the last traces of water away, and his gaze met mine a moment before I turned back to Wrenlock and he pulled my mouth to his.

Hot and smoky, Wrenlock consumed me in a searing kiss, his tongue sliding over the seam of my lips before they parted to allow him inside. Our tongues collided as he lifted me into his arms, and my legs automatically secured around his waist as he carried me out of the bathroom, pausing to prolong the kiss for an extra moment before his mouth broke away from mine and he placed me down on the mattress.

Wordlessly, he sank to the ground between my thighs, pushing my legs apart far enough to hook my knees over his broad shoulders, and then he buried his face between them without a blink of hesitation.

Gasping, I writhed against his mouth instinctively as his tongue made indulgent strokes across my entrance, lapping up my arousal, and then he slipped two fingers inside me while he nuzzled his face against my clit, sucking, circling, and occasionally making the most insanely sexy sounds that vibrated against my body and went straight down to my soul.

Lucais's hands found my breasts while Wrenlock knelt between my legs, playing with them with less urgency and more curiosity. He explored different combinations as he pinched and pulled my nipples, which hardened into extremely tight peaks under his attentive gaze, eyes alight with a fiery gold as he evaluated each of my reactions—one at a time, one after the other, both at once, and then harder, harder, *harder—*

My hands flew up to cover my face, but Lucais's arms were in the way. I clutched him instead, gripping his forearm like the ledge on a cliff face and turning my head to the side as an orgasm crashed into me with a wave of undiluted pleasure, starting in the centre point between my hips before clawing its way up my spine and shooting across every nerve ending in my entire body like strobe lights.

I came floating back to the ground like ash from an explosion beneath light and dark gazes.

Lucais tentatively stroked his length. "Do you want me to glamour it to adjust the size for you this time?" he asked softly.

"No," I blurted. My cheeks caught fire. "No, of course not."

That would be insane behaviour, even if he wasn't already juggling far too many ongoing enchantments in the middle of a power struggle with an unidentified entity in the lapsus. I didn't want to change anything about him, even if certain things took some adjustment for one reason or another.

"Do you want to try it in reverse?" Lucais suggested. "Not—" He let out a breathy laugh. "No, I mean, do you want to try starting with him this time?" He tipped his head towards his friend. "It might help you to feel...ready."

I wanted to say that I would do anything he asked, but that felt too forward, so I just wet my lower lip with my tongue and glanced at Wrenlock with a nod. I didn't know why I felt so nervous, but Lucais's skin was tinged with a faint pink glow that didn't seem linked to any physical exertion, and that was making my heart race even faster. He was nervous, too. He knew that it might actually be it for us the second time around, and I was too far gone to back out.

"Come here," Wrenlock urged, sitting down at the end of the bed where Lucais had perched the night before.

He helped me climb onto his lap, holding himself in place so I could find the right angle. I braced my hands on Wrenlock's shoulders while the High King rested his back against the pillows at the head of the bed, and then I looked down between our bodies at where they were about to join, wondering if there was any way that I could avoid sealing my fate with Lucais. We were doing it on our terms, but it felt as foreboding as it did exciting. We'd made so much progress in such a short amount of time. Eternity seemed like a looming threat—like a playground of opportunity for things to go wrong.

I gulped and settled down on Wrenlock's lap, feeling the sharp stab of pleasure hit me in a deeply hidden and coveted spot as he slid inside me. It knocked the breath from my lungs. The high, unsteady moan that rolled out of my mouth was unstoppable, so I bit down on my hand to muffle the sound as I started to ride him in earnest, chasing that wild, euphoric feeling he'd stirred awake.

"That's it," Wrenlock purred, his hands firmly planted on my hips as I moved up and down on his lap, the wet slap of each thrust loud and obscene in my ears.

I met Lucais's gaze over his shoulder, copped the brunt of the heat in his unrelenting stare as he lay back on the pillow with one hand behind his head, touching himself as he watched me fuck his best friend on the end of the bed.

"You look at him all you like, baby, but you keep riding my cock like that until you come."

I bit my hand again to hold back a raging moan as heat flooded my face, turning my cheeks as hot as the end of a burning poker. Lucais didn't seem the least bit bothered by the comment. If anything, I thought it was likely responsible for the dribble of thick fluid that leaked out of the tip of his cock when his fist dragged upwards. The sheer sight of it had my movements on Wrenlock faltering, and a smirk turned up the corners of Lucais's mouth.

Keep going, bookworm. You're okay, the High King purred into my mind. *You're taking him so fucking well. You should see yourself from my point of view.*

An image entered my mind.

I was straddling Wrenlock, both hands on his shoulders, the strong muscles in his back flexing as I rose up and down, glimpses slipping over his shoulder of my breasts bouncing with each movement. My nipples were tight, hard peaks, the colour matching my lips and complementing the faint blush of exertion that bloomed beneath the freckles on my skin. My hair fell in loose, wild curls, disappearing down my back, though a few strands were sticking to my forehead and caught in my eyelashes.

It was the hottest thing I'd ever witnessed—watching myself riding someone from the perspective of someone else entirely. Better than a movie, better than a mirror.

Moaning, I shifted my weight so my hips were pressed into Wrenlock's body, my thrusts against him morphing into something less forceful and more intense. Tilting my head back, I gripped both of his shoulders while his hands moved to cup my ass, and I picked up a new, steady rhythm as I rocked against him, grinding my clit against his stomach with every movement.

That's my girl, Lucais crooned, and the image he sent me shifted.

It was the same view, but he'd pulled it back far enough so I could see myself fucking Wrenlock with Lucais's hand stroking himself at the forefront of the picture. He matched each pump of his fist along his shaft to the beat of my movements on his friend until we were in perfect sync, and I began to imagine what it would feel like for them to swap places, with the High King's length sliding into me with each crash of my body into his—eternity be damned.

Wrenlock groaned as he felt me tightening around him. "Fuck, baby, that's it."

The waves of pleasure built in my core with every stroke of Lucais's hand up and down himself. I switched between images—the one in my head, watching myself through his eyes, and the one I had of him, watching the expressions cross his face as he worked himself into a state of abandon. His tip glistened with the leaking arousal that dribbled down the sides, and I imagined myself licking the little beads that he was squeezing out of his dick with each pump.

I must have sent the thought into his mind without meaning to because his rhythm stuttered, and he raised his eyebrows at me.

Is that what you want?

Oh, fuck it.

Nodding eagerly, I slowed my pace on Wrenlock until we stopped.

"I want to try something," I whispered in response to his questioning gaze.

The High King was already sitting up, his expression restrained but eager as he waited for me to climb off Wrenlock's lap. Once I had, I put myself on all fours at the end of the bed, glancing over my shoulder to find that Wrenlock was already moving into position.

"You want me to take you from behind?" he asked, checking to make sure that he was reading the situation correctly.

"Please," I begged.

"Fuck yes." He slid back inside me with one perfect thrust, slamming all the way to the hilt, and a low groan escaped my mouth.

The new angle was more demanding, and I had to be careful how I held my posture to keep the pleasure from turning into pain, but Wrenlock slowed his thrusts until he was rocking his hips into me with just a few inches pulling out. The tip of his erection was nudging the detonation zone hidden deep inside of me when he fucked me like that, and I found myself beginning to unravel with each push. He reached around and pressed his forefinger against my clit, stroking it in slow circles, wet with the mess we were making as he entered me.

When I opened my eyes, I found that Lucais was looking at me with the kind of admiration that stripped me bare and convinced me to step into a confessional to give away my sins. His eyes were literal temptation, a distant fire in the dark of night, and I was drawn to it like a moth to a flame. I urged him to move closer, shuffling into the middle of the bed so I could bend my head down and—

"Oh, fuck, bookworm." His words were a low, feral growl as I licked him from base to tip, tasting the hint of sweetness and salt of his excitement before I twirled my tongue around the head of his cock and sucked the first few inches into my mouth.

Lucais threaded one hand through my hair, the other gripping a fistful of the blankets at his side, and I did my best to sync the movements of my head with each of Wrenlock's thrusts as he fucked me from behind, muttering low curses and grunts as he moved one hand to grip my hip and the other to massage the curve of my ass.

"I love the way your tongue turns sweet for me," Lucais murmured, his tone dripping with wonderment and arousal. His words sparked a new wave of heat inside me, and with Wrenlock's movements becoming consistent, I found myself on the verge of another collapse as pleasure so perfect and relentless spread throughout my body like wildfire, and then I was moaning around Lucais as I came. "Oh, Aura." He sucked in a sharp breath, hands on my head, hips jerking upwards with slow, barely restrained thrusts. "*Fuck*, bookworm."

Wrenlock pulled out of me, though I was sure that he hadn't finished yet, and I continued working Lucais with my mouth as the remnants of pleasure dissipated, sinking a little further down his length until he was inside my throat.

"I'm not saying that I don't fucking love this," Lucais uttered breathlessly, "but if we don't stop soon, I am going to come in your mouth so hard you won't stop tasting me for days."

I knew that it was counterproductive, but part of me wished he would. Even so, I relented after making one final attempt to beat my personal best at the number of inches I could choke down before his cock made me gag. Lucais groaned, muttered a few unholy curses, and then reached up to wipe the tears from my cheeks as I sat back on my heels and brushed a hand over my mouth. I could barely manage to look him in the eyes—to see the affection in them, clear as day, powerful as a natural disaster.

"Lay down," Wrenlock murmured from behind me, and I was all too willing to obey. To do anything either of them asked so I didn't have to think or feel. "I'm going to finish on your stomach, and then you're going to take his cock like the good fucking girl you are, okay?"

I nodded, heart racing.

"I need to hear you say it," he demanded, positioning himself on his knees at my side, his hand around his erection as he made slow, shaky strokes above me. I could see his pleasure teetering on the edge of release in the way his muscles trembled, in the burn behind his eyes.

"Okay," I whispered. Lucais moved his hand between my legs, fingers pressing gently against my clit in circular motions. I cleared my throat and said it again, louder. "Okay."

A few earnest pumps later, and Wrenlock's face contorted with pleasure, his cock shooting thick ropes of hot come all over my stomach exactly as he'd promised. I gasped at the sudden feel of it hitting my skin—sticky, warm, and so devastatingly intimate. I watched Wrenlock's face soften, his abdominal muscles flex, his hand fall still, and his erection twitch as the last of his orgasm washed through him and the final beads of come dripped down onto the mess he'd made on my waist.

"Good girl," Wrenlock breathed. The praise lingered in the air even as the energy drained out of his voice. He exhaled in a sigh, eyes becoming heavy and half-lidded when he leaned down to kiss me before relaxing onto the bed at my side.

I gazed up at Lucais, the sacrifice upon his altar.

"Do you need a moment?" he offered, swallowing with effort.

Because I couldn't seem to locate my voice, I simply shook my head.

"Good," the High King replied, and then his fingers were on my stomach, trailing through the sticky mess. To my absolute surprise, he lubricated himself with Wrenlock's come, first with his hand and next by sliding the point of his erection down my stomach, and then, with a low groan, he drove himself inside me—all the way home.

Forty-Two

Just One More

The High King of Faerie stared down between our bodies, one arm beside my head and the other next to my shoulder, fixated on the place where we had joined for one single stroke of fatal pleasure before I'd tensed and shut down, unable to do anything to stop myself from squeezing my inner muscles around him until he'd sworn and pulled all the way back out again.

With wide eyes, I watched the emotions crossing his face as he considered his options—one of which, I imagined, would be to let the Court of Darkness simply have me. We had engaged in all of the more basic activities without too much of an issue, but the one simple little thing that we needed to do to signify to the universe that we accepted the mating bond was causing a problem and dragging out the entire affair.

Eventually, after all of those thoughts had crossed his mind, Lucais met my eyes and pushed himself back inside me as far as he could possibly reach—which was a few inches, at the very most, before I writhed beneath his body and involuntarily clamped down around him again.

"Let me in," he demanded.

Working my tongue around in my mouth, I managed to pull my voice back from where it had retreated to the base of my throat, and then I replied, "You are in."

"No. You shifted your hips," he growled, golden eyes flashing. "Let me in so I can touch that spot again, Aura." Lucais pushed his hips against me, but I was petrified. Tense. His eyes narrowed like a challenge. "I'm not against a healthy dose of edging, but we've been at this since yesterday. Have you changed your mind?"

Panic flared hot in my chest. "*No.*"

"Then if you don't relax, this is going to hurt," he warned, a glimmer of relief shining through the surface of his irises despite it. "Because I'm not going to stop this time, but I want you to feel good."

"You mean you *need* me to feel good," I said quietly. Immediately, I blushed at my own petulance and averted my gaze, selecting a corner of his bedpost and canopy to study as he hovered over me because I honestly wasn't sure what was happening. I wanted it. I wanted *him*.

"I mean I need *you*. Period." Lucais's voice was harsh, but the words were honey-sweet and warm. I felt the impact of them settle in my core, soothing and stretching, and lowered my hips so my back was resting flat against the bed once more. "Now. Let. Me. In." Lucais's gaze was hard and unyielding as he lowered himself onto his forearms, eradicating the space between us, and coaxed the thick, granite-hard length of his erection back inside me with three slow nudges of his hips, each gaining another couple of inches until he was all the way there.

I was at my limit. I was *full*. I suddenly wondered if I was still flesh and bone or simply glass about to shatter inside a furnace.

Taking measured breaths against the crook of my neck, Lucais stayed still until I'd lost count of our heartbeats, giving me the chance to get used to both the size and the sensation of him. It was like nothing I'd ever felt before and prompted a tidal wave of emotion to sweep over me from head to toe, heart to soul. I had the insane urge to cry, which triggered a flush of shame, and in turn made me want to squirm beneath him so he didn't feel the rising temperature of my skin pressing into his.

"You're okay," he whispered into my ear, sensing the escalating discomfort. "Hold still, bookworm. It's okay. You're perfect. Just a few more moments to get used to this, and then we'll find our rhythm, okay?" He pressed a kiss to my temple, and I squeezed my eyes shut against the threat of tears. "You're doing so well. So perfect, Aura."

Lucais slid one hand behind my head, holding me to him as he moved his hips back. The lack of him was an immediate, palpable ache deep in my core. When he slid back in straight to the hilt, I gasped, the sound high-pitched and wonderstruck as an unrivalled form of ecstasy took hold of my nerve endings and applied pressure. I felt the pinch of euphoria running all the way between my sternum and my lower belly, warm and smooth and alive.

Beginning to rock inside me, he moved back and forth, gradually increasing speed until the bed started to jostle along with us.

A loud, sudden growl ripped through the air—

Lucais covered my mouth with his hand to muffle my laughter as we both looked over to where Wrenlock was lying on the bed beside us, fast asleep and snoring.

He chuckled silently and bent down to whisper in my ear, "You must have given him one hell of an orgasm."

I stifled my amusement and shook my head free of his hand. "What do we do now?"

Lucais's eyes crinkled at the corners as he glanced around the room. "Floor?" he suggested dubiously. "No..." He turned his head towards the other side of his space. "Wall? Window?"

Nodding, I prepared for him to pull out of me and help me to stand, but he didn't do either of those things. Instead, Lucais pressed his mouth to mine, drawing me into an explorative, indulgent kiss, and then he wrapped his arms around me with one hand secured on the nape of my neck and one behind my waist as he made another lazy thrust inside of me and the bed fell out from under us.

In an instant, we were against the wall across the room, the cool and slightly roughened stone biting into my skin. Lucais was holding me against it high enough to capture my nipple in his mouth and give a gentle, teasing tug before he kissed his way back to my lips, lowering me an inch or two until I was on him again.

He was so hard and I was so wet that neither of us needed to use our hands. I gasped as he pushed himself inside me in one sudden, hard thrust—and he swore so loudly that I was almost afraid it would wake our companion or draw attention from other parts of the palace.

I pressed the back of my head against the wall as he drove himself into me, but I couldn't keep it from banging into the stone with each one of his thrusts. Bending forwards, I pressed my forehead into the crook of my elbow, resting on his shoulder as my arms twisted around his neck.

We fell into a feverish rhythm. He filled me perfectly, found the spot in my body that begged for attention, and rammed the head of his cock into it over and over again. Each movement pushed me closer towards a state of all-consuming, mindless bliss, and he forced moans and cries out of me with every slam of his body into mine. I could not be sure if the sounds would seem more like noises of torture or ecstasy to passersby.

I suddenly didn't care.

The heat reached a climax under my skin and within my skull, and the pinpricks of pleasure began to build like a wave between my hips. I writhed against him, trying to maintain that perfect, flawless angle as he hit that spot inside me over and over again until I was close to madness.

"Oh, fuck." Lucais's mouth was all over me, devouring me with kisses and bites that took pleasure and pain around in a circle until I could hardly remember my own name. “That’s it, isn’t it? Let me hit that spot again, bookworm.” His voice made my muscles shudder, on the verge of folding. “That’s it. Just once, okay? I need you to come for me once, and then I swear, you’ll never have to do it again. You can give me one, can’t you?”

My answer was an incoherent sound, half a whimper and half a moan, because he’d already contributed to putting my senses through so much in the last day, and I was feeling the beginnings of exhaustion. Like if I did it again, I would permanently break all over him, and he may never be able to clean up the last of the mess I’d made.

“Lucais,” I whispered. My orgasm was like a spontaneous explosion, and I’d never forgive myself if I ended up in tears over it.

“I know.” He pressed his forehead to my temple, driving into me again and again, as if we might just melt into each other and cease to exist from all of our problems if we tried for long enough. “*Fuck*, Aura, I know.”

His tip knocked into the detonation zone in his next thrust, and a heat sparked at the base of my spine, triggering a sensation that built in intensity with each subsequent hit. I felt wrung out and spent, but at the same time, like I would die if he stopped.

“Just one more,” Lucais bit out, exertion seeping into his voice. I realised he must have been feeling the same—on the brink of utter devastation with no way to stop himself from falling headfirst over the edge. “You can give me one more, can’t you, perfect girl? You’re so fucking pretty when you come. Let me watch you one more time.”

I was undone in a moment.

He turned his head to the side, blazing golden eyes meeting mine, and his next thrust banished the breath from my lungs. Lucais’s hands were so gentle, but his hips were enough to shatter me, his erection enough to split me in half. I was entranced, unable to look away even as I came apart at the seams, and bit down on my own hand to muffle my scream as I pulsed around him.

With an unequivocal tsunami of ecstasy, I came all over him in a way that I had never experienced before—and almost never wanted to experience again, though part of me wished it would never end. It hit me so hard that it was borderline painful, and I held onto Lucais like I’d disappear inside of a dying star if I let go of him because, suddenly, the wall behind me was gone, replaced by the ice-cold glass of the window, and yet I was still falling.

The same brutal pleasure of the orgasm he was giving me hadn't relented. The sensation assaulted me, prolonged like nothing that could be replicated under any other circumstances, as our bodies stitched our souls together in the kind of way that not even the ends of the universe could break.

Gripping the back of his head as Lucais nestled his face into my neck and fucked me against the window like he'd lost all sense of time and space, I ran my fingers through his hair and curled my fingertips against his scalp before I grabbed a fistful at the roots and tugged. I moaned, the sound low and full of indulgent bliss, as I felt his orgasm follow.

His cock pulsated with an intensity that could have been considered violent as he emptied himself inside me, and he pressed his lips against my throat and let out a long string of moans that crashed into and interrupted each other in the sexiest sound I'd ever heard.

But we were still falling.

The window disappeared, and the sensation of freefalling through time and space and magic partnered with the unrelenting orgasm he'd sent to destroy me from the inside out as we spun through floors and ceilings and doorways. I was torn between trying to escape it and trying to trap it.

Nevertheless, we had a death grip on each other as we knocked into new walls, hitting cabinets that belonged to different parts of the palace, tripping over furniture in other bedrooms, knocking over picture frames and empty lanterns. The whole time, we were desperately kissing, touching, grasping for more like we could find a way to crawl inside the other person if the wave of pleasure lasted long enough to blow all sense of reality into smithereens.

We ended up on a couch in a space many floors below the room in which we had started.

I was on top of Lucais, a hot and sticky mess between our stomachs, and I was trembling as I rode out the last drops of pleasure on him until exhaustion overcame the both of us and we eventually fell asleep kissing.

It was a little while later when I stirred awake. I scowled up at his perfect, sleeping face before I lay my head back down on his chest and succumbed to the intrinsic need for sleep, calling for an overnight ceasefire.

He was such a liar. A conman. A morally grey High King who could not be trusted, even though he was getting sloppier with each of his schemes and secrets. He'd been all over me, inside of me, and lying to my face the whole time.

Just give me one. That's all I need, and then we'll never have to do this again.

I rolled my eyes at him before I closed them.

Yeah, right.

We were definitely going to do that again.

Forty-Three

The Bond

I woke up the next morning with something lodged behind my rib cage.

My breath came with greater effort, the beat of my heart slowed with confusion, and I felt it contract when I sat up—a brutal tension like the twinge of a pulled muscle. The foreign object was magnetic, and it gravitated towards something behind me. I turned my head, careful not to disturb the balance of near pain in my chest. Maybe it had broken off something that I'd been sleeping on—

My eyes fell upon Lucais's face, and I knew.

I simply knew he'd left something inside of me that was permanent and unalterable, and that when he woke up, he would realise that I'd left something tucked inside of his chest, too.

The bond had been solidified. Once. Twice. I thought we might have done it one thousand times in total—or at least, it felt like we had. One thousand crash landings into an explosion of pleasure so acute, violent, and all-consuming that I still felt the echoes of it ghosting across my flesh and bones so many hours later.

One thousand times, I had said yes, more, please.

One thousand times, we told the Oracle that it was right. One thousand times, we carved out tiny little pieces of each other to patch up our respective hearts. One thousand times, we had branded ourselves upon the other with literal blood, sweat, and tears in fragmented dreams and soul stitches.

One thousand times.

Forty-Four

The Urge to Throw Yourself into Fireplaces

I had no idea which room we ended up in—or why we fell through the palace in the throes of passion in the first place—but it was on somebody's cleaning schedule.

A small faerie came bustling into the room carrying a broom, dustpan, and bucket of firewood. When she realised the High King was naked on the sofa beneath an equally naked woman, she dropped everything with a clatter, and I lurched to my feet, grabbing the throw blanket draped over the back of the nearest chair and wrapping it around myself. My actions exposed even more of Lucais's body, and the woman's cheeks turned red, her eyes rounding to comical proportions.

Lucais stirred, presumably from the contact with the cool morning air. He scrubbed at his eyes before he sat up and threw his legs over the side of the couch, bracing his elbows on his thighs. I studied his lean, bare body while he blinked away the sleep, and I had to admit that my eyes would have done the exact same thing as hers if it was my first time seeing him naked, too.

He was hot. He was really quite stupidly hot, and the length of his half asleep boner was almost more impressive than when it was fully erect with the way he was hung. Faelight shone over him in a dim and romantic glow, despite the early daylight infiltrating the fog beyond the large French doors. Lucais was all golden tones and gloom, messy hair and smooth skin—

Bleary-eyed, the High King tilted his face towards mine and smiled.

"I am so sorry, Your Highness." The woman standing in the doorway immediately fell to her knees to pick up her supplies.

That woke Lucais up.

He jumped to his feet, mouth agape and hair sticking up in places like he'd been electrocuted, and when she glanced up at him again, I was afraid the heat under her skin might be flirting with dangerous levels. To her credit, she gathered her items and retreated from the room in record time, and Lucais waved a hand to shut the door behind her. Letting out a husky laugh, he ran his hands through his hair to ruffle it after spending a night on the sofa cushions with my head on his chest and his arms around me, and then his eyes made their way back to my face.

I blinked at him, paralysed in the middle of the room, draped in a blanket, a deer caught in the headlights of his irises.

Apprehension circled us, a heavy tension in the air too thick to be snapped, and we assessed one another inside it with narrowed gazes. My stomach flipped when Lucais's hand absently floated to his side, fingers poking at the same spot around his rib cage that was bothering me on my own body. His eyes darkened as he calculated the severity of what we had done, and then he broke our impetuous silence.

"Are we going to stand here and pretend that wasn't the best sex either of us have ever had?"

"Yes."

A sigh slipped through his lips, and the croaky languor of his voice was enough to make my heart grow phantom wings. "Okay." He nodded in defeat, throat bobbing as he swallowed. "Well...then I'm going to shower and apologise to the staff."

"Okay." I stared at my nails as if my cuticles were interesting and shifted from one foot to the other before looking back at him. "That sounds good."

There was a very long pause as we tried to tear our eyes away from the bewitchment that had locked our gazes together and sealed them with glue.

"Okay." Lucais made the first move to break free of the trance and took a step as if he was about to evanesce from the room, but at the last minute, he turned back to me. "Aura?"

My cheeks flooded with heat for some unbeknownst reason. "Yes?"

"I meant what I said last night." His gilded gaze dropped to the soft rug on the floor beneath us as if the memory was too strong to swallow. "You are perfect, and you did *so* well, and I..." The High King's tongue swept over his lower lip, followed by his teeth. "I won't ever ask you to do that again now."

I cleared my throat. *Oh.*

"Thank you," I whispered. "I appreciate it."

Even if I was a little disappointed, I didn't show that to my brand-new soulmate, who smiled sweetly at me before vanishing from the room. I stood still for a few minutes after he left and familiarised myself with the way my left rib felt as the distance between us extended and stabilised, like the tension on a liferope or a grappling hook, moving and shifting depending on how much thought I gave to it and our relative proximity.

How do we know if it worked?

Lucais heard my question and replied instantly. *If you get the urge to throw yourself into fireplaces again, we'll know.*

Where are you?

In the shower. Why? Would you like to join me?

Ignoring him, I pulled the blanket a little tighter around my shoulders and shook my head free of our mental connection as I shuffled towards the glass doors. They led out into a courtyard on the ground floor, though I could hardly see through the mist. All I knew was that we had plummeted through so many levels of the palace, landing in a small parlour filled with old bookshelves, a fully stocked liquor cart, a neatly organised desk, and the sofa we had slept on in front of a fireplace that didn't have any wood left in the grate.

Deciding that I needed to shower too, I took one last, longing look back at the sofa before I left the room. I only made it to the next floor before my walk of shame was perceived.

"Aura!"

Halfway down a corridor, I came to an abrupt stop and swivelled towards the voice. Morgoya was climbing a staircase at the other end, each of her long strides making the tresses of her beaded gown swish and rustle. I hesitated, hyperaware that I was wearing a borrowed blanket, and wondered if I should make a run for it and pretend I hadn't seen her. Deciding against it, I stumbled a few steps in her direction, clutching the blanket with both hands underneath my chin and trying not to let my cheeks burn like the very portrait of shame.

"You look well," she commented, smiling so widely that a glimpse of her teeth was visible between her blood-red lips.

Morgoya knew.

"So do you," I returned pleasantly.

The High Lady let out a long breath of air as she caught up to me, her smile simmering down into something duller and less intimidating. "I wanted to give you something," she informed me, wringing her hands. A little crease appeared between her sharply sculpted eyebrows. "I don't know whether to call it my condolences or my congratulations."

I chewed on my lip as her meaning washed over me. "Right. You're talking about my father."

"That must have been very difficult for you."

My heart launched into a gallop. There was no polite way to explain how desperately I wished not to talk about it, but her good intentions permeated the air between us, impossible to offend or escape. I swallowed down the urge to vomit all over the pretty lace corset of her dress. "There are worse things," I pronounced at last.

"I see." Her expression transformed, the hard angles softening as she let her shoulders drop and risked another baby step towards me. "Did it help?"

I gave her a quizzical look.

"With reconnecting to your magic?" she prompted, and then she laughed at the look on my face.

"I haven't tried," I admitted, blushing at my own idiocy. *When did that stop being a priority?*

"He's quite distracting, Aura. Even I can admit that." Morgoya shook her head in an endearing sort of way, a kind smile reshaping her mouth. "I would love for you to spend some time with me in the palace training rooms. Batre will be there. We'll ban the boys from entering and see if we can help." Her viridescent gaze searched mine. "Would you like that?"

My eyes must have betrayed eagerness because Morgoya's entire face lit up in relief before I'd even opened my mouth. "That sounds great," I decided. "When and where?"

Forty-Five

Ground, Open Up and Swallow Me Whole

I met the High Lady at the agreed time and place so she could show me to the palace training rooms, and while we walked, Morgoya gave me a brief political update. It looked like the Court of Wind had settled in for a long stay—much to the High King's chagrin—and the carousal was beginning to wind down in the city at last, no thanks to Enyd's men.

"I've been doing the rounds, trying to get a read on public opinion after the Malum attack," she enlightened me as we climbed a steep, narrow staircase. There were numerous small windows high above us, smothered with fog and barely illuminating the dreary space. "Most faeries were too preoccupied with drink and dance to notice that anything unordinary was happening. The sirens were loud, but only the sober faeries picked up on the fact that they were a warning alarm and not part of the festivities, and the faelight outage occurred while many were sleeping."

A chill ran down my spine as we paused on the next landing.

The Malum had been right outside their homes, and nobody had known how much danger they were in that night. The clandestine nature of faeries was so extreme they didn't even ask questions amongst themselves.

"There are, however, a few particular factions of the High Fae who are discussing the missing lights," Morgoya went on, lowering her voice into a conspiratorial whisper. Her slim-fingered hand drew me into the shadows against the wall, and I felt like concrete had been poured down my spine. "There are rumours that the repeated instances of vanishing lights are connected. There is talk of the High King losing his power."

Her words froze my blood.

"Does he know?" I choked out.

In the shadows, Morgoya's features were severe. "He doesn't care. He thinks he's immune to public opinion because of what he experienced as a child, but I've ordered my spies to see through the rest of the discussions. I'm taking this seriously, Aura, even if he won't." Her feline eyes glowed with an emerald viridity through the dark as she appraised me. "I think you should, too."

A painful throb smashed into my chest, and it took me a moment to realise that it was anxiety affecting the beat of my heart.

I understood what she was trying to tell me.

We both knew Lucais's power was impeded by the lapsus—though I didn't think she was aware that the entire city was being held together by one of his spells—and he was under more strain than normal, which was a risk neither of us wanted to continue taking. We also knew that I was supposed to have access to a certain type of magic, which might be helpful to him if I was able to master it, and my inability to do so had already incurred a cost to his reputation.

But there was one part of her warning that bothered me more than the rest.

"Don't these faeries know I'm the one who took the light in Sthiara?" My voice took on an unfamiliar, harsh edge that surprised me. "They saw me in the Oracle. They've heard the prediction of a union between light and dark—not to mention the fact that he basically outed me to everyone at the meeting in the throne room."

"I wondered that, too," she assured me. "I believe the narrative they're trying to spin is that he's covering up for the fact that you're a human without powers. Two spells with one stone, so to speak."

I was already shaking my head, a foreign rage simmering beneath my fingers as I flexed them to try to remain calm. I'd felt anger before, but the things Morgoya told me were making me absolutely livid.

How dare they? He's their High King—

"That bond really does something to you, doesn't it?" The High Lady's smile was rueful but momentary. "I'm not saying any of this to upset you. I truly believe you need to know...because there's more."

Forcing myself to swallow despite the tension in my throat, I asked, "What else?"

"If you're not a faerie with magic, as they're suggesting, then that begs the question of what the darkness portrayed inside of the Oracle actually means." Her mouth flattened into a red slash across her face. "Some think it signals the end of Lucais's reign, but others have started asking about Blythe."

"Fuck."

"My thoughts exactly."

My gaze hit the ceiling, watery and unstable. "I see why you've invited me to train with you," I said with a forced laugh, trying to lighten the oppressive mood that was cloaked around us in our secret corner of the palace staircase.

Morgoya curled her hand around mine and tugged me along beside her. "It's not only for that," she remonstrated. "I've been wanting to reconnect, but I respected your need for space."

"That was on me." I sighed. "Every time I wanted to say something, I froze."

She squeezed my hand before exchanging it for the handles of a double door. "I never should have allowed him to take it that far," Morgoya insisted, glancing over her shoulder as she shoved against the wood.

An enormous, open space was revealed with high, arched windows and a dome ceiling that merged a fair distance above a viewing balcony; it had indistinguishable carvings on the railing and spanned all the way around the top of the room. Reminiscent of a ballet studio, an entire wall was covered with a mirror, magnifying the reflection of the gloomy stone, and showcasing a figure sitting in the middle of the polished floor.

Batre was cross-legged with hands on her knees and her eyes closed.

Forgetting my reply, I paused on the threshold, entranced as I watched the earth faerie rising from the ground. Her ascension was so precise I couldn't discern what was happening for the first few minutes as her girlfriend and I observed her in a respectful silence—until the vines began to build up around her sides.

Batre didn't show any signs of exertion as her magic worked to create a throne beneath her, using foliage and tendrils pulled up through the cracks in the floor. Olive-coloured and flowering with little white petals, the vines wove in and out of each other as they grew in length and thickness, stitching together to create the chair that raised her until she was perched atop it like a goddess of nature.

Her eyelids fluttered gently as we approached, cracking open once the throne of vines settled into the foundations of the stonework.

"Hi." She beamed at me. "I'm so glad you're here."

My jaw slackened. "You are *incredible*."

Batre snorted, flicking her long twin braids over her shoulder as she wriggled her legs out from beneath her and rose from her creation. "I do parlour tricks like this when I'm not rescuing damsels in distress," she informed me, winking.

"Thank you again," I blurted, a wave of shyness washing over me. "I do hope you never have to rescue me again, though."

"Well..." Her gaze flicked towards Morgoya before returning to mine with a sheen of shrewdness. "I don't suppose the Court of Darkness will be interested in you anymore, will it?"

For a moment, my lower belly tightened with the memory of everything I had done with the High King in order to achieve that hopeful outcome. The sound of Lucais's voice echoed in my ear—how he praised me, begging me for one more, the feeling of his hips as they rocked into me, as he touched a part of my body that I could have sworn had never been noticed before...

"Aura?"

Shit.

"Um." Blinking furiously, I rubbed my temple and swallowed down the filthy memory, praying to the High Mother that he wasn't able to eavesdrop through our newly cemented bond. "I don't actually know." I dropped my hand. "I guess not?"

If I hadn't been so spooked when we woke up in a completely different room to where we'd started, maybe Lucais would have stayed a bit longer to talk me through the next steps. As it was, though, I didn't even *think* to ask him for the specifics, simply being so relieved that we'd managed to do it successfully after all of that effort.

"I feel like a soulmate," I confessed in a whisper. "I don't feel like a High Queen."

But I didn't feel like the High Lady of the Court of Darkness, either.

Morgoya patted me on the shoulder as she strode past me to greet her girlfriend properly. They shared a sweet, chaste kiss before she told me, "There is a separate ceremony to the mating bond required for the coronation of any High King or High Queen."

"You're kidding." I slouched as all of the blood drained from my face. "They didn't mention that."

Morgoya's head whipped towards me so fast it could have flown right off her shoulders. "*They?*"

Ground, open up and swallow me whole.

If Batre could conjure up a throne of vines through the stonework, perhaps she could do the same with a sinkhole or quicksand. The earth faerie did no such thing, but she did speak up so I didn't have to keep my foot wedged inside of my mouth, and for that, I was thankful.

"It's not a really big deal if you're the *adjacent* leader," she promised me. "If you've solidified the bond, then the hard part is over—no pun intended—and you've secured your place at his side as a ruler of Faerie. It just isn't completely official until they weigh it down with all of the bells and whistles." She nudged Morgoya in the ribs, who was staring at me like she was trying to read my mind. "Is it enough for the Court of Darkness to back off, though?"

"The Court of Darkness, yes," the High Lady mused distractedly.

I crossed my ankles, wishing that I could access the power of time travel. I'd go all the way back to the day I left Brynn in the human world, take her with me instead, and then I'd make sure this particular conversation never happened.

"It should release some of the pressure on you," Batre persevered encouragingly. "For now, let's focus on getting a feel for your magic again. I haven't experienced this myself, but I hear that when a prospective leader is coming into their full power, they're usually unable to access any other parts of their magic."

Rubbing the space between my eyebrows, I made an effort to physically shake my shoulders, imagining that I was freeing myself of the regrets that plagued me and the horrors that haunted my subconscious mind. Like the memories from the Court of Darkness and the Court of Light, where magic had sent me into a spiral on more than one occasion. And the lingering echoes of my childhood, where I had befriended an entity that abandoned me in my time of need and left me with countless scars on my heart.

If I was going to take magic seriously, I needed to understand it—how it could build a throne of vines beneath a woman with peace all over her face and bring light into the streets, instead of only seeing how it could paint walls black and leave whispers in the dark.

"Help me figure out what that means," I pleaded.

Forty-Six

Glass Rose

"Levitation." Morgoya picked up a small glass orb from the cart of wares Batre had hauled out of a hidden storage facility on the other side of the training room. It was thin, reflecting the fog-tainted light like a pearl, and extremely fragile.

She let it drop.

Her hand flattened in the air above it, halting the descent. The orb floated a few inches away from an untimely death upon the floor. With a glance at her girlfriend, she withdrew her hand, and the orb wobbled midair but remained in place. Batre had extended her own palm flat and horizontal, accepting the transfer of power and keeping it safe.

"Any faerie can do it," the High Lady informed me as Batre's bare hand guided the orb back to its place on the cart. "There are a number of basic abilities that *anyone* with magic can complete, though everyone has different strengths and weaknesses. It doesn't matter which Element you were born to inherit."

"I did that once," I announced, pointing to the orb.

Morgoya's face betrayed mild surprise. "You did? When?"

"I was a child. I didn't mean to do anything like that, but during one of my"—I searched for the right name—"*episodes*, all of the objects in our living room started levitating. I had no control over it." Bile rose in my throat, the familiar prickle of abhorrence triggering the hairs on the back of my neck, so I took a deep breath. "Like...I *couldn't* put them down."

"Hmm." Morgoya tapped a manicured finger against her upper lip. "Is that the only instance of baseline magic you've experienced?"

Ignorance jerked my eyebrows up. "Um... What are the others?"

The High Lady elevated one arm, sharply clicking her fingers as she brought her fist towards her face like she was pulling a string. A book appeared on top of the cart.

"Summoning," she declared simply, and then proceeded to let her arm fall back to her side, releasing her fist into a flat hand as if she were wiping a table, and the book disappeared. "Vanishment."

I watched as she summoned the book once more, then twisted her hand as if to flick an invisible switch. Immediately, the hardcover book flipped open, and pages began to turn of their own volition.

"Enchantment," she announced, and then the orb was in her hand once more. "Summoning," she reminded me with a pointed look, before she tossed it into the air.

I braced for another round of levitation, but Morgoya let the glass shatter upon the floor, and it was all I could do to keep up as she brought her hands together above it as if she was praying. The broken shards of glass morphed back into the original item without a single crack or scratch.

"Restoration."

The High Lady made the motion of lifting a string and the orb floated up to rest on the waiting palm of her free hand. A moment later, she made a pinch towards it, and the glass orb was once again shattered into hundreds of tiny pieces.

"Destruction."

Keeping her fingers in place above the remnants of glass gathered on her palm, she rubbed them together like she was seasoning a pot with salt, and I stared open-mouthed as the glass refashioned itself into the shape of a rose. The delicate petals shone in the low light, the transparent stem harnessing a bluish hue. With a theatrical curtsy, Morgoya handed the glass rose to Batre—who took it while fanning her face with her other hand and batting her eyelashes exaggeratedly—and then she twisted back to face me.

"Transformation," she concluded.

"You're already aware of trans*portation*," Batre added, kissing the rose before she sent it floating back to the cart of magical supplies. "That's what we do when we evanesce, but we can also do it with items. Certain faeries are skilled enough to do it to other people, too, but that's often frowned upon."

"Necromancy is another one," Morgoya mentioned, swishing her hips as she walked over to the throne. "That isn't just frowned upon, though. It's a banned magic, commonly viewed as a practice that only the Witches still acknowledge."

"Oh, and don't forget telekinesis!" Batre exclaimed.

The High Lady clicked her fingers as she sat down on the throne of vines. "Yes, that one, too! Thank you." Her gaze settled on me. "I tend to forget telekinesis because I'm fairly weak in that area, but it's the practice of mind-reading or mind-sharing—which is what you and Lucais are able to do through the mating bond's magic—and memory-scraping." She shrugged, a reticent look in her eyes. "The last part of that is controversial, but it's not actually banned unless you're permanently removing the other person's memories. It's also one of the most uncommon skills, second only to necromancy. Lucais's father was a very talented telekinetic, actually."

"Healing!" Batre threw in as she rustled through a cabinet. "So common we always forget it. Everyone can heal themselves to a degree, but only some have mastered it well enough to be able to heal others." She straightened, pensive. "I think that one ranks about third on the list of uncommon talents—for being able to heal other people, that is."

Head spinning, I held my hands out in front of me to beg for pause.

"Let me go through this from the beginning," I beseeched, feeling foggy and warm as I displayed a hand to count on my fingers. "The most common forms of baseline magic are levitation, restoration, destruction, transportation and trans*form*ation, enchantment..." With both hands in the air again, I trailed off with uncertainty.

"Summoning," Morgoya added.

I lifted another finger.

"And vanishment," Batre concluded.

Another finger.

"Right." I nodded like my mind wasn't swimming through muddy waters. "So there are eight, plus three forms of less common magic that include necromancy or healing, and then all of the mind-reading stuff."

The High Lady clapped her hands gleefully. "You've got it!" she applauded, grinning as she crossed her legs.

I raised an eyebrow at her. "Hardly."

"There is a whole new world of layers and rules that apply to all of those forms of magic, but we don't need to get into them right now," she assured me. "The most important thing is that you know what your options are so you don't feel pressured to follow through with the only form of magic you've ever been shown—which was dark and kind of messy, no offence."

"None taken." I swayed a little on my feet, woozy. "I feel like this is a lot, though."

"Here," Batre offered, picking up the glass rose that Morgoya had transformed. She smiled as she approached me, but I saw the panic flaring in the depths of her eyes, like she was concerned they might lose my interest or scare me away. Like they'd be damned if they did. "You said that you've levitated in the past. Why don't we see if you can do that again?"

Inhaling deeply through my mouth, I accepted the glass stem. It was cool and so devastatingly fragile between my fingertips, the distortion of the world through its translucent, ice-blue surface too pretty to be handled by someone who had touched so many horrors. Batre reclaimed my attention, pulling me from the intrusive thought, and I understood the look she was concealing. She'd pledged the commitment of her lifetime to Morgoya, who was irrevocably tied to Lucais in ways I still didn't fully understand, and losing him would be catastrophic for the both of them—even if it was only in title.

Rulers in Faerie generally die at the end of their reign.

I straightened my spine. "What do I do with it?"

"First, imagine there is a link between you and the flower," the earth faerie urged. "Picture it as an extension of yourself, the stem another part of your hand—a limb you can hold and control with calculated movements. Focus on that feeling, and let me know when you think you've got it."

I did as she instructed.

The rest of the room faded from my mind; everything from the High Lady on the edge of her vine-woven seat to the maroon smudge of my hair in the mirror. The ceiling disappeared, and the floor fell away from under me. I stared at the glass rose until I knew exactly how many petals made up its flower, until the stem felt like a part of my hand, until I felt a sense of familiarity with the single leaf and thorn that peeked out from one side. Rolling it in my hand, the sharp angle of the thorn glinted as I turned it, and I could imagine my own blood running through it like a vein that would fill with the colour of my insides, a crimson flood linking my body to the flower—

"Apply pressure if there are any open wounds while you wait for someone to come, preferably with a clean bandage if you think you can find one. But the first thing you do is call us, even if you need to leave the house

to do it, even if you think she really needs your help. Someone will always come if you call, Auralie. Okay? You did really well tonight."

—and making us one. I squeezed my eyes closed, keeping the visual in the forefront of my mind as I gripped the glass stem and imagined that I could manipulate its movements the same way that I flexed my fingers.

There was a pressure in the air, an invisible thread stitching us together, as corporeal as the tendons in my hand or the muscles in my jaw. Opening my mouth to tell Batre—

The blood was everywhere, all over the floor and her clothes. The room was destroyed, our belongings strewn around the space like it had been ransacked, so many broken things I'd dropped without ever picking up. I heard a roaring in my head, shouts coming from all sides, but I couldn't make out a single word of what they were saying or what was happening. The only thing I could hear was the wet, raspy breaths she was taking as she lay with her eyes closed on the living room floor. My hands trembled as I ran to her, stumbling over my own feet in my haste. The shaking was so violent it was in my teeth. Inside my own skull.

"Ma—mam—mama—" My tongue slipped between my molars as they slammed together and blood poured into my mouth. I fell to my knees at her side, hands hovering over her body, trying to find the wound. The nurse told me to apply pressure to open wounds. So where was the wound?

There was swelling in her face, but her nose had stopped bleeding. I touched it lightly, fingertips red and unsteady. Then the cut across her cheek. I forced my stiff limbs to work—forced them because they weren't cooperating, they were barely attached to my body anymore, feeling like objects that I'd discarded on the ground and couldn't pick up again—and moved her head from side to side, checking for an open wound.

Nothing.

I did the rounds like the paramedic showed me last time, hands following her body from her neck down to her swollen belly, which was scarred but otherwise clear from injury, to her legs and feet. There was nothing. Nothing that I could see caused all of the blood on the floor...

"N—n—n—no, no—no, no—no, no—"

"Aura, please, baby," someone was saying.

Their hands were on my shoulders. Their hands felt more real on my body than my own hands did, so I decided to do the only thing I could and screamed at the top of my lungs. The person's hands fell away from me, but my body started to jerk, and I couldn't control it.

I moved one of her legs. That was where the blood was coming from—it was coming from between her legs. On shaky knees, I rose to stand, stumbling into the kitchen with blood-coated hands to find a clean bandage so I could stop the bleeding.

"She's waking up!"

The sound of glass shattering forced my eyes to open, and I swore, instinctively lowering myself to my knees so I could clean it up, though my hands were bare and empty.

"Hey." Morgoya's face was in front of mine a moment later. "Are you okay?"

I shook my head. "I dropped it."

"You levitated it for a moment first, I think," she whispered. "It kind of fell out of your hands in slow motion."

"Damn." I laughed without humour. "I was really trying, too."

She stroked my hair back from my face before cupping my cheek. "I know you were. You did well for your first meaningful attempt. We'll try it again tomorrow, okay? Something a bit different." When I nodded, she proceeded to offer, "Would you like to come with us for some tea? You can leave all of this here. We'll send someone up to deal with it later."

"Uh..." I sat back on my heels, exhaling in a huff. "I appreciate that, but I think I need to sit here for a minute and think. That brought up some things for me, which is"—I swallowed—"why I dropped it. You two go ahead."

Morgoya hesitated for longer than I expected her to, but she eventually conceded to my hint and placed a gentle kiss on the top of my head before standing up. I didn't take my eyes off the broken glass to watch either of them leaving because I didn't trust myself not to cry or show some other kind of emotion if I did. That would make them feel bad about it, even though I really did think I needed to process the resurfaced memory.

But when I was certain that I was alone, I tried to manipulate the glass shards back into the beautiful rose it had been before I dropped it.

I felt so silly doing it that I'd never even attempt it if I wasn't by myself, but it was the part that had upset me the most—the fact that the item I'd damaged had been so delicate and pretty before I touched it. If Morgoya and Batre had handed me a glass toothbrush, I probably wouldn't have experienced quite the same surge of untempered emotion in the wake of its demolition.

If destruction was a form of magic that all faeries should be able to access, then surely restoration wasn't far behind as an attainable skill, and I was already so good at destruction.

The eerie, unsettling sensation of being watched fell over me as I tried different gestures and hand positions over and around the mess of broken glass in a series of failed attempts to coax it back together. Eventually, I gave in to my frustration and scooped the glass shards up in my hand, determined to clean up my own messes even if it was the mortal way, but a particularly large piece of a broken petal slid too close to my thumb, slicing the skin open.

"Ouch. Fuck!" I dropped the glass shards, staring at the gash on my hand as the blood pooled.

Are you okay?

My head snapped up, the pain forgotten as I stared at the empty training room in front of me and heard Lucais's voice in my mind. *How can you possibly know that I hurt myself?*

Have you already forgotten that we are fated mates who solidified the fuck out of the bond last night?

You can see when I hurt myself through the bond?

No. He laughed into my mind, the sound soft as wind chimes. *Don't be ridiculous. I can see when you hurt yourself because I'm standing behind you.*

I whirled, sending glass shards spinning out across the floor as I searched the room for a blond head and exasperatingly sexy smirk.

Lucais emerged from the shadows in the doorway, hidden from view while he watched me for the Oracle only knew how long when I thought I was alone.

"This is becoming a habit for you," I complained as he closed the distance between us, and then I gasped as Wrenlock entered the room behind him. "Not you, too!"

Wrenlock rolled his lips together to suppress a smile. "I've missed you, too, baby." He waved a hand at the floor, and all of the broken glass disappeared. "In my defence, I didn't want to interfere with your concentration."

While Lucais took my injured hand in his and hoisted me to my feet, I rolled my eyes at the both of them, although I had to admit that their appearance was an instant mood booster. I was so happy to see them that I didn't even flinch when Lucais started to remove shards of glass from my flesh, which normally would have made me feel unwell.

"We've been in a meeting with the Court of Wind," Wrenlock apprised me. He was wearing his usual attire—grey tunic, black pants—and had a dagger strapped to his hip. "Enyd found out we weren't technically even in the city when she arrived, so she's been on a rampage all morning."

"What does she want?" I enquired.

"Oh, she wants to swap spit and create a secret handshake," Lucais groused, squinting at my hand. "You've got tiny little shards of glass in here, bookworm. I need to get them out before I can heal the wound."

Before I could even reply, he brought my palm up to his face and placed his mouth over the cut. My stomach flipped with an alien feeling of arousal and disgust as I felt the suction like a kiss—so similar to the way that he had sucked on my neck, my nipples, and my clit, but so different as blood and glass shards were pulled into his mouth—and when his eyes met mine, aureate and filled with so much heat, I felt a wet warmth sliding between the apex of my thighs. Lucais withdrew and spat onto the ground, which made it even worse.

I gulped as a flare of light magic stretched between our hands, the colour rich and vivid, the warmth stronger than ever, and my skin was stitched back together as if the injury had never happened. It was a magic I'd seen before—a magic I resented and coveted at the same time for all the good it could have done me, but never did.

Unfortunately, I couldn't say the same for the glass rose, because Wrenlock had already made the remnants of it vanish, but when Lucais kept his suggestive gaze locked with mine, I found that my train of thought was beginning to derail completely. A feeling overcame me—hot, needy, and essential—and I couldn't name it other than to admit that it made me want to be ruined and repaired by the man standing in front of me, over and over again, until I was no longer the same person I was when we first met. His touch could remake me in ways that I had craved my entire life...

And if he didn't stop looking at me the way he was looking at me, I was going to fall onto my knees and start humiliating myself in front of an audience again.

"Bookworm," he purred, eyes narrowing even as the gold exploded into a firestorm of desire. I couldn't separate the warning from the invitation in his tone as his fingers flexed around my healed hand, an involuntary tug that had me inching closer to him. Lucais cocked his head, a spark of surprise alight in his gaze that had to be fabricated because I *knew* he felt it, too. "Stop that," he warned carefully.

I shook my head, my lungs working overtime to bring in fresh gasps of air. "Stop what?"

He faced Wrenlock, his grip firm on my hand. "Tell her to stop."

His friend chuckled darkly, feigning consideration. "You know, I'd really rather not, to be honest."

An incredulous expression crossed the High King's face as he turned back to me in slow motion. His eyes glimmered with a completely melodramatic sense of indignation, as if we were betraying him with an unspoken proposition that he'd started all on his own by spitting like that. "I made a promise to you. Do you want me to break that promise?"

I pursed my lips. "Aren't you kind of a liar, though?"

The High King's eyes flared with genuine outrage at that, even as I sensed the escalation of desire caressing the surface of his restraint, and he let out a disbelieving laugh while his grip tightened on my hand. "Alright, that's it," he declared, sliding his hand along my arm.

Biting the insides of my cheeks, I let Lucais pull me towards him like I was a hostage tied up and bound at the end of a rope, and I fell into his arms with the fervour of someone who had checked and tightened all of the knots themselves.

Forty-Seven

Irrevocably

I didn't realise how gentle Lucais had been the first or even second time we were intimate together until I goaded him into the third by aiming a hit directly below the belt.

Wrenlock kissed me while the High King stripped my clothes off, discarding them in a haphazard pile before dropping to his knees between my legs. His face pressed against me in the most obscenely provocative position we had tried while Wrenlock stood behind him with one hand gripping my thigh, the other in my hair, and his tongue tangling with mine in the most deliciously sensual way.

For a moment, though, I was unable to feel anything but astonishment.

Lucais had struggled to bow to Wrenlock at the House. He hadn't been able to let go of most of his mannerisms as the High King of Faerie, even though doing so would have supported his own agenda, and until recently, I'd assumed it was due to the fact that they were habits. However, with the newfound knowledge of how deeply pride impacted the rulers of Faerie, I'd started to form a different opinion. Lucais was unwilling to even pretend to worship another person for his own benefit, yet he so easily got on his knees for me—and in front of the same man he'd barely been able to kneel before in the House.

Any feelings of surprise were quickly dispelled as he lapped at my entrance, fucking me with his tongue while Wrenlock left a hickey on the side of my neck. I moaned helplessly at the high dome ceiling like it was there to forgive my sins. As soon as he slid two fingers inside me, I was falling to pieces all over him, and Wrenlock was the only thing in the world holding me up as I climaxed hard and fast on Lucais's face in the middle of the training room.

That's my girl, he crooned into my mind. His mouth was still devouring me through the aftershocks. *You taste so perfect coming all over my tongue.*

I moaned as his words made a dull, aching tightness form between my hips, riding out the last of the waves and creating new ones at the same time. When the final flickers of pleasure subsided, Lucais slipped out behind me. Panting unsteadily, I leaned against Wrenlock for support.

"Sit on the throne," Lucais instructed his friend. He scooped me up in his arms, cradling me against his chest. I was promptly reminded that they were both fully clothed while I was utterly naked, which made everything feel infinitely more erotic. "Pull down your pants."

While Wrenlock undid his pants, freeing his erection as he lowered himself onto the seat as instructed, Lucais carried me over to one side. Placing my feet back on the cool ground, he bent me over the arm of the throne, forcing my hips up so I was on the tips of my toes with my ass in the air. He threaded his hands through my hair, tightening his grip around the roots, and then he leaned over my shoulder to watch as he guided my mouth down towards Wrenlock's stone-hard cock.

"I thought you said this was a hard limit," I reminded him, all too willing but confused.

Lucais's voice was a devastating, velvety growl. "I changed my mind."

He pushed my head down onto Wrenlock's lap, and I opened up eagerly, licking the beads of come that formed on the tip, tasting the salt and soap of his delicate skin.

"Fuck, baby." Wrenlock's voice was a rasp. "This is so fucking hot."

Lucais yanked my head back, and Wrenlock's cock made a wet sound as it slapped against the hard planes of his stomach. "You're going to suck him off while I fuck you, but you're not going to let him come before I do, or I'm going to make sure that this really is the last time we do this. Understood?"

I couldn't nod, but wanted to. *Yes.*

A moment later, my legs were spread apart and Lucais was shoving himself inside me, the force of his thrust bending me further over the edge of the throne's arm. I cried out, then wrapped my lips around Wrenlock's thick erection while Lucais drove into me from behind, faster and harder than he'd taken me before. The sound of Lucais's balls slapping against my clit, the motion of my head bobbing up and down as I sucked on Wrenlock's length, and the combination of our stifled moans filled the room and brought us into an entirely new world of pleasure as we coaxed each towards the edge of an unending precipice.

When Wrenlock released a deep, unhinged groan, I felt as though he might be on the verge of exploding, so I raised my head and let him fall out of my mouth. He let out a loose breath, running his hands down his face as he gazed at me, eyes heated and full of adoration. Swearing softly, he flung his head into the back of the throne, his stomach contracting as he worked to calm himself down.

"Atta girl," Lucais purred, hands gripping my hips as he nudged his cock back inside me with gentler, slower, deeper thrusts. His body inside of mine set off a blazing heat, an electrical fire. "Fuck, bookworm, think of all the drama we could've avoided if I'd known that all I had to do was fill you with my cock to get you to fucking listen to me."

With my mouth empty, I had a retort on my lips. "I—"

The words, along with the memory of whatever they were going to be, were immediately banished from my mind when Lucais took a fistful of my hair again and forced my mouth back down onto Wrenlock's erection. I couldn't help the wide grin that lifted my cheeks despite the thick, firm heat sliding back into my mouth, and he moaned as a delighted laugh escaped, muffled against him. Lucais's hand remained in my hair, guiding me as my head moved in indulgent, rhythmic motions on Wrenlock's lap, sucking him into my mouth until his tip hit the back of my throat and then circling my tongue around the head before Lucais urged me to slide all the way back down his length.

The hinges of my jaw started to ache, and tears dripped from my eyes, but I was yearning to feel and taste more of them, so I refused to stop.

"You look so fucking good taking us at the same time like this," Lucais purred.

He released my hair and slid his hand down the side of my neck. I felt the rigid muscles on his chest pressing into my back as he leaned closer, each thrust hitting a slightly higher spot, and the pinpricks of ecstasy began to build at the apex of my thighs, buried between my hips and disturbed with every divine movement he made.

"You're going to be the death of me," Lucais vowed, and then his hand was all the way around my throat, pulling my head away from Wrenlock, and I was pulsing around his length uncontrollably with barely a whimper escaping from my mouth. "I want to die with my cock buried inside you and my hand around your throat, Auralie. I want the last thing I hear to be my name on your lips."

"Lucais—"

"*Fuck.*"

In an instant, the tension in the room snapped, and every single one of us was undone. Wrenlock's eyes were on Lucais's face, watching him coming inside of me as he gripped onto my throat and pressed his mouth to the back of my head, moaning so loud the foundations of reality might have quaked as I pulsated around him with a fanatical intensity. He fucked me the whole way through his orgasm, each thrust a little less than the last until I felt the sticky heat of his come spilling down my inner thighs. Barely a moment later, my hand found Wrenlock's erection, pulling once, twice—and suddenly, his cock was jerking as he came, the thick heat of his orgasm dripping down the sides of my hands, and I was coming again as Lucais slipped out of me, replacing his dick with his fingers.

Fucking Elements, he swore into the bond, a split second of shock quickly replaced by greedy lust as he slipped his arm around my waist and slid his fingers back inside me. *Ride my hand, bookworm. There you fucking go.* He groaned, the sound echoing through the cavernous training room as I ground my clit against his palm. *Give me one more. That's my girl.*

I felt like I was going to die, too.

When we were finished, and they'd collectively squeezed the very last drops of euphoria from my body, they worked together to clean me up and carry me back to Lucais's bedroom, one bringing me some water while the other covered me with a blanket.

It dawned on me as I sipped my drink that I'd never seen them operating in sync before. Everything had always been disjointed with the identity swap creating a rift—except for when they were intimate with me. When we were all together in that way, they barely needed to exchange a word, both so dedicated to fairly inflicting pleasure, making me feel satisfied and special. It was the only time I caught a glimpse of the way they must have been as friends and colleagues before I'd come into their lives. It was strange, but there was no jealousy or competition. They were familiar with one another in the way of lifelong friends, only they had an element of trust on top of that—the kind that only two people who went through the same trauma and came out of it alive could claim.

Like the Gift War.

Like the loss of their family members to the Malum—Lucais had lost his parents, and Wrenlock had lost his sister.

I drifted off to sleep feeling safer than I ever had in my life, with a smouldering warmth in my heart and a comforting pressure against my rib cage. My last conscious thought haunted me through my dreams—that perhaps the best thing I had done, after the catastrophic lashings their friendship took while we were in the House, was to fall in love with both of them so irrevocably and unconditionally that I had forgotten how to hide it.

Forty-Eight

I Am Sick of This

Two days later, I sprawled across Batre's throne of vines and tried to concentrate on what she was teaching me instead of the erotic things I'd done bent over the side of it.

It was all I'd been able to think about ever since it happened. Phantom echoes of Lucais and Wrenlock moaning resounded in my mind as I closed my eyes and kicked my feet, resting my head on the same arm of the throne that Lucais had positioned me over before he fucked me into the following week.

"Your baseline magic skills generally surface as a child, before you start to discover your abilities in line with your Element," Batre was saying. "Once a faerie hits adolescence, they usually learn how to apply certain attributes of their Element to their existing magic. For example, I could summon a book when I was a child, but I couldn't do *this* until I was almost an adult."

I opened my eyes, craning my head to watch as she directed her attention to one of the tall, arched windows in the training room, hand outstretched like she was trying to shield her face from the sunlight. The problem was that the fog had not relented, so there was hardly any light, and I had no idea what she was doing beyond the glass.

Moments later, a collection of small plants appeared in a circle around her; a variety of flowers, succulents, ferns, and exotic carnivorous plants with long, curly roots and soil set in a slightly dishevelled cylindrical shape.

She'd taken them straight from someone's garden—straight from someone's *pots*.

"Being an earth faerie, this side of my magic allows me to summon things that most other faeries can't accomplish without our help," she explained. "Anyone can summon mundane objects, but controlling flora is borderline impossible unless it's your Element or you have the power of a ruler. A water faerie might be able to do what I just did, but the plants would come with their pots because a water faerie would have to focus on them as an item rather than a living element. The same way that I could summon a candle if it was already lit, but I can't summon a naked flame."

I swung my legs down off the side of the throne. "I'm supposed to start with the basic things, then? And once I've mastered those, the way to handle the dark Element is supposed to come naturally?"

"That's the hope," Batre agreed with a smile that didn't reach her eyes. Truthfully, I didn't blame her or her smile for that.

I spent the rest of the day trying to forget that I was meant to be a dark faerie, regardless of whether the Court of Darkness wanted me to become their evil leader, and instead listened to Morgoya and Batre talking me through magic they performed as effortlessly as breathing.

It was hours before I was ready to make another attempt on my own, and by then, I'd only made a small amount of progress in separating my ideas of magic from my experience with the voice at my side. I'd never felt power when I was alone. The voice had always been there, curled around my wrists, whispering in my ears—even when the Little Folk visited me.

"Try to convince the pen to write on the page," Batre entreated as I glared down at the notepad and pen in my lap with my hands firmly behind my back. "An enchantment is more about intent than it is impact, meaning that you don't necessarily need the strongest set of magic if you have a strong, isolated desire. It does make them risky, so there are additional requirements for larger and more complex spells, but not for the basic ones like this."

I blinked down at the blank page.

I AM SICK OF THIS.

The thought circled my head for what felt like hours before the sting of my eyes became too much, and I broke my concentration so I could shoot an exasperated look at my friends.

"Okay. That's okay." Morgoya brushed her hands down her floor-length, black velvet gown and went over to the teapot sitting on the magical cart. "Let's take a little break. Have some tea."

While she made up three cups, I tossed the notepad and pen aside, feeling a rising sense of dread filling my throat.

We had tried levitation and enchantment, and I'd attempted restoration on my own. At the House, I'd also tried to master teleportation the day I'd blacked out, so we all agreed to leave that one out of our practice sessions in case it had the same outcome. Nothing we tried was even the slightest bit fruitful, which left us with summoning, vanishment, transformation, and destruction. And I had the worst feeling that I'd only do well at the last form of magic.

I sipped my tea and sat cross-legged on the floor, hoping Morgoya had dosed it with a sleeping pill or poison. "Do you remember what we talked about on the staircase?"

The High Lady hummed into her teacup from where she sat perched on Batre's lap as they relaxed on the throne. "Which part in particular?"

"The part about Lucais not caring what people say," I clarified. It had struck a chord with me at the time, but I didn't get the chance to question her about it—like I hadn't been able to question Lucais on something he told me in his bedroom the first morning we woke up together. "What exactly happened to him when he was a child?"

The High Lady's impenetrable mask of kindness momentarily slipped into something cruel. "I don't know how much you've been told, but Lucais was a child when he became the High King."

"He told me the story of Hugo," I offered, taking another sip. "I have the vague gist of how he obtained the crown—the coronation and the countdown and all of that."

Her shoulders rose and fell incrementally. "Hugo, along with Gage and Raella, tried to keep things calm and amicable during that time," she conceded. "But nobody can really force a child that young to stop being a child, no matter how hard they might have tried. Lucais was a toddler, so he had tantrums, and the crown doesn't place age restrictions on a ruler's mood. He unwittingly caused a lot of damage in the early days, usually due to the incessant attempts made to separate him from the crown as if the magic didn't supersede all of it. There were storms so violent that towns flooded, lightning set farmlands ablaze, and cyclonic winds tore apart a lot of important infrastructure in Faerie. It wasn't his fault.

"He was a minor, and his parents were acting in the crown's interests without legitimate authority, aside from that spineless Hugo telling them to cover it up no matter the costs. In the end, it was so bad that there were calls for his execution. There were people who wanted him dead—who planned to murder an *actual faeling*—simply because they were so desperate for the weather events to cease. Gage wouldn't stand for it," she recalled, frowning into the reflection in the mirror as if it were a window into the past. "Raella wanted to run, but I told her the crown would only follow. At the time, I was already High Lady, and it was a big deal for us to have a light faerie rise to power. Lucais's family weren't much for the city or civilisation, so I often visited them here.

"The palace was overrun with fire faeries, and I didn't want them to feel alone. The human world didn't even exist, the Aboveworld was off-limits due to the war, and we were on shaky ground with the Underworld. They stayed and fought for him in the end, but Hugo didn't," she lamented. "He was so worried they wouldn't be able to quell an uprising that he killed himself and left Lucais as the sole High King of Faerie—at the mercy of his politically challenged parents, and in a palace of staff who travelled here in order to serve Hugo and would leave as soon as he was gone—when he was barely out of his cloth. It took me *years* to build back public confidence in what they were calling the *Era of Infancy* and the *Boy King* even after Lucais grew up. He was still a young man when they began to trust him again, but he was no longer a child. I left him to his own devices with his parents then, and I watched the same faeries who had marched through the streets calling for his execution begin to fall in love and chant his name in exultation."

I hugged my knees to my chest. "What went wrong?"

"He was still too young." Morgoya's eyes were worlds away. "He was given the most power for the least effort, and it made him arrogant. He saw a problem in the way the High Fae treated other faeries and immediately removed it. He acted first, apologised later—or not at all—and refused to consider the potential blowback from some of the more influential members of his Court, which led us straight into the Gift War. It didn't help that his parents were still around, vocalising their eccentricities about switching to pure magic and inventing tools that could do the things we traditionally used our gifted magic on. Lucais was smart to shut them down, but again"—she grimaced—"I think he was too brazen about it. I often wonder whether his parents would have rebelled if he showed more tact. If he was patient, the Malum might not even exist."

"Do you really think that?" Batre piped up, tilting her head to gaze into her lover's face.

"I'll never know."

I pushed my teacup further to the side and moved so I was sitting on my knees. "I've been wondering about something like that myself," I started, a burn in the back of mind. "Lucais said something to me about the enchantment he placed on the Forest of Eyes and Ears, and I haven't been able to make sense of it."

"What is it?" the High Lady pressed.

"The enchantment was a mistake," I remembered, squinting at the foggy windows. "He wanted to hide from his parents, but he combined a mind-reading spell and a...cloaking hex? He said the end result was that the Forest became sentient, but he mentioned that it reads the minds of travellers and moves things around depending on who they are and where they want to go," I confessed. "It attacked him when we were there together because we were arguing. The part that bothers me is that the cottage predates the enchantment, which means that Gage and Raella were the only ones who knew where it was when it was set on fire..."

The High Lady gracefully rose to her feet and began pacing in front of the throne. Batre leaned forward, eyes narrow and lips slightly parted.

"They would never." Morgoya turned to me with horror painted all over her face. "Gage was a highly-strung scientist. All of his notes and inventions were stored in the cottage, even after they moved into the palace. There is no *way* he would have burned his life's work, and Raella wouldn't dare."

"Were they living in it when it burned down?" I queried.

She started pacing again. "They had recently moved back. The fire happened some time after Lucais publicly denied his father's request to harvest the essence of the Witches to complete a trial only days before they became Malum."

A heavy silence fell over us, so dense I could hear the ticking of my heart like a time bomb in my chest, counting down the moments until I worked up the courage to say what all three of us were thinking out loud.

"His parents knew the person who burned their cottage down," I mumbled. "They trusted them."

Forty-Nine

Mmhmm

We had two questions, and absolutely no answers.

Who burned down the cottage that night, and why?

The Forest would have read the intent of arson in the mind of the visitor if they required the Forest's help to find the cottage. I was sure of it, even though it meant the Starfires had to have escorted the arsonist to their destination personally—or at least given them directions.

Batre floated the notion that it might have been Gregor, but Morgoya was dubious. I enquired about Blythe's relationship with Lucais and his parents back then, but again, the High Lady was not convinced there was a motive. According to her, Lucais's parents had not integrated well into the political landscape, but that was a good thing for their social lives. It meant they were on friendly terms with all of the other rulers because they were never equipped to take point on contentious issues—so they never made enemies within the Courts.

Eventually, we drifted back to my magic training, though the atmosphere was a little darker and more suffocating than it had been before our conversation.

"Visualise something that you want to bring into the room with us right now," Morgoya suggested. "Are you hungry? Thirsty?"

I stared at the chalk cross she'd marked on the stonework as a guide for our summoning practise, and my mind went blank. We'd tried vanishing to no avail, and I wasn't having any greater luck with its counterpart. Destruction was next, but I was afraid to even attempt it in case I finally succeeded.

"I'm frustrated," I admitted after a moment. "How do you materialise frust—"

Lucais appeared in the middle of the cross and sketched a bow. "I heard you were summoning the things you want," he announced, winking.

"That's how," Batre muttered, and I covered my mouth to conceal a small laugh.

"I *know* that I did not just magic you in here," I stated, forcing my lips to flatten. I shot him a reproachful look, pointing at the chalk. "I wasn't even thinking about you."

He gave a slight shrug. "Perhaps it worked backwards, then. I was thinking about you."

The space between my hips heated, a molten liquid pooling in my core. "I'm busy."

"You're about to be, yes." With an atrociously attractive wink, he whirled on Morgoya and Batre. "If you don't mind, the High Queen is required to attend to some urgent business before dinner this evening, so I'd like to take her to go and…finish it."

Morgoya frowned at him, but Batre began to pack up the supplies from the magical cart.

"We *have* been at it all day."

That was all Lucais needed to hear, but I didn't miss the urgent look that crossed Morgoya's face before he snatched my hand and we disappeared.

When we materialised in his bedroom, I wasn't at all surprised. The three of us had slept in the High King's bed every night since the afternoon we had spent in the training room together, but nothing else had happened, and I'd barely seen either of them during the days.

Morgoya and Batre kept me busy from dawn until dusk with their magic exposure therapy. According to the faint grumblings that came out of Lucais's mouth whenever he traipsed into his room late at night and collapsed into bed next to me, Enyd had been doing a similar exercise with him and Wrenlock, demanding they spend lengthy meetings together to discuss their plan of attack for the Malum and the Court of Earth. Wrenlock was equally fatigued.

"I thought you said you wouldn't ask me for this again," I reminded him, even as my voice strained while I watched him undo his pants with haste. They fell to the floor, and the sight of his erection springing free had me sighing unbidden.

"I thought you said I broke that promise," he countered.

"Technically, no." I adjusted my shoulders as my nipples hardened, incredibly sensitive against the fabric of my shirt. "I asked *you* for it last time, but this"—I gestured to him as his hand went to his length, stroking it once and then again as he stifled a groan—"looks a lot like *you're* asking."

Lucais pumped his fist along his shaft and grinned at me like a man on the verge of total chaos and collapse. "Take it or leave it, bookworm, but I am going to stand here and get myself off to the sight of you right this fucking second because if I don't, I am going to commit a murder."

"Enyd?"

He closed his eyes. "Do not *speak* the wretch's name."

My eyebrows elevated as I pulled in a deep breath, but I gradually lowered myself to the ground. It was cold and hard beneath me as I crawled towards him on my hands and knees, preparing to surprise him by taking him in my mouth.

"Fine. What has the wretch done to you now?"

He stilled, and I almost thought he was listening to me approach until he finally said, "She's taking me away from you."

"Oh?" I tried to suppress the tremble in my voice. "I would've thought you'd be thanking her for that."

"Maybe before," he allowed, still fisting his cock. "Not anymore. I can't think when I can't see you, even if I know where you are. We had to move our meeting room all the way over from the other side of the palace to be closer to you because I was going out of my fucking mind—" He let out a small gasp as I stopped at his feet and licked the slit on the head of his cock, causing a dribble of arousal to trickle out.

I licked that, too, and then I sucked his tip into my mouth and moaned a little, "Mmhmm?"

"I cannot stop thinking about you," Lucais admitted as I wet the entirety of his length with my tongue. "I'm in these damned meetings all day being pushed to make hasty decisions. Wrenlock wants me to draft proposals to our prospective allies, and Enyd is demanding I make commitments to an invasion strategy should we fail to talk sense into Gregor, if we can even—" Lucais broke off, groaning as I pushed his hand away from the base of his shaft and slid my mouth along it, taking him as deep as I could manage. When I felt him nudge the back of my throat and my eyes watered, I compensated with my hand for the inches I couldn't quite fit any further down. "Fuck, Aura, forget it. Keep doing that."

Pulling him all the way out of my mouth, I kept one hand around his girth and tilted my head to peer up at him. "No," I protested. "I want to hear about your meetings. I want you to tell me why you were so desperate to kidnap me from my own commitments."

Especially because I was up there trying to help you.

Gazing down at me, half a smile on his face, Lucais shook his head with glimmering adoration. "Put your mouth back on my cock, start sucking on it, and I'll tell you anything you want to know. You want political secrets? Blackmail material?" He grunted, the sound low and gravelly. "Do that thing with your tongue again, bookworm, and they're all fucking yours."

With a little laugh, I did exactly that, twirling my tongue around the tip of his cock, sliding it beneath the base of the head, and then applying pressure as I jerked him off with my hand and lapped up the trace amounts of his excitement pooling in the line at the end. Lucais's moans were a series of sexy sounds that spurred me on, beautiful and vulnerable as they echoed through his bedroom and dove inside my heart.

Moving my hand down to the base of his shaft again and squeezing, I sucked until my cheeks hollowed out and the taste of him was the only thing I could remember ever having on my tongue.

"All I can think about is the way it feels when I'm with you," he rasped. "Fuck the Court of Earth. I want to bury myself inside you so deep that I'll never be able to crawl back out." His hand slid into my hair, pushing me a little deeper onto his erection and groaning when I obeyed, though I gagged and tears spilled down my cheeks.

"I don't want to go to war," Lucais breathed, his voice shaky as my movements increased in speed. "I want to go to bed with you. I want to rail you until you can't walk, until your pussy has coaxed every last drop of come from my body. I want to make you see stars. I want to make you"—he grunted as his release spilled into my throat—"*fucking*"—he took my head in both hands and held it in place while he pushed one last, long thrust into my mouth as deep as he could go, so far that it forced some of his come to spill out of the corner of my mouth—"*mine*."

My heart did a pirouette as I swallowed the taste of his climax.

Once he had pumped the last of his come down the back of my throat, Lucais bent down to wipe the mess from my chin and placed a kiss on my mouth.

Before I could even swipe the moisture away from my lashes, I was on my back on the floor and he was kissing his way down my body, ripping and tugging my clothes out of his way with nearly feral ferocity so his lips could clash against my bare skin. A raging heat burned in my core. His teeth grazed my nipples, sucking them into his mouth as his hands fumbled with the waistband of my pants, clumsily pulling them down. Then, he worked his mouth over my stomach until he had undressed enough of my body that he could force my knees apart, exposing me to himself and the cool bite of the air.

"This." His eyes were a wild shade of gold as they devoured me. "This is what I fucking need."

It would be a lie to suggest that I didn't know exactly what he was talking about. I felt it, too—an all-consuming, constant, maddening desire. Like I was incomplete until he was inside me. Like my vision was blurred until he came back into focus.

"You should have warned me it would be like this," I uttered breathlessly. While he worked my pants free of my legs completely, I brushed the sweat-dampened hair back from my forehead. "I didn't know it would be like *this*."

"Oh, yeah," Lucais grunted, spreading my naked legs all the way apart and sliding a finger down my centre until it was wet with my arousal. He gave me a sardonic look as he slipped that finger inside of me, eliciting a quiet moan before he slowly bent his head between my thighs. "Because I knew in advance from all of the other fated soulmates I've had."

Then, his tongue was on my clit, and I was unravelling again.

I was halfway through a moan, on the brink of an indelicate release when the door opened and Wrenlock strode over the threshold. He paused, an unreadable expression on his face as he looked down at us, but it was enough to send me over the edge. My squeal of surprise as I stared at him upside down morphed into a moan of ecstasy as Lucais's mouth and hand brought me over the edge, and I was grateful that Wrenlock waited to speak, watching with delayed interest while I settled into the aftershocks.

"Enyd is demanding that everyone has dinner together," he said, looking a little regretful. I couldn't tell if it was because he'd missed out on our bedroom floor activities or if it was because he didn't want to dine with Enyd, either.

Maybe both.

Lucais's tongue gave me one final, lazy stroke before he lifted his head and groaned. "*Fine.*" He rose to stand, then scooped me into his arms. "After we've cleaned up, we'll come downstairs to meet the wretch. What's her favourite food?"

"Uhh..." Wrenlock shrugged, his mouth turning down at the corners. "I *think* she's partial to seafood?"

Tutting under his breath, Lucais carried me into the bathroom, and shouted over his shoulder, "Make sure we serve anything but that!"

Fifty

The Court of Water

"I have a question."

"Yes, bookworm?"

We had been mostly silent for the whole shower, applying soap to each other with professional concentration. Lucais stood behind me while the water ran over my back, his hands massaging my scalp as he washed my hair.

"The bond changed some things..." I ventured. "Has it changed the way you feel about Wrenlock being with us? Do you mind? Sharing, that is."

The High King angled his head so that his eyes met mine, a crease forming between his brows. "Are you comparing our life to those books again?"

Scrunching my nose, I blinked away the droplets of water sliding over my face. "I suppose so."

Lucais sighed and leaned back, returning to the task of rinsing my hair. "You're aware that I could've had him tried and hung for the things he wants to do to you?"

I scoffed. "He's your best friend."

"Yes, and I'm your *mate*." Lucais clicked his tongue, lost in thought for a moment. "We live for a long time, Aura," he finally answered. "Even those of us who find our intended soulmates often engage in other intimate relationships, together or separately. You saw what it was like at the party we threw at the House. We're very fluid beings, and generally not fussy about who shares pleasure with us. Nor do we believe that an individual is only capable of loving one person, sometimes even when there's a mating bond in place."

Frowning, I stated, "You were annoyed at the House, though."

Lucais's fingers stilled in my hair for a moment before he cleared his throat and continued to massage my scalp. "That was different. You didn't know he wasn't me."

"And now that I do?"

"Our dynamic with Wrenlock is not unusual. If you wanted to kick me out of it, I'd be annoyed, but otherwise, I'll carry you to whoever's bed you wish to sleep in for the night. Assemble a harem, if you like." His tone shifted, taking on a dark edge. "The second a hand touches you without your consent, though, I'll remove it—from your body *and* their own."

I braced against a shudder as Lucais finished with my hair, cut the water off, and turned me around to face him. His eyes were smouldering as they searched mine.

"Do you want me to physically remove him the next time he touches you?"

"No," I answered carefully. The confession was already in my throat. "I...*like* seeing the two of you the way you have been over the last few days."

Lucais smiled as he scrunched the water out of my hair. It was edged with sadness and distance, but his voice was relieved. "Good. I like it, too."

After we had dried and dressed, we made our way downstairs holding hands. The gesture felt so natural that I hadn't realised we were doing it until after we let go to take our seats.

I was surprised to see that Lucais had permitted Enyd back into the warm space of the dining room and wasn't trying to ice her out by serving dinner outside in the fog. The room was cosy as ever—a set of teapots steaming on the table, plants crawling all over the bookcases and walls, orbs of light floating around in the corners, and a fireplace crackling in the hearth. I skirted it, taking the long way around to my seat on the far side of the room beside the window, which I noticed had been cracked open. A tiny wooden windmill was placed in front of the gap, drawing in a breeze just strong enough to spin the slanting blades around.

Enyd was sitting alone, tapping a fingernail against the table. When we entered, she glanced up, and I could have sworn that her features relaxed. But in the next blink, it was gone, and she was back to holding herself with the hard, fiercely honed posture of someone who was gearing up for a fight.

The High King pulled my chair out for me and waited for me to sit down first.

"Aura," Enyd murmured. "How are you feeling?"

"Much better, thank you." I smiled, forcing my eyes to steer clear of the burning wood over her shoulder. The room wasn't filled with many other risks—unless I threw myself out of the window or tried to impale myself with a butter knife—so it was my main concern. Lucais squeezed my hand on top of the table. "How are you?"

The High Lady relaxed back in her seat, laughing lightly. "I'm about to rip your mate a new one, so please accept my apologies in advance."

"Anything I can help with instead?" I asked, though I immediately questioned myself for it.

Out of the corner of my eye, I saw Lucais smirk.

"Maybe," Enyd murmured, thoughtful. She was wearing her usual plain clothes—a grey shirt over leather slacks, a weapons belt slung over the back of her chair—and had her hair slicked back into a low bun. "You might understand my nervousness. You see, I lost some of my best men at the House, and they were like family to me. They were *important*. So, if Gregor was responsible for letting those atrocities into our Courts, I'd want to take my retribution sooner rather than later." Her eyes darted to the High King. "Upon my arrival in the city, however, I discover that not only am I the *sole* potential ally that Lucais has recruited, but he's actually keeping a platoon of the murderous beasts in his throne room like some kind of museum display." Her stormy eyes drifted back to mine. "You understand me, don't you?"

I threw an apologetic look at the High King because even I had to admit it wasn't a good look.

He rolled his eyes at me and leaned forward, clasping his hands beneath his chin with his elbows resting on the table. "Enyd, my darling. You have my *word* that I will dispose of the nasty creatures within the next few days," he vowed. "I wanted to renovate the palace, so I thought that trying my hand at zookeeping might help me to raise the money for it, if only the locals would pay a handsome fee to glimpse the beasts in their rotten flesh. Thank the High Mother, you've helped me see the error in my ways—"

"You insufferable fool," she snapped. "What about everything else?"

Lucais pushed away from the table with a long-suffering sigh and rubbed the stubble on his chin. "We will contact Ulyssa once the caenim are gone, like we discussed."

Enyd mimicked his movements, but she also crossed her arms. "You might want to dispose of the caenim tonight, then, because I've already sent word to them."

"You did *what*?" The shrill voice came from the doorway as Morgoya's lithe figure appeared. "Nobody authorised that! You cannot just—"

"It is already done," Lucais cut in wearily, holding up a hand like a white flag. He levelled Enyd with a sharp look, leaning forward to shove his hands through his hair. "The caenim will be disposed of before Ulyssa arrives, but the next time you decide to go rogue—"

"What?" she sniped, the word as harsh as the crackling fireplace behind her. "You'll do what to me, Lucais?"

"Not to you." His voice dropped into a low snarl, brimming with a threat so powerful the glassware rattled on the table between them. "I'll do it to your *men*."

My stomach rolled over as I observed the colour draining from Enyd's face until her cheeks were the same grey as the ribbon tied around her forehead. I liked Enyd, but she was strong-arming Lucais into decisions he wasn't ready to make. And although I'd only just figured out the reasons behind his impulse control issues myself, I thought that she really ought to know better.

Before something—or someone—broke, the sound of Wrenlock bursting into the room ripped everyone's attention back in the direction of the doorway. Fury shredded his expression, eyes hot enough to raze the entire room as he scanned the faces at the dining table and slapped his hands down on the wooden surface.

"Who the *fuck* invited the Court of Water here?"

A collective sigh gathered in all four of our chests, diffusing like the breeze spinning Enyd's windmill as the High Lady and I stared at each other across the table.

"Well, they're really fucking early," the High King grumbled.

Enyd sniffed, picking up a silver spoon and beginning to scoop up the watery vegetable soup she had been served. She blew gently to cool it, and then commented innocently, "Everyone is early when you're always late, Your Highness."

Fifty-One

Ogres Will Fly

The surprise announcement at dinner had sent everyone into a tailspin.

I'd never seen the High Fae quite so panicked, though it wasn't in the familiar way of humans. There were no screams or tears. Rather, a newfound sense of urgency fell upon them like a second skin, like they'd finally started to hear the ticking of the clocks as time passed and realised with a start that not all things were infinite. The need to act—and to do so quickly—hit all three of them at once just as soon as Enyd retired to her room.

While Morgoya went to greet Ulyssa and the Court of Water, Wrenlock paid a brief visit to the armoury before meeting the High King outside the throne room. As always, I went with Lucais, and Batre had never shown up to dinner in the first place, so I had no idea where she was.

The pungent smell of the caenim was nearly enough to bring my soup up again as I followed the men into the throne room. Enyd was right—there was a whole platoon of foul beasts stored in iron cages, and the sight sent a cold chill down my spine. If I didn't know better, I would also be questioning whether the man keeping caenim like circus tricks in the middle of his palace wasn't actually the real enemy.

While the High King and his Hand decorated themselves with weapons, I counted the caenim in the room.

Twenty beasts divided by five Courts meant Lucais planned to release at least a few into each one—unless he was truly insane enough to think that he could recapture them to use again and again. I sincerely hoped he didn't, but I also knew better than to hold my breath.

When the double doors to the throne room swung open with a loud bang, I was so distracted staring into the teeth-filled eyes of a nearby monster that I nearly jumped out of my own skin. Morgoya rushed into the room, waving a hand above her shoulder to command the doors to slam shut in her wake, and stalked straight between two cages of particularly large caenim positioned near the entrance.

"Ulyssa and the water faeries are settling into their rooms, but it won't be long before they expect a host," Morgoya announced, cheeks flushed as she fought for breath. Misunderstanding the fascination in my eyes, she glanced at me and explained, "We can talk freely here under the suppression spell. It covers noise and smell *outside* of this room, but not inside, unfortunately." She threw Lucais a revolted look.

"You'll have to play host," he muttered obliviously. Lucais's gaze was averted as he secured something onto his weapons belt. "I have to adjust the wards so our smelly little companions can do their job."

"Where are you taking them first?" the High Lady enquired, her voice nasally as she pinched her nose shut with two fingers and glared sideways at a caenim drooling at her through the bars. Saliva dripped from its eyes, sizzling as it hit the iron.

"The Court of Water," Lucais declared, hands going to his hips as he lifted his head to look at her. "We may as well start there since Ulyssa is already here—"

"No," Wrenlock interjected, stepping between them. "That's way too suspicious. I know you're pissed, Lucais, but we're logistically better off starting at the Court of Fire and working our way down the Map. It borders the Court of Darkness, which is where everyone's going to assume they're coming from, and besides that, Ulyssa's Court is too random. It's not even adjacent to Gregor's Court, and to hit it first the night they arrive?"

Lucais hummed, considering. "Ulyssa's going to fuck this up."

"Not if we stick to the original plan."

The sound of the caenim breathing heavily in the background was all we heard for a long moment as the men surveyed one another and contemplated strategy.

"Fine. Yes, you're right," Lucais agreed at last. Anxiety darkened each word. "The Court of Fire it is."

The tension bled out of Wrenlock's stature, and he returned to whatever he was doing before interrupting the conversation.

Striding over to me, the High King placed his hands atop my shoulders and studied me with warm, loving eyes. "Here's the thing, bookworm," he said softly. "You didn't get as much time in the training room as you needed, but I can't be more than three feet away from you without going out of my mind. It's dangerous to bring you with us, but it's even more dangerous to leave you behind, so which—"

"You're not leaving me here," I cut in firmly. The very thought made me feel weak and queasy. "There is no way."

The High King smiled. "I'm not leaving you here," he agreed, but then a shadow crossed his face. "I need you to understand that the cloaking spell I'll be using to conceal the caenim will be quite labour-intensive. I have to remove every last one of them before Enyd does something stupid—like give Ulyssa a tour of the palace when I'm not looking. Once I've done that, I have to focus on manipulating the wards, so I can't have my eyes on you the whole time." His smouldering gaze flickered to Wrenlock's face, hovering beside us, and then back to me. "I want you to take a weapon, Aura. You need to have one to defend yourself if something happens to either or both of us—especially if magic is still off the table."

My heart beat so loudly that it hollowed out my chest, but I managed to nod, even though I almost wanted to keel over and vomit on the ground.

Within seconds, Wrenlock was slipping a dagger into my limp hand and forcing my fingers to curl around the hilt. "Here," he murmured. "I've enchanted it so the blade will win your favour in a fight to compensate for any difference in skills between yourself and your opponent."

I stared down at the red jewel encrusted in the hilt, sparkling with a depth and glimmer so strong it almost took on the illusion of an eye. "You mean you spelled it to cheat," I mumbled thoughtlessly.

Lucais's fingers grabbed my chin and jerked my head up to look at him. "Cheat, Aura. Fight dirty. Break the rules." His thumb dragged over my mouth, flicking my lower lip, and I felt his gaze like a physical touch while it wandered across my face as if he was memorising every blemish and freckle. "I don't care what you do to keep yourself safe as long as it works. If there's a cost, I'll pay it *tenfold*." His eyes landed on mine. "Do you understand me?"

I understand you.

The High King's voice was in my head as I weighed the blade in my hand. *You've been using your magic like a weapon, as if it's a sword that you can pick up and put down. Remember what I told you. You are power. It is not a separate thing. Stop thinking about it like it is.*

I've been trying.

I know, my love. He pressed a swift kiss to my forehead.

I wished that he was right, but I only had one type of baseline magic left to experiment with—and it was destruction. Exactly like the Court of Darkness showed me...

Breaking my trance before I became totally numb, Morgoya pulled me into a hug so tight I felt something crack. "You'll be okay," she promised. "We'll resume our practice as soon as you come back."

Part of me wanted to thank her for all of her help, but the words felt like goodbye on my tongue, and I wasn't sure how to get them to sound any differently.

A moment later, the doors banged open and a succession of heavy footsteps echoed on the floor. The familiar warmth of Batre's arms encircled me, and I no longer needed to say anything. She squeezed me even tighter than her girlfriend had. As I felt the High Lady slip out of the embrace, I heard her drop her voice to speak to someone nearby.

"You'd better bring her back to me."

If Morgoya threatened Lucais like that before the bond was solidified, I would have understood completely, but it seemed a little redundant after everything had been said and done. Still, I appreciated the sentiment. I appreciated *her*.

"I'll buy you as much time as I can, Lucais." Morgoya's eyes were filled with regret as Batre and I pulled back from one another, and her green gaze settled on her lover. She tilted her head towards the doors in a question, but Batre motioned for her to go on without her.

"I'll be there in a second," she said, and then she pulled a notepad out of her large pocket, holding it in front of me. "I was late because I went to get this."

My lashes fluttered with uncertainty as she turned it over to a page with the words I AM SICK OF THIS written in a messy scrawl right in the middle of the paper. I started to shake my head, but she was already ahead of me.

"No, I'm serious," she insisted, tilting the page so that Lucais's inquisitive eyes could assess it, too. "I had a feeling that something like this would happen after the incident with the rose. You're not going to tell me this wasn't what you were trying to write down, are you?"

Torn up on the inside, I made a long, choking sound before I relented. "Yeah, no." My free hand came up to rest against my forehead as my thoughts began to spin, the other curled around the dagger in a fist on my hip. "That's what I was thinking."

"Sweetheart, I need to go," Morgoya called from near the doors. "They cannot be permitted to find this room before the caenim are all gone, and I don't trust Enyd as far as I could push her down a staircase."

Batre's eyes seared into mine like a brand. "We'll pick it up when you get back," she promised, tearing off the page with the writing and pushing it into my grasp before she spun on her heels and hurried to join Morgoya at the door.

She threw one glance over her shoulder before the doors closed, and I fell back against the nearest wall when the echo rang out.

Enchantment. The pen had done as I intended it to, but there was an absurd delay. So I *was* capable—yet faulty.

I cringed against the stonework, cradling the dagger against my chest, scrunching the paper into a ball in my fist. I could feel the enchantment in the blade—a slight difference to the weight and feel, a twinkle that blinked back at me in the stone—but not on the paper. As I re-examined the hilt and its richly coloured jewel, I searched for a bond with it the way that Batre and Morgoya had taught me to do when I had been trying to access levitation magic. I felt a spark, but it was like grabbing soap, and it slipped out of my reach.

"We need to go." The High King's voice jerked me out of my fixation. I stuffed the page into the side of my boot so my hand was free to take his. "You're about to see a lot more of Faerie, bookworm. Each Court looks very different," he warned me.

Lucais was a vision of violence with two broadswords crossing over his back and a plethora of different devices strapped to his waist. When I peered around his tall frame, I realised the caenim had already disappeared from the throne room. We were all moving so fast that I wondered if the High Fae had actually been slowing down on purpose for me the whole time.

"The Court of Fire kind of looks like it's been blown up when you're on the outskirts. There's a little forest surrounding it that they use for kindling reserves, situated between the outlying towns and the Ruins, so that's where we'll take cover while I work on manipulating the borders." He moved to pull me into his arms, but hesitated. "We *cannot* be seen, Aura. If we're discovered doing questionable things around the borders, it's all over. We'll have to explain ourselves to everyone and hope the High Court can be convinced to see reason."

Wrenlock snorted as he sauntered over to us, equipped with as many weapons as the High King, minus the broadswords. "Yeah, right. Ogres will fly."

Fifty-Two

Please Choose Wisely

Elera was waiting near the stables as the three of us snuck out of our own palace like fugitives under the cover of nightfall and fog. I questioned the decision to take her—I was questioning absolutely everything at that point—but I was given mixed answers.

"She hates to miss out on the fun," Lucais informed me with a playful wink.

"She'll get you out of there fast if things go wrong," Wrenlock added, raising a brow at the High King.

The unicorn nuzzled her soft, furry muzzle against the crook of my neck as I approached, so I gave her snout a quick peck before Lucais helped me onto her back and climbed up behind me. Elera broke into a canter before she launched into the thin mist. I held my breath the whole time we were evanescing to stifle the rising sickness in my stomach, and found my lungs were burning by the time we landed on solid ground. For whatever reason, Wrenlock chose not to bring his own mount and travelled alone behind us.

We landed in a strange forest, dark but not quite nighttime. Without the fog to suppress any light, the evening sky peeked through the canopy of overhanging trees in a mixture of ashy greys and deep oranges, like the sunset was a fire in the sky.

On the ground, the trees were so close together that they barely allowed Elera the space she required to slow to a stop. After a near miss with a giant log, she turned in a tight circle inside of a very small clearing, and then doubled back to exact vengeance by ripping at the bark on a nearby tree.

"The caenim will go straight for you if given the chance, so stay alert and wait for me," Lucais instructed as he helped me down. "If we do get approached, there is a good chance that my title and standing will be respected, but if it looks like it's going the other way, I'm going to need you to bolt for this clearing. Elera will take you back to Morgoya."

My stomach twisted at the thought of there being such an uncertain assortment of allies and enemies in Faerie, even amongst those who didn't know about the Malum. But the fact that Lucais mentioned it eased some of my worries. He knew about the rumours and the unrest, so I prayed he was factoring it into his decisions. Logic told me that he was Lucais, so he definitely wasn't, but the mating bond seemed to have dulled some of my logic in favour of lust.

Wrenlock appeared on the ground nearby with the grace and silence of a cat, his footsteps nothing more than whispers against the forest floor as he approached. Lucais pressed a finger to his mouth when he looked at me, bestowed a gentle pat upon Elera as she gave the tree bark a piece of her mind, and then motioned for us to follow him into the trees.

All three of us tried to keep our steps silent, avoiding branches that might snap underfoot or piles of rustling leaves because there wasn't another sound for miles.

My ears strained to pick up something. The silence was unnerving. There weren't birds in the trees or insects flying through the air, let alone the sound of voices or activity, and the atmosphere was so dry that my skin immediately felt the impact.

The forest was perfectly average at first glance, but every second or third tree had been cut down to a stump, and there were stacks of kindling all over the floor, which was covered in little twigs, pine needles, and trace amounts of ash and charcoal.

After only a couple of minutes, we came out of the thickest part of the trees to the very edge. Immediately, I smelled smoke, like someone had a bonfire burning nearby—but it was the entire Court that was on fire. Owain's Court was exactly as Lucais had described it; like a meteor had crash-landed in a red desert and the civilisation of fire faeries had been built on top of it.

As far as my mortal eyes could see, there were small fires burning through stacks of wood, lighting the entire landscape up in a warm, orange glow. The atmosphere was a haze of smoke spread thin across the roads into town, almost like Lucais's fog if it was diluted to allow for normal visibility levels, but the smoke curled into thicker wisps as it rose into the sky and took the place of rain clouds.

"I'm going to lower the ward long enough to slip the caenim through," the High King informed us quietly. He came to stand behind me, leaning down so he was at eye level with me, and pointed ahead at a small building with a tin roof. "Do you see that little hut in the distance? That marks the furthest corner of the first town. Once the caenim are loose, they tend to go for the nearest source of food, but these ones have been programmed to follow you."

I stared at the little tin rooftop—and then the penny dropped.

"You need me to lead them towards the town," I realised, unsurprised. I should have known there would be a price to pay for wanting to come with him.

"I would have done it alone, but they won't follow me if they know you're here, so we'll have to do it together."

I twisted my neck to look up at him, unimpressed, but he simply placed a kiss on the tip of my nose and grinned at me like a fiend before he strode off towards the tree line. He left me battling a deeply rooted sense of distrust with a new, more potent sense of infatuation and lust, and I was afraid the mating bond would always win.

While Lucais worked, I tried to distract myself in some productive fashion by attempting to make sense of the magic he was wielding. The Ruins were a deadzone, which meant that the forest we had entered must have been part of the very outskirts of the Court of Fire. And if that was the case, we were already inside of the wards. Wrenlock hung back, leaning against a tree in the shadows provided by the canopy overhead. I turned my back on him so I could watch Lucais.

His hair was so gold it was nearly red beneath the fiery skies. Adorned with so many weapons glinting in the waning light, he looked like a High King and a God of War enchanted into the body of a single man who was simply trying to do the right thing the only way he knew how. I felt a pinch in my chest, stretching all the way down to my rib cage and stomach as I watched him standing completely still except for the slow, deliberate movements of his hands as if he were moulding invisible clay into the shape of a key. The air around him shimmered like the distortion of heat.

Summoning, perhaps.

He hadn't explained the finer details to me, so it was all I could do to assume that Lucais had the caenim cloaked inside of a spell somewhere, and he was going to use summoning magic once he'd manipulated the wards to allow them to enter. As far as I knew, the individual leaders of each Court weren't attuned to the wards, so it wouldn't alert anyone to the threat—

I felt movement behind me, shifting the pine needles on the ground, but my gasp was muffled as a large hand cupped my mouth at the same time as the sharp edge of a blade kissed my throat.

Warm lips pressed a kiss to my temple, and smoky breath whispered against my ear as a male voice said, "I'm sorry."

Wrenlock.

Lucais whirled on us half a heartbeat later, the shifting of the wards falling away as he completely dropped his hold on it, and his eyes burned like the molten core of the sun as they settled on us. I held perfectly still, refusing to even breathe. His glare would have torn my captor to ribbons if he were literally anyone else in the world, yet his voice was menacing and cold as ice.

"What. The. *Fuck*. Are. You. Doing."

The blade was steady against the delicate skin of my throat, even as I felt a shudder ripple through Wrenlock's chest with my back pressed into him. "I will do this if I have to," he warned, his tone severe. "It would hurt me to lose her, but not as much as it would hurt you." He swallowed, and it was audible. "Take all of your weapons off and put them on the ground."

Lucais was shaking his head even as he obeyed. His eyes locked onto mine, a whirlpool of emotion swirling inside them, and I found myself struggling to breathe with the hand over my mouth as fear stuffed itself down the back of my throat and made everything feel swollen.

"Take your fucking hand off her mouth," the High King swore viciously, unbuckling his weapons belt and casting it aside. "She cannot breathe."

Wrenlock hesitated, but his hand retreated a moment later. The blade remained against my neck, and I winced as it made a tiny slice into my skin, caused only because my throat expanded to accommodate a huge gasp of air. Lucais's eyes raged, and he took a step forward, but Wrenlock responded by moving the blade to the centre of my throat, poised ready to slash it clean across, so the High King's steps faltered to a clumsy halt.

"I'm going to kill you," Lucais promised. His voice was calm and still as undisturbed water, yet lethal as the monster hiding beneath the surface. "I'm going to feed those hands to the caenim, finger by finger and bone by bone, and then I'm going to cut off that soft cock and wrinkly ball sack and jam them down your throat until you choke on your own semen."

The imagery made me blanch, but I held still, knowing my focus needed to remain on minimising the breaths I took while a blade was angled against my throat.

"The rest of your weapons," Wrenlock prompted, blatantly ignoring the threat.

Obeying with a poisonous expression, Lucais continued removing the last of his weapons, keeping his eyes on me as he bent to retrieve small blades from his boots, and then he flung his arms out to the sides to display that he was officially unarmed.

"This doesn't have to go the way you think it does," the traitor behind me insisted, his voice low but firm. "I need you to trust me."

"Take your filthy fucking hands off her and we'll talk."

"Turn around."

"The fuck I will."

Wrenlock shoved me forward, aggression seizing his posture and his voice for the first time since he had turned on us. "*Turn the fuck around.*"

Lucais's hands were trembling at his sides, but he gave me one last glance before he did as Wrenlock demanded and turned his back to us. His breathing became ragged, and I felt a sharp spike of panic in my mind that wasn't solely my own.

Is he hurting you?

Not really.

I just need him to lower the blade for a second—

"Stop with the silent conversations," Wrenlock snapped. "I can sense the way the bond flares up when you talk to each other through it, so cut it out. If you want to say something, say it out loud, or don't say it at all."

"I was just telling Aura about all the ways I'm going to make you scream when this is done," Lucais replied pleasantly, though his voice shook with the same tremors of an earthquake. *You have a blade, bookworm.*

My eyes flared when I heard the thought and remembered that I did, in fact, have a dagger strapped to the belt at my waist. Fingers twitching towards it, I held my breath carefully as I calculated the distance and time it would take for me to reach it. Then again for what it would take to use it.

"What is this about, Wrenlock?" Lucais questioned, still standing with his back to us.

"Put your hands in the air."

"What, are you going to shoot me?" He laughed once. "How human of you."

The insult made Wrenlock stiffen, and I only understood it myself because of a book I'd read at the House. Faeries didn't use guns. They were created during the Gift War by the faeries who relinquished their magic, and they were widely considered signs of significant weakness and cowardice by the High Fae.

"You're not in a position to be making snark—"

I took advantage of the distraction and moved to yank the blade from my belt, twisting it with only a single moment of opportunity to lodge it straight into Wrenlock's side. My wrist bent at the wrong angle, resulting in a slight shot of pain, but the worst feeling was in my heart as I felt the blade sink into his flesh all the way down to the hilt. His shirt brushed the side of my little finger as I drove the dagger in as far as it would go, but the only sound he made was a deep sigh.

"Aura, you're damn well lucky I didn't just open your throat by accident."

I stood there, holding my breath, paralysed when I realised that he hadn't even flinched, and his own blade was still poised to slice open my neck. From experience executing my father and Hanson, I knew that I should have felt blood leaking from the injury, but I didn't.

"Baby," he crooned softly, "I am really sorry. I didn't mention that the weapon I gave you only works on people who are not me."

I pulled it away from him with no resistance, and would have dropped it if I didn't want to check the blade for blood out of sheer, dumbfounded curiosity. It was clean. Wrenlock took it from me before it fell from my loosening grip and secured it back onto my belt.

"No matter," Lucais said through his teeth. His head was turned as far to the side as possible in order to look back over his shoulder without technically turning his body around. "I have a whole arsenal of weapons over there that should work just fine. Be a good sport, Wrenlock, and let her have a second go with one of those."

"You are failing to see the gravity of the situation once again, Lucais."

"No, I'm not." He straightened his head, shrugging his shoulders as if to loosen them. "I'm committing it to memory, actually, so that it doesn't matter where you go or how long it takes before I get to enforce a punishment fit for your crimes."

Wrenlock scoffed. "The three of us are going to walk into the Court of Fire. There are dozens of soldiers waiting for us inside this forest, and they're going to come out as soon as we're in the open. They are armed with execution orders if you try to do anything risky, and it's not placed on your head. Everything you do from this point on determines what happens to the girl in my arms, so for everyone's sake, Lucais, please choose wisely."

Fifty-Three

The Court of Fire

It wasn't hyperbole. There really was a small army of soldiers waiting for us once we cleared the last of the trees. About fifty steps out into the open, we stood exposed and vulnerable beneath the burning skies as they poured out of the forest—so close they had to have been watching us the entire time—and every last one of them looked as though they were prepared for a bloodbath.

With the colour of the dirt beneath their feet, I could have easily been convinced that there had already been one.

"Owain's militia," the High King said in greeting as a group of soldiers clad in red and black marched forward with a set of iron manacles. His tone betrayed his ire, but it was tainted with a flicker of genuine intrigue. "Where are all the women?"

"Things have changed here since the last time you paid a visit to us, Lucais." Wrenlock's tone was clipped, and he urged me to take a few steps forward, but the firmness of his hold relented by a fraction once the soldiers had the High King in chains. The hissing as the iron seared Lucais's skin made me want to scream. "He's banned anyone who isn't male from enlisting."

I was still in a daze, stuck on the way he had said the word *us*.

"I'll see about that." The High King gave a disappointed head shake, turning in a slow circle. My gaze landed on his hands, bound at the waist, as steam billowed out from between his wrists and the irons. "Fancy showing bookworm here the first proper army in Faerie, and it's your lot of burned leftovers."

"I've seen your army," I found myself mumbling in an effort to make sense of a single thing that was happening around me. It was so trivial, yet I got stuck on it, and the white and gold uniform of the Court of Light was engraved into my memories after everything that had happened with Hanson.

"You haven't seen the real armies," Lucais countered, his tone conversational even as we were pushed into a walk that felt like a death march by our captors. "Enyd keeps a certain type of men around her because she sleeps with them, and I don't station women as guards because they thrive in intelligence, but if you'd met Ulyssa before we left, you'd find that their assembly consists mostly of women or queer soldiers. Owain used to have female guards, at the very least." He turned his head, surveying the soldier closest to him. "Don't get me wrong. It's not that I find any of you handsome gentlemen disappointing, but it is odd after what the Court of Fire used to represent."

"Lucais?" Wrenlock called over my shoulder, causing me to cringe away from the sound.

"Yes, dearest?"

"Just shut the fuck up."

For once in his life, the High King of Faerie actually did what he was told, and the rest of our walk was spent in a reflective silence. I didn't risk sharing a thought with Lucais again, but it wasn't necessary for me to know that he was thinking the same thing as me.

He was wondering how we had gotten into such a mess, and how we were going to make sure at least one of us got out of it alive.

The soldiers from the Fire Army escorted us into the outlying town beyond the little tin hut. The smoke was stifling; ash gathered in my throat, triggering my muscles to tense around a cough, though nobody else seemed particularly disturbed.

Eventually, a cobblestone road appeared through the centre of the village, cutting a long, straight line between rows of houses that glowed with a subdued red tint reflecting off the numerous fires that lined the streets. Stacks of wood were littered between buildings carved from stone and topped with slanting tin sheets or straw, a practise that would have raised alarm bells if the occupants of the township were human beings because there was a significant risk that half of the town would go up in flames if the wind took a turn in the wrong direction.

No other signs of life were present as we marched onto the cobblestone, the sharp impact of boots against the ground the only sound brave enough to encroach upon our silence. On the other side, there was an expanse of dead land where fires burned like bushes in the place of any flora.

Beads of sweat started to gather against my hairline until they were heavy enough to slide down my temple. I couldn't move my hands to wipe them away, and I found myself silently raging at Wrenlock's hypocrisy. He had criticised Lucais for chaining me to his carriage, but he was holding my wrists bound at my back after putting a knife to my throat. The knife, at least, was no longer resting against any part of my body—it remained in Wrenlock's other hand, an ever-present threat.

Two carriages waited for us up ahead, and that was when Lucais broke his vow of silence.

"No," he snarled. In an instant, he'd shrugged off the hands of both of the soldiers escorting him and whirled on Wrenlock. His hands were still bound in the iron chains, dulling his magic, but the wind picked up around us. "You are not separating us in those carriages, Elumos. I swear to the High Mother—"

Wrenlock was calm when he cut him off by saying, "We're all travelling to the same place. It's just a precaution."

Before the High King could speak, one of the soldiers crept up behind him and pulled a thick black bag over his head. Lucais shouted and swore viciously, pulling against his constraints so hard it looked like he was willing to sacrifice his own hands to break free, and I found myself needing to turn away when they kicked him to the ground.

I wanted to scream. I wanted to stop them. I wanted to do something, *anything*—

But I was immobilised by my own mind, slipping into a dreamlike state that incapacitated me, though I would have clawed my way out if only I could feel my own hands again. All I could do was look away.

Sheathing his blade, Wrenlock put his hands over my ears to block out the sound of Lucais being beaten into submission and forced into the carriage waiting behind us. I was guided into the first one. It was carved from a gold frame and glass wheels, pulled by a trio of black stallions without any horns, with cushioned red leather seats on the interior. The maroon-coloured velvet curtains were closed, restricting my view of the world outside and allowing only the faintest light to illuminate the interior of the carriage.

Once inside, Wrenlock released my hands and crouched in front of me. I rubbed my wrists and turned my head when he reached up to sweep my damp hair away from my face, revulsion churning my stomach.

"Aura," he whispered. "Please look at me, baby."

There were vipers in my stomach, biting me in the places I used to feel the wings of the butterflies in his voice.

I closed my eyes, and I didn't open them again for the entire carriage ride, even when I heard him sigh and settle back into the seat across from me.

Fifty-Four

Surprise, Bitch

A kaleidoscope of onyx and glitter monopolised my vision while the carriage sped over the flat, dirty landscape of the Court of Fire. The stress was getting to me, and yet I suspected the sweat dampening my skin was caused by the rising temperature. With it, the smell of smoke intensified.

Are you okay? I whispered to Lucais through the darkness in my mind, over and over again.

He did not reply.

The carriage jostled us around a bend, taking up a steep incline, and the sensation made my stomach flip like a rollercoaster as we climbed. I was grateful that Wrenlock didn't try to speak to me again. Even though I had questions—like what had happened to the High King, where we were going, and why he had betrayed us—I couldn't bear to hear the sound of his voice. I was so categorically furious that I trembled uncontrollably from head to toe—little tremors that seized my muscles and shook until I felt my bones rattling—and I genuinely didn't think I still had the ability to speak.

Hands wrapped around my wrists before the carriage came to a stop, and I opened my eyes to glare into Wrenlock's expectant gaze as he urged me to move ahead of him. I wanted to punch him in the throat, to slap him until he undid everything he was doing to us, to find my voice and use it to shred his eardrums until they bled, but I was in a nightmare, unable to do anything but breathe, listen, and obey.

The landscape took my breath away when I stepped outside. Vengeful as I was, I had to admit that there was a cruel and mesmerising type of beauty in the expanse of obsidian streaked with cracks of molten ochre. In the air, there was so much ash that it turned the entire sky grey in clouds that circled the peak of a tall, single mountain before us.

We were at the base of a volcano.

It towered high above us, proud and menacing, with ribbons of smoke dancing into the sky from the crater. Lava trickled down the sides, snaking into rivers that hissed and bubbled in various sizes and depths all around us, like veins of fire that fed into the atomic bomb of a landscape upon which we had intruded. Every so often, a tiny fire caught alight when a dribble of lava overflowed onto the burned earth, or a piece of rock fell into the magma. But the sounds were soothing—a calm soundtrack of white noise inspired by one of the most incredible natural wonders I had ever witnessed.

Fighting against the desire to ogle for longer, I wiped the sweat from my brow and turned in search of Lucais. For some reason, Wrenlock stood back patiently and allowed me to take in the monstrosity of fire and ash, but as soon as I altered my focus, he grabbed me and spun me into the aether through a wall of heat so intense I felt like it grabbed for us with proper hands. My eyes closed on instinct, and when I opened them, I found that he'd taken us inside the volcano—

No. Inside the *palace*.

The volcano is a palace, I realised with no small amount of horror, and the crater was a throne room.

We stood in the centre of a large, circular platform, surrounded by the rough interior walls of the crater's peak—a fatal drop straight down into the magma chamber below us that flowed in waves like an ocean of fire. Sizzling, red-hot lava climbed the walls like vines in a forest, alight with an orange glow that made me extremely uncomfortable.

A small, narrow bridge crossed the gap between the circle in the centre of the volcano and a door built into the far wall, extending behind an enormous wooden throne with six heavenbound spikes carved into its back. Soldiers from the Fire Army flanked it, one on either side, large pitchforks clasped in their hands before them, and an emptiness in their eyes as they stared straight ahead at absolutely nothing.

With painstaking slowness, I turned around as other faeries appeared on the platform with us. Two additional soldiers brought Lucais in—unconscious—and threw him onto the ground. I lunged for him, but Wrenlock held me back, and I couldn't find the strength to make even a sound of protest. I was stuck in a lucid dream, trying to wake up, to push through the wall of glass from the other side and feel the tassels of my throw blanket in my hands again—a tether to the reality I needed to reclaim before it was too late.

Because it couldn't be the one I was in.

Shoving Wrenlock's hands away, I stepped out of his reach to make a statement, and as I did so, my eyes fell upon a figure hunched beside the wooden throne. His head was lowered like he was trying to make himself invisible, his hands and feet bound in irons.

Despite my state of mind and the horrors that were seizing control of my reality, I recognised him. I took two careful steps forward, squinting to get a better look at his face. He shuffled backwards, aware of my presence, so I ducked my head and—

"*John?*" I blinked. Heatstroke symptoms aside, I recognised the old man. He was unmistakable with his large hands, greying hair, and the dark eyes that reluctantly rose to meet mine as I took another step forward. "John Dante," I gasped. "What in the blazes are you doing here? What have they done to you?" *Why have they done it?*

He hung his head, the manacles around his wrists fizzling as he tried to retreat. "Wasnae the plan, lass."

The sight of John cracked the surface of the dream, bleeding one reality into the next, and I felt my voice humming in my throat as if it had never been suspended. "Wrenlock—"

A figure emerged from behind the throne, stopping me in my tracks. She had long, brown hair, brown eyes, and a chocolate bar half covered in the wrapper in one hand. My head fell forward so fast it might have rolled clean away from my shoulders, and my eyes became saucers while my brain struggled to reconcile with the sight of my childhood best friend standing inside an active volcano in Faerie.

"*Amelia?*"

She rolled her eyes between long lashes and gave me a less than friendly wave. "Surprise, bitch."

"What..." I trailed off into stunned silence as the pieces of the puzzle clashed. Amelia looked exactly the same age as she had when I left for Faerie, but that was more than eight years before in the human world. "What the *hell* are you doing here?"

As if on cue, Lucais began to stir. He groaned as he sat up, rubbing his temple, and blinked his golden eyes a few times before they found my face, and his eyelids stilled. Awareness lit his gaze as he processed my expression, then immediately searched the room for the cause.

Finding John cowering beside the wooden throne, he frowned—the crease on his brow would have been adorable under any other circumstances—but when his gaze landed on Amelia, there wasn't even a hint of recognition in it.

"John and Amelia are here," I stated, wildly thrusting a hand towards them. It was equal parts confusing and inconvenient for me, and it showed.

Lucais's head swung towards me. "Who's Amelia?"

"My best friend."

He screwed up his nose, eyes flicking back and forth between us with a strong dose of judgement and distaste evident on the surface. "Your best friend is a Hobgoblin?" he asked.

Every part of my body was hanging on by a thread—from the air in my lungs to the blood in my veins. Especially my eyes as I whirled on Amelia once more, confusion and anger blurring until all I could see was a wall of black and red adamant. "You're a *Hobgoblin*?" I screeched.

My best friend sighed, popping the last piece of chocolate into her mouth before she floated the wrapper away on a phantom wind. It spiralled over the edge of the platform like a leaf falling from a tree, and the lava below hissed as the flames devoured it.

"Well, I'm certainly not a fucking human," she replied, licking the corners of her mouth clean with a tongue that suddenly looked a little too long. "My old man couldn't get as close to you as he needed to get the information for the job, so I came to the rescue." She sketched a bow. "You're welcome."

I blinked a few times, stupefied. "*Job?*" I exclaimed. "I was your best friend!"

"Oh, please." Amelia waved me away, her expression as animated and overly dramatic as always. "Did you even think of me *once* after Prince Charming whisked you away to his House?"

Irritated as I was, the question loosened another chunk of guilt free from the graveyard of mistakes I kept locked inside of my heart. She was right. I hadn't thought of her at all after leaving Belgrave, but that only stirred up more of the confusion lingering like a cloud of smoke in my head. We had been *so* close. We spent so much time together. Her family knew mine. She was my only friend in the entire world for a long time, and vice versa, yet we had nothing in common.

My best friend—and I hadn't missed her for a second after leaving home.

"Exactly." Amelia shrugged with her shoulders and hands. "Don't take it personally. That was the job. I had to follow you around, make sure you stayed alive, and report back on your magical abilities. Which, spoiler alert, were practically nonexistent your entire life because you are actually the most *boring* person on the whole planet."

I felt a tingling sensation beneath my skin as if my soul was separating from my body, and there wasn't a single thing I could do to defend the connection.

"What did you say to Brynn?" I demanded, eyes narrowing.

I noticed it then. For the very first time, there were faerie traits in my best friend's demeanour; the way she smiled like a serpent, the nonchalant gestures, the callous expressions reshaping her rounded features, and the pitch of her laughter an octave too high for a normal human being.

There was an evil glint in her eyes as she taunted, "You should really be more concerned about what *she* said to *me*."

"Alice?" I pressed, barely able to string a proper question together.

Amelia picked some melted chocolate out from underneath one of her nails with her teeth. "Not related," she said offhandedly, as if pretending to have a sister for the last couple of decades was really no big deal. "A glamour here, a glamour there. I had to get deep enough to stick around for the long haul, you know?"

Swaying on my feet, I nodded foolishly, light as a feather and yet impossible to lift. Desperate to avert my gaze from the face pictured next to mine in the photos of every birthday party I'd ever had, I looked away only to find that Wrenlock was standing next to me with his attention on the owner of the bookstore, still chained on the ground.

Wrenlock was staring at John Dante—staring like he knew him.

I shook my head, trying to remember which direction was up and which was down as my entire universe tilted on its axis. The worst part was that John returned Wrenlock's familiar stare, but to my knowledge, they'd never met.

Has Wrenlock ever been to Belgrave? Has John done something to the Court of Fire?

"Why is one of you in chains and the other isn't?" I questioned, fatigue slipping through.

“Simple,” an unfamiliar voice replied, booming throughout the volcano. “One committed a crime and the other didn’t.”

There was no opportunity for me to enquire after the details of the crime. Lucais climbed to his feet with a sense of urgency, hands still bound in irons, and two guards closed in around him as the doors opened on the far side of the volcano and a tall, broad-shouldered man with flame red hair strode into the room with a huge smile on his face.

“Aura! Lucais!” He clapped his hands, and the sound was like volcanic lightning. “Wonderful to see you both conscious and standing upright. That will save us time.”

“I have a bone to pick with you, Owain,” Lucais seethed.

The High Lord of the Court of Fire.

Owain shuddered theatrically, his dark eyes alight with a wild thrill. “Then by all means, Your Highness, let’s open the closet, shall we?”

Fifty-Five

Insignia

"John Dante is in custody under suspicion of treason. The sacred insignia on his privately owned establishment in the mortal realm was vandalised, and John failed to take the appropriate measures to correct the situation," the High Lord recited, answering my question. "Furthermore, he has been accused of aiding and abetting known rebels acting against the interests of this Court, using a second privately owned establishment in the mortal realm for the purposes of conducting meetings, facilitating unauthorised inter-realm transport of prohibited persons and prohibited goods, and he has refused to give up the locations or identities of his accomplices."

I glanced at Lucais. The Court of Light insignia had been scratched off the rosewood on Dante's Bookstore, but—

He warned me not to look at it for too long, lest ye see the flame start to flicker and ye lose yer wits.

"Belgrave's insignia was flame," I whispered, glaring at John with tears burning my eyes. The slight shift of his head was my only clue that he heard me. "It really was enchanted to deter people from looking, wasn't it?"

"The day ye asked me about it 'twas the day it stopped appearing to ye as flame, lass." John Dante's dark eyes lifted to my face, sorrowful and wide. "Flip the Court o' Fire around, and it willna take much to convince ye that it's Light."

An image flashed across my mind, blurred with static.

Dante's Bookstore looms high above me as I stand outside the front door waiting for the Closed sign to turn over to Open. The polished rosewood carving is striking, a larger-than-life depiction of a single flame curling towards the west. A breeze stirs, and the outline of the etching shudders and bends.

"What are ye standing out in the cold for, ye wee lass? Yer early today."

"How long has it been doing that?" I ask the old man in the doorway.

He steps over the threshold with a grunt, craning his neck so he can look up at the insignia's carving, too. Our breath clouds in front of us in the bitter morning air as we stand out the front of the bookstore, and I'm sure that he can see the way it's moving, but all he does is let out a really long sigh.

"Been like that since I was a boy. And my father before me..."

"That's it!" Lucais exclaimed, yanking me out of my reverie. He stalked into the middle of the platform and started to pace in a small circle. "That is fucking *it.* They're always confusing our two Courts, and I've had it." Pivoting, his golden eyes landed on the High Lord with perfect aim. He dipped his head, a serious crease forming between his brows as he pointed to him with both manacled hands and declared, "You're changing your insignia."

Owain snorted. "Why us?"

"Because I don't want to change mine," Lucais replied, a snarky emphasis on each word.

"But yours is the one everyone thinks is a flame," Owain protested in a voice that made the whole thing sound utterly ridiculous.

"Yes, and yours *is* an actual flame," the High King argued, "but nobody really seems to know that, do they? So it can't be that good a depiction of flame! They're constantly mistaking it for something else, and they think mine belongs to this hellscape. Why is that, huh?" He twirled in a circle, scanning the small crowd of faces. "Who works in advertising here?"

"Lucais," Wrenlock began, raising one hand in the air. "We have more important—"

"No." Lucais spun to face his friend. "No, we will get to those life and death matters in due course," he avowed with a deadly look, "but right now, Owain and I need to settle this vexing ordeal about the insignias once and for all."

"Lucais," he tried again. "You're being ridiculous."

The High King looped around in another circle, throwing his head back with his eyes squeezed tightly shut as he groaned at the ash-tainted sky. "Am I?" he rebuked. "Don't you see how much trouble this fucking thing has caused us?"

"I can settle this for you," Owain offered casually.

He was deeply tanned, tall, and broad-shouldered—though not as toned as the other men—and his face was lined with a greater number of years. His clothing was plain and black, though embroidered with red flames along the collar, and it shifted as he strode over to the throne and settled into the seat, flicking his hands up.

“It’s not happening,” he announced, utterly blasé. “I’ve seen the future, Boy King, and there is no Court of Light in it.”

Lucais had the nerve to roll his eyes. “Forget your iron-thread, did you? When did you become a Secret-Keeper, Owain?”

The High Lord shook his head and signalled to one of his men. “Not me,” he replied, and then he glanced up. “*Her.*”

We followed his upturned gaze and found an enormous bird cage being lowered to the floor. It appeared from within the clouds of smoke high above us, the metal chains anchored to something obscured way up in the sky. To my horror, a girl was curled up inside of the cage, bony and frail, with dull strawberry blonde hair and worn features. She was older than me, but much smaller, like the growth of her bones had been stunted.

There was something that reminded me of an archaic torture device on her head; it was metal, tightly fitted around her temples and beneath her jaw, and rose in spires over her scalp in the shape of an old crown. Small flickers of purple light swirled between the metal rods, like she was wearing a static electricity ball on her head for sport.

Her eyes were as blue as mine, but lacking cognisance. Despite the recognition in her gaze as she looked towards us, there wasn’t even a spark of hopefulness left in them, and she couldn’t speak even if she wanted to because her mouth was sewn shut with rusted iron-thread.

She was a Secret-Keeper.

“My little Oracle,” the High Lord stated with a lot of pride and no apparent regret. “I’ve seen it all, Lucais. From the start of the world to the end of it—and I know how this goes. Your insignia really is the least of your problems.” He gestured to the cage. “Take it from Siah.”

Lucais glanced between them, understanding crawling its way over his face. “Siah…” He took a step closer to the girl, peering at her through the bars. “She’s your daughter,” he said, a lilt in his voice. “I remember now.” Crouching down a careful distance away, he looked over his shoulder at Owain. “So you’ve found a way to circumvent the restrictions of the Temple?”

Owain shook his head, grinning like a madman with eyes alight and wicked. “Not me,” he corrected. “Your father.”

Lucais's brows flicked up. "My father?" he repeated, incredulous. "You don't say..." He cocked his head towards the girl again. "And it really works? She's able to feed you the future?"

"Yes, she is." The tone the High Lord adopted made my stomach churn, as if the girl were a machine and not a person, and it worsened as he approached the cage, pointing to the metal band on her head as if he were identifying the selling points. "See that? It's your father's invention, Lucais. He was a very talented memory-scraper, that man, but the price his magic demanded of him was too high. So, he found a way to create a machine that could do the work for him. There's a loophole in everything if you look hard enough, and Gage dedicated his life to this. By *taking* the memories from Siah, we overrode the agreement she made inside the Temple of All to keep her knowledge to herself. She doesn't have to consent—"

"Because she never would," Lucais muttered.

"—and she doesn't have to do anything. It's brilliant! The Temple of All ensures that no living creature can access the knowledge by force, but this invention is artificial. It can do what your father couldn't by taking his magic and developing an artificial intelligence. This is a scanner, pulling everything she knows out of her head and feeding it into a separate device that stores it for me to look through whenever I wish. Like an Oracle of my own."

The High King's expression was as granite-hard as his voice. "What's the catch?"

"Gage couldn't make it permanent," Owain admitted, tilting his head from side to side as if he were trying to reckon with the moral consequences. "In order to truly beat the safeguards of the Temple, Siah has to wear the device at all times so it can continuously scan her memories. Otherwise, the visions completely disappear from my orb and the memories of anyone who has ever peered into it."

Lucais's expression softened before he faced the girl again. "Siah," he crooned, a delicate croak in his velvet voice. "You must be in an immeasurable amount of pain."

Siah was incapable of speaking through the iron-thread, but a single tear slipped from the corner of one eye and rolled down her cheek. The sight caused my heart to flare with a long, poignant ache.

With a profound sigh, Lucais stood, pivoting towards the High Lord with his fists clenched beneath the iron manacles. "How could you do it?" he implored, an acidic bite to his tone. "How could you do this to your own child? She's your *daughter*."

Owain was unaffected. With a deep laugh, he said, "What do you mean, how could I do this to my own child?" His dark eyes were scrutinising, and I detected a sliver of authentic perplexion inside them. "Don't you remember that I had two children, Lucais? Has it really been so long that you've forgotten my son?"

An itch crawled over my skin like ants and spiders in the silence that befell the room as Lucais churned through the words. The quiet in my mind was intolerable, but I didn't risk reaching for the bond, even though my agony magnified the moment the High King figured something out before I did, and I had to watch it dawn on his face in isolation.

"No," he whispered.

"What?" I hissed.

"Yes," Owain affirmed, utterly unbothered by the fury simmering in Lucais's golden eyes. "Siah is the *lucky* one. Not only does she get to play a pivotal role in this, but she gets to be the one who lives to see it all play out."

"How did Alaric really die, Owain?"

The High Lord smiled cruelly. "He died during a training exercise with the caenim."

Lucais brought his hands, still cuffed together at the wrists, up to his face and started banging the knuckles of his thumbs against his forehead. "Why? Why? *Why* would you *do* that?" he beseeched, voice edged with hysteria. "Why would you *kill* your own son?"

Owain rolled his eyes, amusement replaced by a sudden surge of anger. "Because he fell in love with the bitch, didn't he?" he returned, thrusting a hand into the air as he spun on his heels and stalked over to the wooden throne. The High Lord's voice became mocking, his hands moving in wild motions. "He wanted to *stay* with her in the human world. And, worse than that, he developed grand plans to steal her away from that pig of a mortal husband she had so they could raise their faeling together here in Faerie. That was certainly never going to happen because that would have ruined *everything*." He shook his head, heaving a harsh breath as he sat down. "He would have ruined everything."

"How?" the High King demanded.

"Because the child was the perfect hiding spot so long as it remained in the mortal world," he snarled, slamming his fist down onto the arm of the throne. "The baby being conceived was the whole *point*."

Visions sliced across my mind like broken windows into the reality that Lucais had uncovered, fleshing out the inflections in the High Lord's words, but none of them made any sense. I scanned the faces in the room for clues, though nobody was looking at me. Wrenlock stood behind me wearing a mask of stoicism, John hung his head so low I would have had to lie down flat on the floor to be able to glimpse it, Amelia was oblivious as she filed her nails down with a pocket knife, Siah was unable to move, and both the High King and the High Lord were staring each other down.

I stumbled a step forward. "Can someone *please* tell me what is going on?" I begged, and everyone turned to look at me as if they had forgotten I was ever there. Irritation nipped at the corners of my mouth. "I get that John and Amelia were spies, but which baby are we talking about? What happened to it?"

Brynn? My brother?

Fear and hope battled to the death in my heart.

Owain examined me, looking at me properly for the first time since he had strolled into the crater of the volcano. There was a calculating darkness around the corners of his eyes that seemed so familiar to me, like I'd glimpsed it before in the reflection of the mirror, and I could have sworn I saw the shadows recede for a moment. In the next second, they came flooding back, and he broke our stare with a bitter chuckle.

"What baby do you think we're talking about? And what do you *think* happened to it? Are you telling me you have no idea who I am?"

I blinked once, the battle abandoned. "Why would I have any idea who you are?"

"Really, Auralie?" The High Lord of the Court of Fire put on a look of mock offence. "You don't recognise your own grandfather?"

Fifty-Six

The Malum's Curse

"My son, Alaric, is your biological father."

The words went straight through me. I was a ghost on a prairie, and the High Lord of the Court of Fire was throwing things at me. Things that shouldn't have been real, but felt like physical blows to the head and the heart.

"He's dead now," he added, feigning a grimace. "He became a liability when he developed real feelings for your mother. Who knows what he would have wanted to do about you once you were born." Owain gave me a meaningful look. "In the end, his sacrifice helped attune the caenim to your scent, prepping them for the day they went looking for you, so it wasn't all for nought."

I felt like cotton candy was being stuffed into my head—puffy, sticky, and overloaded with sugar to the point it made me sick. My hands shook at my sides uncontrollably as I stared at the High Lord and struggled to make sense of a single thing he was saying. In my peripheral vision, Lucais was watching me, his expression a steady portrait of quiet rage—but there was no trace of confusion as he waited to see how I would react.

All of a sudden, it hit me.

Lucais was waiting to see if I *would* react, to find out if I already knew or suspected any of it.

I blinked into the open space, utterly befuddled. The beat of my heart ticked over like the hand of seconds on a clock.

I had to say something. They were all waiting for me to say something.

"Why me?" I whispered into the thick, smoky air.

Owain's eyes flickered with surprise, a flame when the wind changed direction. "Well, it's bad luck, I suppose," he answered in the voice of a commentator. His tone didn't match the malicious admissions he was making, but my question seemed to have been the last thing he expected. "It was never about *you*." His eyes fell over me like a meteor shower before sliding to my mate. "It was always about *him*."

"Me?" the High King cried, outraged. "What did I ever do to you, Owain?"

The question had me suppressing an eye roll because he was a million times more likely to have done something to the High Lord—considering that he was Lucais Starfire, and I had never even met Owain—but I let him put on a show, praying he had a plan.

The High Lord gave him a withering look, but I saw a firestorm brewing in his eyes behind the façade. "I honestly don't know how to take you seriously sometimes, boy. Do you mean aside from the fact that you disrupted the status quo after single-handedly ending the very first reign of a High King from the Court of Fire by driving him to bring shame upon our people by *suicide*?"

Lucais stood with an open mouth and murder in his eyes. "Hugo kills himself and leaves all of Faerie to an infant ruler who was nearly executed *twice* before his first birthday, and you think *you're* the victim in that situation?"

"That infant ruler drowned my wife!" Owain thundered, shooting to his feet. His large frame loomed over us, double the size of the figure who had strolled in to greet us so casually, and a heat flare almost knocked me to the ground.

The lava in the magma chamber roared, rising in waves that cascaded around us, brushing against the walls and twisting until it sealed over the sky, trapping us like we were inside a whirlpool. The temperature burned through my body while my skin reddened and sweat dampened my hair, making it heavy as it stuck to my nape. My human lungs could hardly breathe through all of the magic and fire.

"Calida was killed by a water faerie," Lucais contended, pacing between the throne and cage. A hint of doubt crept into his voice as he recalled a memory that surely didn't belong to him, given the timeframe, but his eyes remained fierce. "You had her murderer tried and executed."

Owain sniggered, the sound dark and destructive. "Hugo orchestrated that! He insisted, in fact, and I think it was because of your mother." His features morphed into a scowl. "Do you think I could do anything about you back then? No! I had to *watch* and *wait* along with everyone else who was put at the mercy of a babbling leader who would raze entire townships if he was told to eat his vegetables! A leader who wailed so hard about a lost rattle that he caused a rainstorm in the south that washed away one fifth of my entire Court! My sweet Calida went to help with the rescue efforts the day she was caught in a flash flood and washed into Ulyssa's territory, where she drowned in filthy floodwaters and was dragged out to sea through the estuary between the Ruins."

Lucais stilled. "I didn't know."

"Siah was so devastated by the death of her mother that she went to visit the Temple without even telling me," Owain went on, and the whirlpool of lava around us slowly began to withdraw as he settled back into his throne. "It wasn't until she returned with the iron-thread and a certain look in her eyes that I realised the opportunity I'd been given. Everyone knew your father was an eccentric who was determined to create abominable creations to take the place of magic in our everyday lives. With all of his mundane notions and ideologies, some might even say that he was the first real human being. But where they saw a pariah, I saw potential. In all of your father's creations, he had to have struck gold with one of them, right?"

The High King didn't respond.

"When you destroyed the natural order of things by banishing the inferior beings from our employ and allowing the females to train in your army for frontline combat, I knew it was time for me to act. Your parents and I became fast friends, and it wasn't long before Gage was inviting me to examine some of his creations. The Memory-Scraper was his pet project—the closest to his heart, given his condition..." Owain cocked his head to the side and inspected Lucais with narrowed eyes. "Did you even know your father was sick?"

The High King shook his head, barely. "He always said the price of his magic was too high. My mother told me that he suffered from an imbalance."

"I think it was all in his head, to be perfectly honest with you, but he did experience stronger-than-normal side effects from the use of his magic. I witnessed it for myself. It was to the point where it couldn't be countered with talismans or charms."

Lucais's eyes flicked to his hands for half a second before they snapped back to the High Lord's face, and my stomach bottomed out as I put it together. It took every last ounce of strength left in my body to hold my composure, but nobody else had seen the momentary glitch. Lucais hadn't told anyone why he wore so many rings. Not even me. And

I would not be the one to give him away—even though the prickling sensation of tears welling in my eyes felt more real than anything had in the past few hours.

"Your father gifted the prototype of the Memory-Scraper to me when I showed interest. The plan was always to swap the devices over if he ever found a way to make the effects permanent, but he never did—"

"You burned the cottage down," I breathed.

Owain didn't look at me, but he said, "I had to destroy all of his records to ensure that nobody would discover what we had done."

"But the cottage was destroyed during the war," Lucais insisted.

"No." Owain tapped his fingers on the wood. "It is easier to blame everything on wars, though, isn't it?"

"You're a hypocrite, Owain." Lucais took a step forward, flanked by the guards. "You are well aware that I had nothing to do with the lights in the sky."

The Dragon War.

"You're a light faerie, though. I can't blame them for making the connection, even if I don't subscribe to superstition myself." Owain shrugged. "Besides, it was perfect timing. Your parents had agreed with me that you weren't cut out to rule Faerie before the Gift War even began, so it wasn't hard to convince them to approach you with the Witch Experiment. Your father was the most excited about it, because I gather it would have solved a lot of problems for him personally, and he was the most disappointed when you dismissed them. His disappointment was what crushed your mother, I think, but I already knew your answer would be no. You see, I'd watched it through Siah's visions. After you killed Calida, my little Oracle returned to me with a list of ingredients for your downfall stored in her head. Since you were a child, Lucais, this is what I have been doing—waiting."

"Waiting for what?" I whispered.

Yet I already knew the answer.

Owain turned his unfeeling gaze on me. "For you to be born."

My face felt numb, my lips shaking as I forced out a single word. "Why?"

"Because Siah saw that the High King was destined to take a human mate long before the Oracle's prophecy was ever revealed to the public.

And what better hiding place is there for *noxaeterna* than in the mortal girl with whom he cannot help but fall in love?"

Everything fell into a state of slow motion, suppressed by the single word with a lifetime of power behind it.

Noxaeterna.

The Malum's Curse. The Malum's Curse. The Malum's Curse—

My head was foggy, stuffed full of images and sounds that spiralled crosswise inside of transient blinks and muffled echoes, like I was struggling to swim through the shipwreck of my own thoughts and memories at the bottom of a midnight ocean. I was looking at everything through ripples and aftershocks. It was suddenly *freezing*. And it had been so much easier to focus on the picture above the surface, the vision of what my life should have been like breaking through the light above me on dry land—a warm, clear, attainable reality that I had never grasped because it didn't truly exist.

And then it shattered.

Noxaeterna. The name of the Malum's Curse.

My curse.

I was all alone at the bottom of the ocean, looking up at the world through the pieces of a broken mirror, distorting the shadows and shapes around me. Some of them might have been clouds eclipsing the sun, but some of them were definitely sharks, and my lungs burned as I dragged my tired body to the surface while memories dove for me with wide-open jaws filled with sharp teeth.

"It is the most intricate spell I have ever seen, as a matter of fact, and it was placed on Auralie Roberts before she was born," Owain announced to the room, as I stood paralysed in the centre of the platform. "It was woven with the brilliant little caveat that she could not think or speak of it until the curse was named. It's always risky to embolden a spell with something like that because, at any point in her life, someone might have said it without even realising what they were doing. Then, she would have figured the rest of it out."

My head was spinning so fast that my vision was nothing more than a smear of colours, shapes, and stars within an endless darkness. I lost all sense of gravity. I could have been floating upside down for all I knew as I burrowed into the recesses of my soul and *finally* picked up the thing that had been inside me all my life. It was small, dark, and slippery, wriggling like some kind of leech as I snatched it with my mental hands and snapped it in half.

The sensation was liberating and crippling at once.

In the distance, I heard a scream that I thought was my own, but I was too far gone as my soul raced over two decades back in time to the day that someone put the curse inside me. I knew my throat was being shredded by my own voice, although it felt like no more than a delicate hum as I lost my hold on time and space, and I named it in every corner and every moment of my existence.

Noxaeterna.

Power seared through my veins as I wrestled back control—knowing it, naming it, banishing it. I stepped out of the curse like stepping out of layers of clothing that I'd been wearing for my whole life without realising they were making me overheat—until, finally, I became aware that they were suffocating me. Through years and years of my life in the mortal world, I named the nameless friend that had spoken to me through the dark, and vanquished it.

And it was like breathing.

My whole life, I'd been choking, unable to fill my lungs, unable to keep my head above water, unable to clear my mind. And then, all of a sudden, I was on dry land, and there was fresh air *everywhere.* So much air that I didn't even have to *work* for it anymore. I was light as a feather. I was free from the stifling darkness of my confines.

When I finally caught up to the time and place I had been in when I learned of the curse's true name, I found myself on my hands and knees on the floor, panting heavily as I faced a puddle of blood and black ink that spilled out beneath my body. I was lighter than ever. My vision was clearer. My head was no longer plagued by thoughts that were not my own and could not be controlled.

I lifted my head with a smile, only to find that Lucais was being restrained by five guards—one for each limb, and one for his throat—and the look on his face immediately switched from horror to relief when our eyes met. Wrenlock stepped between us, brow creased, and a shadow rose from beneath me, pushing him to the ground and out of my way.

"What the fuck?" the former Hand muttered, brushing ash from his hands as he scrambled back to his feet.

"Hmmm." Owain's face was wrinkled as he perceived me from the distance of the throne. "Well, that's going to be a problem." He gestured to one of the guards holding Lucais. "Bring me Cacindra and the little dark faerie, would you?"

The guard bowed, then vanished. A moment later, he returned to the same spot with a woman on either side. He held ropes attached to iron collars that were secured around each of their throats.

One woman had hair as white as starlight and skin as pale as the moon, tinged with an ethereal sapphire hue. She held her posture, spine straight and shoulders back, and the fierceness in her silver eyes told me that she was doing it as a statement of strength and defiance. The iron collar didn't seem to be scorching her flesh, and her ears didn't protrude from the curtain of her hair like the High Fae. In fact, she looked more human than any of them—smaller in stature and frame, with fewer enhancements to her physique, and much rounder eyes with thicker brows—but I didn't need to see any of that to know what she was anymore.

A Witch. Cacindra.

The other woman was High Fae, and reminded me of Delia before I had turned her white hair black. Her skin was many shades darker than the Witch's, though her tresses were white as paper. She was broad-shouldered with delicate features, slumped against the iron collar with an expression of pain cutting into the beauty on her face. She wasn't a Witch or a Secret Keeper, though.

The dark faerie.

"Cacindra," Owain called pleasantly. "Care to explain why there's magic pouring out of that redhead over there?"

I frowned, shooting him a glare. "The curse is broken. You named it. *Noxaeterna.*" Saying its name out loud sent a thrill rippling through me, and I had to bite back another smile.

"The curse remains intact." Cacindra's voice was robotic, rehearsed.

Owain let out a frustrated sigh. "Naming the curse doesn't break it, you stupid girl," he muttered. "It simply removes the block that prevents you from being aware of it, and thinking or talking about it." He paused, as if he wasn't sure whether to speak the next words. Then, with a shrug, he added quickly, "You might also find that one or two of the reality distortion hexes start to fall apart at the seams. And..." He squinted at me. "What is that?" he asked the Witch, leaning forward with his elbows on his knees. "Is that a *love* spell?"

The Witch remained silent.

Owain threw his hands up in the air. "Never mind, Cacindra. Focus! If the curse remains intact, why isn't her magic still being suppressed?"

"The fire magic is void," Cacindra recited politely.

Owain lifted a palm in the air, fire blazing to life against his skin. "If you don't say something helpful—"

The High Lord was interrupted by the pealing sound of someone's laughter. At once, every head turned to Lucais and found him bent over in a fit of hysterics with the most deranged and jubilant smile I had ever beheld upon his perfect face. Raising his bound hands, Lucais pointed to Owain with a single finger as if he was about to say something, and then he laughed even louder.

Owain gestured to one of his guards, and a moment later, I was staring at the pointy end of a pitchfork. A snarl curled on my lips, but as I considered trying to wrestle it away from him, the High King's laughter subsided.

"I wouldn't do that if I were you," he warned. "You fucking idiot, Owain. She doesn't *need* your fire magic. She doesn't need any type of Elemental magic." He glanced over at me, a gentle crease forming around the corners of his mouth as his eyes simmered down into the gilded smoulder I loved so much. "Can't you see it? Aura has been absorbing the magic of the curse this whole time. And now she's learning to control it. She *owns* it." He looked back at Owain. "Where did you store the *noxaeterna* prior to Aura's conception?"

"Me."

For a second, I had no idea who had spoken, but then Lucais was staring into the face of the dark faerie, and I realised that she had spoken for the very first time despite the iron sizzling against her throat.

"He stored it in me."

"What is your name?" Lucais requested softly.

"My name is Bethanne, Your Highness," the dark faerie replied. "I am the High Lady of the Court of Darkness. It's an honour to finally meet you."

Fifty-Seven

Dreams

"Bethanne," Lucais crooned, moving towards her. "Oh, I am so sorry. I am so, so sorry. What happened to Blythe?"

"She's dead, Your Highness." The dark faerie tried to swallow, but the motion made her throat flex against the iron, so she let the saliva trickle out of the side of her mouth instead. I noticed that it was tainted with blood. "I was taken a long time ago—long before Blythe knew that I was destined to be her successor, and I'm afraid she did not react well when she finally discovered me here. She gave her life trying to save me."

Lucais tilted his head to the side. "She was murdered?"

"Yes, Your Highness."

He blew out a long breath, taking it like a hit to the face. "Oh, the sneaky bitch..." He shook off the news and glanced at me over his shoulder before turning back to Bethanne and asking, "You're the reason the Court is covered in shadows, then?"

"Yes," Bethanne agreed. "I am afraid there is very little that can be done about them while I am here. The shadows persist while the Court is forcefully separated from its leader, but nobody can take my place while I am still alive."

Lucais retreated a few steps closer to me, and two of the guards followed him. "And I never would have suspected this Court with the former General of the Fire Army acting as Hand to the High King for so many years." He fixed Wrenlock with a hard look. "How long have you been a spy?"

The other man stared at him impassively, giving nothing away in his depthless brown eyes.

"He almost failed in his task," Owain remarked.

"What do you mean?" The High King kept his eyes on his former friend's face.

"He was supposed to bring the two of you together much sooner than he did. Even in Siah's visions, it was hard to tell which way you'd go in the end. So, when Aura was old enough to see the Oracle's prophecy in her dreams, Wrenlock was meant to find her and bring her into Faerie, but he delayed it by months."

"Owain," Lucais chastised. "Why don't you speak less in riddles and more in words that might actually make you seem clever?"

"I'm talking about the decision you need to make, Lucais." Owain tutted under his breath. "Now that you understand the reason you couldn't fix what your parents did, what will it be? You can save your family, or permanently condemn them to the *noxaeterna*."

Lucais stared at the High Lord, panic and confusion flaring in his eyes. My heart thundered.

"Who are you going to kill?"

The High King shook his head feverishly.

"Her, or them?"

Before the *noxaeterna* was named, I might have been surprised to learn the cost of breaking it, but deep down, I'd already known what it would take. It was buried at the bottom of a still lake in my mind alongside everything else the curse suppressed—including the fire in my veins that the dark voice around my wrist had snuffed out.

I couldn't speak through the curse. I couldn't even *think* through it. But I knew—I had always known in one way or another—that I carried life and death inside of me. That I was destined to do something so impossible it didn't matter if it was good or evil. And that Lucais would love me enough to choose me and damn the millions of consequences trapped in flesh and bone, living within houses, greeting the sun and bidding goodnight to the moon as if a selfish, redheaded girl from a bookstore didn't stand with a pair of scissors hovering over the thread that tethered their souls to the realm. The thread that gave them a right to life, the thread that would one day *snap* beneath her razor-sharp edges whether she meant for it to happen or not.

Like the vision the Court of Darkness had shown me.

The Little Folk had known, too.

The trinkets they used to bring me as a child were bribes. I remembered with sudden clarity the pleading of their little eyes as they approached me with caution in the backyard of my first home, beseeching me to find fantasy in books so that I might never go searching for it in the real world. So that the bomb inside of me may never be activated.

But I never liked fantasy books. I never liked them much at all.

There was always a beginning, a middle, and an end. There was always a problem that required a resolution, and a team of characters would work together to figure it out in some kind of impossible scenario. It was tense. There were close calls. Sometimes, there were heavy losses, and I followed different plot points around in a maze until I reached the one inevitable conclusion—

That it was going to end.

That not even magic could make things last forever.

I didn't want to read about that, so I closed those books, and I moved on to contemporary romances and thrillers—

Until fantasy found me.

Like it was always going to.

Because the page could not be turned over unless it did.

The mask of defiance on Lucais's face melted away. "No," he whispered, and his eyes were pleading as they bored into Wrenlock's. "No," he repeated desperately. "Tell me he's wrong, Elumos. Tell me right now that he is *fucking* wrong—"

"It's true." Wrenlock's throat bobbed, and he averted his gaze from both of us, tucking his hands behind his back. "The only way to break the curse on the Malum is for Auralie to die, and they are aware of it."

That's why they killed all those girls.

Lucais laughed bitterly. "So all of that was for *nothing*, then?" he yelled at his former Hand's side profile, pointing at me with his bound hands as he stalked Wrenlock's guilt-ridden eyes. "Everything you ever said to me about loving her and wanting to protect her—that all gets thrown out the window now? For what? For *Margot*? Answer me!" he bellowed, and the very ground beneath our feet shook.

"Guards!" Owain called. "Restrain him!"

"Unhand me, you crispy slices of mutton!" Lucais shouted, shrugging them off with his shoulders. His eyes were blazing with power, but he lifted his arms, shaking his bound hands in the air for emphasis. "The only threat I pose is to your fucking egos! I'm in irons, for the love of the Elements! Stand *down*."

The guards halted their attempts to force him to his knees, exchanging a fleeting glance.

Lucais gazed at me with such burning desire and intensity that I thought it might kill me. "You are, without a doubt, the worst thing that ever happened to me," he said. Then he paused, his eyes ablaze. "But if anyone tried to change it, and they tried to take you back from the absolute train wreck that catapulted you into my life, I would hunt them to the end of the world. I would hold their hearts in my bare hands and squeeze until they threw you back to me, little beast."

"What are you saying?" I hissed. "What are you *doing*?"

He shook his head gently, smiling at me like he was in love. "Even knowing how this ends now, bookworm, I swear to you that it is the truth this time."

"Lucais," I said, panicked. "Lucais, stop—"

"I tried to avoid it." He sighed. "I tried to avoid you for the most agonising weeks of my life so I could be the High King my people deserve, but it's not working either way, Aura." His golden eyes darted to Wrenlock. "They can't kill me because someone else will just take my place, so they're going to keep you here in order to control me. That is how this will work. They will force us apart, and I will not be able to stop the things they do to you, even if I do everything he says. They might cease the torture sooner. They might make it a little bit less gruesome. I will be able to keep you alive, but you will never be safe."

By the time I realised what he was planning to do, it was too late for me to think of a way around it. I tried to summon the parts of the curse I controlled—like I had done when Wrenlock obscured my view of Lucais—but it required a level of anger and concentration I couldn't access while my eyes were glued to Lucais's face and my heart was splintering into pieces.

"This is the only way," he told me.

It hit me like a punch to the gut. "No," I protested. "No, you don't *know* that—"

But I had seen it in my dreams. The prisoner in the dungeon who was being tortured while I stood there, powerless to save him. And I had shown him those visions, so he knew it, too.

"I do."

"I saw Wrenlock, too," I blurted, my hands and teeth trembling violently. I had. I'd seen Wrenlock in the dark first, but I'd called Lucais's name. "I know it doesn't make any sense. In the dungeon with you when we kissed, I showed you the dreams I'd had in the human world of you, but the night we came to Faerie, I swear, I dreamed of Wrenlock instead. You both had the same injuries." I deliberately left out the part about them having the same tattoos because the reality distortion hex was falling apart at the seams like I'd been warned, but I was desperately clutching at straws. "You don't know that this is the only way, okay? You can't possibly know—"

"Aura. *Bookworm.*" His voice was going to break my heart. "Those dreams you were having?"

"Yes, exactly—"

"I was having them, too."

All the hope gathering in my chest deflated like a balloon, replaced by sadness—and fear.

"What?" I breathed. The cracks in my reality were irreparable. "Why didn't you say anything? You *knew* the whole time that this was going to happen, and yet you brushed me off when I tried to warn you? You let me keep going like we even had a future—"

"Aura, my sweet girl." He did it. He broke my heart with his mouth. "I am not the prisoner in the vision," he whispered gently. "I never was."

Frantically, I glanced at Wrenlock, but he was staring at a fixed spot on the volcanic floor.

"It's you," Lucais murmured. "It's always been you."

"No," I pleaded, but as the tears fell down my face and I shook my head to disprove it all, the memory rose up. It was as clear as anything I had ever seen.

The picture of the dreams morphed from a male body to my own as the magic fuelling the illusion fell away like pixels on a screen in my mind, and I realised the curse was embedded so deeply inside of my identity that there were still layers to it I hadn't even touched.

"The dungeons in Faerie are reinforced with iron," Lucais explained. "They're designed to suppress magic. The only reason you were able to show me your memories of the dreams down there was because the iron weakened the magic of the curse just enough to let it slip through, but the reality distortion hex on it was too strong, so you were never able to see for yourself who was really pictured in the vision. But you see it now, don't you, bookworm?"

Sadness branded my cheeks. My lips trembled.

"The *noxaeterna* made her forget the visions once the prophecy's lifespan ended. But the reality distortion hex was still required as a safeguard because she never would have come to Faerie if she so much as suspected what would happen to her when she did," Owain explained. "But you complicated it unnecessarily when you refused to give her your real name."

Lucais didn't move his eyes from my face. "I know," he said quietly. "I'm sorry."

And then he rushed at me.

The High King of Faerie broke free of the iron manacles, and for a fleeting moment in time, I really believed that we might be okay—

Until his hands closed around my arms in a familiar embrace that smelled like the rain and the muddy portal outside of Caeludor.

His body against mine was like a jolt of adrenaline straight to my heart as we collided, and I screamed for him to stop. To find another way. To give me another chance. But once again, he pushed me into Wrenlock's waiting arms, and the man who betrayed us locked his hands around me like a python, and then my heels were being dragged along the floor as he spun us around.

Shouts rang out from all sides.

Orders were fired left, right, and centre, and I wanted so desperately to chime in and agree—

"Stop them!"

Stop us.

They were too slow for the men who didn't have to share words or thoughts to understand each other, even in the trenches of a devastating betrayal. Lucais turned back, a flare of his light magic buying us time as Wrenlock lunged out of the reach of a nearby guard, tackling me over the edge of the platform.

I screamed as we fell into the heart of the volcano, headfirst into bubbling lava that growled at us like a hungry beast, and rose up as if to break our fall—

We landed back in the kindling forest on the outskirts of the Court of Fire, and the last thing I felt through my bond with Lucais was the sensation of his body collapsing on the platform in relief before the string around my rib cage went slack.

Fifty-Eight

It's Not Forever

I barely had time to gather my thoughts before I heard the sound of Elera screaming.

Whipping my head around frantically, I searched for her, only to find that she was being accosted by a group of men wearing plain clothing and carrying an array of weapons and ropes.

"No!" I screamed, the pitch so loud I felt my eyes reverberating inside my skull like porcelain ornaments. I struggled to get to my feet, fighting dizziness as the sky became the ground, and Wrenlock appeared in my peripheral vision, looming above me. "No! Let her go! Give her back! She's not yours! She's *not yours*!"

Elera bucked wildly, and the sound of her squeals cut through the forest like sirens, like needles aimed straight for my heart. She pulled against the ropes with all of her might, her large, dark eyes reaching for me hopelessly as I struggled against Wrenlock's arms, and she ducked her head, trying to hit her assailants with the ends of her horns as they secured the ropes around her neck and *yanked* on them.

"We're not hurting her," Wrenlock swore, grunting as he heaved me onto my feet. "She's all yours, I promise. If you come with us peacefully right now, I'll tell them to let her go, but you cannot go near her until we know you will stay with us."

"You bastard!" I yelled, the words searing my throat. "You *fucking* bastard! How could you? Who's *fucking* side are you on?"

His answer was immediate. "The rebellion."

I was too disoriented to ask which flavour of rebellion he was flaunting, considering there were two opposing sides between Lucais and Owain, and the men stealing my unicorn seemed to have betrayed both of them in the same breath.

The rebels stumbled from one side to the next as they worked in a group of seven or eight to lead Elera away from me. She snorted furiously, ears flattened against her head, hooves digging into the dirt as she resisted. Three additional men came jogging out of the shadows, and one of them was carrying a whip.

My eyes widened in horror. "No!" I screamed. "Wrenlock, no!"

"Fuck." He dropped me, leaving me to crumble onto the dirt like a sheet ripped from a washing line. I couldn't see straight, let alone stand upright. "Stay here—"

The sound of the whip cracking split the air, followed by Elera's enraged screaming, and I rolled over and wretched onto the ground, though nothing came up except for saliva and the misery leaking out of my nose. I dug my fingers into the ground, desperate to haul my body closer to her even if I couldn't stand up, coughing and spluttering as dust filled my mouth and lungs.

"Abello! Stop!" Wrenlock roared, and his voice was already a fair distance away from me. There was a scuffle of shoes and incoherent shouts from all around, but the crack of the whip didn't sound again, and when I peered up through tear-filled eyes, I saw that Elera had stopped fighting them so hard.

Abello.

I took the name from the air and seared it into my brain.

Abello.

I'd make sure that Abello died first. After he suffered.

"It's not forever." Wrenlock's tone was a cruel taunt when he returned to me, though I knew he was trying to be gentle and sincere. It simply didn't matter; I'd never be able to stomach his voice again. "As soon as you're ready, the dagger will guide you to me wherever I am, and I will make sure you are safe."

My head tilted up, hatred overtaking the water in my eyes, burning through me like a fever at the height of illness. In my delirium, the spinning of the universe ceased to mean anything, and a counterfeit strength returned to my limbs. "Like you kept *her* safe?" I snapped.

Wrenlock's eyes were depthless, but his mouth turned down at the corners, and his shoulders lowered ever so slightly. "I am so sorry about that. Abello didn't realise she was for you, and she was trying to stab his friends with her horns—"

"Because they were *kidnapping* her!" I scrambled to get to my feet and pulled the blade out from where it was tucked into the side of my belt. "This stupid blade is going to show me to you?" I demanded, shaking it in the air between us.

He nodded warily.

"Then I don't *want* it!" I whirled, breathless and dizzy and furious, and stabbed the dagger into the trunk of the nearest tree. To my absolute shock, the entire tree went up in flames a second later. A raging fire devoured every last inch of bark and leaves, but left the dagger untouched.

I watched on in awe and horror, panting heavily.

I wish I could've stabbed him instead.

"You'll see why I'm doing this," Wrenlock promised, sounding like he was trying to reassure himself more than he was me. "I know you will, and when you do, I'll be waiting for you."

"Your promises aren't worth anything to me."

"Please, Aura. I know it's not the City of Light. I know it's not High Queen of Faerie, but if you come with me, you could be my Queen. *Our* Queen. You could have the Court of Rebels to yourself, and I would worship at your feet. Aura—"

"Go away," I commanded weakly, my eyelids fluttering as they waged a war on my exhaustion. "Go after them. At the very least, make sure they don't hurt her again. You owe me at least that."

"Find me," he stressed, his face torn even as he glanced behind him. The forest was empty and quiet with Elera and the rebels already making tracks away from us.

Fuck yourself, I thought, but I kept the sentiment quietly tucked away in my mind because I needed him to prioritise my unicorn even when I wasn't watching. I needed him to keep her safe until I could equip myself to take her back and kill every last one of the monsters who had taken her from me.

And from Lucais, who—

The thought was a knife to the stomach. I couldn't finish it. I held myself together with my arms locked around my waist, feeling like I'd unravel into a pile of string if I took pressure off the space around my left rib where the bond had gone quiet and still. I pressed my pointer finger against it, feeling the tension flicker faintly inside my flesh and bones.

If he was already in the dungeon, he was surrounded by iron.

Lucais wouldn't be able to hear me. He wouldn't be able to feel me, either.

I tried to suck in a breath of air, but it was so sharp it felt like broken glass as it went down. Holding myself still instead, I searched the forest for any trace of life—anything beyond the slow death of my own heart knocking to be let out of my chest.

It wasn't until long after Wrenlock had disappeared into the trees that I allowed my knees to buckle and the vertigo of my unravelling curse to win. The forest floor was littered with tiny stones and jagged rocks that dug into my flesh as my body crashed onto the ground. I braced my hands on the dirt in front of me, my fingertips curling into the earth as I forced myself through a series of deep breathing exercises that did nothing to placate the panic.

I squeezed my eyes shut, bringing my fists to my chest as my heart screamed through an impossible pain. It tore through me—mind, body, soul, and bond—until I couldn't take it anymore.

Folding in on myself, I rocked back and forth on my knees, and I whispered into the devastating silence.

"Tommy. Tommy. Tommy."

The End

Thank You For Reading!

I am so grateful that you chose to pick up this book and disappear from reality with me for a while. ~~If you hated it, I'm sorry—but you're not going to like the next book either, so you'd best cut your losses and—~~

Hold on. *What is it?*

You can't say that.

What do you mean I can't say that? It's my book.

Do you want to be a successful author or not?

Yes. Obviously.

Then you can't say that. You can't outwardly warn people not to buy your books.

Why not? If they're going to hate it—

Then they'll leave a review telling everyone how much they hate it. It's good for the book. Just... trust me.

Fine.

Book Club

Scream Into the Void:
Loren's Reader Group, Love Letter Sign Up

Stalk Me on Socials:
Instagram, TikTok, Facebook

Website:
Loren Little Books

Official Author Profiles:
BookBub, Goodreads, Substack

Acknowledgements

Well, the fact that I get to do this again is absolutely mind-blowing. I cannot believe that I am sitting here writing the acknowledgments for my *second published book*—and so soon after the first one! Is this real life? On that note, actually, I can't believe anyone read the acknowledgements for my first published book. But I saw quite a few comments on social media referencing some of the details I left in the back matter of A House of Cloaks & Daggers, and it made me laugh. I feel like we have little inside jokes now, and it's really cool.

So much goes into a book behind the scenes, and as an indie author, it's been my job to learn how to do all of those things alone. It wouldn't be a proper acknowledgements section if I didn't do a shout-out to myself because, yeah, I fucking did it again and I am *so* proud of myself for chasing my dreams and holding onto them for dear life. I am endlessly grateful for the small circle of friends who keep me alive and sane while I do my best to bring plotlines together and get my line spacing and margins right at the same time. I am also very thankful for the resources available to independent authors—from the software to the blog posts—and for the wisdom offered by other authors and industry professionals on their own platforms.

To B—for the food and water. And the coffee. Utterly essential, life-sustaining aspects of my creative process that I would absolutely forget about if it were not for you.

My wonderful alpha team—Krystal and Caitlin. You read my messy first drafts and kept up with my eccentricity like true friends, and I am so lucky to have you. Thank you so much for listening to my frequent crises and graciously talking me off the metaphorical ledge. They don't know this, but all of my readers owe you a debt of gratitude for stopping me from trashing this entire book throughout the draft process... More than once. I love you both infinitely.

My lovely beta team—Krystal (again, you absolute superstar!), Madison, Casey, Belinda, Kirsten, and Jo. I agonise over these early versions, and I am extremely fortunate to have so many volunteers willing to read through my work before it is ready to be polished and published. Your feedback and opinions are so valuable, and I could not go through with this without your support and void-screams into our DMs. Thank you.

My street and influencer team, both the official and the unofficial members. I see you, and I love you, and I am so thankful for you. Every single comment, share, and mention you give to my work makes the world of difference to these books. You're all such extremely talented creators, book reviewers, and book club admins. I admire you greatly and appreciate you for all that you do, not only for my corner of the romantasy realm, but the whole reading community.

My editor, Brittany Bitossi, from BLD Editing. Thank you for diving into this world with me again. Your professional processes are so fun and respectful, and you match my frequently unhinged energy to perfection, which never fails to leave me looking forward to our next session. I am extremely grateful for the time you take to detail and update our working documents for this series, and for every little "NO EDIT" comment you leave in the margins for me. You are the champion of indie authors, and I don't know what we did to deserve you.

My cover designer, Laura, from Covers by Aura. You created the most stunning designs for these books, and it has been so fantastic to work with you!

My echo and my shadow—the anchors in time and space, fixed in one reality so that I can keep travelling into the others. I love you always.

And Lucais, my beautiful idiot. You didn't let me break even though I came so close to it this time somewhere between thirty and sixty thousand words, and then again between one-thirty and one-fifty. You picked me up when I was down, as you have always done. There may be speculation as to whether or not you're real, but your impact on my life is one of the realest things I've ever experienced, no matter what.

Lastly, I would like to take a moment to acknowledge the devastating impact that artificial intelligence (AI) is having on this industry. There are billion-dollar corporations stealing intellectual property from artists all over the world to train these programs without a lick of remorse, and it is sucking the soul out of a creative community that has suffered long enough. When I was an aspiring author, I flipped to the back of previously published books to see what the acknowledgements were supposed to look like. If this is you right now—side note: I'm honoured—please know there is not and never will be a single word or suggestion that AI can give you that is worth taking. Your voice is the magic essence of your writing, and nobody can replicate it. The agony of this craft is worth it. Embrace it. Own it. Please protect it at all costs.

About The Author

Loren Little is an Australian indie author who writes tales of romance in fantasy, dystopian and contemporary settings based on her imaginary friends. Her stories are filled with banter, steamy scenes, and a lot of wishful thinking. She likes to flirt with the line between light and fluffy and dark and depraved, and she is in an ongoing love affair with morally grey characters and plot twists. Also, she simply adores cliffhangers, and she's not sorry about it.

Also by Loren Little

The Gift War Series:
A House of Cloaks & Daggers
A Palace of Smoke & Mirrors

Glossary

Proper Nouns

High Fae

- A race of faeries descended from the High Mother.

High Mother

- The deity worshipped in Faerie, creator of magic,

High King

- The ruler of all rulers.

High Lord

- The ruler of a specific Element or Court.

High Lady

- The ruler of a specific Element or Court.

Secret-Keepers

- Faeries who give up their voice in exchange for answers to all of life's greatest questions.

Dragon Master

- The riders and owners of sky-dragons in the Aboveworld.

Hand

- The trusted advisor of the High King or High Queen of Faerie.

Prince

- The title used to describe an heir of royalty.

Princess

- The title used to describe an heir of royalty.

Faerie

- Ruled by the High King Lucais Starfire.

Caeludor

- The City of Light and Faerie's capital.

Court of Light

- Ruled by the High Lady Morgoya Maudgold.

Court of Wind

- Ruled by the High Lady Enyd Windfall.

Court of Darkness

- Ruled by the High Lady Blythe Darkcloud.

Court of Fire

- Ruled by the High Lord Owain Everspark.

Court of Earth

- Ruled by the High Lord Gregor Woodburn.

Court of Water

- Ruled by the High Lady Ulyssa Pondrop.

Belgrave

- Auralie's small hometown in the human world.

Dante's Bookstore

- Auralie's place of employment in the human world.

The Water Dragon

- A public house in Belgrave.

Sthiara

- A small town in Faerie.

Forest of Eyes and Ears

- The sentient forest that will protect those who enter at all costs.

House

- The High King's safe house, enchanted to care for guests in the ways their lives have lacked.

Opiate Desert

- A bone-dry, barren expanse of land.

Metal Mountains

- The mountain range that splits Faerie down the middle, bordering the capital city.

Temple of All

- The High Mother's place of worship.

Ruins

- The outskirts of Faerie to where creatures like the Malum and the Banshees are exiled.

Aboveworld

- The world that belongs to faeries who live in the sky.

Underworld

- The world that belongs to faeries who live under the sea.

The Watch

- A wall and watchtower in the Court of Earth that oversees the mountain range.

Malum

- The creatures born of Banshee and High Fae.

Banshee

- A non-magical race of faeries exiled for draining magic from others.

Hobgoblin

- A race of faeries known to be grumpy and anti-social.

Ogre

- A race of faeries who are larger than life and talented cooks.

Witches

- A race of faeries who believe in using pure magic derived from the earth.

Vampyrs

- A race of fanged faeries who drink blood for pleasure and sustenance.

Sprites

- A race of small, winged faeries who are kind to the people they like.

The Little Folk

- A race of miniscule faeries who bring gifts to human children that still believe.

Swapling

- A race of faeries who can shapeshift.

Merfolk

- A race of faeries who live in the Underworld.

Goblin

- A race of faeries who values privacy and do not like to be observed by strangers.

Wolf-Folk

- A race of faeries who can transition at will from humanoid form into wolves.

Basilisk

- A race of faeries who can shift between snake and humanoid forms.

Wood Nymphs

- A race of small, winged faeries of ethereal beauty who inhabit woodlands.

Bogeyman

- A race of faeries who can possess the minds and bodies of others.

Spectre

- A group who represents the ghost of deceased faeries, usually as a result of murder.

Centaurs

- A race of faeries who are part horse and part humanoid.

Trolls

- A race of faeries who usually dwell beneath bridges.

Cyclops

- A race of faeries with one large eye, taller than most other races.

Elves

- A race of faeries who are short, fast, and quick-witted.

Leprechaun

- A race of faeries who are often found at the ends of rainbows.

Pixies

- A race of faeries who are known to be beautiful and cruel.

Elements

- Variations of magic gifted to faeries.

Coven

- The name for a group of Witches.

Witch-Lapis

- A weapon that can duplicate a killing blow up to five times without taking energy from the carrier.

Blood Lock

- An amplifier that will give the wearer the combined strength of all parties who willingly bleed onto it.

Guard

- The High King's personal regiment of sentries, soldiers, and spies.

Oracle

- The prophetic magical entity that appears at random to offer glimpses into the future.

The Sins of Stars

- A book without a known author, detailing a story of how the Aboveworld might have ended during the Dragon War.

Gift War

- The fight between High Fae, which resulted in the creation of human beings and split the world into one magical and one non-magical realm.

Dragon War

- The fight between land-dragons and sky-dragons that occurred when the risk of land-dragons becoming extinct was first identified.

Map

- The Map of Faerie.

Nouns

Caenim

- A type of creature that can be kept like pets or trained like soldiers.

Land-dragons

- A type of creature who lived in Faerie like dinosaurs, but are now extinct.

Sky-dragons

- A type of creature who lived in the Aboveworld like dinosaurs, but their status is unknown.

Lochgrub

- A type of winged creature with unparalleled beauty that lives in the ocean and is hunted by Merfolk for sport.

Paperdove

- A type of creature, like a bird, that lays eggs to be consumed purely as food.

Locust

- A highly venomous type of creature that loses a stinger to its victims, but regrows them.

Faelight

- A magical form of light wielded by the High King.

Fae-lily

- A faerie drug designed to render humans who inhale the substance unconscious.

Faerie

- The species of magical beings when referred to as a group of people.

Unicorn

- A magical type of horse.

Sixty

Bonus Scenes

The following scenes occurred at the end of A House of Cloaks & Daggers.

LUCAIS

Ah, fuck.

When Auralie's lips curved into the most faerielike smile I'd ever seen on that gorgeous, spiteful mouth, I knew I was in trouble. An incoherent shout came from behind me as she cocked her head to the side, those seastorm eyes stabbing relentlessly into my heart, and then she—

Oh, bookworm.

The light glitched, a flash of onyx shattering the moody gloom, and my world plunged into darkness as deep as the middle of the night. I knew it was Aura's doing because I felt her imprint across the spell as clearly as I would feel her hands all over my body. The woman had a touch of madness, tempting me to chase the heat in her gaze before it turned ice-cold on me at the last possible second, and I was addicted to every lingering glare and stolen glance. I thought about her all the damn time—the blue oasis of her eyes, the shivers that danced along my skin beneath the brush of her fingertips, the delicate pout of her touch-starved mouth, and those strands of sunset-red hair always blowing out of my grasp.

When she reached into the core of my magic and ripped out the lights in the sky, it was a very familiar ache.

"Lucais!"

Enyd's voice came from somewhere in the shadows, an irritatingly shrill note of accusation in it. Internally, I groaned at the inference. *As if I would shut down my own fucking magic. Why are we not beyond this yet?*

Deep down, I understood it was because the passage of time was a tricky thing to balance against the impact of world-altering events. The ones that created realities, and the ones that destroyed them. Lights were a sore spot for faeries, and they probably wouldn't be able to heal from the trauma until someone from the Court of Light no longer possessed the crown. Fear took no hostages in right and wrong.

I suppressed a sigh, knowing my options were slim—and that the behaviours and feelings my people had about the matter were not entirely unjust. Consequently, my next move would be taking responsibility for the future High Queen's darkness leaching into my

Court. Aura had ripped light magic out of the sky, and the last time something even remotely similar happened, it signified the beginning of a long and brutal war.

They still blamed me for that, too.

"What the *fuck* is going on?" the High Lady from the Court of Wind demanded.

Pinching the bridge of my nose, I raced through a mental list of acceptable explanations, but I kept stumbling over the one truth I couldn't tell.

She turned the lights out. Aura found a literal switch for my magic and fucking flipped it.

The beautiful, clever little fool and her disastrous magic. Wren tried to stop her, but there was a dead body between them, and he was still reeling from her rejection. It made him hesitant and clumsy.

I knew what had happened immediately, but I couldn't speak. I couldn't bring myself to twist the truth, even if it would stop Enyd from screeching out redundant statements or quieten the surprised rumblings from her men. The sound of gravel shifting underfoot accompanied the commotion as soldiers staggered through the sudden dark, forgetting that a corpse was lying somewhere in the middle of our group—quite separately from its head—and I blinked in a futile effort to help my eyes adjust.

Standing in the courtyard, encased in the pitch-black expanse of night falling in the middle of the afternoon, I rubbed my temples and counted to three. Someone nearby shouted an obscene curse after having stumbled over the decapitated head, and that was when I finally let light flare in my palms.

I kept it dim and tight, enough to illuminate my silhouette and prevent anyone from tripping over Aura's figure. She was on the ground beneath me, her hair splayed around her head like a maroon curtain, her expression peaceful as she dozed inside complete and utter magical burnout.

I fucking warned her.

Sighing, I sent the light from my palm out in a wide orb, swallowing the two of us in a bubble while the others stumbled around in the dark. They could wait. I needed a minute or two to summon the strength to fix what the love of my life had damaged.

My light gilded her face, partially covered by auburn curls, her chest rising and falling with every deep and even breath. Auralie Roberts was out cold. I crouched down beside her, my mouth in a tight line as I swept a lock of hair back from her forehead, and made a quick assessment to ensure she hadn't sustained any serious injuries on her way down.

By the Elements, I had fucking *warned* her.

It was only a couple of days prior when she had started to hoard magic like a Goblin with treasure. I could sense it gathering around her, stagnant and unused. The reserves of my own powers were stretched so thin that I felt starved myself—of magic *and* her touch—so any spark of rogue power seemed to linger near me like a feast to which I was not invited. Hers was...painful. The excess magic blooming around her chafed because it was so opposite to my own, and yet so deliciously abundant. She tempted me with her mind, body, soul, and magic. Still, I warned her away from it. I told her that she risked imploding and taking out Sthiara, and she ignored me.

Of course she ignored me.

I gazed down at her and I knew I'd fucked it all up.

From the moment I first saw her until the moment I told her I loved her—everything was wrong and backwards and deeply regrettable.

Except... There had been those glimmers.

We'd had moments where it felt like she was tripping over me—despite my mistreatment and her attitude, and the fact that she believed she had to fall in love with Wrenlock—and my arms ached in the most euphoric way from being constantly poised to catch her. Waiting. Always waiting. Waiting for her to fall, and then to accuse me of pushing her.

It was deplorable, but I'd admit to it. I'd confess that I would gladly spend the rest of my life deliberately tripping her over if it meant she would spend more time in my arms when I inevitably broke her fall with my body. Over and over again. Like a dance. Like a rehearsal for the performance of a lifetime. Aura would call me clumsy, and I'd neglect to correct her so she didn't see how pathologically in love with her I was.

She could look at me with hatred in her icy blue eyes just so long as she kept looking.

"Aura," I whispered, selfishly reinforcing the light barrier against sound so my words to her were private. "You beautiful little idiot. I don't think your fall is responsible for the blackout." I actually suspected her magic had gently guided her to the ground after knocking her out because she hadn't made a sound and there wasn't a single mark on her body. "I think your magic burned through your system so fast that it caused you to short circuit. I'll bet this is all self-preservation," I murmured, adding the last part more for my own benefit than hers. I doubted she could hear me through the magic fog, anyway. "That's what it always is for you, isn't it?"

Self-preservation.

Staying alive. Even when she...

My hand tightened into a fist around a strand of auburn hair as the memory surfaced, as it had been doing at random ever since I found her kneeling before the caenim, ready to die in the field. She had followed me into a portal willingly because she wasn't satisfied with her life in the human world, but something had followed her through it—something that wasn't tangible or traceable.

Something even I couldn't fight.

I hoped to the High fucking Mother that she would decide to be strong enough to fight it herself when she woke up.

My beautiful, lonely, haunted girl.

The bane of my existence in the very same breath.

My undoing.

Heaving a long breath, I stroked one finger down Aura's cheekbone before I pulled her into my arms and rose from the ground, cradling her limp body against my chest. I counted to three again before I let our private little bubble of light stretch and expand—first to incorporate the others, and then Sthiara, before finally spreading it out across the entirety of my Court. I was about to have a lot of explaining to do, and the demands on my magic made me feel light-headed. I needed to get inside, away from prying eyes and droning voices—even if only for a few minutes.

Turning my back on the rest of the world as my light bled into it, I carried Aura into the House. Morgoya's lilting voice drifted on the wind as she dissuaded Enyd and her men from following me with the threat of petty blackmail and illegal sanctions. Wren would deal with the body before he tracked me down—whenever he felt brave enough to revisit the subject of my soulmate with me.

I wanted a private moment with Aura when she didn't consciously hate me. A moment where I could feel guilty for everything I'd done, and I could tell her all about it. Explain why I did things that broke my own heart. Confess that I broke hers on purpose, but only so the damages would be limited to things I could control. And then admit I was losing control.

I loved her, but I was losing control.

WRENLOCK

The body left a trail of thick, black blood on the stones and grass as I dragged Enyd's fucking sentry to the graveyard at the back of the House. A melancholy grey had reclaimed the sky once Lucais's power bled the darkness out of his Court, but the atmosphere was charged with a quiet sense of dread, accompanied by the bitter chill in the too-still air. The only sound for miles was the suppressed thump of my boots hitting the ground, and the eerie scrape of the corpse ruining the well-kept grounds.

I gripped the decapitated head by the roots of his dirty brown hair, holding it to the side with my arm fully extended as I stalked away to carry out my unspoken orders. My proximity to the noxaeterna gave me the heebie-fucking-jeebies. I'd never been a superstitious man before the curse, and I'd fought through years of bloodshed and magic bombings in the Gift War without so much as flinching away from the gore and violence, but the swollen veins covering the carcass of Enyd's toy soldier were far more disturbing than anything a war could conjure.

High Fae simply shouldn't *be* that shade of green.

Lucais believed the Malum were reproducing. I hadn't heard anything about that happening yet, and I fucking hoped I never would. Things were bad enough without a full-scale apocalypse falling on top of us, too.

If the last couple of months had demonstrated anything to me, it was that the High King was more than willing to let both worlds fall to ruins as long as the shield he created around Aura held fast. *Typical.* The man had a one-track mind, proven to us time and again. He made it incredibly fucking difficult to get anything done when I had to spend so much time preventing him from dropping the metaphorical match before the accelerant was flushed. And, unfortunately, time was the one thing I was short on when it came to Aura and the Malum.

There was a hair-trigger on another war. I just needed a little more time before someone decided to pull it. Until then, there was a chance. There was *hope*. After that, I would have to start making some pretty heartbreaking fucking choices.

Sometimes, my mind wandered back to the day the High King wove the notion of an apocalypse into human history before he sealed off their new world at the end of the war.

Zombies—that's what he called them. He had based a monster created solely to star in human nightmares on my sister and his own parents. Lucais's reasons for it were equal parts noble and insulting, like his reasons for doing most things were. Objectively, the conceptualisation of new mythology protected the image of faeries. It stopped them from resurfacing in human dreams and breaching the spell between our worlds, but by the same token, I was convinced he genuinely believed that mocking the fate of our families would make it hurt less.

I stifled a sigh.

He was wrong. He was often wrong, but he was the High King.

The garden bed came into view, the colours dulled and muddied while the graveyard flowers lay dormant. I approached it, releasing my hold on the sentry's ankle with a grunt, and then shook my hand as if the motion would cleanse my palm, though I knew it was useless. The noxaeterna wasn't a contagion; it couldn't be transferred from one being to the next through innocent contact even when it was in its worst form. If it could, I'd be well and fucking truly doomed.

"Dinnertime," I called to the graveyard flowers in a low, sing-song voice. Notes of wisteria and thyme filled the air as a gentle breeze swept through the garden while the flowers awakened. They lifted their sleepy heads, blinking at me curiously, and I grinned through my disgust. "Who's hungry?"

There were a variety of carnivorous flowers in the graveyard, but only one was large and bloodthirsty enough to devour the sentry's skull whole—the vibrant, crimson trap-flower at the end of the first row. Stalking over to it, I held the head out in front of me, jiggling it above the closed blossom. When dormant, the buds were small and curled in on themselves, the stems short as they burrowed into the soil at their roots; but when tempted by the meat of freshly deceased bodies, they sprang to life, capable of growing up to twenty times their size.

I wasn't sure if they'd want an infected corpse, though. I'd never had to feed one to them before. During the Gift War, the bodies were often slain by the blade. Occasionally, the humans were armed with guns and iron bullets, and those were the dead bodies the graveyard flowers had always rejected.

The chill in the air was biting as I stood alone on the House's grounds with a corpse and a bed of carnivorous flora. I shifted from one foot to the other impatiently as the trap-flower's petals unfurled, revealing the blood-red core of teeth masquerading as seeds to unsuspecting visitors. Beady eyes studied me, evaluating the offering in my hand. Graveyard flowers seldom attacked the living. They much preferred the ease of digesting bodies already in rigor mortis over the violent struggle of subduing live prey, but they would devour me if they felt it necessary. We had that in common, at least.

The flower swayed, delicately sniffing the air—then, in the blink of an eye, it pounced. In a whirlpool of green and red, the trap-flower rose up from the ground and opened its jaws, snapping at the head in my fist.

"Shit." I let it go and leapt backwards, a sick kind of thrill sparking through my veins. "I'm out of practice, then, aren't I?" I muttered, giving the graveyard a sidelong look as I shuddered to dispel the nervous energy. "That should be a good thing."

The graveyard didn't talk back. I watched with a grimace as the sentry's face disappeared, swollen mouth agape and eyes closed as it sank down the inner stem the way large prey would roll through the body of a snake. With disturbingly little effort, the flower petals folded over the seeded core, and it slowly retreated to the safety of the soil to digest the sentry's head. I whispered a little prayer for his last rites in soft tones, but it wasn't anything special.

I didn't know the man. He and I were not the same.

While I had buried bodies for Lucais up and down the countryside, the soldier in the garden bed was one of the many who travelled with Enyd, taking turns fucking her before and after the meetings she attended with the other leaders. It eased the stress of the job, I supposed. Honestly, I'd long thought Lucais should give her methods a shot himself. I'd much rather do *that* than play the part of his undertaker, adding to the burial grounds we planted all over Faerie because of his political indiscretions.

Enyd was annoying as shit, but she was a good conversationalist after a couple of drinks, so I imagined the men she kept close to her couldn't be all that bad, either. I hoped he didn't have a family, though. His skull would rest beneath the garden bed safely and in good company once the trap-flower had finished cleaning it up, but they'd never get it back—if they ever found out what had happened. I doubted they would.

With a resigned sigh, I turned to the rest of the body. It was disrespectful to burn the entire thing when a graveyard was accessible. On top of that, the remaining unfed flowers had perked up and were glaring eagerly at me, so I wiped the invisible traces of noxaeterna from my hands, holding them out to either side as fire blazed on my palms. For a moment, I let my magic burn. It was one of the greatest fucking feelings in the world—the best before I'd met Aura—and it gave me false assurances that my skin would be seared clean of the corpse's malady.

A guilty pang hit my heart.

Keeping the best side of myself hidden from Aura was fucking painful. I couldn't risk using my fire magic when she wasn't looking in case it had an adverse effect on her, given the condition of her own magic. So, it had been building up inside me for weeks. The glimpses she showed me in her eyes—the deeply protected, unknown fire smouldering beneath the surface of her soul—were punishing. I felt an ache building in the core of my being, desperate to ease the torture in her beautiful mind, to share some of the magic that was her birthright, and embrace the connection between our souls that hummed without any expectations or demands. We owed the world nothing. We owed each other nothing—but we could be everything.

She wanted to know what she saw in me?

Fuck. I wanted to show her. I hated myself for keeping it a secret, but it was a necessary precaution. Aura would have to understand when it was finally safe for me to confess everything. She would have to understand.

I hoped.

Once I finished burning the sentry's bones clean of his clothing and flesh, I tossed the last of him into the garden bed. The noxaeterna couldn't be burned away completely, but fire helped. Thankfully, the soil shifted like sand, taking hold of the bones and slowly dragging them under the surface.

“Bon appetite,” I muttered to the graveyard flowers. Then, I turned on my heels and stalked back towards the House, mentally reaffirming my vow that I would share my magic and my secrets with Aura as soon as possible.

There were days when I hoped she would discover it on her own—my part in it, at least. I didn’t know what would happen to her if anyone hit her with the whole, terrible truth unexpectedly, and it wasn’t a risk I was willing to take. Selfishly, I waited for someone to mention my magic to her in passing, and I imagined I’d try to play it off like it was no big deal because she had never asked me. But I had no such luck. She was attracted to me, drawn to me—and led to believe it was due to the bindings of fate, which left her impossibly conflicted when she learned that it was completely her own doing.

Aura’s rejection of our connection stung, though I understood her reaction. It didn’t change the fact that the link between us was the most natural thing in the entire fucking world.

Mating bonds were both sacred and fair game. Lucais’s feelings for her were legitimate, and I didn’t discredit his relationship with her—if it could even be called that—but nobody sat in the same room with their fated soulmate and his best friend and felt more connected to the other man.

Nobody.

Yet Aura had.

Brushing off the icy outdoor air from my shirt, I entered the House and found the two of them in the front parlour on the ground floor. Lucais had placed Aura on the sofa, her flame-red hair billowing out on the cushion beneath her head as she slept through the repercussions of hitting her magical self-destruct button. Lucais’s shoulders were hunched as he knelt on the ground beside her, his silhouette cast in a rectangle of gloomy light that streamed through the window above them from his weakened sky.

I couldn’t read him beyond the outward melancholy. Lucais’s stature appeared smaller, his shoulders tensed and tucked in the way they had been in the months after he first broke his wings, and his golden locks were a shade closer to a dirty bronze without the excess of power at his disposal. For a moment, I felt a flutter in my chest, like our connection was being revived and I could go to him to provide some solace.

But his temperament was never more volatile than when Aura was in the room with us, so I refrained.

Besides, he didn't need me to tell him what went wrong.

It wasn't hard to fathom that the moment Aura found out what we had done, she started planning to leave. I thought part of her stayed simply to know that Lucais was going to be okay—because, deep down, she always cared at least a little about him, and because it would prove beyond doubt that he was the true High King—but she had one foot on the threshold of the front door. She just didn't realise that the noxaeterna wouldn't let her activate her magic. She didn't know that everything she'd ever done had been the result of the curse defending her in the face of danger.

Her father. The fucking Banshee. Even Delia, though I still hadn't quite figured out what caused that particular glitch. Delia wasn't a threat, but she was the closest Aura had been to the real threat since the day she was born.

Chest pulling tight, I gazed at her angelic face. My lungs felt weightless, breathless, because—*fuck.* I loved every one of her freckles, and I could stand there counting them until they made up their own numeric system. But I couldn't. Not yet. Not until things began to turn around, heading for a long overdue change that she would help me bring to fruition.

Leaning against the doorframe, I cleared my throat to be polite, even though Lucais had heard me coming from a mile away.

"Thanks," he murmured without turning around. His voice was rougher than normal. "Morgoya's helping Enyd pack up. They can't transport the body, and I can't have it lying around here for someone to stumble on while they sort it out."

"No problem," I answered in a low voice. Lucais hadn't turned, so I pushed away from the doorframe and took a few precarious steps towards the sofa. When he didn't react, I knelt at the end, peering down at Aura's sleeping face. My throat was tight, but I forced the words to come out sounding even and loose when I asked, "What are you going to do with our girl?"

A muscle on the side of his neck flickered. "She needs to sleep." His forehead was resting against the edge of the sofa, the top of his head nuzzled against Aura's waist. Eventually, he lifted it, meeting my gaze with bloodshot eyes. "I'll take her to Caeludor as soon as she feels strong enough to travel."

I knew he didn't mean when *she* felt strong enough to travel. He could sense things through the bond that I could only dream about, and it would only get worse if she ever accepted it. The narrowing of my eyes was all it took for him to know my thoughts, and I braced myself for his elaboration.

"I can feel it," he answered softly. "Her entire system is being suppressed. It's like she's on life support, but every so often, there's a ripple of something—"

"Of what?" The words were out before I could stop myself.

"I don't fucking know!" Lucais snapped. Shuddering through a long, harsh breath, his eyes slammed closed as he threw his head back, and he dragged a shaky hand through his hair. I felt the familiar sympathy surging up once more, wanting me to comfort my brother or at least explain why I wasn't, but I held it at bay. Ignored the demands, the questions, the nausea. Lucais groaned quietly. "Sorry," he mumbled. "I don't know what. And I *hate* that I don't know."

"Look." I bit my lip, aware that we were balancing on the brink of another fight, but unable to submit to his need to be in control all of the fucking time. "Why don't you go and get some air—"

"I don't need air."

I choked down a humourless laugh because I was unsurprised. "Luc, I am perfectly capable of staying with her while you take a walk and remove whatever the fuck went up your ass while the lights were out."

He met my gaze with soft, corn-yellow eyes. They were exhausted, but the faintest of glimmers told me that he knew what I was doing and he was *trying* to take the bait. "I know," Lucais replied, bringing his elbows up to the couch and folding his hands beneath his chin. He sighed, forcing a pathetic smile that lacked all of his usual mirth. "I just think that I should be the first one she sees when she wakes up. She *is* less mad at me."

"Oh, that's a bit rich," I returned lightly. There was a lump of tension in my throat that I tried to dislodge by swallowing, but it hurt. I sucked in a mouthful of air instead. "You're the one who brought her here under false pretences, and she's pissed that you betrayed her with your name."

The High King pulled a face at me. "You stripped her bare on the dining room table and then scared her out of the room."

"Ah." I chuckled, pinching the bridge of my nose as I squeezed my eyes shut against the memory of that day. I'd never handled something so fucking awfully before in my life, and I still hadn't been able to make it up to her. "Yeah," I lamented. "I did do that, didn't I?"

He bared his teeth at me in a smile, a dark flash of humour evident in his tone as he stated, "You're an asshole."

"You're a hypocrite."

"You're excused."

Fuck.

We lost our balance and fell back into that awkward pit where human traits, provoked by our mutual interest in a human girl, clawed at our ankles in an effort to pull us down. Lucais bent to rest his head against the sofa again, effectively dismissing me, and I silently cursed myself for the attempt at lightening his mood. We weren't boys play-fighting in the fields behind my home or in his Forest anymore, and sometimes the reminder was like a slap across the face. Especially when we were both so deeply in the wrong.

Before rising to my feet, I placed a gentle kiss on my girl's forehead. He didn't comment on it, and I didn't speak again as I walked out.

I didn't speak again for days.

I knew Aura would be fine, but it killed me to stay away from her. Lucais didn't leave the room. Thankfully, he didn't call a healer, either. He realised she didn't need one, yet I still paced across every floor of the House while I waited for him to do something else. Anything else. Like answering the door when Delia knocked—*anything*. But Lucais didn't make a sound, and he didn't let anyone into the parlour to see Aura.

And when he finally left the House with her, he didn't fucking tell me.

"Fuck!" My shout echoed through the House as I kicked the thick hall runner outside the door to the empty parlour. The action flipped a corner over, creating a crease down the middle of it. My hands threaded into my hair, fingers clawing at my scalp as I paced in a tight circle and seethed. "He is such a fucking *child*."

I had played nice with him for long enough. Given him chance after chance after *fucking* chance. Somewhere along the way, I'd let my feelings about our friendship cloud my judgement, and it had almost cost me the whole damned world. Aura was the key to everything, and I'd nearly fucking lost her. Not once, but *twice*.

I was not going to let it happen again.

Made in the USA
Monee, IL
22 August 2025

23945521R00328